Changeling Press LLC

ChangelingPress.com

Arcane Heart (Arcane Talents 3)
An Arcane Talents Dark Fantasy Novel
Angela Knight

Arcane Heart (Arcane Talents 3)
An Arcane Talents Dark Fantasy Novel
Angela Knight

ISBN: 978-1-60521-816-8

Publisher:
Changeling Press LLC
315 N. Centre St.
Martinsburg, WV 25404
ChangelingPress.com

Printed in the U.S.A.

Editor: Treva Harte
Cover Artist: Angela Knight

The individual stories in this anthology have been previously released in E-Book format.

Table of Contents

Arcane Heart (Arcane Talents 3)
An Arcane Talents Dark Fantasy Novel
Angela Knight

The wildest passion has claws.

When a pair of cops with magical abilities become the target of a hate group, they must unravel the plot against them before it costs them their lives -- and love.

Deputy Erica Harris is a witch who can see the magical auras of those around her, a talent which helps her determine when someone intends to commit a violent crime. Her partner, Deputy Jake Nolan, has a psychic link with an African lion that allows him to manifest the animal's powers.

But it's tough to serve and protect when demagogues stoke public fear of you. As the two cops fight to unravel a politically motivated web of hate and deceit, Erica and Jake are targeted by a magical assassin hired by the plotters.

While dodging murder attempts, they begin to fall in love. But as Jake's desire makes his inner lion more possessive, his self-control erodes. Can they afford to take a chance on love when so many lives hang in the balance?

Chapter One

It was sheer, stupid impulse, and she knew better. But when Deputy Erica Harris's gaze fell on the Potions sign, she whipped her patrol car into the nearest empty parking space. For a moment she sat there, listening to the cooling engine tick and staring at the nighttime crowd streaming past her cruiser. "You really are an idiot."

Shaking her head, she picked up her radio's handset mic and clicked the button to call dispatch. "Laurel County, Alpha 22, going 10-8 at Potions."

"10-4, Alpha 22." The dispatcher sounded bored. No surprise; it had been a slow night.

So now Jake knows where I am. Question is, will he show up? Yeah, Potions was Jake Nolan's favorite restaurant, and she hadn't heard him go 10-8 -- the Laurel County police code for "out of service" -- to take a dinner break. That didn't mean he'd take one now and join her.

So go for it. Call the man and ask him to meet you...

Yeah, no. Much as she wanted to see him again, only a masochistic twit would want another ride on the Nolan merry-go-round. The last time had damn near destroyed her. Yet here she was, masochistic and twitty, with the need she'd felt for months threatening to overwhelm her sense of self-preservation.

Screw it. If he shows, he shows. If he doesn't, I'm still hungry. Erica got out, a spring breeze sighing cool against her cheeks. The Friday evening crowd surged around her, heading in and out of the bars and restaurants along Faraday Square. Her stomach growled, and she headed up the sidewalk toward Potions. She'd been too busy working a traffic accident to grab dinner. It was eight o'clock now, and she craved the greasy goodness of a cheeseburger combo.

Almost as much as contact with Jake Nolan. Her two Mideast tours as a member of his Arcane Corps team had turned the man into an addiction. Hunting terrorist sorcerers together built emotional connections that were hard to break.

The thought of the war made her automatically check the crowd, though she shouldn't have to worry about terrorists in Laurel County, South Carolina. Still, last year's attack by the polar bear Feral and his witch partner proved even Laurelton wasn't immune to psychos. The Faraday Square Massacre had occurred months before Erica had joined the department, but even she could tell the whole community still suffered the aftereffects.

Breathing in to center herself, she opened her awareness to her Talent. Most Arcanists had to close their eyes to see the arcane energies surrounding all living things, but Erica was much more sensitive.

Suddenly those around her wore glowing overlays of healthy blue and green, though splashes of red here and there indicated pain -- headaches, feet hurting from pinching high heels. That poor bastard on the right probably had a bleeding ulcer; that shade of red wasn't right for cancer.

All pretty standard. She started to close her Talent down…

A block ahead, the crowd parted, revealing a tall man just as white light exploded across his aura like a bomb blast.

Erica froze. For an instant she was back in Iraq, watching helplessly as a Caliphate sorcerer detonated his suicide vest, its explosives amplified by intricate spells. The terrorist's aura had flared exactly like that the instant before the blast killed him and a dozen innocents.

Too late, too late… Erica braced for the explosion.

It didn't come.

This isn't Iraq, dumbass. There's still time! She lunged toward the man, dodging through the crowd, pushing people aside, ignoring startled shouts and drunken curses. No sign of a weapon blocked the shine of his aura -- no black silhouettes of guns, knives, hand grenades, or a suicide vest's wiring. Nothing but the shadows of zippers and buttons. *I can still stop him.*

Because he had to be stopped. Every time she'd seen someone's aura flare like that, they'd attempted murder minutes later. The weapon might not be on the asshole now, but it was somewhere nearby.

Erica thumbed the button on her body cam, activating it as she plowed ahead. Grabbing her shoulder mic handset, she keyed her radio. "Laurel County, Alpha 22. Officer needs assistance in front of Potions on Faraday Square. Possible 10-68A." Which was the ten-code for mentally ill suspect, possibly violent and armed. "White male, approximately six-three, weight 230 to 240, dark haired, dressed in jeans and a black trench coat. Out with the subject."

"10-4, Laurel Alpha 22," the Laurel County dispatcher replied. "Dispatching units."

Hope they're in time to do me some good, Erica thought, slowing to a cautious walk as she moved up behind the man. He had a good six inches on her, along with sixty or seventy pounds. On the other hand, she was good at hand-to-hand, and the guy looked a bit chunky, which should slow him down. Unfortunately, given the way his head was glowing with fifty shades of crazy, she wasn't confident she'd win. Not without shooting him, anyway.

She'd rather not have to shoot the unfortunate batshit bastard. Judging from the furious currents whirling around his head, he was already hip deep in hell. He needed help, not a bullet. Erica could kill if she had to -- she certainly had during the Caliphate War -- but she'd rather avoid it.

Just as she was about to reach for him, Burning Man stepped off the sidewalk and started across the street.

Meaty shoulders bunched, big hands curled into fists, he headed for the cars parked along the narrow strip of park that occupied the center of Faraday Square.

His weapon must be in his car. Erica's hand tightened on her pistol, her thumb on the snap of the retention holster. She didn't draw the Glock. It would be way too easy to miss and kill an innocent bystander in this crowd.

"Sir!" Throwing up a hand to stop oncoming traffic, she jogged across the street. "Sir, I need to speak to you."

He didn't turn, didn't appear to hear her at all. The white blaze surrounding his brain intensified. *I really don't like the looks of that aura.* It wasn't just murderous-asshole-white. You could reason with a murderous asshole because he didn't necessarily want to die.

Burning Man was *I'm-going-to-die-and-take-you-all-with-me-white.*

Yeah, this isn't going to end well. She was right behind him when he reached a battered Honda Civic, parked diagonally in a patch of darkness between the street lamps. As he paused to fish in his pocket for the keys, Erica slapped a hand down on the trunk with a hollow metallic bang. "Sir!"

Burning Man jumped, shying like a startled horse. She had to concentrate hard to see his face through the hectic shine of his aura against the night. His dark hair stood up in sweaty clumps, as if he'd been raking his fingers through it. He stank of sweat and stale beer, and his round face was stubbled, as if he'd forgotten to shave for a couple of days. An intricate tattoo crawled up the side of his neck, something serpentine with wings.

"What?" Burning Man rocked back on his heels at the sight of her black sheriff's deputy uniform, and his eyes took on a hunted rat gleam. "I didn't do nothin'!"

Yet. "You were jaywalking." She hated to fall back on the excuse of harassing cops everywhere, but it wasn't like she had a choice.

He glowered. "You gotta be kidding."

"Crosswalk's back that way. Can I see some ID?" She needed to distract him long enough for her backup to arrive. At least that murderous white had dimmed around his head, taking on a yellow tinge of fear. Burning Man could still blow, but she'd bought a minute or two.

Cursing, Burning Man dipped in a pocket of his coat. She tensed, but he only pulled out his billfold and fumbled for his driver's license. Still no sign of a gun.

No sign of probable cause either. The Supreme Court had ruled information gained through magical means about non-magical crimes wasn't admissible in court. She badly wanted to draw on him, but he was unarmed and not visibly violent. Instead she moved in closer and *reached* with her magic. Blue tendrils of her aura brushed his roiling energy, curled into it like fingers, trying to slow it down, cool it off.

Burning Man handed over his license with a shaking hand, his aura going a brighter yellow as her magic shifted his emotions away from suicidal determination to the fear of going to jail. Keeping her voice low and soothing as she wrapped her power around him, Erica went into a cop's questioning patter -- who was he, where did he live, what was he doing in town.

As she spoke, she darted a glance down at his license in the illumination of a nearby streetlamp. Assuming the information was accurate, his name was Richard Carson, age twenty-eight, brown hair, blue eyes, address 132 Mason Avenue in Cotton Ridge. "This address still correct?"

"Uh, yeah." Carson fidgeted, rocking from foot to foot, his eyes darting.

"That's forty-five minutes from here," Erica said, even as she poured more magic into calming him. Her head began to ache with effort; he was too damned close to the edge.

"I was just going to get a beer," Carson began. "I work at…" He broke off.

She sucked in a gasp as the psychic currents of his aura dragged harder against her magical grip.

Which was when she realized he was staring at the gleam of the gold pentagram pin on her collar. An expression of fury dawned on his face, eyes narrowing, lips pulling off his teeth.

Oh, shit.

"Witch!" Carson's aura flashed blinding white, detonating like a Molotov cocktail. "Witch!" And he dove at her.

Erica went for her gun.

All two hundred plus pounds of him plowed into her like a runaway truck. She hit the sidewalk flat on her back hard enough to click her teeth together. Erica tasted blood and glimpsed a tattooed fist flying toward at her face. She snapped both arms up in an automatic boxer's block an instant before big, inked knuckles rammed into them.

"Witch, fucking witch! Trying to cast a fucking spell on me! I'm gonna *kill* you!" Screaming in fury, Carson loomed over her, raining punches over her head, his expression crazed, the whites of his eyes showing all the way around his irises. She could only ball tighter behind her blocking forearms, pain blasting through bone every time he struck. *Opening, I need an opening…*

He paused an instant, frustrated at his inability to hit her.

Erica rammed her fist into his mouth hard enough to rock his head back on his shoulders. Whipping both legs around his hips, she wrenched sideways, fighting to wrestle him off her as she gathered her magic. If all else failed, she'd…

A fist the size of a canned ham powered past her guard. As it slammed into the side of her face, Erica saw stars and tasted blood again. *Oh, fuck this!*

She reared up, slapped her palm against Carson's forehead and fired a magical blast right into the center of his skull. Though she didn't have the power to knock him cold, she could induce a blinding burst of pain in his cerebral cortex.

With a startled scream, he rocked back on his knees. Erica released his hips to slam both feet in the center of his chest, knocking him flat. She clawed for her Taser...

The roar echoed off the surrounding buildings -- a shattering leonine blast of sound that made them both jump.

Jake Nolan. And he sounded seriously pissed.

Oh, thank you, God. With the Feral in the fight, Carson didn't have a prayer.

"Shit!" Pale-faced, terrified, the big man scrambled to his feet and ran for his life.

Despite her aching jaw, Erica leaped up and charged after him. Something gold and blazing bounded past her with another ear-ringing roar. Bystanders screamed in terror, fleeing in all directions. *Probably remembering the polar bear...*

Glowing like a halogen bulb, the magical African lion leaped, knocking Carson on his face and pinning him there with massive golden paws. The man writhed, fighting to escape, screaming until his voice cracked. "Get off me! Getoffgetoff! *Don't eat me...*"

"I'm not going to eat you, you idiot," Jake growled back, magic giving his normal baritone an inhuman reverberation. Erica could just make out the familiar broad, muscular body inside the blazing shell of his cat. "But I am going to kick your ass if you don't quit fighting me!"

"No no no..." With a sob, Carson went limp, his aura burning red with pain, probably from a combination of her blast and getting tackled by a fully manifested Feral.

None of the red was intense enough to indicate serious injuries, though. Probably just bruised all to hell. Eyes squeezed shut, he started babbling about demon cats and witches interspersed with fragments of prayer. Waves of terrified yellow rolled across his field's scarlet background. He really did think Jake was going to eat him. Erica might have felt sorry for him -- if she hadn't suspected he'd been planning mass murder.

"Hey, Jake." She stepped up behind them as Jake pulled a pair of handcuffs off his belt and started cuffing the sobbing man. "Thanks for the backup."

The big deputy glanced over his shoulder at her. Feral-gold eyes shone through the outline of his manifestation's mane as he gave her a tight nod. Judging from the muscle flexing to the right of his mouth, he was still pissed. "Why the hell was he trying to kill you?"

"My winning personality. Also my pentagram pin. Don't think he likes Talents."

"Witch!" Carson moaned, his voice muffled by the grass he was pressed into. "'Thou shalt not suffer a witch to live!'"

"I'll see your Exodus 22 and raise you a 'Thou shalt not kill,'" Erica said dryly. Bullies had been throwing Exodus in her face since kindergarten. The verse had lost all power to sting by the time she was in high school.

"Cat demon in the shape of a man..." Carson panted, but made no effort to resist as Jake patted him down. He might be crazy, but he wasn't stupid. Fully manifested, a Feral was four or five times as strong as a Norm the same size, not to mention damn near bulletproof.

"Okay, Mr. Carson, you're under arrest for assaulting a police officer," Erica told him. Then, just to cover her ass, she started reciting the Miranda Warning. She might need to interrogate him, and she didn't want the case thrown out if she was right about what he'd intended. "You have the right to remain silent..."

As she finished her spiel, Jake banished his lion manifestation, letting it dim until only someone with Erica's Talent could see it at all. Though the deputy's attention was focused on Carson, his Familiar's ghostly head turned toward her. Glowing eyes studied her with interest. Clarence's physical body was several miles away at Briggs Feral Sanctuary, but thanks to the mystical bond between them, Jake and his cat could draw on one another's magic even at that distance.

"*Rrmmmmm.*" Clarence butted his big, maned head against her hip, creating a ghostly sensation of fur brushing over her aura.

"Hi, there, Clar." Smiling at the familiar psychic contact, she reached down to scratch behind one round leonine ear. He chuffed -- the soft puff of air big cats used as a greeting. With a soundless mental click, their wartime psychic bond activated again.

Like all Familiars, Clarence had been bred for magical ability, intelligence, and physical strength. His thoughts might be nonverbal, but he had the same ability to reason as a human four-year-old.

While Jake dealt with Carson, Clarence circled Erica, rubbing his head against her hip like the world's biggest house cat, sampling her aura, tasting her emotions. Marking her. And making her acutely aware of Jake, whose spirit was so entwined with Clarence's it was hard to tell where the cat left off and the man began.

Jake looked around at her, Feral gold gaze narrowing. She'd have known what he was just from the eyes alone. Ordinary humans just didn't have irises that color. As their stares locked, she felt the intimate mental connection between her, the lion, and the man -- a holdover from the Corps. She drew in a breath at the emotion she felt ringing through that bond: *Approval. Hunger. Need.* Too strong to ignore.

And then the impression was gone, the connection

vanishing as though snuffed out like a candle.

Damn it, Jake, I want you. And she'd have to go on not having him, because nothing had changed.

Swallowing, Erica forced herself to ask a halfway professional question. "Have you found Carson's keys?"

"Yeah." Jake jerked his chin at a pile of items he'd put on the grass just out of the suspect's reach. A wallet, a cell phone, a pocket knife...

And a key fob.

Erica scooped it up. "Mr. Carson, do we have your permission to search your car?"

Carson turned his bruised, dirty face until he could look up at her. He sounded sullen, if a bit more coherent. "I don't give a fuck what you do."

Erica pointed the fob at the Honda Civic she suspected was Carson's and pressed the button. The car's headlights helpfully flashed, confirming its ownership. She pushed another button and watched the trunk pop open a couple of inches. But as she started toward it, a nasty thought made her break step. *Suddenly I feel the need for a bomb suit.* Damn, but she wished she could see through the metal of a trunk the way she could fabric...

"I smell guns." Jake frowned as he followed, dragging Carson along with one big hand fisted in the man's collar, the other gripping his handcuffed wrists. The Norm was five inches taller than he was, but that made no damned difference whatsoever to a Feral.

Erica eyed their prisoner, watching his aura for deception. "Did you rig your car to blow?"

"No." Judging from his tone, Carson wished he had. But there was no sign of the swirling orange shade she associated with lying.

Taking a deep breath, Erica raised the trunk lid.

"Shit," Jake growled. "What the hell were you planning, World War III?"

There was an AR-15 rigged for automatic fire with a

bump stock, two sixty-round magazines, three tear gas grenades, and an H&K semiautomatic .45, as well as a bulletproof vest and a gas mask.

Erica studied the armory grimly. "Who were you planning to kill, Carson? And I know it was somebody. I could see it all over you."

"I wasn't gonna kill nobody." His aura flashed orange with the lie.

Jake just looked at him, his magic vibrating the air around him, producing a deep leonine growl. Clarence flared into full manifestation again, lips peeled back to reveal fangs the length of a man's forefinger.

Carson recoiled, eyes rounding in horror. "Had to! Drank one of their fucking magic beers. Bitch put a spell on me, made me think things..." He jerked, trying to escape Jake's hold. The deputy growled again and cranked up on the handcuffs. Carson yelped and dropped to his knees as the cuffs bit into bone, threatening to break his wrists.

"You're talking about Potions?" Erica demanded. The bar was the only place on Faraday Square that sold magical microbrews. It was also where she'd been headed for the cheeseburger and fries she'd had in mind for dinner. *Good thing I got him before he hit the bar, or I might be dead now.*

Carson hesitated. Clarence snapped his jaws, and the man jerked. "Yeah! Fuck, yeah, Potions. It had to be cleansed. Andy said if I killed the witch, it'd break the spell." Orange, yellow, and red roiled his aura like a pot coming to a boil.

Erica and Jake exchanged a quick, hard glance. She dropped to one knee beside Carson. "What kind of spell?" She kept the question low and controlled. She couldn't let her fury show if she wanted to get the truth out of him. "What witch?" *The son of a bitch had planned to murder everyone in Potions.*

"That bitch bartender cast a spell on me to make me kill kids!" Carson's eyes were so wide, white showed all the way around the irises. His aura burned in a furious swirl of hot color that grew brighter by the second. "She wanted me to go to that Talent elementary school and shoot up the place. I could hear her talking at me all the time, she wouldn't let me sleep, she wouldn't shut up. Always muttering and chanting. *I had to shut her up!*"

He's either a paranoid schizophrenic or he's been on some very nasty drugs for a very long time. Either way, he intended to kill Barb. Erica knew the cheerful blonde bartender well, and she'd always liked her. "Barbara Miller's a Norm, Mr. Carson. A Norm with two little kids. She has nothing to do with brewing those microbrews. And even if she had, all the beer does is make you feel a little blissed. The voices in your head are all *in your head.*"

"It was her!" Carson insisted, voice spiraling higher. "I told Andy, and he said it was the beer, and she served me the beer so she had to die to break the spell." He was talking faster and faster now, all but babbling. "Andy said I'd be a hero. Cleanse the evil. Save the kids. No more demons and witches and glowing eyes in the dark, no more screams and chanting... Quiet. Quiet. Just quiet. *I need some fucking quiet...*"

You need some fucking antipsychotics. Ruthlessly, Erica cut into his babble. "Andy who?"

At that, the whirlpool of yellow coiled tighter, reddening in a way that told her a lie was about to come out of his mouth. "Andy... Kelly... Andy with the ink."

"You're a fucking liar," Jake snarled, in a voice more lion than man. He twisted the cuffs so ruthlessly, Carson yelped. "Andy *who*?"

"I don't know, man, just Andy. I didn't want to do it, but I couldn't take the chanting, and the kids... Better the witches die than the kids... but the kids have demons, we need to save them. The dark has teeth, teeth and dragons and skulls on fire... and dark, blood dark, screamingwon'tletmesleep..." He began to gibber, the words running together.

Erica traded a look with Jake, who shook his head. She stepped back and keyed her mic. "Laurel County, please dispatch the crime scene unit and I-9 to Faraday Square."

As she waited for Dispatch to confirm the detective and the crime scene investigator were en route, Erica glanced around. Looked like the crowd had dispersed back to whichever bars or restaurants they'd been headed for when all hell broke loose. *Thank you, God.*

Carson cowered at Jake's feet, rocking slowly back and forth, muttering to himself. Judging by the writhing currents of his aura, this encounter hadn't been particularly good for his mental health. Then again, it hadn't done a hell of a lot for hers either.

Still better than being dead. *And a hell of a lot better than a bar full of murdered people.*

Jake slanted her a grim smile. "Glenda the Good saves the Lollypop Guild again. What told you he was a flying monkey?"

"Happened to be scanning the crowd when his aura blew white." She blew out a breath and grimaced. "His head looked like a mushroom cloud."

The Feral winced, knowing what that meant as well as she did. "Shit. You probably saved a hell of a lot of lives."

"And you probably saved mine -- again. How many is that, anyway?" She grinned at him. "I lost count somewhere around the second tour."

"About as often as you saved mine." He gave her the grin that always made her heart beat a little faster.

Even in the dim light from the surrounding streetlights, Jake was ridiculously handsome. His square-jawed face was all chiseled contours, with an aquiline nose enhancing its stark masculinity. Thick blond brows slanted over Feral gold eyes that glowed in dim light. His frequent crooked grins were sometimes cynical, even downright sarcastic; you knew he meant the smile when his dimples came out. He wore his bright hair in a ruthless buzz cut, yet it somehow managed to tempt her fingers anyway. It had been long enough to curl in Afghanistan. Sometimes it had been all she could do to keep her hands off those curls.

Yeah, Bobby wouldn't have taken *that* well.

Jake's body was just as impressive as it had been during their tours, all broad shoulders and powerful muscle. Jake wasn't that tall -- only about five feet ten inches -- but between his build, bulletproof vest, and duty belt, he looked like a tank. Given what he and Clarence could do, that was just truth in advertising.

RRRrrrrr? The lion appeared again, glowing softly, barely manifested even to her senses. He was a big beast, the top of his head level with her ribcage. The cat's physical body weighed almost six hundred pounds.

Erica reached out and stroked a hand through Clarence's transparent mane. He rewarded her with a soft leonine moan of pleasure. As she touched the Ferals' blended auras, it was all Erica could do not to moan herself. The psychic contact felt so damned good, so familiar. God, she wanted him. Wanted him despite the grief, despite the guilt, despite knowing she shouldn't.

When she glanced up from the cat, Jake's golden eyes glowed faintly with his magic. Reminding her far too much of his brother's.

Bobby's lips moved. He shouldn't have been able to make a sound given the damage, but his magic spoke for him. "Sorry... Love you... sorry... so..."

Pain shafted her so savagely it was all she could do not to cry out. She jerked her gaze away. Clarence moaned again, this time in distress, as if he'd felt her pain through her aura. He probably had.

As she fought the agonizing memory, a white van

rolled up and parked in the fire lane just down the block. A sheriff's star gleamed on the door in metallic gold paint, and black lettering read "Laurel County Crime Scene Unit."

An unmarked car that probably belonged to the detective pulled in behind it. Erica started toward them. Much better to focus on the present than the bloody, painful past.

Chapter Two

And there she goes again, Jake thought, watching Erica Harris walk away, her assorted gear framing that delightful, heart-shaped ass. *Every time I think we're getting somewhere, she runs like a rabbit.*

Clarence made an impatient sound from the depths of his head.

It's not that simple, furball. If I could, I would. But human women get to tell you no, and she ain't having it.

RRumphhhhh. An image flashed through his mind: a snarling lioness striking out with a lightning-fast paw. Clarence's way of pointing out that at least Jake didn't have to worry about taking a set of claws across the muzzle. *MmmRRRRR.*

Translated from the lion: *Grow a pair.*

Maybe the cat had a point. God knew, Erica Harris had tempted him from the first day she'd been assigned as their team Arcanist five years ago, back when they'd all been in the Arcane Corps.

She was damn near as tall as he was, with a lean, athletic build that contrasted sharply with her delicate features. She still wore her chocolate hair in the same short, layered cut she'd had in the Corps, probably thinking it made her look like a hardass. Epic Fail. The pixie style called attention to the gentle contours of her oval face, with those big, dark eyes and that soft, full mouth.

Jake could think of a lot of things he'd like to do with that mouth. He might have suggested a few, if it hadn't been for the scent of pain hanging in the air, lingering like a particularly astringent perfume over the acrid stench of Carson's madness.

She still wasn't over Bobby. But then, neither was Jake. It wasn't the kind of thing you got over.

Ever.

Brooding, he watched her approach Detective Grant Sawyer as the man got out of his car. Despite his muscular build, Sawyer was a hair shorter than Erica. That and his cap of curly brown hair made his handsome face look boyish. He had a habit of speaking in a low, slow southern drawl that made people underestimate his intelligence.

Sawyer wasn't above suckering people ruthlessly in the pursuit of justice. Jake liked that about him. He was also one of the reasons they'd gotten through that mess with the terrorists a year ago without a higher body count.

Erica started to speak, gesturing as Sawyer listened intently. Beneath the professional focus, Jake thought he saw a flash of personal interest in her brown eyes.

RRRRrrrr.

Shush, Jake told his Familiar. *She's not standing too close -- she's giving him a report. Don't be an asshole.*

Mmmrrrrrr   rrrooooollll.   Mmmmrch   Ooomffff. Translation: *Tell it to some cat who's not in your head. Let's get over there before he asks her to mate.*

It doesn't work like that, Clar. Anyway, we've got to keep an eye on the asshole.

The gunman still sat at his feet, dirty, bruised, face bleeding from being slammed into the pavement during that flying tackle. Jake felt zero sympathy for the fucker. If they hadn't gotten lucky, Carson would have shot up the bar with Erica in it.

I could have lost her.

Nrrroooommmm? Translation: *When did you have her?*

Before Jake could retort, a black and white pulled up and double-parked beside Sawyer's vehicle. A moment later, a familiar figure got out and started toward them.

Jake suppressed a curse. Johnson. *Fan-fucking-tastic.*

Tall, graying, and spare, Sergeant Roger Johnson cultivated a Sam-Elliot-playing- Wyatt-Earp look, complete with ruthlessly short hair and thick mustache.

Completely humorless and convinced of his own moral rectitude, he hated the fuck out of Jake.

The feeling was mutual.

Johnson stalked over to interrupt Erica in mid-word. As the sergeant started snapping questions, a frown gathered on her pretty face. Bastard was probably being his usual douchenozzle self. She always did have a low tolerance for bigots.

In the depths of his mind, Clarence chuffed.

Yeah, I'd better get over there before she tells him off and gets fired.

Reaching down, Jake grabbed Carson by one arm and hauled him to his feet. "Come on, let's get you in the car."

Crazy or not, the man knew better than to push a Feral any further than he already had. He didn't resist as Jake marched him to the patrol car parked a couple of blocks down the street.

Five minutes later, Carson was buckled in the back, sitting slumped and sullen as Jake parked behind Johnson's cruiser. When he got out, he saw the Honda's trunk was open again, revealing its armory to the crime scene investigator documenting it with an expensive Nikon.

As Jake approached, Johnson glowered at Erica. "So why did you stop this guy to begin with? It doesn't sound like you had probable cause."

Look who's joined the ACLU, Jake thought. *You're never this worried about civil rights when you're kicking a Talent's ass.*

"His aura showed the explosive white pattern that's a known indicator of someone planning a mass casualty attack. I saw it several times during the war." Erica's face was so expressionless, Jake knew she was about a minute and a half from telling the sergeant what he could do with his probable cause.

Johnson curled a lip. "You saw it in his 'aura'? What

kind of magic power is that? You sure you didn't just overhear him bragging about it?"

In the depths of Jake's mind, Clarence growled softly. Johnson had treated them just as contemptuously until Jake's dance with that fucking bear Feral. Funny how saving the SWAT team's ass gave some people a whole new attitude.

Damned if Johnson was going to dis Erica if Jake had anything to say about it. "Actually," he said with a little too much Clarence rumble, "All Talents can see auras. Harris is just much more sensitive than most of us."

The sergeant shot him a glare of cold displeasure at the interruption, then ignored him. "How'd you get him to confess? Cast a spell?"

"No sir, I did not," Erica said, icily respectful.

"But you Arc witches did that kind of thing all the time in the war."

"Not to American citizens -- it's a violation of the Fifth Amendment. Even if it weren't, it would require a spell circle that takes an hour to cast. Besides, I doubt I could have pulled it off. My strength is in sensing and disrupting magical structures, not brute force magic."

"Then why did Carson confess?"

Okay, that's enough of that. Jake reached down into the white-hot core of his bond with his cat and let Clarence spill out. The lion manifested around him in a crackling surge of magic, glowing so bright even the Norms could see it. When he spoke, his voice rumbled an octave deeper than normal. "Because I scared the shit out of him."

Johnson flinched a heartbeat before his fear morphed into anger. "Yeah, well, I'd better not hear of you using your magic in violation of department policy…" Glancing at his fellow Norm, Johnson registered Sawyer's cool, disapproving stare and broke off.

Yeah, you're letting too much of your hate-on show, Sarge.

"Still, you probably prevented a mass casualty event." The praise sounded grudging at best. "Good work."

The air around the sergeant smelled astringent with the telltale scent of deception. But was it their methods he disapproved of? Or the fact that they'd prevented a bloodbath that could have forced Potions out of business? Johnson didn't approve of Talent-owned establishments.

The cynicism in the thought made Jake wince. The sergeant might be a prick, but he was still a cop sworn to protect the public. Even Talents.

You're getting paranoid, Nolan.

* * *

Sergeant Roger Johnson thrust his key into his cruiser's ignition with a hand that shook. Grinding his teeth, he checked behind him and pulled out, forcing himself not to stomp on the gas. *Sawyer and those fucking Talents are probably watching.*

He listened to the scratchy background chatter on his police radio as he drove out of Faraday Square. As he passed the towering statue of Colton Faraday, an image flashed through Roger's mind: the bronze figure standing silhouetted under a bright blue sky, puddles of red smearing the emerald grass around its base.

Roger's gut wrenched as the events of a year before reared up and smacked him with a flashback so vivid, so intense, it didn't even feel like a memory...

The air trembled with the deep, shattering roars of the Feral terrorist, Virgil Ford, almost drowning out Steve Jenkins' horrified scream. Twelve feet of glowing polar bear pounced on the deputy, biting right through his body armor as if it were taffy. Steve shrieked as the monster ripped him open, spilling scarlet guts on the spring grass.

Driven by his best friend's dying howls, Roger charged out to help. Before he'd taken two steps, a thundering fusillade of rifle fire deafened him. A bullet punched his vest like the swing of a baseball bat, forcing him back into the shelter of the alley with the other cops of the SWAT team. Anguished, listening to Jenkins die, he scanned the rooftops for the witch sniper and her assault rifle. *I've got to do something!*

He'd attended the Academy with Steve, busted up bar fights, chased drug dealers, even been Steve's best man. But if he broke cover, he'd never even get to the bear before the sniper gunned him down.

Another roar whipsawed over the bear's, and Roger's heart leaped. Jake Nolan barreled past, running hard in full lion manifestation, all glowing muscle and inhuman power. Bullets smacked into his magical shell, but he never even broke step as he hit the bear like an eighteen-wheeler, knocking him away from his limp victim.

He'd still been too late.

Four people had died that day: Steve Jenkins, Deputy Al Keller, and two civilians. The butcher's bill would have been much higher if not for Nolan and his Feral buddy, Kurt Briggs. They'd fought Ford to a standstill, and Nolan had damned near died doing it.

Roger had been helpless. His gun and his badge and all his experience hadn't been worth shit because he was a mere human. Nolan had saved lives because he'd been born with abilities Roger would never have, no matter how he worked and sweated. Roger had never liked Talents. Never trusted them. But Faraday Square had taught him how dangerous they really were.

Humans couldn't afford to just sit back and let Talents keep taking over their military, law enforcement, government -- even entertainment, for Christ's sake. They had to be stopped. Even if that meant innocent Talents paid the price.

He frowned as he drove toward the Laurel County Sheriff's Office. *Even if that meant innocent Talents paid the price…* His stomach twisted.

No. No way. She wouldn't have…

Fuck. Yes, she would. There wasn't much Virginia Laurel wasn't capable of.

Roger drove downtown until he found a local park, empty and dark this time of night. A perfect place for a conversation he didn't want anyone to overhear. Plucking his private cell phone off his belt, he thumbed in her number. It was close to ten, and he half hoped she wouldn't answer.

No such luck.

"You'd better have a good reason to call at this hour." Virginia's low drawl was all well-bred southern matron, though her tone was frosty with disapproval.

"We narrowly avoided a mass casualty event at Potions tonight. Thought you'd be interested."

"What happened?" She didn't sound particularly concerned. Not that she ever did.

He sketched the situation out in a few clipped sentences as devoid of emotion as he could make them. She'd often told him she didn't want color commentary. "So it's a good thing Harris can see auras, or we have a lot of dead and wounded."

"Dead and wounded who pollute their bodies with magic. Perhaps it would have taught the survivors a useful lesson about being more careful with whom they associate."

He asked the question before he had time to think better of it. "Did you have anything to do with this?"

The icy silence that followed made clear he'd overstepped. "Are you actually asking me if I sent that lunatic to murder the citizens of Laurel County?"

A bead of sweat began to roll down his spine. He forced any trace of doubt from his voice. "Of course not."

"I'm relieved. It would be political suicide if such slander ever got out -- for both of us. Or have you given up on running for sheriff?"

Roger swallowed. *Damn it, I should have kept my mouth shut.* If he had any intention of running against Gable next year, he needed the support of the Humanist Party. Virginia Laurel could make that support a reality… Or she could block it completely. Her connections went all the way to the White House. "No, ma'am."

"Then you certainly don't want our party associated with a hate crime."

"That goes without saying."

"I'm glad to hear it. The Humanists are doing a lot of good with our education and anti-poverty programs. It would be a shame to hand the Constitutionalists the ammunition to stop us." Her voice took on a silky note. "And it wouldn't do your aspirations a lot of good either."

He licked his lips. "No, ma'am."

"In the meantime, I suggest you keep an eye on those Talents of yours. All of our lives would be a great deal simpler if they could be encouraged to find some other line of work." Her voice dropped to a growl. "Especially that 'hero,' Nolan."

"I'm working on it."

"Work harder."

His phone screen flashed *CALL ENDED*.

Blowing out a breath, Roger tucked the phone back into its belt holster.

And tried very hard to believe South Carolina State Representative Virginia Laurel had nothing to do with sending Richard Carson to commit mass murder.

* * *

Dropping her phone into her lap, Virginia curled her fingers around the cut crystal glass of Kentucky bourbon. She lifted it to her lips, drained the glass, and then sat back in her armchair. Listening to the fire crackle, she stared sightlessly at the portrait over the fireplace. Her great-great-great-great-great grandfather William Laurel stared coolly back, his oil-painted features stern under his tricorn hat and powdered wig, looking every bit the Revolutionary War hero he'd been.

At one time the Laurel family had owned most of the county that bore their name. Their sprawling plantation had included thousands of acres used to grow everything from tobacco to indigo, then later, cotton. The family had been among the richest in the state.

But that had been before the Civil War. Before General Sherman torched the plantation and freed hundreds of slaves. Before Alexander Laurel had been forced to sell thousands of acres to that carpetbagger Colton Faraday, who'd used the land to lure his fellow Talents to Laurelton.

More than a century and a half later, the descendants of those magic-users were still here. Still using their powers against normal people to cheat, enchant, and kill. And pose as heroes.

But they weren't going to stay here if she had anything to say about it.

Her jaw tightening, Virginia punched a button on her phone. "Call Adrian."

The cell beeped a series of tones, obeying. He answered on the second ring -- as well he should.

"Is there a problem?" Adrian Fleming's voice was smooth, cultured, without a trace of an accent to reveal his origins. Which amused her, since she knew he could sound like he'd just crawled from the depths of a trailer park. He was very good at pretending to be whatever the mission required.

Just now, though, she was less than happy with him, and she damn well wanted him to know it. "Carson failed. It seems he encountered the department's one witch deputy, who was able to divine his intentions just by looking at him. Evidently she sees auras. She and the Feral stopped him before he even got in the door. Will he talk?"

Adrian laughed, nothing at all cultured in the harsh bark of amusement. "Not after the spell I cast. The more they question him, the crazier he'll get." Fleming paused a moment, considering. "But I've still got some of his blood. I can always induce a heart attack."

Virginia made a mental note to ensure he never got his hands on any blood of hers. "Would the magical tampering show up on an autopsy?"

"Only if the pathologist is also an Arcanist. Unless the FBI takes an interest, that's doubtful."

"What about the witch?"

"She got lucky. Next time, she won't."

"If she does, I expect you to take care of the problem."

"That is what I do." He hung up the instant before she could.

Disquieted, Virginia stood and began to pace the library, watching the silken peach skirt of her nightgown kick around her slippered feet.

Like all Talents, Fleming was a magic-using snake, but he'd come highly recommended by those who knew the best tool for the job. Otherwise, she wouldn't have hired him.

Once she'd never have lowered herself to work with any Talent, no matter how highly recommended. The events of Faraday Square had taught her that squeamishness was a luxury she couldn't afford.

As she turned to pace in the other direction, Virginia's gaze fell on the photo of Victoria hanging over her desk. Her granddaughter's eyes were as big and blue as her own had been in her youth. Just four years old, the child was all blonde curls and chubby hands, her innocent spirit blazing in her joyous smile.

Even in Virginia's current grim mood, something about that smile made her smile back.

Her granddaughter deserved to live in a world free of Talents. Free of people who could use their powers to hurt her, steal from her, or lord it over her because she didn't have magical abilities. Free of those who had robbed her of her birthright.

Virginia meant to ensure her grandchild got the world she deserved.

* * *

Erica's field training officer had told her once that police work was forty percent boredom, two percent stark terror, and fifty-eight percent paperwork. On nights like this, she realized his figures were off.

The paperwork was closer to eighty percent.

"Look at the newbie!" Katilia Sharp sauntered over. Slim and short, black hair pulled back from a sharp-boned face, the young deputy grinned, flashing white teeth against dark skin as she presented her knuckles. "Saving lives and kicking ass. Good job."

Erica grinned at her friend and gave her a fist bump. "Thanks." Katilia had the zone adjoining hers; she, Jake, and Erica frequently backed each other up in situations where more than one cop was needed.

Katilia turned the grin on Jake, who sat at the desk next to Erica's in the Alpha shift bullpen. "I hear Lee Harvey Asshole thought you were going to eat him."

Jake looked up from his laptop. "He had nothing to worry about. I'm on an asshole-free diet. They give me gas."

"And sighs of relief sound all over the department." Katilia chortled and gave them a wave. "Well, I'm done for the night, folks. See y'all Monday." She frowned. "I think it's Monday. I lose track." She wandered out.

As they finished off the paperwork, other cops stopped by with a thumbs up or a slap on the back. It gave Erica an unaccustomed warm and fuzzy feeling.

Speaking of warm and fuzzy, Clarence kept brushing against her legs or sniffing her hair, blowing ghostly lion breath over her nape, keeping her entirely too aware of his Feral partner. *A matchmaking lion. God help me.*

Sawyer stuck his head in the bullpen door. "Nolan, Harris -- could you two give me a hand? I'm getting ready to question Carson. I'd like to know what he lies about."

Jake hit a button and stood, stretching his big body. It took all Erica's willpower not to stare in yearning at the curve of his ass. "What do you have in mind?"

"Just sniff for bullshit. Shake your head when he gives me any."

"Yeah, I do know that smell. After two years as a cop, I'm practically a bullshit connoisseur." He inhaled noisily. "Ah yes, smells like grass-fed Holstein with notes of Longhorn."

"Yippee ki-yay."

* * *

They questioned Carson in Interview B -- a small room furnished with a table bolted to the floor, a pair of chairs, and a camera set up in one corner of the ceiling. Television cop shows notwithstanding, there was no one-way mirror. Instead, Erica and Jake stood against the rear wall while Carson lied about the same thing he'd lied about before -- only louder, faster, and even less believably.

This time he claimed the man who'd sent him to shoot up Potions was named Tommy Miller rather than Andy Kelly. He also swore on a stack of Bibles he didn't know any Andy.

Sawyer rolled his eyes, and Erica knew what he was thinking. The minute a suspect started swearing on Bibles, he was lying his ass off.

The detective questioned him skillfully, circling back to the information he wanted, asking the same questions in different ways.

Carson went right on lying. That is, when he wasn't babbling, ranting, or quoting so-called Bible verses Erica knew didn't exist. Apparently his mother hadn't made him read the Good Book as often as Erica's had.

The whole time, orange patterns of deception spun through his aura like swirls of sherbet racing through the lemon yellow of his fear. She watched the energy flow intently, trying to match what he was saying to the color shift to determine which statements were lies. It wasn't easy -- his aura was seriously weird, swirling from his chest to his head and back again. She'd never seen anything like it. Which was why she spent more than two hours shrugging at Sawyer's inquiring glances, aware Jake was doing the same.

Finally, the detective called a break and they all retreated into the hall, leaving Carson sitting with his handcuffs bolted to the table in front of him. His restless jittering made them rattle and clank against the metal table.

"As my DI used to say, that man is crazy as a shithouse rat," Jake muttered as they all collectively slumped against the wall. Interrogations were exhausting even without using magic.

"Which doesn't make him legally insane. If he didn't know right from wrong, he wouldn't be lying his ass off." Sawyer leaned one muscled shoulder against the wall as he scrubbed both hands over his face. "Thoughts?"

Jake raked his hands through his blond brush cut. "I smelled so many lies, I couldn't tell which was which."

Erica nodded. "If we had a roster for Human Heritage and rattled it off at him, I could probably narrow down who was involved."

"Assuming the asshole in question is an HHer," Jake pointed out.

"Is it possible there *is* no Andy or Tony or whoever the fuck he says it is?" Sawyer asked. "This is a guy who thinks a witch is telling him to shoot up an elementary school. He could have imagined 'Andy' too."

Erica considered that. "Possibly, but the fact that he knows he's lying about the guy's name suggests there is a guy."

Sawyer grunted, his expression brooding. "I don't like the way this situation smells. It's one thing if a lone gunman does something like this. It's something entirely different if someone put him up to it."

Jake gave Erica a smile. "Either way, we're damn lucky Harris stopped him."

"Yeah, but I'd be happier if he doesn't have friends." Sawyer frowned at them, his gaze concerned. "It's not a good time to be a Talent in this town. Too many people are scared, and that makes them mean. Some of those people are cops."

Erica eyed him. "You mean Johnson."

"And his buddies." Sawyer scrubbed his knuckles over his jaw meditatively, then sighed. "Look, you've got good instincts, Harris. You played tonight's situation just right. You didn't get anybody killed, not even the asshole suspect." He grimaced. "Whether or not he needed killing."

She rolled her shoulders, a little uncomfortable with the praise. "Thank you, Detective."

"My point is, the same thing that makes you an asset to people like me will make you a threat to anti-Talent types. You and Nolan would do well to watch each other's backs."

Watching Jake's anything isn't exactly a chore, chimed in small voice in the back of her head. She told it to shut up. "We'll keep that in mind."

Sawyer nodded and straightened away from the wall. "I think I've dug as much out of Carson as I'm going to get. I'll tackle his friends and family tomorrow, see if they've got any ideas who put him up to this. In the meantime, we need to get him booked into the county jail."

"I'll take care of it," Jake said.

Erica pulled out a dog-eared notebook out of her back pocket. "What are we charging him with?"

"None of the weapons he had were registered, and possession of tear gas grenades is illegal. So let's start with that." Sawyer rattled off a string of charges as she scribbled them down. "The Solicitor's Office may add or subtract some after they interview him and look at your body cam footage. I'm going to call the ATF on the grenades tomorrow. The Feds may want a crack at him too."

"Works for me." Erica flipped the notebook to a clean sheet and scribbled her cell number, ripped it off, and handed it to him. "By the way, I'm off for the next three days. If you've got any questions, feel free to give me a call."

Sawyer took the sheet, giving her a warm, pleased smile. "I'll do that. See you, Harris, Nolan. Nice work tonight."

"Thanks." Erica watched the detective stroll off toward the Violent Crimes division. He did have nice shoulders. Maybe not as nice as Jake's, but not bad, either.

From the corner of one eye, she saw Jake fold muscled arms, his body tensing, a frown darkening his face. Before she could ask him what his problem was, his cell rang. He plucked it off his belt, looked at the screen, sighed, and put it to his ear. "Hi, Mom."

Erica's lips twitched.

Jake grinned back, self-depreciating humor bringing out a dimple. "Mom, I survived the Caliphate War. Some HHer fruitcake is not going to hurt me. He was way too busy begging me not to eat him." He laughed, his voice deep and rich. "Yeah, yeah, you are what you eat…"

Erica grinned, remembering getting calls like that from her own mother…

Her smile faded. She'd never get one again.

Dropping her gaze from Jake's laughing eyes, she looked down at her shoes.

"I'll tell her. Have a nice night, Ma." He thumbed off the call and clipped the phone to his belt. "I wish I could talk her into not watching the eleven o'clock news."

"She worries." *And you have no idea how lucky you are she's around to do it.*

"Yeah, but she doesn't need to. I'm a lion Feral, for God's sake. They don't call us Tooth Tanks for nothing." He shook his head, then added, "By the way, she said to tell you 'Good work.'"

"Thanks. Let's go put Carson in a cage."

As they started toward the interrogation room, her stomach gave a demanding rumble. Jake lifted a blond brow at her. "Was that you? Because it sounded more like Clarence."

Erica grimaced. "I'd planned to stop off at Potions for a burger earlier tonight, but Carson had other ideas."

"You want to stop by The Cauldron after we get Batshit Boy booked?" The question sounded casual, but there was a gleam in his eyes that suggested otherwise.

Erica hesitated, looking up into his handsome, angular face. The gold of his eyes reminded her far too much of his brother's. "It's a little late."

"So? I know you, Harris, you're a night owl. Besides, I need to talk to you about Johnson."

Well, she couldn't disagree with that. "The Cauldron it is."

Chapter Three

By the time they got Carson booked into the county jail on all those counts, Erica's stomach was indeed beginning to sound like Clarence in a very bad mood. The fact that their prisoner had grown increasingly violent hadn't helped. Jake had finally been forced to manifest his cat just to get him fingerprinted, booked, and into a cell.

It was 1:30 in the morning by the time Erica parked next to Jake's cruiser in the restaurant's parking lot. One of the few diners in Laurelton that was open 24/7, the Cauldron's food was both delicious and reasonably priced. All of which made the place beloved of cops, partying teenagers, and drunks looking to sober up after the bars closed.

The long narrow building had brick walls painted white, the better to showcase an eye-catching mural celebrating Laurelton's history that swirled across one wall. Revolutionary War hero William Laurel struck a heroic pose, musket in one hand; Colton Faraday stood beside one of his trains; and Laurel County's BMW plant sprawled across manicured emerald grounds. Dancing sigils surrounded all three elements in shades of green, blue, and gold. The symbols weren't just for show, either; magic glowed beneath the paint, a spell to attract hungry customers and put them in the mood to tip well afterward. The Arcanist who'd painted it had been damned good.

"I hope you don't mind if I order an embarrassing amount of food. Working magic always makes me hungry." Jake's smile took on a sensual tilt that gave his words a note of double entendre as his eyes lingered on her mouth.

Erica swallowed, trying to fight her body's vivid reaction to the thought of his hunger for anything.

Especially me. She cleared her throat. "Yeah, I was famished even before I started slinging power around."

Something in his smile triggered a memory of walking beside him during the war. She could almost taste the desert air, feel the weight of her body armor as she, Jake, Kurt, Dave, and Bobby hunted sorcerers through the Iraqi night. Their cat manifestations moved along with them, alert, utterly silent, the air almost pulsing with their magic, knowing that at any moment they could walk into a firefight or trigger a MEED -- Magically Enhanced Explosive Device.

Those nights had been the first time in her life Erica had felt accepted. Valued, instead of a freak suspected of striking a deal with the devil. Living her first eighteen years as an outcast had sucked. Going to war had been a small price to pay to get away from her self-righteous Norm neighbors.

Jake stepped ahead to open the door for her in one of those habitual gestures of southern gallantry his mother had drummed into his head. As Erica passed him, her gaze lingered on the span of broad shoulders that looked even wider in that bulletproof vest. Need heated her blood.

But then, she'd lusted for Jake even in full body armor, wearing the stink of dirt, blood, and combat sweat, his expression grim, his gold eyes alight with an adrenaline junky gleam...

The voice of common sense muttered a warning: *This has epic fail written all over it. Kind of like stopping off at a bakery on the way home from a Weight Watchers meeting.*

Just like a big piece of chocolate cake, Jake was both tempting and bad for her -- and Erica wasn't likely to be terrific for him either. She and Bobby had done this dance, and it hadn't ended well for either of them. *If I had any sense, I'd go home.*

But here she was -- staying. *Idiot.*

As they paused just inside the door, a twenty-something server bustled over, trim in the Cauldron's white and green uniform, her long blonde hair tied back in a ponytail with a green ribbon. She gave Jake an appreciative smile. "Just the two of you?"

"Right." Jake flashed a hint of lady-killing dimple.

The woman's gaze fell on the F on his uniform sleeve. Blue eyes widened. "Come... Come right this way." She sounded nervous.

As they followed her toward a booth, Erica eyed her. *Really? This is a Talent town. You need to get used to dealing with us.*

The server -- Betty, according to her name tag -- handed them a pair of laminated menus. As they slid onto opposing green-upholstered benches, she blurted, "Are you him? The Feral who fought the bear in Faraday Square?"

He shrugged, a little uncomfortable. "One of them."

"My mother was there that day having lunch. She might've died if you hadn't..." Breaking off, Betty clutched her menu pad to her chest. "May I... may I take a selfie? Mom will never believe I met you."

"Sure." Jake didn't even blink, evidently no stranger to being treated like a celebrity.

The woman whipped her phone out of an apron pocket, sank to one knee beside the booth, and angled the cell to aim it at herself and Jake. Studying Betty's aura, Erica realized she'd misread her. Judging by the swirl of pink pleasure, her nervousness was a product of hero-worship rather than fear.

Grinning, Betty bounced back to her feet. Gaze falling to the pentagram on Erica's collar, she asked, "Were you there too?"

"Uh, no. I wasn't a member of the department then."

"Oh." The server looked briefly disappointed, then slid the phone back into an apron pocket and pulled out a menu pad. "What can I get you two to drink?"

They both ordered water -- the last thing either needed at the end of a shift was caffeine. The waitress all but danced away in her excitement. Erica lifted a brow at Jake. "Do you get that a lot?"

"Enough." His smile turned dry. "It can come in handy. You'd be surprised how often pissed-off people calm right down when I roll up. If they're drunk or Human Heritage, they might give me some passive aggression, but that's about it. Not many people try to pick fights once they spot the F patch."

"Good to know the public has some sense of self-preservation."

When Betty came back for their order carrying a single glass of water, another server accompanied her, also carrying a glass. He was a tall young man, his long, bony face bright with the excitement of someone meeting his hero. His nametag read "Shannon."

Eyeing his aura, Erica realized he was a Talent. A Bard, based on the strong, glowing violet of his magic. Looked like he had a lot of ability -- the kind that would eventually lead to recording contracts and hordes of adoring fans.

"I hate to bother you," Shannon said in a deep, beautiful voice that didn't match his thoroughly ordinary face. Yep, definitely a Bard. She'd love to hear him sing. "But can I take a selfie?" His eyes flicked to her collar pin. "With both of you?"

"I wasn't there," Erica told him.

"But the sheriff hired you, so you must be pretty good." The smile drained from his face. "And you're keeping the rest of us safe." The flat way he said it had her checking his aura again. The red of pain flowed through it like blood in the water. Somebody had been making the kid's life hell.

For just a moment she was five years old again,

and... Erica cut the thought off and forced a smile. "Of course I don't mind."

Shannon grinned like a boy and took the selfie, angling it and snapping off four shots.

"Somebody been giving you trouble?" Erica asked.

"Since last year, we've *all* been catching a lot of shit." His smile a shade forced, he nodded and turned away. "I'll let y'all eat. Thanks a lot. Have a nice night."

The waitress watched him walk away. "Somebody painted a pentagram on his mom's front door this morning. His neighbors are assholes." She shook her head and took out her pad and pen. "Do y'all know what you want?"

Jake ordered a quadruple stack of pancakes with a loaded omelet -- he hadn't been kidding about the caloric needs of Ferals. Erica made do with a double stack.

As the waitress hurried off to put in their order, Erica leaned back in the booth. "Bet that pentagram's not the worst thing Shannon's suffered lately."

"Probably not. The town's collective mood has grown ugly since the terrorists killed Kurt's dad. Even my mom caught some of it, at least from the people who don't consider her a hero's mother."

He looked so grim, Erica decided to cheer him up. "So how big a stick *do* you have to use?"

"Stick?"

"To beat the women off." She tucked her tongue in her cheek. "Or do you just sacrifice your body for the good of Norm/Talent relations?"

"That's me -- martyr to the cause."

Erica smiled in pleasure at the flash of dimple she'd gotten out of him. This felt so... right. Giving each other gentle hell, the way they'd done on deployments.

What does it say about me that I felt more at home in a war zone? But life had seemed simpler then, and she'd had Bobby. Though sometimes that had been a mixed blessing…

Yeah, don't go there. Erica cleared her throat. "So what the hell is going on with Sergeant Johnson?"

Jake drained his water as if it were a shot glass. "He wants to run for sheriff with the Humanist Party. Which means he thinks all Talents are closet terrorists. Or at least, he has to pretend he does." He curled his upper lip in a snarl so impressive, it deserved fangs. "Kurt told that fucking bear Feral if he and his bitch Arcanist tried to work that spell, they were going to trigger a literal witch hunt. But noooo. They were convinced they could terrorize President Roth *and* Congress into leaving Talents alone."

"It's tough to intimidate a guy with the nuclear codes."

"Which is why Congress passed that damned National Talent Registration Act. Exactly what the Fords were trying to discourage." He shook his head. "And now Indigo's dead, Virgil's headed for death row, and the rest of us are glowing in the dark from the figurative fallout."

Betty and Shannon reappeared carrying trays loaded down with their meal. Jake and Erica promptly tabled the discussion in favor of refueling.

Once her stomach was full, Erica said, "So Johnson hates us."

"And he's got friends." Having demolished his pancakes, Jake went to work on the omelet. "There are four deputies that share his attitude toward Talents: Tom Green, Scott Clary, Mary Hampton, and Bob Martin. If you ever have one of them backing you up, you need to keep a closer eye on them than whatever asshole you're dealing with."

She frowned at him over the rim of her coffee cup. "Are there a lot of Humanists in the department other than just those four? I've only been out of the academy a couple of months, but most of the guys have seemed pretty friendly to me."

"They are." Chewing a bite of omelet, Jake shrugged. "As far as I can tell, most deputies either like Talents, have Talented relatives -- which means they have some weak ability themselves -- or they're neutral. Though I will admit, some Norm cops do give Talents a higher threat assessment than they would've last year." He paused, chewing as he thought it over. "Then again, *I've* been giving Talents a higher threat assessment than I would have last year. Though I'm a hell of a lot more paranoid about Norms."

"Not much most Norms can do to a Tooth Tank."

"*Oo-Rawr.*" It was an old Corps joke, a variant on the Marines' "Oorah."

As if her reference to him had captured the lion's attention, Clarence's gold eyes appeared over his head, surrounded by softly glowing mane. It was hard to see the big cat in the restaurant's bright light, but Erica could just make him out. He stretched his great head across the table until she felt the brush of ghostly whiskers against her face. Grinning, Erica extended both hands and gave him a vigorous scratch. From the corner of one eye, she saw a Norm diner stare as if wondering what the hell she was doing. He wouldn't be able to see the lion at all, which was probably a good thing for his peace of mind.

She buttered a piece of toast and ate it, returning to the problem of Johnson and his Talent-hating cops. "If the sarge is such a problem, can we transfer to another shift?"

"Nope. Sheriff Gable assigned me to Alpha specifically to keep an eye on them. And I strongly suspect he wants you to watch my back."

"So what the hell have these guys been doing, and why doesn't the sheriff fire them for doing it?"

"Because Scott Clary's brother-in-law is Gary Stoneman."

Erica's brows lifted. "The county council chair?"

"Yep. Six months ago, a handcuffed Talent tripped and fell into Clary's fist. Three or four times. Gable was all set to suspend him, but Stoneman hinted he'd be a lot less supportive of the sheriff's plan to give his deputies a five percent raise if Gable didn't cut his in-law some slack. Gable wants me to see if I spot something outrageous enough that he can fire the lot of them without Stoneman retaliating."

Erica grimaced and rubbed her hands over her face. "Jesus. What's Johnson's story?"

"He's been with the sheriff's office for thirty years -- he was a captain in the last administration, but he got demoted when Gable was elected."

Ah. She considered that. Unlike police chiefs, sheriffs were elected officials. Traditionally, a new sheriff gave senior admin posts to his supporters, a bit like the president and his cabinet. Rank and file deputies up to sergeant weren't affected, but lieutenants and above got shuffled around. "I'm surprised Johnson didn't quit after a demotion like that."

Jake shrugged as Betty stopped by to refill their water glasses. "Johnson's too close to retirement. He wouldn't be able to get hired anywhere else, and he's got too much time in." When Betty vanished with her pitcher, he continued, "So we're stuck with him until and unless I can find proof he and his bunch are abusing Talents. Something beyond the petty crap they've been doing so far."

"What kind of petty crap are we talking about?"

"Mostly beating up Talents who had too much to drink for 'resisting arrest.' Talents have also filed complaints about nasty comments, threats, trumped-up charges, even groping. Which would be reason enough to can at least a couple of them, but Clary's bunch are too smart to do anything in front of witnesses with cell phones. As it is, we've got a lot of 'he said, she said,' stuff, which makes it almost impossible to bring charges."

"But if they're collecting that many complaints…"

"People make complaints all the time against cops. Hell, I've had them made against me, generally by some asshole who was outraged I'd dare arrest him for beating the fuck out of his wife."

"Too bad about that asshole-free diet… What was the problem again?"

Straight-faced, he replied, "Gas."

"Maybe you should consider Beano."

As he chuckled, a soft, low rumble sounded, and Erica felt the sensation of a furry body butting against her legs. Never mind that there wasn't enough room between her and the table; Clarence was only partly manifested. Most Arcanists wouldn't have been able to detect him at all without closing their eyes, since the well-lit room would have overwhelmed his faint glow.

With another inquiring rumble, the lion laid his big, insubstantial head in her lap. She reached down and absently ran her hands through his mane, enjoying the ghostly brush of the thick, coarse strands against her palms. The effect was an illusion, of course, a product of her aura interacting with the blended one he and Jake produced.

Glancing up, she froze. Jake was watching her, heat and need so stark in his eyes, it reminded her that Clarence wasn't the only one who could feel her caress. Hastily, Erica dropped her hand from the Familiar's big, regal head.

Jake's expression shuttered.

* * *

Jake watched in frustration as Erica retreated behind a mask of cool self-control. His hand tightened around his fork. Pain prickled his palm sharply enough to make him drop the utensil. When he glanced down, he saw four points of blood smeared over his skin. *Damn it, manifested claws*. It was never a good sign when he started doing that without intending to.

Erica's chocolate brows flew up. "What's wrong?"

"Nothing." He suppressed the urge to shake his stinging hand, knowing he'd fling blood everywhere. *The punctures aren't that bad, but it'd serve me right if they were. Moron.*

RRrroorr, Clarence told him. Translation: *Let me handle this*. Through their bond, he felt his Familiar butt his big head against Erica's chest, rolling his jaw across her breasts. Scent marking her.

For a moment it seemed Jake could feel the soft mounds pressed against his own face, and yearning hit him so hard he had to lower his gaze to his plate. He'd never touched her like that, but he'd wanted to. God, how he'd wanted to.

They all had. Jake, Bobby, Dave Frost and Kurt Briggs, otherwise known as Arcane Corps Whiskey Team. Or, as Dave called them, "Whisker Team."

He vividly remembered the day he'd met her, five years ago at Bagram Air Base in Afghanistan. They'd all gaped like idiots. Erica made even camo look good. Tall and long-legged, she had full breasts that rounded her tan T-shirt with intriguing curves. Her grip had felt smooth and surprisingly strong as she shook his hand, flashing a brilliant smile. "Glad to be here."

Dave had shouldered him aside, grinning, toothy as his Familiar. "Not as glad as we are to have you."

From then on, the members of Whisker had vied like smitten twelve-year-olds for her attention. She'd kept her distance from them all, refusing to flirt, silently demanding to be treated as a fellow soldier rather than a woman.

It wasn't until they watched her disarm a MEED one afternoon on patrol that they'd learned she was a hell of a lot more than a pretty face.

Dressed in a seventy-five pound bomb suit that made her look like a robot in a '50s monster flick, Erica lumbered over to the mine Jake had scented buried in the sand. A Caliphate sorcerer had inscribed complex magical symbols over its case designed to trigger and amplify the MEED's Semtex explosives.

Three months before, the team's previous Arc had been killed trying to disarm a booby trap just like it. They'd all watched in tense silence as she'd knelt in the clumsy armored suit, only her pale, lovely hands bare. You couldn't work magic in armored gloves, and disarming a MEED called for a delicate touch.

Staring through closed lids, Jake had watched her aura wash over the Caliphate spell, picking apart sorcerous symbols with delicate precision. For the next hour, she'd labored in the broiling heat. If she'd touched one magical symbol out of order, she'd have triggered a blast that could have killed her on the spot. At the very least, she'd have lost those pretty hands. In theory, the bomb suit would have protected her, but maybe not. MEEDs had had been known to take out tanks.

Erica had successfully disarmed the bomb.

Whisker Team had whooped and cheered like maniacs as she lumbered back to them in the bomb suit. They'd had to help her out of it, since the helmet alone weighed thirty pounds. Jake had no idea how anybody worked in one of the things, especially a woman.

As it was, by the time she was out of it, her clothes had clung to her sweating body as if glued there, and her perspiring face was beet red.

Dave, being Dave, teased her about smelling like a goat. She'd grinned and shot back, "What's your excuse, furboy?"

That was the moment Corporal Erica Harris truly joined Whisker Team.

Three months later, Bobby had somehow talked his

way into her bed. Jake had been irrationally jealous of his brother. Even Clarence was pissed. But Erica had made her choice, and they'd all respected it.

To make matters worse, Bobby had been an insufferable shit about the whole thing, at least in private where she couldn't hear him gloat. He'd done a lot of crap behind her back. Though in retrospect, Jake supposed he couldn't begrudge whatever happiness his brother had managed to find. God knew he'd paid dearly for it.

"Stop that," Erica said.

Jake jolted back to the present as she took Clarence's half-manifested head in her hands. It felt as if she cupped his own face. "Quit rubbing on me like that," she scolded. "No other lions will be sniffing me, so there's no point in scent marking."

Clarence chuffed, refusing to cede the point. Jake had no idea whether she could hear the cat or not. Probably. Erica was incredibly sensitive where anything magical was concerned.

"About that." Jake hadn't intended to say it, but somehow it came out of his mouth anyway. "I'm going to BFS tomorrow to see Clarence. Want to come?"

She looked up, the flicker of panic in her eyes disappearing behind the emotionless mask soldiers learned in Basic. "I don't think I'd be welcome."

"Bullshit. Nobody who disarmed MEEDs is that big a coward." He hid a wince the minute the words were out of his mouth. *Way to alienate her, moron.*

Her chin snapped up. "I'm not a coward."

Rrrmmmm, Clarence rumbled.

Yeah, yeah, I know. Working on it. "Nobody blames you for what happened."

"Tell that to Dave."

"*Especially* Dave. Either way, don't you think you owe him a chance to say his piece?" He snapped his mouth closed and held up one hand. "Okay, that last bit was dirty pool. Sorry."

She blinked, looking torn between holding on to her outrage and being mollified by his apology.

MRRRmmmmmm. Clarence planed a huge paw on her knee and rubbed his head over her thigh.

Jake caught his breath as the illusion of tough polyester uniform pants seemed to rub across his cheek. It felt like his chin was two inches from her groin. An image flashed through his mind: licking her there, tasting the plump, wet flesh, breathing in the seawater-and-sex scent of her pussy. *Don't you dare, Clarence.* God forbid his Familiar take the thought as a suggestion.

Clarence chuffed a lion laugh.

Erica stared down at her lap full of invisible cat, brown eyes going wide. Her gaze flicked back up to him, and for minute he was afraid she was about to bolt from the restaurant. *Crap.* Had she picked up his conversation with his Familiar? He wouldn't put it past her.

Settling back in the booth, Erica deliberately relaxed tensed shoulders. "Maybe you're right. I do owe Dave a chance to tell me whatever he thinks I've got coming." She sighed. "Besides, I want to tell Kurt how sorry I am about his dad."

"He knows you'd have come to the funeral if you'd been able to."

"Yeah. I all but begged, but my boss wouldn't let me take the time off. I sent flowers and called, but it's not the same." She broke off and shook her head. "Never mind. Coulda, woulda, shoulda. Bullshit. Yeah, I'll come with you. What time do you want to go?"

Jake barely managed to suppress a delighted grin. "Around ten?"

Erica smiled, but it looked forced. Well-developed sense of duty or not, it was obvious she wasn't looking forward to this. "Sure."

He was asshole enough to take advantage of her guilt. "Great."

* * *

At her surrender, Jake gave Erica both dimples full blast in one of those wide grins that reminded her a little too much of Bobby's.

This is a mistake.

Maybe, but he's got a point. Avoiding Dave is cowardly.

It had been one thing when she'd lived in New York or attended the South Carolina Criminal Justice Academy in Columbia. But she'd lived in Laurel County for two months now, and she damned well should have visited BFS.

Being gutless was the one thing Erica couldn't tolerate in herself. The fact it was emotional cowardice rather than physical didn't make it any more acceptable. But then, she'd always found physical threats a lot easier to deal with. After a childhood of getting the shit beaten out of her, disarming MEEDs and magical booby traps hadn't seemed all that intimidating.

She'd still rather face a dozen Caliphate sorcerers than Dave Frost.

Erica had always had a soft spot for the tall, lanky Texan. For one thing, she'd enjoyed the way he, Bobby, and Jake vied to see who could fire off the worst puns, bad jokes, and acid snark. Dave generally won, though Jake could give him a run for his money.

That he'd live the rest of his short life as an animal because of her... Well, it was tough to take. Better than being dead, maybe, but not by much.

As she brooded, Betty came by to refill their water glasses again. Jake asked for the check and she gave him a sunny smile. "Manager said to tell you it's on the house, y'all being law enforcement."

Jake lifted a blond brow. "The *manager* said that? Or was it you?"

He was right, Erica realized, studying the server's

aura. Patterns of pale swirling sherbet orange blended with cucumber green embarrassment. "Um..." Betty swallowed. The orange cleared away. "Me and Shannon."

Jake shook his head. "The sheriff doesn't allow us to accept freebies." He gave her enough dimple to have her looking dazzled. "But thanks for the thought."

Sighing in defeat, Betty produced the check, then started gathering up their empty plates as he reached for his wallet. "Forget it," Erica told him, pulling out her own to extract her debit card. "You're not picking up the check."

Jake shrugged in a fluid movement of impressive delts. "Can't blame a guy for trying." Pulling out a twenty, he added it to her card.

Erica managed to ignore Betty's longing sigh as the server retreated to process the payment.

Side by side, Erica and Jake strolled across the parking lot toward their cruisers. As they walked, a big, furred body bumped her thigh. Her gaze slid to Jake's handsome profile. The lion shouldered her again. Raw sensation jolted through her -- a sudden vivid awareness of Jake, his size, his sheer maleness, his intense awareness of her.

His need. A need she shared.

I am so screwed.

Chapter Four

When the lion butted her hip for the third time, Erica almost fell on her ass. Jake caught her elbow. She was sharply, acutely aware of the warmth of his big hand cupping her through her uniform shirt.

"Clarence, cut that out," he told his Familiar, then added to her, "Sorry about that. He can be really pushy."

"I noticed." Her voice sounded a bit breathy as the cat circled their legs.

Despite her better judgment, Erica's attention fell on Jake's mouth, lips full and tempting under that strong cleft chin. Dragging her gaze away, she tried to think of a more neutral topic. "Did I thank you for saving my ass?" The words came out throatier than she'd intended, so she added a smartass grin. "Tooth Tank to the rescue. Ooo-Raar."

"Yeah, you thanked me. But I don't mind hearing it again." His voice dropped into a seductive rumble. "I'm interested in anything you want to give me." His eyes fell to her lips, and his blond head lowered. "In fact, I have some suggestions."

Erica could have stepped back. God knew she'd done it often enough when her ex-boss had tried to force an unwelcome kiss. But Jake wasn't forcing anything, and the warm, gentle brush of his lips was the opposite of unwelcome. She'd been craving this for months. Years.

With a sigh, she parted her lips under his, wanting to taste him. To drink him in, as she'd longed to do for the past five years. His mouth tasted of maple syrup and Jake. Heat gathered in her belly, the tips of her breasts.

An uneasy voice spoke from the back of her mind. *But what if it all goes sideways again? I barely survived losing Bobby. I wouldn't survive losing Jake.*

The thought made her draw back a few inches, breathing hard, to meet the burning gold of his eyes. *This is stupid,* her common sense insisted.

"Erica," he murmured softly, cupping her face in one broad hand, his thumb brushing back and forth over her cheekbone. "I want you." A wave of heat rolled over her body at the stark, simple need in his voice.

And she realized she didn't care about common sense or guilt or simple self-preservation. Not with the touch of his aura triggering a wave of hot, carnal awareness that made her catch her breath. Something deep inside her seemed to flower, a delicious quiver of sensation rolling from her head to her toes.

Oh, fuck it. I want this. I want him. Rising onto her toes, she kissed him, eager, hot.

Jake growled softly against her mouth -- a human growl rather than leonine. His tongue explored her lower lip in a wet velvet stroke.

And God, it felt so good.

It had been too damned long. Too long since she'd felt the swirl of a lover's magic rousing her body to desperate, trembling heat. Too long since she'd felt alive.

Opening her mouth, Erica let him in. His tongue stroked along hers, and her breathing roughened. So did his.

He licked deep, once, twice, then retreated, inviting her to explore his mouth in turn. She closed her teeth on the soft pillow of his lower lip in a teasing bite, then licked his gently thrusting tongue. His hands came to rest on her hips, drawing her close as he angled his head, deepening the kiss, offering her more.

And God, she wanted more.

Rrrrrrollll rumf. Clarence's psychic voice held a moaning note of warning.

They jerked apart.

For a moment, Jake stared down at her, breathing hard, gold eyes glowing. Erica stared back, her heart slamming in her chest, need a hot, dark burn in the base of her belly. As if from a great distance, she heard a car rumble past. Which must have been what Clarence was trying to warn them about.

"We can't do this standing out in the parking lot." Erica's gaze focused on his lips, the damp, full curves of them, the hungry, eager way they parted. "Somebody's going to report us. We'll get fired."

"Not sure I care." Jake sounded hoarse. "I need more of you." Feral eyes flashed gold, reflecting the parking lot lights, the glowing not quite human. "Now."

Despite the cool spring wind, a wave of heat poured through her. She'd thought she wanted Bobby, but it had never felt like this. As if she were under a spell that stole her will and self-control, leaving only aching lust. And yet…

"You know how it is with a cat's libido." She shook her head hard, trying to banish the memory of Bobby's sneer.

Jake's eyes narrowed, taking in her reaction. "Do you know where the Greenbriar Mall is?"

The strip mall stood a block away, closed and unoccupied since its big box anchor store went bankrupt. "Yes, but…"

"We can talk there."

"Is talking really what you have in mind?" She'd intended the question to sound arch, but breathlessness sabotaged the effect.

His mouth curved in a smile so hot, she felt a responding fire leap in her own blood. "What I really want is you in my bed all night long, but I strongly suspect you'd chicken out before you got there."

Her inner twelve-year-old was offended. "I've never chickened out of anything in my entire life."

A dimple flashed in one corner of his sinner's mouth. "Then you'll meet me behind the Greenbriar in five minutes." He pulled out his key fob and unlocked his patrol car.

Erica watched him slide in and slam the door. The engine roared as he looked up at her, lifting a brow in challenge before he pulled out.

"Damn it, Nolan, if somebody spots us, we'll get fired." Never mind that they were technically off duty. Shaking her head, she dug out her own keys and unlocked her cruiser.

As Erica followed Jake's taillights onto the strip mall's property, her sense of self-preservation was still bitching. Muttering curses under her breath, she trailed him around the long, low building, past an AVAILABLE sign, its paint peeling in strips off weather-beaten wood.

The cruiser's tires thumped over the cracked pavement as they headed for the rear lot with its concealing border of pine trees. Several security lights had burned out there, leaving an inky patch of darkness that Jake headed for like a homing pigeon. Erica followed, parking her cruiser next to his.

He slid out of his car and looked down at her, a broad-shouldered silhouette. His eyes caught a beam of light from God knew where, reflecting gold. Heart pounding a crazed rhythm, she got out to join him. "If you think I'm necking in the back of the patrol car…"

"God, no. Way too many drunks have yarked in my cruiser. I keep my car clean, but there's only so much you can do."

She could only grin. "And Dave says there's no romance in your soul."

His teeth flashed. "Give me a try and see for yourself how romantic I am."

Erica swallowed at the erotic challenge in his tone. *This is not a good idea.* She found herself moving closer anyway until they stood chest to chest.

Which would have felt *much* sexier without the two bulletproof vests they were wearing.

Jake's big, broad hands came up and cupped her

cheeks to cradle her head, tilting her chin up. His palms felt calloused, deliciously warm. His mouth felt just as seductive as he kissed her, his lips feathering a soft brush across hers.

Erica groaned and let herself lean into his chest. Though Jake wasn't a tall man, his muscular breadth made her feel almost delicate. Feminine. The ASP baton hanging from his belt tapped her thigh, and the plastic buckles of their duty belts clicked as they eased together.

He slid a hand behind her back to grip her belt and pull her closer. Angling his head, he deepened the kiss, his tongue tracing the seam of her lips. She opened with a soft, yearning groan.

He tasted of the Cauldron's maple syrup, smelled of something dark and wild that made her think of deep woods and cat musk. Arousal tightened her belly, kicking off a honeyed flare of heat through her blood. Behind the thick padding of her vest, her nipples hardened. God, she wanted to feel his hands on her bare breasts. Ached for it.

He rumbled, a delicious vibration. Thick, coarse fur brushed against the back of her thighs, a psychic impression of a leonine body.

"Go away, Clar," he murmured against her lips.

The impression of fur disappeared.

Shivering in helpless arousal, Erica spread her hands over his chest. Felt only tough uniform fabric and the thickness of the Kevlar vest. *God, I want him naked.*

He drew back from her mouth, looking down at her with hooded eyes. "I want to touch you."

"God, yes. But this isn't the…" His big hands stroked up over the rise of her breasts. She closed her eyes and swallowed, wishing it wasn't so damn cold. Wishing she was naked, so she could feel his skin on hers.

Fingers brushed the bare skin of her collarbones as if her bullet-resistant vest had turned to mist. An electric jolt of pleasure zinged through her, so intense it almost stung.

Erica's eyes sprang wide. Jake watched her hungrily, gold eyes glowing as his thumbs brushed back and forth over her uniformed chest. One hand slid down, and she rocked back, instinctively giving him room. Room to trace down her sternum, dance across the upper curves of one breast, then down the slope of it...

Fingers brushed nipples with a sensation so vivid, she looked down, half-expecting to find her clothes had disappeared.

Both uniforms were still there. He was using his feral magic to manipulate her aura. "Oh," she breathed. "That's... incredible. I didn't know you could do that."

"You'd be surprised what I can do." Jake's smile took on a darker cast as he magically toyed with her, fingers brushing over the vest.

His left hand paused, tracing the curve of her ribs, dancing over thin skin, gliding downward to find the jut of a hipbone. And across.

Between her legs.

A jolt of magic shot right into her clit. Erica inhaled and caught his shoulders to keep from falling on her ass.

"Like that?" Jake's voice seemed to brush across her senses like velvet, rich and tempting. He went for her lips again, sipping at her tongue, as one hand played between her thighs and the other danced delicate spells over her breasts as though she was naked. Deliciously naked and aroused.

Well, part of that was true.

Jake purred against her mouth -- a sound that became a gasp as she slid a hand down and sent her own magic questing. To find the thick shaft of his erection pressing against his fly. Cupping her fingers over him, she danced a feather of magic the length of his cock from balls to head.

"You're living dangerously." His voice sounded

rough.

She smiled wickedly and closed her teeth over his lower lip, tugging it as she intensified the magic whirling around his eager shaft. "Yes, well, so are you."

His lips curled against hers. "Sometimes a little danger can be fun."

Erica froze as the words triggered a dark association: *Sometimes a little danger can be fun.* That had been one of Bobby's favorite sayings, used before missions, bar brawls, or jumping out of an airplane. He'd even said it the first time he'd taken her to bed.

And the morning she'd caught him cheating. "*Sometimes a little danger can be fun.*"

Jake's eyes widened in dismay as he felt her recoil. "Erica, I..."

She stepped back out of range of his hands, his magic. Suddenly the spring breeze felt icy over her hot cheeks. "I'll... see you later."

Jake took a step toward her, one hand lifted, then aborted the gesture. His broad shoulders slumped. "What about BFS?"

Erica wanted to say no. Wanted to at least put him off. Instead she heard herself say, "I'll meet you there."

Idiot!

Relief brightened his gaze, and he tried out a tentative smile. "Why don't I pick you up instead. Ten o'clock?"

She turned away and headed for her car. All she wanted was to get home. "Sure, whatever. Fine."

But it wasn't fine. *Why the hell didn't I tell him no?*

She knew exactly why. *I've never been smart when it came to any Nolan.*

* * *

Why the hell didn't I tell him no?

The thought was still circling Erica's mind as she unlocked the door and stepped into the little two-bedroom apartment that was all she could afford on a deputy's salary. She was determined to hang on to her savings from her last job, so she had a strict budget.

If she'd learned anything from six years in the Arcane Corps, it was that you never knew when things would go sideways -- but you'd better be ready when they did.

She felt stiff, aching, as if now that she no longer had Jake to distract her, her body remembered the brawl with Carson. Biting back a groan, she hobbled past the sectional couch and the butcher-block counter that separated the kitchen from the living room.

She had the ugly suspicion Carson had left behind an impressive set of bruises, though she hadn't been aware of them until now. It was damn lucky Jake had charged to the rescue. Maybe she could have taken Carson, but it was likely one of them would have ended up badly hurt.

Probably her. She was good, but a guy that big was a guy that big.

As she hobbled down the hall, her gaze fell on a cluster of framed art and photographs hanging in geometric patterns. There was the photograph of her mother before she'd gotten sick: a tall, wiry woman with a tired face and kind brown eyes, her graying hair loose around her shoulders. The woman who'd healed everyone else hadn't been able to heal herself. And as hard as she'd tried, Erica hadn't been able to save her, either. Her heart twisted.

Next to her mom's photo hung one somebody had taken of Whisker Team, the men gathered around Erica, all of them in body armor and holding their M-4 rifles. Bobby Nolan leaned in close to her wearing that familiar smartass grin, Feral gold eyes crinkled in laughter.

Jake stood next to his brother, but his gaze was fixed on Erica's profile as she laughed at whatever Bobby was saying. There was such longing in his eyes.

Sighing, Erica scrubbed both hands over her face and

limped into her bedroom. It was tiny, barely big enough for the oak queen-sized bed and bureau. A cream comforter sprigged with tiny yellow roses covered the bed, matching the drapes on the window looking out over the back yard.

Colored pencil sketches hung on the walls, pieces she'd done in idle moments on deployment. Jake posing with Clarence, his hands buried in the cat's mane. Kurt and his tiger Familiar, Stoli. Dave Frost kneeling beside Smilodon, wearing a grin almost as toothy as his tiger's.

But the sketch that never failed to give Erica a pang of grief was the one she'd done of Bobby and Selena shortly before their plane was shot down. The rest of the team and their Familiars had escaped serious injury, but Selena was hit by shrapnel and bled to death. Bobby managed a hasty magical fusion with the lioness that had saved her spirit, if not her body.

Unfortunately, sharing a body with a wild animal proved every bit as hard as fused Ferals always said it was. Bobby found it difficult to control Selena's animal temper and instincts 24/7, instead of only when he drew on her magic. His good-natured attitude quickly gave no way to an unpredictable temper that forced Erica to walk on eggshells around him.

Until the night in Afghanistan it had all really gone to hell.

Staring at the sketch now, Erica's mouth twisted in pain. Even after two years, the memory had lost none of its merciless, crystalline detail...

* * *

As Erica approached the B-hut that was her home on base, a female voice moaned in pleasure, the sound carrying clearly through the thin door. Great. One of her roommates was getting some. Grimacing, she started to turn away.

A deep male voice growled, "Yeah, that's right..."

The blood drained from her face, leaving an icy cold

that was followed a heartbeat later by a white-hot blast of raw fury. Whirling, Erica grabbed the doorknob and jerked it open. *They didn't even bother to lock it.* Stalking inside, she slammed the door with a gunshot bang. "What the fuck is going on?"

Bobby, bare-assed between Tammy Eckhart's thighs on her roommate's narrow bunk, glanced back at her over one shoulder. "Isn't it obvious?" His golden eyes glittered, and his teeth flashed as his lip curled.

Erica clenched her fists, wanting to punch him right in that perfect nose. "Yeah, I guess it is."

"Oh, shit, Erica!" Tammy bolted from the bed and start scrambling around in a desperate search for her clothes. "Sorry, sorry, I knew I shouldn't have..."

Erica made a mental note to find a new roommate -- among other things. "How long has this been going on?"

Bobby rose slowly to his feet, thoroughly naked. At least he was wearing a condom. Though, adding insult to injury, his erection showed no signs of deflating. He shrugged in a negligent lift of one powerful shoulder. "Only since I fused with Selena." His eyes glittered as his mouth pulled into a tight smile. "You know how it is with a cat's libido."

"Bullshit. Selena is female. The only time she gets horny is when she's in heat."

"Yeah? What your excuse?"

"What the hell are you talking about?"

"You think I don't see the way you watch Jake? I'd kick his ass, but you'd probably like that."

Her jaw dropped. "I have never cheated on you. I would never cheat on you."

"Maybe it would have helped if you had. Sometimes a little danger can be fun." He smirked. "Always worked for me."

She rocked forward, fist cocked. And stopped, eyes burning with unshed tears. Punching him was beneath her.

"Go ahead. Do it." For a moment some emotion flashed over his face, but she couldn't tell what it was.

Automatically, she checked his aura to find it blood-red. Pain. He was hurting almost as much as she was.

His lip curled again. "Never mind. You don't care that much."

Eyes stinging, Erica whirled to stalk out of the cabin. His harsh bark of laughter was the last thing she heard before the door slammed shut behind her. She was heading for the enlisted club with every intention of getting hammered when Dave called from behind her, "Harris! We've got a job."

Perfect. Just perfect.

An hour later, Erica found herself on a Huey trying to ignore Bobby as they flew into a barren stretch of the Hindu Kush mountains. The hills there were riddled with limestone caves, and Afghanis had been using them to live in and fight from for thousands of years.

The American military had spent the past year digging the local branch of the Caliphate out of those mountains. Now they had to clean up the mess -- the weapons caches, the pockets of resistance, the MEEDs and spell traps. A team of Marines had discovered a cave that had evidently been a Caliphate base, judging by all the MEEDs they'd found. Erica had been ordered to disarm them while the rest of Whisker searched for more.

She'd gone into a lot of nasty spots, but none of them made her as twitchy as these fucking caves. The only illumination came from the flashlights mounted on her rifle and that of her Marine guide. The cave floor was littered with loose rocks, and the rough limestone walls narrowed unpredictably, studded with outcroppings that could snag a uniform or gear.

And then there were the bats. She could hear them squeaking and fluttering somewhere in the dark.

As if that wasn't nerve-racking enough, the caves stank of human waste and the reek of malevolent Caliphate magic, a smell compounded of the herbs they used and the chickens they sacrificed. They used human sacrifices for the seriously nasty spells. There was a reason good Muslims hated the rebel sorcerers. The Caliphuckers wanted power, and they were willing to murder and terrorize their own people to get it.

All in all, this wasn't the sort of mission she liked tackling in her current frame of mind.

It took her the better part of an hour to break all the spells, but at last Erica and her guide headed back to the tunnels to rendezvous with the rest of Whisker, who were still searching for Caliphate traps.

Barely a hundred yards away from Whisker's reported location, she heard Bobby's full-throated roar, followed by a man's dying scream and Jake yelling his brother's name.

Erica's heart catapulted into her throat. Ignoring the Marine's warning shout, she broke into a run, chasing the bouncing light of her rifle flash. A heartbeat later, the tunnel filled with the echoing thunder of a single rifle shot. "Medic! I need a medic!" Kurt bellowed over the radio.

Rounding a bend in the tunnel, Erica stopped dead in horror.

Kurt and Jake knelt by Bobby's side as he writhed on the rocky ground, the two men fighting to stanch the red, gaping wound pumping in his throat. Just beyond them lay a crumpled body that could only be Dave.

"Shit!" Erica charged past them to drop to her knees beside her fallen friend. Which was when she saw why they weren't trying to help him.

Dave lay flat on his back, eyes staring sightlessly upward, his head twisted at an impossible angle. Checking for an aura, she saw nothing at all. He was already gone. *God, I hope he fused with Smilodon!* Blinking away tears, she leaped up to join Kurt and Jake as they worked on Bobby.

"We need transport for these men," Kurt snapped at the Marine without looking away from his patient. "Direct your people here, and make sure somebody called for that chopper!" The man nodded and ran back the way they'd come.

"Can you do anything?" Jake demanded as she shouldered in beside him. His blood-splattered face was too pale, set with pain, dazed with shock.

"I'll damn well try." Taking a deep breath, she reached for her Talent, though she knew she didn't have the raw power it would take to keep him from bleeding out. And even if she had, she didn't have time to draw a healing spell. Arcanist magic took too fucking long.

It didn't matter. She'd do whatever the hell she could.

Bobby stared up at her, his eyes wide, his mouth working over the ruin of his throat. Erica pushed Kurt's hands away and pressed her own to the wound. Blood seeped around her hands as she poured power into the injury, fighting to slow the bleeding. "Damn it, Bobby, hang on! Hang on, the chopper's coming…"

His lips moved. He shouldn't have been able to make a sound given the damage, but his magic spoke for him, vibrating the air around him. "Sorry… Love you… sorry… so…"

And he was gone.

* * *

Erica turned away and started stripping off her uniform, eyes stinging. After this long, it shouldn't hurt this damn bad, but guilt had a way of making sure some wounds never healed.

If she'd finished disabling the traps ten minutes sooner, she might have arrived in time to warn Bobby before he triggered the spell. If she'd had the power, maybe she could have slowed the bleeding long enough for him to make it to a hospital.

But even beyond that old, aching guilt, she was left with the same agonizing questions. *Why hadn't he spotted the spell? He should have been looking for it.* It was a Caliphate sorcerers' base, for God's sake. They'd all known there were spell traps. Hell, that was why they were there. Except she knew exactly why Bobby hadn't seen the trap, didn't she? He'd been too distracted by what had happened between them that morning. Jake had told her later that he'd seen his brother's shoulders brush the wall, seen the sigils burst into the air as the trap sprang. Bobby had frozen in shock as the Caliphate spell rolled over him, maddening his cat.

Then Dave had bumped into him -- and he'd whirled, manifesting with a roar of rage. He'd broken his friend's neck with a single swipe of one paw. Bobby had gone for his brother next. Frozen with astonished horror, Jake would have died too, had Kurt not shot Bobby in the throat.

In retrospect, it was astonishing he'd managed to put a bullet through the manifestation at all. The magical shell should have deflected the bullet, allowing Bobby to kill Kurt and Jake in the same maddened attack. And probably Erica and the Marine too.

Jake believed that when he killed Dave, Bobby had regained just enough self-control to realize what was happening -- and deliberately thinned his manifestation. If that was true, he'd basically let Kurt kill him. And yes, that did sound like something Bobby would do.

"Sorry… Love you… sorry… so…"

"Damn it, Bobby," Erica muttered, blinking away tears. She'd cried enough. It was time she was over this.

Chapter Five

It didn't matter how many times Adrian Fleming killed a man with magic, he never got tired of it. True, there was something to be said for the hands-on approach. He loved being there to watch as a target went from human to a lump of meat. It didn't matter how -- stabbing, shooting, beating someone to death with his bare hands -- it all gave Adrian an incredible buzz.

But killing with magic was like being God. To touch the target's bright spark of life -- and snuff it out. Feeling the target die, drinking in his or her liberated life force, the raw stuff of the world's magic. Adding it to Adrian's own power...

No other high could touch it. Not smoking Tink or Stroll. Not jumping out of an airplane or surviving a firefight or strangling a woman as you fucked her -- nothing else was as intense, as addictive.

Best of all, once you'd established a mystical bond with your target, his life was yours. You could drop him at a whim. And he had no idea he belonged to you. No idea you'd become his personal god.

Every time Adrian tattooed a target, he had to be careful they didn't see the erection it always gave him. Wouldn't do for them to get the wrong idea.

Fucking idiots.

For people who hated Arcs, those Human Heritage morons were quick to let perfect strangers tattoo God knew what on them. Yeah, Adrian's work was beautiful, but they only had his word he wasn't an Arcanist. And he lied like a motherfucker.

True, he'd made a profession out of it for twenty years, so he was good at it. But still, it took a dumbass. That and their combination of ignorance and viciousness made fucking them over an absolute joy.

His cock hardened as he headed for the basement

that was the sole reason he'd rented the house. When you were suckering a bunch of anti-magic bigots, you couldn't afford to let them spot your spell circle or magical paraphernalia. Thus the deadbolt that opened with a key, newly installed on the battered door.

The house otherwise had little to recommend it. Having been built in the 1970s, the brick split-level was in desperate need of renovation, between peeling paint, chipped linoleum, and filthy, matted carpeting. Strategic yard sale purchases enhanced the trailer trash effect: a sagging couch, a recliner upholstered more in duct tape than anything else, and assorted other scratched and dented particle board furniture. All of which perfectly suited his cover identity of Andy Jones, scuzzy HHer tattoo artist.

Flicking on the bare bulb that illuminated the stairs, Adrian started downward. As always, he had to ignore a niggle of claustrophobia as he descended into the windowless box with its cinderblock walls and poured concrete floor.

He'd laid out the intricate spell circle in colored chalk after Virginia Laurel told him she wanted Carson gone. Then he'd waited, giving the man plenty of time to get settled into his cell at the county jail. It wouldn't do for some guard to resuscitate him.

It was icy in the basement, and gooseflesh rose on Adrian's bare arms and chest, pebbling the skin under his intricate tattoos. Any Norm looking at them would see only the surface images that covered every inch of his skin: wolves, snakes, eagles, dragons, skulls, demons, and ghosts. There was something hypnotic in the intricate line work, in the flowing rhythm of each shape swirling into the next. His Arcanist mother was a hell of an artist, and she'd been treating him as her living canvas all his life. Adrian had returned the favor, since she'd started teaching him the art when he was in kindergarten.

Only another Arcanist would recognize the gorgeous images as camouflaged magical symbols designed to amplify his power, direct the flow of his aura, and protect him from magical attacks. All of which was why he considered Marion Fleming a major reason he'd been so successful. And so deadly.

She'd taught him to kill not long after she'd taught him to tattoo.

He paused to study the spell he'd inscribed on the floor, checking to make sure every line was where it was supposed to be. A sigil curling left when it should have curved right had killed more than one Arcanist. Satisfied everything was as it should be, he stepped over the chalk lines, careful not to smudge the symbols. Accidentally erasing one of them would be just as suicidal as getting a sigil wrong.

Finally he knelt before the heavily engraved golden bowl that sat in the heart of the design. It held only a wad of paper towels smeared with rust-brown stains.

People bled when you tattooed them. That blood carried the client's DNA -- genetic material an Arcanist could use to anchor any spell he wanted. Not even the most paranoid HHer thought twice when you wiped blood and ink away with a paper towel they assumed you'd throw out. Which Adrian usually did.

But he made an exception for those special clients for whom he had plans.

Breathing deeply, slowly, Adrian hooked bare feet over his thighs and straightened his spine. The lotus position was damned uncomfortable -- particularly on icy concrete -- but the discipline it took helped him focus.

Magic was all about focus.

He let his eyes slide shut and began to hum, activating a spell. Behind his lids, he watched the glowing symbols on the floor lift into the air and begin to revolve around him. Each sigil warped the currents of the planet's aura like a stone jutting through the surface of a lake. He could see the tortured energy patterns hazing the air like the heat from a campfire.

Breathing in through a slow count of three, then out for a count of four, Adrian concentrated on his body's sensations: the chill, the smell of musty earth, the ache of his bent thighs. Then finally, the slowing beat of his heart.

When his mental preparation was complete, he reached out, eyes still closed, and plucked the bloody paper towel from its bowl. Wrapping both hands around the wad, he cupped it between his palms and concentrated.

And felt the answering reverberation of his own magic miles away, where a symbol lay tattooed on Richard Carson's chest. Right over his heart.

Like his own, the sigil was hidden beneath the swirl of non-magical ink. A flaming skull blazed the width of Carson's torso in brilliant golds and reds, concealing the sigil beneath the black ink of one eye socket. Even an Arcanist would have difficulty spotting it against the burn of Carson's aura.

Adrian concentrated on the intricate whirls of that distant sigil. Focused on it until a slow, rhythmic beat filled his ears: Carson's heart.

His cock hardened in anticipation.

It had been months since he'd tattooed the sigil. The ritual he'd used to create the magical ink involved his own dried blood. Of course DNA would point the finger right at him if the ink was found and tested, but since spotting it would require an Arcanist pathologist, he wasn't worried. The county didn't have anyone like that on staff.

Good thing he had friends in high places who could be counted on for a vigorous cover-up. Magical murder was a death penalty offense.

Adrian focused all his attention on his sigil, listening

to the rhythmic pulse of the man's blood through his magical connection to the tatt. Once he felt Carson's heartbeat as if it was his own, he willed the rhythm to change.

His target's heart skipped one beat. Adrian tightened his magical grip, and it skipped again. Another squeeze, then another, faster and faster, until the organ's muscle fibers began to spasm, losing rhythm, no longer pumping in concert.

Carson gasped in agony, the sound as clear as if he was in the same room. "Fuck... oh fuck..." Behind his closed eyes, Adrian watched his target lurch to his feet, mouth working as he tried to yell. "Guards!" His barely audible croak didn't even wake his cellmates. His knees gave under him, and he fell.

Adrian didn't feel him hit the floor.

The magic of Carson's life force blasted him in an electric rush more intense than a hit of the purest Tink. Adrian threw back his head with a bellow as his cock pulsed, balls tightening as he came.

* * *

Erica was waiting in front of her apartment building when Jake pulled up in a white F-150 pickup the next morning. Must be his civilian vehicle. The sheriff's department might let deputies take their patrol units home so they could respond to emergencies, but you weren't supposed to use them for personal business.

"Morning," Jake said, eying her as she got in. "You're moving like you're a bit stiff."

"Bruises from my tango with Carson." She winced at the ache as she put on her seatbelt. "Poor bastard."

"Poor bastard?" He snorted. "Yeah, right. I should have hit him harder."

Erica lifted a brow at him. "Didn't you watch the news this morning? He had a heart attack and died in his cell last night."

Jake blinked. "Well, shit. That was convenient for

somebody."

"Wasn't it, though."

"Think it was a coincidence?"

Erica hesitated before shaking her head. "Got to be, unless there's an Arc involved we don't know about."

"Like HHers would work with an Arcanist." He threw the truck into gear.

"Doesn't sound likely." But she frowned as they headed for BFS.

* * *

Briggs Feral Sanctuary was located on a hundred acres of farmland that had been in the Briggs family for generations. Which, to some, still didn't entitle it to exist.

"Great. Kurt's got company again," Jake growled as they rounded a curve in the tree-lined road.

A ragged line of ten men and three women stretched across the entrance to the park. Their hand-lettered signs read "Kids and tigers don't mix!" "Laurel Co. is for Humans!"

"Who the hell is that?" Erica demanded, frowning.

"HHers," Jake told her, his jaw tightening.

Human Heritage was one of the more extreme fringe groups connected to the Humanist movement. They used the Internet to spread lunatic conspiracy theories, such as the idea that melded Ferals like Dave were demon-possessed. They also agitated for government mandated exorcisms for all melded Ferals, whether in animal or human form. If that didn't work, HHers thought killing them was justified to protect the public from demonic influence.

He gave her a narrow grin with absolutely no humor in it. "Want to stop and say hi?"

"Let's." She jerked her chin at the pot-bellied middle-aged guy with the AR-15. "We can make sure they've got a permit for that. And is that a bump stock?"

"Looks like it. But this is South Carolina, so it's perfectly legal." He pulled off onto the shoulder of the road, parking behind two cars and a pickup that apparently belonged to the protesters.

Erica slid out of the truck and joined Jake as he started toward the thirteen glowering Humanists. "Considering the odds, it's a good thing we're armed," she murmured. The department required off-duty deputies to carry weapons. Like Jake's, hers was holstered on her hip.

"So are they."

Taking a closer look, she realized every one of them wore a holstered handgun, including the one with the rifle. "Oh, goody. We're outgunned."

"I'd be intimidated if I thought any of them has ever shot at anything that could shoot back." As they got within earshot, Jake tapped the badge he wore clipped to his belt and called, "Y'all know better than this. You can picket all you want, but it's illegal to block the park entrance."

"We ain't blocking shit," replied the guy with the AR-15. "Anybody dumb enough to want into that devil's park can get by."

"Do you have permits for those guns?" Erica demanded.

AR-15 had a thick, graying beard and a gorgeous tattoo of a dragon wrapped around his bald head. The ink was so vivid, it had to be new. "We got a right to protect ourselves against any tigers that get loose."

"The cats are in cages, sir," Jake rumbled, his voice going dangerously deep. "You sure you're not planning to flash those weapons at buses full of school tours?"

"Kids don't need to be anywhere around demon animals." AR-15's beard shifted as his jaw worked, hazel eyes narrowing. "Which is why we're gonna get this place shut down."

Erica had heard enough. "The man who runs BFS damn near died last year protecting this town. He's a veteran, and so are the Familiars who live here. They deserve --"

"Yeah, right," AR-15 sneered as the others muttered agreement. "Briggs was in on it with the terrorists -- everybody knows that. We don't want 'em here. We got a right to protest, and we got a right to protect ourselves."

"That's..." Erica swallowed the hot words she badly wanted to say. *Damn it, Harris, you're supposed to be a professional.* If there was one thing she'd learned over the past two months as a cop, it was that you couldn't reason with idiots.

But you *could* put them in jail if they gave you an excuse. She was surprised how cool and polite she sounded when she said, "I need to see your ID and weapons permits."

AR-15 glared. "We don't have to show you a damn thing."

"You do if you don't want to go to jail. Identification and permits."

The protesters muttered among themselves.

Jake turned to Erica. "Call dispatch and have them send a transport. Seems these folks want to spend Saturday in jail."

"All right, damn it." AR-15 pulled out his wallet.

As Jake examined his ID, the man drawled, "I recognize you. You here to see your pussy?"

Jake looked up, one blond brow slowly lifting. "Would *you* like to see him, Mr. Garrison?"

His voice sounded deceptively mild, but AR-15 -- Garrison -- took a step back, eyes widening. Which proved the man was smarter than he looked.

"You have a right to protest," Jake continued in that same silken tone. "But if I find out you're threatening school kids or tourists, you're going to jail." His long, steady stare had the whole crowd shifting nervously. Erica suppressed a grim smile. Nobody with a brain wanted to piss Jake Nolan off -- including her.

There are so many better things to do with him, purred a treasonous little voice in the back of her mind.

Shut up, she told it.

It chuffed, sounding a lot like Clarence.

* * *

Having determined all the protestors had indeed brought their carry permits, Erica and Jake returned to the truck. As the Humanists parted resentfully to let them pass, she glowered. "Ungrateful fucks. You and Kurt almost died protecting this country. And they have the gall to say you *colluded* with Virgil-fucking-Ford?"

"Actually, I'm less worried about that than the fact the protest is working. Tourists don't like to cross picket lines, especially when the picketers carry guns. Kurt's worried BFS is going to go out of business if this keeps up."

"What the hell is he going to do?" And what would Jake do if BFS closed? He couldn't exactly keep Clarence in his backyard.

"I have no idea."

The roadway wound through stands of oaks, pines, and maples before turning into BFS's sprawling parking lot. A surprising number of cars occupied the spaces, considering the armed protesters outside.

"Well, at least somebody's here," Erica commented as Jake parked between an aging Toyota Camry and a big white van, its driver's door painted with the BFS logo: a lion's head with Feral gold eyes. The cat's flowing mane formed the figures of tigers, lynxes, jaguars, ocelots, and mountain lions. "Considering the asshole brigade, I'm surprised."

"Most of these cars belong to the volunteers who help take care of the cats. And some of those have quit. Kurt's started picking them up in the BFS van so they don't have to drive through the picketers by themselves."

Erica frowned. "Is he afraid the Humanists would do

something to them?"

Jake shrugged as they got out. "Maybe, maybe not. But with Kurt behind the wheel, there's a lot less risk of somebody screaming 'Talent fucker.' Even nuts hesitate to pick a fight with Kurt."

"Well, duh. He beat the hell out of a terrorist *polar bear*."

Erica and Jake strolled along the looping walkway, past the ticket booth and a souvenir shop, both painted with the BFS logo. Beyond them, the walkway wound between clusters of one-story buildings and a series of curving enclosures built of interlocking galvanized steel wire panels. Designed to withstand a thousand pounds of charging, pissed-off cat, the structures were fifteen feet tall and enclosed enough territory to let the occupants climb trees, run around, and generally entertain themselves.

Smaller structures were roofed with additional galvanized panels, while larger ones had overhangs angled inward to keep cats from escaping. They housed everything from huge Amur tigers to sand cats that weighed no more than a Siamese. Erica knew that despite the park's name, most of the animals at Briggs Feral Sanctuary weren't really Ferals. The majority were rescues from abusive backyard breeders, roadside circuses, or zoos that couldn't provide for them. Kurt, like his murdered father before him, considered the cats' well being his mission in life.

A deep, moaning roar echoed between the trees, making Jake grin in delight. "Sounds like Clarence is getting impatient." He lengthened his stride until Erica had to hustle to keep up.

"*RRrrooofff*!" Clarence bounded across a particularly big enclosure toward them, his magnificent mane flowing behind him, muscle rolling under rich, sandy fur. He was easily the most beautiful cat she'd ever seen, even after years of working with Ferals and their Familiars.

As if he wasn't impressive enough by himself, two lionesses ran at his heels. Though they were much smaller than Clarence, there was still a muscular power to them, a wild beauty.

"You got Clarence a harem?" Erica gave Jake an amused blink.

"Well, he's a lion. Cat's got his pride."

As she groaned at the pun, Jake jumped over the low fence that separated the path from the enclosure and headed to the padlocked guillotine door. Pausing, he looked back at her. "I'd invite you to come in with me, but the girls don't know you."

"Since I have no desire to end my life as a chew toy, I concede the point." Besides, she had absolutely no desire to cross the walkway fence.

Which really wasn't like her.

Frowning, Erica looked down at the cement walk... and sensed a swirl of magic. The sun was so bright she had to close her eyes to see the shapes of glyphs inscribed on the sidewalk in ultraviolet paint. Studying the sigils, she realized the spell was designed to discourage people from getting too close to the enclosures.

Probably the work of Genevieve Briggs, the Arcanist Kurt had married. Who must have a *lot* of juice, to have such a strong effect on another Arc. "How do the volunteers get in to take care of the cats with these wards?"

Jake looked around from unlocking the padlocked guillotine gate that led into an empty section of the cage. "Oh, you mean the spell? Gen gives the volunteers charms that nullify the effects."

She knelt, examining the sigils. "Pretty strong work. I'm not sure I could break it."

"Kurt'll be glad to hear it. His worst nightmare is some child sticking a body part into a cage and getting it bitten off. The volunteers watch the tour groups like hawks, but kids are kids." He stepped into the unoccupied portion of the enclosure, then walked over to unlock the guillotine gate into the half the cats occupied.

Erica found herself tensing. Clarence wouldn't hurt him, of course, but those lionesses might be a different matter. Presumably, his Familiar would protect him -- and given his Feral Talent, Jake could touch the minds of non-Feral animals too. But even so, big cats were wild animals, and wild animals were always dangerous.

Which was why even Clarence had to be kept in an enclosure. You could never tell when something would set a Familiar off, no matter how intelligent he was.

Yet Jake showed no sign of fear as the lion butted up against him and the other cats pressed in close. She didn't want to imagine what they'd do to somebody they didn't love.

"I'd hoped that was you. I knew Jake was here when I heard Clarence roar."

"Dave!" She turned with an automatic smile at the sound of her old friend's voice. And froze, her heart in her throat.

A huge Amur tiger stood on the walkway not five feet away, a distance it could clear in one bound. And if it did, she was so dead.

Erica froze. *Oh, fuck.* She might be used to working with magical manifestations, but a flesh-and-blood tiger was still a flesh-and-blood *tiger.*

The big head came up, ears pricking. "Hey, it's me, Dave. Got the vest and everything." Belatedly, Erica realized the cat did indeed wear an orange safety vest emblazoned with her friend's name. She'd seen him wear it doing standup on the *Tonight Show* once, not to mention his YouTube appearances.

"I just..." Erica had to stop and swallow. "... wasn't expecting you."

"I do live here." His mouth didn't move when he spoke; tigers didn't have the anatomy to produce human speech. Fortunately, melded Ferals could produce sound by magically vibrating the air, just as Jake did when his lion manifestation roared. Dave was even better at it; his comedy routine included startlingly realistic imitations of everything from multi-car pileups to Judy Garland. "In fact, I've been living here a couple of years now."

"Yeah." Erica stared at him, helplessly remembering the tall, rangy blond man who'd been her friend. He'd lost his human life, at least in part, because she hadn't been there to detect the spell that drove Bobby insane. She opened her mouth...

His ears flattened and his tail lashed. "If you say it, I swear to God, I'll bite you."

"Say what?"

"*I'm sorry*. I can almost see the words floating over your head in a giant tear-shaped thought balloon. And it pisses me off." Dave spun with a furious flick of his tail and stalked down the walkway. "You don't have anything to be sorry about."

She followed him, aware of Jake watching them go, his expression concerned as he scratched one of the lionesses behind the ears. "That's not what you said the last time I saw you."

Dave tilted his big striped head to look up at her. "I was in a really bad mood."

"That's putting it mildly. Thought you were going to eat me."

"I always wanted to eat you, baby. Rrrowl." That last bit was delivered in mock sexy growl. "Which goes without saying, since the whole damn team wanted you as our own private dessert tray."

"All four of you?" She wrinkled her nose and managed a joke. "I don't think there'd have been enough to go around. Like Mickey Mouse at a cat convention."

"I don't know about that. Have you seen the size of that rat? No wonder the kiddies run in terror." Dave slid into a flawless falsetto impersonation. "Hi, boys and girls!" He promptly answered that with a chorus of shrill, realistic screams. "*Ahhhhh!*"

"Damn it, Dave!" a volunteer yelled from the empty section of a nearby enclosure. "Don't *do* that! You almost gave me a heart attack!"

"Sorry, Karla," the tiger called back.

"Not good enough. You'd better *grovel* if you ever want to see another pork butt again."

"Don't be that way! You know how I love your butt."

"Ewwww! Too. Many. Legs."

"Oh, come on, baby! Once you've had stripes, pink and hairless doesn't get it done anymore. Just ask Angelina Jolie."

"Dave, you did *not* break up her and Brad Pitt, I don't care how many times you say it." Snorting, the woman went back to scooping cat poop.

Suddenly Erica felt a little better. "You haven't changed a bit."

"Nope. Just a new fur coat on the exact same asshole."

"There's a mental image I could have done without."

He grinned toothily. "Psychic scarring is just one of the many services I provide."

"Nope, no change whatsoever."

"What, you expected me to mope around like a six hundred-pound Eeyore?" His voice deepened and slowed until he sounded just like the donkey from *Winnie the Pooh*. "I've turned into a tiger and now my life suuuucks." He returned to Dave's usual Texas drawl. "Yeah, fuck that. I don't have time for that shit."

He really didn't. Tigers only live twenty years at most, and Smilodon had been ten when Dave's human body was killed. He was twelve now. The math made her wince.

"Cut it out." The words were accompanied by a rumbling tiger growl that was no imitation. "I'm *so* sick of smelling everybody's fucking guilt. Damn it, it wasn't your fault! It wasn't Kurt's fault, it wasn't Jake's fault, it wasn't Bobby's fault. Hell, it wasn't even my fault, though I could've been a little damn quicker to get the hell out of the way when Bobby lost his shit. You know whose fault it was? That Caliphucker sorcerer who set the booby trap spell. And since you helped Kurt and Jake kill his ass, that bastard paid for what he did."

Erica eyed his aura. Though anger flowed through it in blood-red swirls, there was no sign of deception. Dave meant what he said. *He really doesn't blame me.* The sweet relief the thought brought was a surprise.

But the cat wasn't done. "In the meantime, I'm going to wring all the joy I possibly can out of every minute I've got left."

She blinked. Though the bad jokes and humor had sounded just like the old Dave, this vehemence was new. "You mean that."

"You bet your ass. I made television appearances with Kurt after that shit with the terrorists last year. I even did *Saturday Night Live*. I've built more than a million followers on YouTube and Twitter, and I'm using that platform to raise money for BFS." His tail lashed. "I'm making my life count for something, Erica. I don't care if those damn HHers do think I'm demon possessed, or if other idiots think I'm a hoax or a curiosity. When I head for the big litter box in the sky, I'm damn well going to leave the world a little bit better than it was when I put on this fur coat."

She studied him thoughtfully. "I don't think I've ever heard you talk like this."

"That's because when you knew me, all I cared about was hunting terrorists, getting drunk, and getting laid --

not necessarily in that order." He paused, tail flicking, eyes narrowed as he glared up at her. "And speaking of wasting time... You need to stop."

She stiffened. "Stop what?"

"How somebody with as much physical courage as you've got can be such a pussy when it comes to her own emotions..." He shook his head. "What are you, male? That's our shtick."

Erica sighed. "Yeah, I should've sucked it up and come to see you months ago and cleared the air, but..."

He produced a loud game show buzz. "Not what I'm talking about. Not even close."

"Then I'd like to buy a vowel."

"Are you certain you're not a guy?"

"Dave, I'm not dropping my pants."

"Damn. I was sure that would work."

She was starting to feel a little irritated. "If you're going to call me an emotional chicken, I'd like to know what you think I'm clucking about."

"Jake."

"What about Jake?"

"You want him, but you don't have the guts to do anything about it."

"And this is your business why?"

"It's not. I just don't care that it isn't. I've been watching you want him without doing anything about it for years. It's getting old."

She stiffened. "I cared about Bobby."

"Cared about him, yes. But you *wanted* Jake. You only picked Bobby because you figured he'd be safer. He was perfect for having a good time with, but you weren't going to fall for him. Jake's a lot of things, including a pain in the ass, but you never saw him as safe. We all knew it, even Bobby. He wouldn't have been such a shit to you otherwise."

It felt as if her face was on fire. She must be beet red.

"You don't know what you're talking about."

"I know better than you do. If you keep wasting time protecting yourself and making excuses, one day you'll discover there's no time left. It'll be too late, and there won't be a fucking thing you can do about it anymore. So I'm telling you as a friend. Grow a pair while you can. Reach out for what's there before you end up having to make do with what's left."

Dave turned and walked off, the tip of his tail flicking back and forth. She stared after him, feeling like he'd slapped her in the mouth.

Chapter Six

Dave glanced back over his shoulder at Erica. "Kurt and Gen are expecting us. You coming, or are you pouting?"

"Where?" She sounded sullen to her own ears.

"Kurt's house. Gen's doing a healing, and Kurt figured you'd want to watch. Do you?" His narrow gaze challenged her.

"Yes." It came out grudging.

"Okay then, come on."

Off-balance, caught somewhere between anger and bewilderment, Erica followed him. Her immediate impulse was to chew him out, but her eyes fell on the metronome flick of his tail and she swallowed the hot words. "Do you really think I'm that big a user?" The question came out less challenging than she'd intended.

"A user? Of who, Bobby?" He looked up at her, considering. "No. Or if you were using him, he was using you right back. But everything went to shit when Selena died, and it wasn't a game anymore."

Erica grimaced. "Has anybody ever told you that you have a real gift for understatement?"

"Nope. They usually just say I'm an asshole."

"Well, that too." They walked on in silence for a moment as she remembered the aching sense something was missing. Not just Bobby or Dave, though God knows she'd missed them too.

Over the past two years, Erica had slowly grown aware of just how empty her life had become. Hell, every time she patrolled her slice of Laurel County, she'd secretly hoped to run into Jake. "Maybe you're right."

"I usually am. Mind telling me what I'm right about this time?"

"Maybe it *is* time I grow a pair."

"Only if you enjoy bathing in the tears of the entire

heterosexual male population."

"Smartass."

"That *is* pretty much my job description."

They headed deeper into the park. Enclosures loomed on either side. A black leopard paced them from the other side of the galvanized fencing of one of them, a blue sheen rolling over his coat with every fluid step. He watched Dave as if enthralled. Which wasn't surprising; even non-magical cats were attracted to Ferals.

As Erica watched the leopard, she found herself blurting the truth. "There's another reason why I was reluctant to get involved with Jake."

"He's a smartass?"

"Yeah, but I like smartasses. You know how a strong Talent gives an aura density?"

"Sure. That's how you can tell a Talent from a Norm at a glance."

"Right. Yours is much more intense than it used to be, since a melded Feral has a greater magical density than any other kind of Talent."

"Makes sense, given that it's me *and* Smilodon in my head now."

"Exactly. Pain gives a density, too." A lot of Dave's probably came from pain, though she had no intention of saying so. "So do responsibility and determination. Bobby was all bright colors and laughter. Jake is more like a storm front. When I first met them, that was one of the reasons I chose Bobby. Assholes have dense auras too -- and I knew a lot of those back home."

"Jake isn't an asshole. Most of the time."

"No, but it took me time to realize that. You're right about me thinking Bobby was safer. And since he was Jake's brother..."

"... If you got involved with Bobby, Jake would keep his distance."

"Which *was* kind of a prick thing to do."

"Not given that you really didn't know us. But you're not that scared kid anymore. You know who you are and who Jake is. Now you've got to decide what you're going to do about it."

"Trouble is, I have no idea."

He gave her a dismissive tail flick. "Yeah. You do."

She tried to think of a counterargument, but nothing whatsoever came to mind.

* * *

Dave led her to a sprawling Victorian farmhouse presiding over a generous lawn at the back of the park. Its wide wraparound porch and wooden siding was a soft dove gray with a hint of green, set off by shutters and gingerbread trim in slate gray. Erica recognized it from pictures she'd seen over the years. This was the house where Kurt had been raised by his father after his mother abandoned them.

Fred Briggs had been an Arcane Corps veteran who'd melded with his lion after serving in the first Gulf War. When he'd returned home, he turned the family farm into a sanctuary for Familiars.

Before Briggs Feral Sanctuary, Ferals had few alternatives when it came to housing their big cats. The federal government maintained a facility for veteran Familiars, but it was chronically underfunded, and Fred felt they deserved better.

So when Kurt left the Arcane Corps at the end of the Caliphate War, he returned to BFS to help his father run the park. Barely a year later, Fred was murdered as part of a vicious spell cast by magic-using terrorists.

It had taken Kurt, Jake, Dave, and an Arcanist named Genevieve Reyes to foil the plot. From what Erica had heard from Jake, it had been a very near thing.

And holy fuck, what the hell are they up to now?

Erica stopped in her tracks, staring in awe and alarm. The Briggs family home seemed to blaze as magic swirled around it like a windstorm. *Someone's working one hell of a spell.* It was Arcanist magic, though Arc magic normally wasn't that intense. You had to lay it down in layers over a long period to get anything with any real juice to it. "What the hell is that?"

Dave looked back at her with a chuff of amusement. "Genevieve's healing a kid."

"Here? I thought healers usually do that kind of thing at a hospital." If one was available. Erica's mother hadn't had access to medical facilities in the poor Appalachian community they'd lived in.

"Gen usually does," the tiger said, heading around the house to the backyard, where a high wooden privacy fence blocked the view. "Unfortunately, Jaida Garza has a brain tumor that hasn't responded to treatment, and she's in really bad shape. As in comatose and dying. Gen had to use the permanent spell circle she's got here. Which took fast talking on her part. I gather the pediatric oncologist wasn't crazy about the idea of bringing a child that sick into a wildlife park. But without the permanent spell circle, Gen said there was no way she could save Jaida. And since Gen is pretty much the kid's last resort..." He tilted his big head in a gesture like a shrug "... Dr. Riley decided they had nothing to lose." He nosed the gate in the slate gray fence, which swung open at the pressure.

Erica followed him inside and closed the gate behind them, curious to see what the other witch was doing and how she was doing it.

The privacy fence encircled the entire backyard, enclosing a thick carpet of verdant grass, towering oaks and azaleas in full bloom. In one corner, rosebushes surrounded a pile of weathered gray stones. Water tumbled down the stones into a pool in which bright orange and red koi lazily swam.

But Erica barely noticed those details, all her attention locked on the blazing spell circle that lay in the center of the lawn. Its sigils glowed bright blue and gold as they revolved over the grass, circling a stretcher where Jaida Garza huddled under a pile of blankets.

A woman stood at an easel by the stretcher, one hand moving in fluid gestures as she drew. The details of her face were obscured by the blaze of the surrounding spell, but Erica recognized the tumble of auburn curls gleaming in the afternoon sunlight.

Kurt's wife, Genevieve.

Erica had seen television interviews with her about the terrorist Talents. Given her role in the battle, maybe it wasn't that surprising Genevieve had been able to create such a powerful circle. Even in the daytime, the sigils glowed like a laser light display. She'd seen bigger circles on Arcane Corps bases, but never one backed by so much juice.

"Damn," Erica murmured, keeping her voice low to avoid distracting the healer. "What the hell *is* she -- Gandalf's love child?"

Dave laughed. "Nope. She just reverse-engineered the spell the Fords cast."

"The one designed to kill President Roth?" Andrew Roth was the leading light of the Humanist party, who'd pushed the National Talent Registration Act that required Talents to register with the government. The two terrorists had thought killing Roth and the Congress would kill NTRA. Instead, the assassination attempt had assured the act's passage.

"No, the one designed to *power* the one to kill Roth. Indigo Ford figured out how to draw on the earth's magical field to keep a spell permanently operational. It amplifies whatever magic you work inside it."

Erica's brows flew toward her hairline. The idea of drawing on the magic of the entire planet was fucking terrifying. "Is she nuts?"

"Don't worry, Gen only uses her power for good.

Come on, I want a better view."

As the hair rose on the back of her neck at the intensity of the magical field, Erica wasn't sure she wanted to get closer. But since that smacked of cowardice, she followed the tiger past the circle with its blazing magical energies. *Crap. Remind me not to piss off Genevieve Briggs...*

They walked around the circle's edge to a slate gray deck built onto the back of the house. The broad wooden platform appeared to be a recent addition to the thoroughly Victorian structure. Several white Adirondack chairs were clustered at the deck railing, most of them occupied. Erica didn't recognize all the spectators, but it was obvious who were the kid's parents.

A wiry young Latino man with a scruffy beard stood with his arms around a painfully thin woman. Both Garzas wore tight expressions blending hope and terror as they stared at the stretcher.

A well-dressed black woman stood talking to them in a quiet voice. Probably the pediatric oncologist. Two others wore the uniforms of an ambulance company.

Kurt Briggs sprawled in one of the chairs, watching his wife with an air of proud confidence. He was a big man, several inches taller than Erica, with a muscled build, curly dark hair, and the striking gold eyes of his heritage. His aura was a deep swirl of blues and greens, dense with the magic of a melded Feral.

Erica winced, remembering Kurt's tiger. She'd always liked Stoli. Most tigers were touchy and solitary, but Stoli had been almost as friendly as Clarence.

Indigo Ford had shot the big cat the same night her terrorist partner, Virgil, had murdered Kurt's father. The cat's death had forced Kurt to fuse with Stoli while coping with Fred's murder. The stress must have been horrific.

Fortunately, if anybody could come through a mess

like that with his sanity intact, it was Kurt Briggs. He was one of the strongest men Erica had ever known.

Kurt looked around as Erica and Dave climbed the deck steps. Handsome face lighting in a grin, Kurt rose to meet them, one hand extended. "Erica! Damn, it's good to see you." His handshake was firm and warm. To her relief, there wasn't even the faintest hint of resentment in his eyes over the months she'd ducked him.

"It's good to see you, Kurt. I'm sorry I wasn't here sooner."

"What matters is you're here now." There was such understanding in his smile, she knew he meant it.

"I was so sorry to hear about your dad. He was a hell of a man."

Kurt's smile faded. "Yeah, he was." He gestured her to the wooden chair next to his. "Have a seat. Want some coffee?"

"God, yes."

He lifted a thermos from a nearby table and poured her a mug, dark, steaming and fragrant, then indicated a pair of stoneware containers and a set of nested spoons. "Cream and sugar."

"Thanks." Erica doctored her coffee and seated herself in the low, sloping chair. Dave flopped down on the deck beside her like the world's biggest house cat. The child's parents didn't even glance around. Either they'd already met the tiger, or they were so focused on their little girl, they hadn't even noticed him. Possibly both.

Erica sipped her coffee. It was rich and sweet, just the way she liked it. "I hate I had to miss Fred's funeral." Corry Winston III, CEO of Winston Dynamics, had refused to let her have time off to attend.

"So do I. Your former boss sounds like an asshole."

"That was just a preliminary pucker. He later hinted it would be helpful if I cast a spell on the owner of a company he was trying to buy out. To make the guy a little more… cooperative in the negotiations."

Kurt frowned. "That's illegal as hell."

"And that's why I quit."

"Did you report him?"

She shook her head. "He never came right out and ordered me to do it. Besides, the government is far more likely to believe a Norm CEO than the Talents who work for him. Arcs have ended up sued and bankrupt over blowing the whistle on that kind of thing. So I told him I really didn't want to work in corporate magic anymore and quit."

"I wondered why you were working in law enforcement for a fifth of the salary you'd get in the private sector."

That, and I wanted to be closer to Jake.

"Speaking of money, I checked the website this morning," Kurt told Dave, his tone going grim. "Internet donations are down. I think those conspiracy theories about BFS are having an effect nationwide."

"I've been thinking about this." Dave sat up on his haunches. "We really need to reconsider that reality show idea. My agent says it's --"

"Oh, fuck no!" Kurt interrupted. "Have cameras follow us into the bathroom? Have them script a bunch of stupid shit for us to say, or edit what we do say to have an entirely different meaning? I don't think so."

"Shelly says we can structure the contract to avoid that. Look, the best way to combat HHer propaganda is to put the truth out there. Besides, I'm sick of people saying I'm a demon."

"A reality show isn't going to stop that," Jake announced, striding onto the deck and making a beeline for the coffee. "They'll just say you're some guy doing a voice-over for a CGI tiger."

"They say that anyway. I'm willing to put up with it, if it gives us enough money to feed all these cats. You can't cut Feral calorie intake without fucking up their magic. And without the magic, we're just animals."

"Nobody's going to cut your caloric intake even if I have to get a fucking job at McDonald's," Kurt growled. "Anyway, Genevieve is keeping us afloat."

"And you hate asking her to do it," Dave retorted.

Jake had told Erica once that Kurt's wife made a hell of a lot of money doing magical facelifts for the wealthy. The results looked far more natural than plastic surgery and didn't distort the features. Though many Arcanists did such spells, Genevieve was considered among the best in the country. She had a long list of media stars and wealthy clients seeking her services.

She could have made even more money as a healer, but Gen's sense of ethics didn't permit her to charge for her healing. Most of her patients were children with fatal diseases that hadn't responded to conventional treatment.

Jake, coffee in hand, settled into the Adirondack chair on Erica's left. He, Kurt, and Dave continued the reality show argument in low voices.

She found herself watching Jake's magic as the shades of blue in his aura began to give way to the swirling patterns of dark red she associated with irritation. It was like watching a thunderstorm, flashes of energy playing through the clouds. It made her wonder what it would be like to really make love to him -- to be the focus of all that ferocious energy and passion.

Last night had been the first time in months she'd even touched a man. The time before that had been a one-night stand when she'd been attending the South Carolina Criminal Justice Academy. Bored and lonely, she'd just wanted… something.

Too bad the experience had been so completely forgettable. Her date had been a Norm ex-Marine, handsome and brawny, who'd looked on her as nothing more than a convenient piece of ass. But she couldn't complain, because she'd been no more interested in a relationship with him. She'd just wanted somebody for the night. Now she couldn't even remember his face, only an impression of short blond hair.

Hair the same shade as Jake's... *Oh, God, am I really that shallow?*

No, but you are that far gone.

Erica's eyes drifted to the line of Jake's jaw, the rise of his sculpted cheekbones, the curve of his lip. Almost without intending to, she reached out with a curl of her aura, brushing it against the hypnotic swirl of his.

Jake's gaze snapped to her, eyes widening.

A smile tugged her own lips in response. Wickedly, she sent out another aural probe dancing over the skin of his wrist. He blinked, his lips parting. *Oh, I like this game.* Erica gazed into Jake's eyes as hunger surged through his aura in a spill of violet, growing brighter as it grew more intense. The pupils of his eyes expanded, reacting to his desire.

Just wait till I get you alone. For a moment, Erica thought he'd said the words out loud. But no, it was simply the pure intent reverberating through his aura, loud as a shout.

"Okay, you owe me a turkey," Dave told Kurt. "And I'm not talking about some dry bird either. You're going the full Martha Stewart, complete with fixings."

Kurt held up both hands, laughing. "Okay, you'll get your turkey."

Dave grinned, all teeth. "And when he asks her to marry him, you've gotta find me a girl."

"I keep telling you, there aren't that many women Feral vets with tigress Familiars. Even fewer of those have melded with their cats. So, no, I am *not* taking that bet."

Erica dragged her gaze away from Jake to stare at them in growing outrage. "You two are *betting* on whether Jake and I get involved?" She looked at Jake --

who, damn him, looked hugely amused.

Before she could sputter a suitably scathing opinion, Erica felt the insistent buzz of magic begin to fade. Glancing around, she saw the rotating sigils of Genevieve's spell slow and sink into the ground.

In the center of the circle, Gen stepped back from her easel and stretched, hands braced on the small of her back. She arched, rolling her shoulders, then looked toward the deck and gave them all a tired wave. "I'm done."

The whole group stood, eager to see how Jaida was doing. Mrs. Garza hurried past, eyes wide and desperate with hope. Her husband clattered down the deck stairs after her as she broke into a run toward the circle. The doctor and ambulance crew followed a little more decorously, with Erica, Jake, Kurt and Dave bringing up the rear.

"Did it work?" Jaida's mother called, sprinting across the yard toward her daughter's stretcher.

Genevieve smiled, brushing the hair back from her face with pastel-smeared fingers. "I think so. We'll know for sure in the next couple of days."

The parents and medical crew gathered around, watching as the doctor pulled out a stethoscope and bent to listen to the girl's chest.

Genevieve pulled the thumbtacks from the sketch and removed the drawing from the easel. She dug a can of fixative out of the bag at her feet and shook it, the metal bead rattling merrily as she walked off to put the portrait down on the grass. The can hissed as she began coating the drawing with the transparent spray to protect it from smudging.

Erica walked over to study the sketch over her shoulder. The child who looked so gaunt and ill on the stretcher bloomed with health in the sketch. Her smile shone bright with happiness, curling dark hair tumbling around her shoulders. In reality, the girl's scalp was hairless after so many rounds of chemo, and dark circles ringed her closed eyes.

Even in the sunlight, the magic that boiled around the sketch was so intense Erica could see it. Each pastel line carried such a powerful magical charge she knew Genevieve must infuse the handmade sticks with her own powdered blood. "Damn, that's impressive."

Gen looked up from adding another coat of fixative and smiled. "Erica, right? Kurt said you were coming. I'm so glad to finally meet you."

She held out a hand and Erica shook it. The healer's palm practically buzzed with magic where she gripped Erica's. Her long, tapered fingers felt a little gritty with pastel dust.

Genevieve looked down at their clasped hands and released her, grimacing in apology. "Sorry about the chalk. I can never seem to work without ending up covered in it."

"Occupational hazard." Erica nodded toward Jaida, who'd begun to stir under her blankets. "I wish I could heal like that. Never had a talent for it, though God knows I tried. My mother was a healer." The thought brought a familiar stab of pain. *If I had the kind of power Gen does, could I have saved Mom?* On the other hand, an adult's magical fields were more difficult to manipulate into regenerating than a child's, so it might not have mattered. And the breast cancer had spread by the time they'd found it, so there was that...

"Oh, you have plenty of talent. It just takes a different form from mine." Tilting her head, Gen eyed Erica thoughtfully. "I wonder if we could combine our magic."

"You mean work spells together? Like a coven?"

"It wouldn't have to be that elaborate. There are some techniques we can use that would allow us to amplify each other's spells." She smiled. "Besides, I could use some female company. I don't know about you, but I'm drowning in testosterone."

"Drowning?" Erica snorted. "I spend my whole life bobbing on a sea of it." She considered the other woman a moment and grinned. "Oh, what the hell. I'm in."

"Are you going to dance skyclad?" Dave thrust his big head between them, his eyes as huge and round as a kid's contemplating Christmas. "Ooooo! Nekkid witches! Can I watch?"

Genevieve popped him between the ears. "Too. Many. Legs."

"Awwww, you're no fun." He flattened his ears and came as close to pouting as anyone with three-inch fangs could. Before either of them could formulate a return sally, a dark haired whirlwind barreled into Gen, throwing both arms around her.

"You did it!" Tears of joy ran down Mrs. Garza's face as Genevieve dropped the spray can to hug her back. "Her vitals are better. She's conscious! She *spoke* to me!" The woman's voice sounded choked with tears and her shoulders shook as she curled her arms tighter around Gen. "We'll pay you. We'll get a GoFundMe and..."

"Not if you don't want to offend me," Gen retorted. "You don't owe me a dime. Anyway, we won't know she's really cured for weeks yet." She stepped back and handed the woman the sketch. "Keep this above her bed for the next year at least. It's probably a good idea to hang onto it even after that."

Mrs. Garza took it with shaking hands, a tender smile dawning over her drawn face. "It looks just like Jaida before she was sick, just a little older. It's like it never happened."

Erica's throat thickened at the woman's joy, and she gave Genevieve an approving nod.

Chapter Seven

They stayed for lunch: trays of sandwiches provided by park volunteers, who'd known Genevieve would be starved after the healing. Sure enough, the Arcanist put away a surprising amount of food before staggering upstairs for a nap.

Afterward, Dave and the guys took Erica on a guided tour of the park. Proud as a new father, Kurt demonstrated the systems to keep his volunteers safe while they took care of the cats.

Meanwhile Erica found her attention drifting more and more to Jake. As her gaze lingered on his big, handsome body and strong hands, yearning rolled through her like warm honey. His hand brushed hers as they walked, so close their hips bumped, fingertips tracing over sensitive skin. With each contact, she felt the stroke of his aura, or sent her own ghosting against his.

Excitement crackled along her nerves like flame along a fuse. Dave was right: it was time to go for it. *I'm finally going to do it. I'm going to make love to him.*

It was a bad idea. Chances were good she'd end up regretting it. Yes, Ferals were sexy as hell, but loving a man with a cat in his head could be dangerous. Erica still had a set of claw marks on her left thigh from the time Bobby had gotten carried away. Yet feeling the brush of Jake's intoxicating aura, she was more than willing to take that risk again.

"Oh, for God's sake," Dave said, sounding disgusted, "Would you two get a room? You're making my teeth ache."

Jake smirked. "It's not your teeth that's aching."

"Asshole."

Erica's cheeks went hot as her gaze slid to Jake's. He smiled back with a flicker of dimple and a wicked glitter in his eyes.

* * *

Jake watched Erica slide into the truck next to him. The scent of her seemed to fill his head: a combination of her body, her shampoo, and the sharp electric tang of her magic. But best of all was the arousal that had been building since they'd all sat on the deck. She was turned on. More, she was turned on *by him*. Not by Bobby, not by some other man, but *him*.

He'd wanted her for so fucking long. Watching her buckle her seatbelt, he suspected his aura probably glowed like a torch with the intensity of his lust.

RRrrrrwwww. Clarence's thought sliced into his consciousness, wordlessly demanding that he claim her before some other male got the chance. Lions were territorial as hell, a quality his cat thought Jake would do well to share.

She's not territory, furball.

The lion's reply was a rumbling psychic growl Jake had no problem translating. *If you keep playing by the rules, you're going to lose.* Or maybe that thought was Jake's.

Acutely conscious of her, he drove the Ford toward the BFS exit, his mind working as he planned her seduction. He scarcely even noticed the icy stares of the protesters as they drove past the picket line.

Out of the corner of one eye, he saw a glowing paw reach across the bench seat toward her. *Oh no, you don't,* he told Clarence sternly. *Too Many Legs.*

"*RRRRRRmph.*" Translation: *Then get off your ass.*

He flicked Erica a look. She was fidgeting, shifting in her seat. She quickly turned the other way, suggesting she'd been watching him. Maybe the furball had a point.

As he stopped at a red light, Jake sent a tendril of aura stretching across the distance between them, feathering his power over the life force swirling around her hand.

Erica shot him a smoldering look in response.

He kept his gaze firmly on the traffic ahead, though

his lips wanted to twitch. *I've got her attention. Now I just need to keep it.*

His next magical probe quested up the length of her arm, just barely stirring her aura. The last thing he wanted was to make her feel she was being groped. Which was why he resisted the temptation offered by those beautiful breasts.

He could *feel* her -- the strength and currents of her magic, glowing bright with the intensity of the mind behind it. There was a visible complexity in the auras of Talents that Norms lacked. That was particularly true of Erica's. Countless interconnecting threads created a structure as intricate and lovely as a spider web dewed and glowing in the morning sunlight.

And God, the way it felt. As delicate and arousing as the feeling of breath against bare skin. Intimate. Hot.

His psychic probe dancing over the strands of Erica's aura, he gloried in the freedom to touch her. With every gliding brush, his need grew -- first into hunger, then craving, then stark animal lust.

And all the while, a rumble sounded deep in his mind: Clarence. Lions didn't purr, and yet the deep, thrumming sound could be described no other way.

* * *

Erica bit her lower lip, her gaze locked on Jake's face in fascination. She would've thought he was concentrating on the road, if it hadn't been for the tiny, exquisite sensations he triggered with each brush of his aura against hers. It reminded her of the sensation of feathers swirling over flesh, delicate as a butterfly's wing. Yet somehow the faint flutter was more erotic than hands on nipples or cunt.

A flush rode his high cheekbones, and his gold eyes glittered as he moistened his lower lip with a pass of his tongue. His big hands rode the wheel easily as he steered the truck around curves, passing other cars with a cop's skilled competence.

Imagining those hands on her skin made her heartbeat a demanding thump in her throat. Swallowing, she crossed her legs. Her gaze drifted downward, following the contours of his muscled chest beneath the red flannel shirt he wore tucked in his jeans.

Down to his belt buckle and the bulge pressing against his fly. *Good God, I don't remember Bobby being quite that hung.*

His aura brushed her inner thigh in a tender, silken stroke. Erica watched the bright rose tendril skate across her skin. It teased her with the thought of what else he could do with his magic.

Her mouth felt dry. Her gaze flicked up to his lower lip, remembering the taste of it. Wanting more. Wanting everything she could get. She'd craved him so damn long. Wanted him so desperately but hadn't had the guts to risk it. Now she ached to run her hands along those broad shoulders and feel muscle shift under her fingertips. Burned to touch the hot, intriguing bulge of his erection behind the tough material of his jeans.

Almost shaking with hunger, she reached out a tendril of aura to play it along the muscled length of his thigh. His magic felt so much more intense than hers. Touching it felt like putting a hand into a fast-moving stream, feeling it roil and bubble around her fingers. His head turned toward her, and his eyes narrowed, reflecting hot gold.

Feeling uncharacteristically shy, she looked away, out the windshield. Stiffened. "Jake!"

He whipped back around and hit the brakes, barely in time to avoid slamming into the rear of the minivan stopped at the red light ahead. "Fuck!"

Erica swallowed, gripping her shoulder belt in one white-knuckled hand, heart hammering. "Maybe we'd better ease off on the foreplay until we get to my place."

Foot firmly on the brake, Jake slanted her a look. "*Is*

this foreplay?"

Her gaze slid down to his fly. "It'd be a waste if it wasn't."

He grinned, displaying almost as many teeth as Dave. "Glad to hear it."

Their eyes met in a gaze hot enough to make Erica's nipples ache.

Behind them, a car horn blew. Jake laughed, a soft leonine chuff, and followed the minivan through the intersection. He seemed to keep his mind firmly on driving the rest of way to her apartment. Erica heroically resisted the temptation to play any more games with his aura.

Not that she needed to. Glancing down at his zipper, she saw he was still hard. Swallowing, she crossed her legs again.

"Cut it out," Jake growled. "Every time you do that, I smell…" He broke off.

Her cheeks heated. "You're speeding."

He eased off the gas. She found herself bouncing one foot just to burn off some of the erotic energy. Her imagination wasn't helping. It kept showing her images of how that thick erection might look without a layer of denim blocking the view.

By the time they pulled into the complex's drive, they were both all but vibrating. Erica was reaching for the door handle when a big hand curled around her jaw to pull her head around.

Jake's mouth crushed down over hers. It was a ferocious kiss, all teeth and tongue and unapologetic lust. Erica threaded her hands into short blond hair and fisted them there as she kissed him back, mouth open, tongue thrusting.

He leaned in hard, pinning her against the door. Long fingers curled around her breast, surrounding her in a rough, warm grip that was incredibly arousing.

She groaned as her lust leapt like a flame. At the needy sound, he tightened his grip, thumb and forefinger closing around one nipple through her bra, twisting, tugging just hard enough to pour gasoline on the blaze.

Shivering, she gasped, stroking one hand over the gold silk of his hair, loving the contrast with the rasp of his five o'clock shadow on her skin as he kissed her.

Sweet. Maddening. Not enough.

He reached up under her shirt, making her pant in delight at the rasp of calluses over the flesh of her ribs. Erica let her eyes drift closed to watch his aura blaze against the darkness behind her lids, shades of violet and blue and rose spinning in wild currents.

It took a surprising amount of willpower to drag her mouth from his. "We can't make love sitting in the cab at three o'clock in the afternoon."

Dimples flashed. "Actually, I'm pretty sure we could."

"Not with the school bus coming by." She grabbed the door handle and all but fell out of the truck. Hopping to the ground, she hurried up the sidewalk toward the door of her two-story brick apartment building.

Jake's running shoes scraped on gravel as he jumped out after her. With a sound far too much like a giggle for a self-respecting cop, Erica broke into a sprint.

"Come back here!" The growl rumbled so deep and rough with desire, it sent a shiver down her spine.

"Only if you catch me!" But she had to stop to unlock the unit's door, the keys jangling in her hand. He pounced on her, wrapping long arms around her from behind. One hand caught her jaw, as his teeth closed over the back of her neck, finding an incredibly sensitive bundle of nerves.

An image flashed through Erica's mind, something she'd seen on a National Geographic special: a male lion holding a female's nape in the same grip as he mounted her from behind. *And why does that thought turn me on so damned much?*

Jake's teeth scored her flesh, making her hands shake until it was all she could do to manage the deadbolt. At last the lock turned, and she pushed it open. Scooping her off her feet, Jake swept her inside to the foot of the stairs, kicking the door closed behind them. "Where?" he growled.

"Third floor. Unit's on the left," she groaned back, not at all sure they'd make it.

He carried her as if she weighed nothing, taking the steps two at a time. When they reached the top, he put her down just long enough to let her take care of the lock while he nibbled her ear. She was quivering by the time she got the door open.

They fell through it together. Jake pushed her backward, his mouth ravenous on hers as he steered her into the living room and tumbled her down onto the sectional. Dove gray leather gave under her back as he settled atop her, a solid male weight.

One hand grabbed the hem of her shirt, pushed it to her shoulders. The other caught the cup of her bra, dragged downward to free a jutting pink nipple. His mouth covered it in wet heat as she groaned her pleasure at the ceiling.

Jake suckled in hard pulls, simultaneously raking his teeth over the little point until Erica writhed under him. Both hands fisting in the material of his shirt, she dragged it out of his waistband. "Naked," she panted. "Want you naked."

"Hell, yes!" He pulled away from her, started trying to unbutton his shirt, cursed as the tiny plastic discs frustrated his aroused fingers.

Jake managed to get only three of them open before she grabbed the bottom of the shirt and tugged it off over his head. Tossing it aside, she stared in unabashed lust.

He was every bit as magnificent as she'd known he'd be --
his shoulders broad, muscle forming great curved plates
across his chest and down the length of his belly, rippling
along broad, strong arms. "Good God, Nolan, do you live
in the gym?"

Jake shrugged, doing interesting things with all that
brawn. "As my old DI used to say, 'Spend time in the
gym or get your ass kicked on the street.' You have way
too many clothes on." He caught the shirt already rucked
up over her breasts, pulled it off, and tossed it aside
before attacking the hooks of her bra. A few maddening
minutes went by as they fought to strip off all those
frustrating layers of clothing, dumping them wherever
they fell.

Finally, Jake rose to shed his jeans as she sprawled
on the couch naked, wet, and aching. For a suspended
moment he stopped and just stared down at her, his big
body tense, pupils dilated in the vivid frame of his irises.
There was something in his eyes that wasn't entirely
human.

Erica swallowed, watching the magic roil around
him, the violet desire intensifying among the ribbons of
rose, the two shades driving out the blue. She glimpsed
the glowing outline of a mane. Her pussy felt hot, plump,
drenched. "What we need now…" She paused to lick her
lips. "… is one less pair of pants."

Dimples flashed. "If you insist." He unsnapped the
jeans and pulled down his zipper, struggling a bit with
the bulk of his cock. The metallic hiss made her catch her
breath.

His cock's flushed shaft pressed out through the
open fly, a glint of moisture tipping its mushroom head.
It looked so deliciously thick, she instantly imagined
what it would feel like thrusting to the balls. "You go
commando, Nolan? Why am I not surprised?"

One corner of his lip curled up. "Maybe because I *am*

a commando?"

"*Were* a commando. Now you're a cop. Get down here and I'll show you what I can do with that nightstick."

"*Nightstick*? Really? What, are you channeling Dave?"

"If you don't move that tight ass, I'm going to start doing sound effects."

"What kind of sound effects?"

"What kind of sound effects would you like to hear?" All but quivering in anticipation, Erica watched him kneel.

"You'll find out." Grinning, he grabbed her behind both knees, lifted them, and draped them over hard, broad shoulders. He leaned in until his face was scant inches from the soft, damp hair of her sex, and inhaled, gleaming eyes sliding shut. His mouth covered her pussy, hot, wet, and demanding. Every muscle in her body jerked tight in anticipation.

"Oh, God!" she gasped.

"Yeah, that's the sound effect I had in mind." Lowering his head again, he licked. Slowly. Tracing between her lips, drawing a long, wet line past plump folds, then back up again to swirl a lazy pattern over her clit.

A shudder ran the length of her body as pleasure wound through her like a scarlet ribbon. Wrapping her legs around his broad back, Erica dug her heels into the thick muscle.

His tongue flicked back and forth, up and down, stroking the tiny shaft of her clit with every pass. As sensation made her nervous system reverberate like a bell, Jake caressed each breast in turn, teasing nipples drawn tight and aching. Every touch made her hips jerk, adding to the sweet burn.

He ate her slowly, thoroughly, suckling, lapping, as

if he was in no hurry to bury that thick cock in her depths. As if she were some exquisite dessert he'd craved a very long time.

"Jake! Jake, please!" Erica hunched against his face, one hand cupping the back of his head, the other gripping the nape of his neck as her heels dug into his back. Her orgasm swelled like a storm on the horizon, tightening muscles with every flick of his tongue and skillful fingers. *So close, so close.* "Please!"

His free hand brushed her ass, and a finger slid into her hot depths. Stroked. In. Out. So close to the edge.

"Fuck me," Erica panted. "For God sake, fuck me!"

Gold eyes glittered up the length of her body from between her legs, and he stopped licking just long enough to say, "No."

Before she could protest, his tongue started swirling a complicated pattern around her clit that had her head grinding back into the couch cushion. The muscles in her belly clenched, her thighs flexing as the climax trembled just beyond her fingertips. "Jake!" The word hissed through her teeth. "Now!"

His only answer was a growl.

Just when she thought she couldn't take any more, he surged up between her legs. Bracing one fist beside her hip, he grabbed his cock to aim it between her pussy's slick lips.

And entered her in one driving thrust.

They both groaned.

Panting, Erica bit her lip at the feel of him, shoved so deliciously deep. She could smell her own wet heat mixed with the dark aroma of aroused male -- clean sweat and musk, the ozone scent of magic overlaid with the faintest trace of fur.

Eyes all pupil surrounded by a thin sliver of glittering gold, Jake began to pump, dragging out, then forcing his way in, slow and taunting. Each satin stroke was a tease of sensation rubbing along sensitized nerves, sending sweet curls of pleasure through her body.

Erica arched her back, the movement pressing her nipples against satin hair and hard muscle -- another dollop of delight. Tightening her thighs around his lean waist, she felt the muscles in his ass ripple as he rode her, filling her with every entry, teasing her with every retreat.

His mouth found hers in a fierce, biting kiss that claimed as his cock ground in and out. Erica kissed him back, wrapping her arms around his waist, digging her fingertips into the thick, working brawn. His aura surged against hers, currents rippling the length of her body, making her writhe against him.

Jake fucked harder, deeper, picking up the pace. Erica met him thrust for thrust, grinding upward, clawing for the orgasm that was so close, blazing behind her eyelids, swelling like a thundercloud. Pleasure stacked on pleasure, each layer enhancing the others, and she heard high, sharp cries she realized were her own.

A thousand shades of violet and rose detonated in front of her eyes like fireworks, and she screamed, coming.

Jake roared, the sound deeper and louder than anything human vocal cords should be able to produce. Purple light forked and snapped through their joined auras like lightning strikes.

At last he collapsed in her arms, panting, a glorious male weight. Erica clutched at him, light still popping around them, her thigh muscles jumping and quivering from the force of her orgasm.

"Fuuuuck," he groaned, somehow managing to turn it into a three syllable word. Flopping over onto his back, he scooped an arm under her and pulled her over on top of him like a sheet. "That was…"

"It… certainly was…" Erica panted back, her heartbeat banging in her ears. She combed her fingers through the silken ruff of his chest hair, with its threads of gold that reminded her of a lion's pelt. "I think our magic intensified the experience." Her lips twitched. "A lot."

Jake laughed, his broad chest vibrating against her cheek. "No kidding." He smoothed one hand along the line of the thigh she'd hooked over his hip. His fingertips paused at something high on her leg. Frowning, he twisted his head to look.

Erica lifted her head and followed his gaze to the five short, silvery scars marking her outer thigh. They almost exactly matched the width and length of his fingers.

"Those are claw marks." Jake sounded puzzled. Realization struck a moment later. "Bobby did that a month before…" He clenched his teeth over the rest of the sentence. "I remember when you had to go to the base hospital the next day. I didn't realize it scarred."

Uncomfortable, Erica managed a shrug. "It's not that bad."

"It's bad enough." He gave her a narrow stare, his jaw flexing as if his teeth were clenching. "What the hell happened anyway? And don't try to put me off with that 'he got carried away' excuse. I'd have kicked his ass then if Kurt hadn't stopped me."

"It was the truth."

"You were fighting. I heard you."

She rolled her eyes. "Ferals have no sense of privacy." When he only looked at her, his gaze cool and level, Erica sighed and surrendered. "He really didn't intend to do it. Yeah, we were arguing…" About the way she'd been watching Jake bench press four hundred pounds, pumping out reps with sweat dewing his skin. She'd been taking a break from her own workout when her gaze had fallen on him just a little too long.

Erica focused on the curl of chest hair under her fingers. "Somehow during the fight, we ended up in bed…"

"Did he hurt you on purpose?" His tone was steely.

"Of course not. If he had, I wouldn't have put up with it."

"What could you have done? Even if he hadn't been a Feral, he outweighed you by seventy pounds."

"I'd have gone to the CO. It was an accident, Jake. Bobby would never have intentionally hurt a woman. You *know* that."

"Intentionally or not, he clawed you."

"More than two years ago. And he's…" She broke off.

A tight silence rolled by. "Yeah."

Jake took a deep breath, his broad chest lifting under her body. She felt him begin working to relax rigid muscles in the exercise Ferals used to control their cats -- and themselves. A man with a lion in his head couldn't afford to lose control.

She'd been telling the truth. Bobby hadn't intended to hurt her. The sex had just gotten a little rough because they'd both been thoroughly pissed off. Of course, their best sex had always been makeup sex. Bobby being Bobby, and Erica being Erica, they'd had makeup sex a lot.

Bobby, did you walk into that trap because you were distracted by our fight? Was that my fault too? Another uncomfortable thought lanced through her mind. *And two years later, here I am with your brother.*

She suspected Bobby wouldn't have been surprised.

Am I doing the right thing? Though maybe the real question was, could she really do anything else?

Chapter Eight

Adrian watched the needle of the tattoo machine punch in and out of John Reese's skin, driving the magical ink deep. Each tiny penetration strengthened his mystic connection to his client. By the time he finished the sigil, Reese would belong to him.

Of course, if the ex-Marine had any idea he was being put under a spell, the fucker would kill Adrian with his bare hands. Or he'd try, anyway. So would the rest of the HHers sitting around the shop, drinking beer and talking about Carson's untimely heart attack. "Fuckin' guards let him die," Bill Garrison growled. A fleshy middle-aged man, he ran a local diner and was the group's ringleader.

He was also Adrian's favorite advertisement. A tattoo of a blue dragon with iridescent green scales wrapped around his bald head. Adrian's eyes lingered on it. It really was some of his best work. The beast's red eyes glared from the center of Garrison's forehead, its sinuous body curving back across the top of his hairless scalp, wings spread wide to cup his face. Its tail wrapped around his throat. Not only was the line work and shading skillful, it covered the sigil on the top of his head that made him suggestible as hell.

Jimmy Pell nodded over his can of Bud. "Poor bastard may have been nuts, but he didn't deserve to die like that. They could have gotten him some fucking help."

The others growled in agreement. Never mind that they'd all been more than a little scared of Carson, especially after Adrian had been working on him a while. The thought of what they would have done if they'd known he was responsible for the fucker's heart attack only added to his buzz.

Undercover work was almost as exhilarating as murder.

The group's five ringleaders sat in folding chairs just outside the magic circle he'd painted on the vinyl floor in invisible ultraviolet paint. His tattoo table sat at the center of the pattern, where the circle focused his magic on its occupant like a beam of sunlight through a magnifying glass.

Though not a particularly big shop, the place was meticulously neat, its walls painted white to showcase colorful framed samples of his art. Wheeled carts held bottles of tattoo ink, a wide selection of needles, several specialized tattoo machines for different design styles, and the assortment of oils and lotions he used to lubricate his clients' skin.

The sign over the door read Killer Ink. Under normal circumstances, Adrian would have considered that name a little too on the nose. Given his clientele, however, he'd thought it apt. And he'd been right. The HHers loved it.

Adrian drew the tattoo machine through the next sweep of the sigil. It was a good thing his audience sat too far away to make out the small design. They might not realize what it was -- but then again, they might. John himself couldn't see it, since Adrian made sure to keep his free hand blocking the man's view, supposedly pulling the skin tight as he worked.

The minute the sigil was finished, he'd cover it over with the colored ink of the surrounding tattoo's intricate shading. No Norm would have any idea it was there.

He'd been playing this game for months now. This was the longest job he'd ever done -- at least not funded by the Federal government. Virginia Laurel had a serious hard-on for Talents, or she wouldn't be willing to pay him two hundred K to run them out of her county. Gotta love a rich bitch with a grudge and no sense of proportion.

The conversation died down. To keep them occupied, Adrian asked, "How'd the protest at BFS go today?"

"Cops showed up." Pell was a wiry little man, with a narrow face and a nasty temper. Adrian had given him a tattoo of a mermaid who looked like the man's wife, her tail wound around his biceps. Oddly romantic choice for such a hardass, but everybody had a weakness. Adrian had made note of his. "You were right about us needing our weapons permits. The bastards demanded our ID. Like we don't have a right to protest that goddamn place." His lip curled. "One of them was that fucking Feral."

"You could see the devil in his yellow eyes," Garrison put in. "I wanted to blow his fucking head off. I should've done it."

Not if you didn't want to get the death penalty for killing a cop. Fortunately, these assholes were more talk than action. They might consider themselves dangerous men, but getting drunk and busting up a bar would've been enough to feed that illusion. It had taken months of work on Adrian's part to turn them into useful weapons.

At first the process of cultivating the local HHers had been slow. They were highly suspicious of strangers, so when Adrian had started showing up for meetings, they initially treated him like a possible FBI agent. Which, ironically, wasn't that far off the mark.

Luckily Adrian was a big man, and he could be intimidating when he chose. His willingness to kick ass -- he'd sent one little prick to the hospital -- quickly convinced them he couldn't possibly be a Fed.

Not that they really had anything to worry about as far as the FBI was concerned. The fact was, HH wasn't all that far off the mainstream Humanist movement. He doubted the Roth administration would send anyone to investigate this crowd unless they killed someone.

Of course, Adrian would promptly throw them all under the bus -- after first making sure none of them could identify him. Once the HHers accepted him, convincing them to go under his needle had been surprisingly easy. His work was gorgeous, and he'd told them he was happy to give fellow Humanists a generous discount. They were equally happy to cooperate.

Now he owned them.

Adrian reached out a rubber-gloved hand and dipped the needle of his machine in the plastic cap filled with magical ink. Reese flinched slightly as the needle hit a particularly sensitive bundle of nerves on his chest. The film beneath his body rustled faintly as he shifted. Like everything else in splatter range, the table was wrapped in protective plastic. Tattooing was a notoriously messy procedure, and as with anything involving bodily fluids, there was a serious risk of blood-borne pathogens. Which was why Adrian was as obsessed with cleanliness as any surgeon. If one of his clients died, it wouldn't be by accident. Besides, the risk of contagion served as a good excuse to keep everyone else at a distance.

He'd been working on Reese for three sessions now, beginning with the intricate line work of the armored warrior on horseback, carefully drawn freehand across the man's chest. Next he'd added the highlight effects with paler shades. Today he'd finish the tat with the most vivid inks applied over his own sigil. He always saved the magic for the next-to-last step, minimizing the chance that a client would spot something to make him suspicious.

At this point, though, Adrian wasn't all that worried. Every member of the Laurelton HH wore his sigil, making them more inclined to believe anything he told them.

Finished with the spell, Adrian paused to remove the liner needle from the machine and replace it with a thick, three-needle shader. The one he used for sigils was so fine, the ink quickly became invisible even on white skin.

Once the new needle was seated in the machine, he dipped it in blood-red ink and began to lay down the first of the vivid colors. Reese barely winced as the needle bit deep, though a muscle in his jaw worked.

The kid had possibilities. A Marine Corps veteran, Reese had returned from the Caliphate War with a haunted look in his eyes and a deep and abiding hatred for Talents. That included the ones on his own side, whom he described as "stuck-up Feral fuckers."

Adrian could understand that attitude. Arcane Corps Ferals had a definite strut that always made him itch to put them in their place.

Which was part of the reason he'd agreed to this job -- a chance to settle accounts with Kurt Briggs and Jake Nolan. He'd worked with the Fords back in his CIA days, before Indigo went batshit from torture. Virgil had saved his life once when a Caliphate sorcerer had been about to put a bullet in Adrian's brain. Making Nolan and Briggs bleed for what they'd done to the Fords would balance that debt.

Adrian figured it was only a matter of time before Virginia would send him after the two Ferals she considered her most dangerous opponents. Plus, it pissed her off that they were considered heroes for saving President Roth and the entire U.S. Congress.

Which only proved the old woman didn't know shit about Talents. She should be a lot more worried about Genevieve Briggs. That bitch had power to burn.

As far as Erica Harris went, Adrian didn't consider her much of a threat. If the deputy'd had any real talent, she'd be working in corporate magic. Still, she'd make a nice appetizer. He didn't doubt killing her would eventually become necessary, judging from the way she'd thrown a monkey wrench into the Carson plot.

And to make things even more delicious, she'd served two tours with Nolan and Briggs. Her death should piss that pair off nicely. With Ferals, their Familiars' instincts were a major weak spot. A man driven by emotion was easier to manipulate into a mistake.

As for Genevieve, that was going to take some thought. A simple spell wasn't enough. She'd spot it, break it, and use it to figure out who he was.

Which was basically what had happened to the Fords. They'd made the critical mistake of underestimating Genevieve, and it cost them everything. It was an error he had no intention of repeating.

Fortunately, he had an idea or two about that.

Which reminds me. Adrian looked up from Reese's bare, ink-smeared chest. "What's happening with the march?"

Garrison spoke up, the beer halfway to his mouth. "I just heard from the Atlanta boys. They're bringing a hundred guys."

"Sounds good." He wiped away the excess red ink from the warrior's axe. "How many is that total?"

Garrison shrugged. "If everybody shows, maybe eight thousand." His eyes gleamed. "Enough to scare every devil worshiper out of this town."

Adrian made a noncommittal sound. Talents had lived in Laurelton for generations. It would take a lot more than a mob of HHers to scare them off. Besides, he figured only a few hundred Humanists would show. It was one thing to talk big, but a couple of recent marches had blown up in the bastards' faces. Injuries, arrests, and protestors losing their jobs tended to discourage all but the most hard-core. On the other hand, even a couple thousand fanatics could do a lot of damage with the right inspiration.

Adrian could be very inspiring.

* * *

Erica spent the first few hours of Tuesday driving her usual patrol route, trying to keep her attention on her job and off her three-day weekend with Jake. Her mind kept drifting to the love they'd made, the comic book movie he'd dragged her to, the way they'd shared popcorn and laughter and snark. Best weekend she'd had in… well, ever.

She later realized her happy mood had cursed her, because the rest of the day went straight to hell.

The call should have been a routine stop. But as Erica parked her patrol car in the driveway of the brick ranch, hair rose on the back of her neck. "Oh, shit." Her instincts weren't infallible, but she'd learned not to ignore them. And they didn't approve of whatever was going on here.

Grabbing the handset of her radio, she keyed the mic. "Laurel Dispatch? Alpha 22 10-23 at 401 Miller Court."

"10-4, Alpha 22."

She'd been dispatched to do a well-check on Rachel Bryer, who'd been scheduled to pick up her four-year-old son from kindergarten at one o'clock. When Rachel didn't show, the school called her cell repeatedly, only to get no response. When they tried her job, they learned she hadn't shown up for work either.

The school principal managed to contact the little boy's grandmother, who'd agreed to pick him up. She'd also called 911, since it wasn't like her daughter to forget Christopher or skip work.

All of which might be sufficient motivation for the creeping sensation between Erica's shoulder blades. It was possible her admittedly vivid imagination was masquerading as a psychic impression; sometimes it was difficult to tell the two apart.

Unfortunately, she didn't think this was one of those times.

Getting out of the car, Erica drew her Glock and started toward the carport and the Ford Focus parked there. A glance revealed no one sitting inside.

Turning toward the house's door, Erica stopped, eyes narrowing. It stood ajar, and the doorframe was splintered as if someone had kicked it in. She keyed her shoulder mic. "Laurel dispatch, Alpha 22. Code 5A at 401 Miller Court." Which was the code for breaking and entering. "Requesting backup."

There was a brief pause. "Affirmative, Alpha 22." Judging by the dispatcher's grim tone, he didn't like the situation any more than she did.

The dispatcher repeated her request for assistance, but Erica knew it might be a while before backup arrived. There'd been a bad wreck on Oakland Avenue that had a couple of units tied up, plus a shoplifting call that had come in a little after that. It might be twenty or thirty minutes before anyone could shake free.

What if Rachel Bryer was injured? The woman could die while Erica stood around waiting for backup. "Fuck it." She raised her voice. "Police!"

Pushing the door open with her foot, she ducked aside in case someone opened fire. Nothing happened. She stepped inside, swinging her gun in an arc to clear the room.

It turned out to be the kitchen, neat at first glance, nothing out of place... Except for the pool of milk that spread across the vinyl floor, leading to an empty plastic jug lying on its side in front of the refrigerator. Erica could imagine the scene: Rachel getting out the milk, only to drop it as someone kicked the door in... "Ms. Bryer? Police. Are you all right?"

No answer. An open doorway led into the room beyond. Erica's heart pounded as she sidled toward the doorway. Feeling something sticky under the rubber soles of her uniform shoes, she looked down, half expecting blood. But despite her howling instincts, nothing was visible. Probably drying milk, tracked across the floor when Rachel ran through the puddle.

Weapon raised, she edged around the corner. Only to freeze halfway through.

No, Rachel Bryer didn't need first-aid.

Erica keyed her mic. "Laurel, Alpha 22. Code 1 at 401 Miller Court. Please send an investigator, the coroner, and the crime scene van."

Rachel lay on the beige carpet of the tiny living room in the middle of a pentagram painted in something rust brown. Presumably blood from her own slashed throat. Her hazel eyes stared sightlessly at the ceiling fan over her head, her oval face slack, mouth open. She'd been a pretty girl, maybe thirty pounds overweight, long hair spilling across the carpet around her head. It was blonde where it wasn't soaked with blood.

Sigils were sketched in a circle around the corpse, their shapes clumsily drawn, again in blood.

"Shit." Someone had sacrificed Rachel Bryer to power a spell. Even as her heart twisted in pity at the thought of the woman's orphaned little boy, Erica knew the implications were almost as grim for Laurel County's Talent community. "The Human Heritage wing nuts are going to lose their collective minds."

Well, nothing for it but find out what the hell kind of spell the bastard had cast. She narrowed her eyes and drew on her Talent, meaning to examine the patterns of magic that should linger after such a working.

Nothing.

Oh, there was the usual aftermath of violent death -- the swirl of lingering aural energy hanging in the air like a dark fog, composed of the victim's agony and despair blended with the perpetrator's rage, viciousness, and sickening triumph. But despite the pentagram, there was no sign whatsoever of the magical energy that should echo the painted symbols.

This had nothing to do with magic.

Which was obvious in retrospect. Had it had been a

real human sacrifice, the killer would have painted the sigils with blood from non-fatal wounds *before* Rachel was killed, so her life force could be used to power the spell. Otherwise there'd have been nothing to focus the energy of her death, and the spell wouldn't have worked.

Erica moved to the closest of the symbols and knelt, careful not to touch it. It was clumsily drawn, with none of the skill a real practitioner would have displayed. What's more, it was the sigil for "water," while the one beside it meant "stone" and the one next to that "sky." It was as if someone had strung random words together without any idea how to write a sentence. "You copied this crap from the Internet, didn't you, you son of a bitch?" The murder had been staged to *look* like a magical crime. Which strongly suggested the killer thought the cops would otherwise suspect him or her.

Grimly, Erica studied the whirlpool of psychic energy lingering on the scene -- all the energy the killer hadn't really used in his faux spell. But she could use it... *After* she finished clearing the house, something she hadn't yet done. *Damn it, Harris, get your head out of your ass.*

Careful not to step in the blood, she rose and edged along the wall toward the hallway.

Five minutes later, she'd confirmed there was no sign of the killer anywhere else in the house. In the process, she'd gotten far too good a look at Christopher's room, with its Spider-Man-themed bedspread and plastic toy chest shaped like a football, overflowing with superhero action figures. She could imagine the boy's anguished bewilderment when Mommy didn't come home.

You're not getting away with this, asshole. Stalking into the living room, Erica jerked a notepad and a pen out of out of her back pocket...

Yeah, that's not going to work.

Drawing in a deep breath through her nose, she blew it out from her mouth on a slow ten count. Closing her eyes, she worked to center herself, thrusting aside her impotent, boiling fury. Strong emotions could contaminate the magic, decreasing the spell's accuracy.

Feet spread wide, eyes still closed, Erica reached out her aura into the unanchored energy left behind by the murder. And wanted to recoil at the storm of rage and pain, hate and fear embedded like flies in the amber of the victim's sundered life force. Despite its psychic stench, she drew on that dark energy and began to draw the swirling patterns. Her pen darted over the pad in swift, unhesitating strokes as she worked to capture what she sensed.

Fifteen minutes later, Erica opened her eyes and looked down at the pad. There, in slashing lines of blue ink, a man stared back at her, eyes narrow, his lips curled back in a snarl to show the crooked line of a front tooth. His hair was thinning, swept back from a high forehead, and his face was long and bony with a crooked nose and a weak, scarred chin.

Even Erica had a hard time understanding how she did magical forensic sketches. For one thing, she had to draw them with her eyes closed, so the lines should be all over the place and her pen should run right off the page. Yet her drawings often beat surveillance video when it came to capturing a useable likeness.

True, sometimes she struck out completely, but this wasn't one of those times. She'd been doing sketches long enough to know a good one from a dud -- and this was a good one. She might not have the raw power of someone like Genevieve Briggs, but Erica's sensitivity to magic gave her a keen ability to pull images out of a crime scene.

Unfortunately, the sketch was only a starting place. Though certain types of magical testimony were admissible in court, forensic sketches based solely on magical impressions were not. Even if they found the asshole, they wouldn't be able to convict him on the sketch alone.

"So we'll just have to dig up something else," Erica told the sketch. "Because you're not getting away with this, you son of a bitch."

"What the flaming fuck are you doing?" a male voice roared.

Erica jumped and whipped around, damn near going for her weapon.

Sergeant Roger Johnson glared at her in fury.

Chapter Nine

"You called for backup, Harris. Why in the hell didn't you wait for it?" the sergeant demanded, gray brows drawn down over furious blue eyes.

Erica snapped to attention in a reflex ingrained by years in the Corps. "There were signs of forced entry. I was afraid the homeowner had been injured and needed assistance."

"And you could have ended up just as dead as she is," the sergeant snapped, his mustache twitching with every angry word. "Instead, you tracked through a crime scene, contaminating who knows what evidence. As first on scene at a murder, your job is to string crime scene tape and keep everybody else the hell out to preserve the evidence so we can catch whichever bastard did this. Or weren't you paying attention that day at the Academy?"

"But I..."

"What the hell have you got there?" He took a long step forward and snatched the pad out of her hand. "What the fuck is this?"

"It's a forensic sketch."

His head snapped up and he stared, his face darkening as his anger grew into outright fury. "What, you *saw* the son of a bitch? You got this good a look? Why in the hell didn't you radio in a description? We could've been looking for him by now!"

"He was long gone by the time I got here."

Johnson flashed the pad at her. "So you just pulled this out of your ass?"

She grappled for patience. "No, it's based on ambient magical energy left behind by the murder."

"Ambient magical..." The sergeant gazed around the room as realization dawned. "Oh my God, this is another human sacrifice." A complex blend of emotions flickered across his face: dread, horror -- and the sick triumph of a man who sees his worst suspicions proved correct.

Damn Norm. She fought her temper until she could manage the controlled, polite tone a smart woman used with superior officers. "No sir, though someone went to a lot of trouble to make it look that way."

Johnson eyed her suspiciously. "If it was magic, would you admit it?"

"Yes. Sir."

"But if this was done by people like…"

"I am *nothing* like the kind of people who make human sacrifices… Sir."

"You use magic."

"You use a gun. Does that make you a mass shooter?"

Offended, Johnson lifted the notebook, reaching for the top sheet as if about to rip it out.

"Maybe," a mild voice observed, "We don't want to have a loud argument about a murder case in the hearing of possible witnesses. Like the ones gathering outside." Detective Grant Sawyer stood in the doorway, Jake at his shoulder. A hint of temper steamed under Sawyer's bland expression. Jake looked worried. "I assume that's not evidence you're getting ready to rip up?"

Johnson shot Erica a poisonous look. "Harris was doodling instead of securing the scene."

The detective held out a hand, and the sergeant reluctantly passed over the pad. Sawyer studied it. "Hell of a doodle."

"It's an arcane forensic sketch," Erica said through tight lips.

"That's one of Harris's magical talents." Jake gave Johnson a hard look. "When I served with her in the Corps, she could walk up to the scene of a bombing and draw a dead-on likeness of the guy who did it. We caught a lot of terrorists that way."

Johnson sneered. "If they were terrorists, and not just

some unlucky bastard that happened to resemble whatever she pulled out of her ass."

"The Corps doesn't assume anything when it comes to Arcanists." A muscle flexed in Jake's square jaw, and his eyes narrowed. "Harris was tested extensively before she was certified. They found she had an accuracy rate of ninety percent."

"Which means for every hundred people she fingered, ten of them were innocent."

"Unless I get a strong impression of the guilty party, I don't do the sketch." Erica gave the notebook a tight nod. "I got a very strong impression on him."

"You didn't follow procedure, Harris," Johnson told her, almost biting off the words. "You should have secured the scene, and then asked permission to do the sketch from the detective once he arrived."

"Sir, the psychic energy from a violent crime dissipates quickly. The longer you wait, the more you lose. If I'd waited too long, I would not have been able to do a sketch at all."

"Quit arguing with me before I write you up," Johnson snarled. "Get your ass out there and string that tape, and keep the lookie-loos from destroying any more evidence than they already have."

"Not yet, Sergeant," Sawyer put in, stopping her before she could turn to leave. "Harris, do we have another human sacrifice case on our hands?"

"No sir." Erica outlined her conclusions, pointing out the fake sigils and her belief that they must have been drawn following the murder instead of the other way around.

Sawyer took notes, writing in a rapid scrawl and firing questions at her until he was satisfied. "Go string that tape, Harris."

"Yes sir." She pivoted on one heel and stalked out, feeling as if her cheeks were on fire.

Jake followed her like a big masculine shadow, unspeaking. He watched as she popped the trunk of her patrol car and got out the roll of yellow tape. The words *CRIME SCENE DO NOT CROSS* repeated along its length in black block letters. "You okay?" he asked quietly as she turned toward the road.

"Just awesome." A small crowd of people had already gathered at the foot of the driveway. Evidently neighbors, attracted by all the police cars parking up and down the road in front of the house.

"Why don't I give you a hand with that?" He took the roll out of her hands and they worked in silence stringing the tape across the driveway, then encircling the yard with it, looping it around trees and telephone poles.

"Do you think Johnson's right?" Erica asked at last as they tied off the last section of thin plastic. "Did I contaminate the scene?"

Jake snorted. "Not as much as an ambulance crew trying to do CPR and leaving a trail of rubber gloves and syringes."

She gave him a dry look. "Thanks a lot."

"You miss my point. We try to minimize contamination of the scene, but in real life, shit happens. Did you walk around handling stuff without using gloves?"

"Of course not."

"And if you hadn't been there, would Sawyer have known the scene was staged?"

"Not unless he brought in another Arcanist."

"Then there you go. You did your job, Erica. Yeah, procedure is procedure for a reason. You don't want to hand a defense attorney something he can use to get his client off --"

"I know that," she interrupted.

"Of course." Jake caught her arm and met her gaze, lowering his voice. "The real lesson from this is that

Johnson's gunning for both of us. He doesn't trust us, he doesn't like us, and he doesn't think Talents should be cops. We can't afford to give him any ammunition. So be fucking careful."

In her frustration, she had to work at keeping her own voice low. "It's so damned unfair, Jake. I prevented a mass casualty event at Potions Friday. I saved lives with the magic he hates, and he's still treating me like crap."

"Baby, that's *why* he's treating you like crap. Nothing pisses off a bigot like being proved wrong." He grinned toothily. "Which is what makes it so much fun to do."

"Channeling Dave now?"

"Naw. Dave would bite him on his bony ass." He snapped his teeth together.

Despite herself, Erica laughed.

"What's so damned funny?" The voice was high with fear and anger, its shrill note cutting across her chuckle. The short, chubby blonde pushed through the crowd and charged toward them, her arms pumping. She wore green hospital scrubs printed with the grinning faces of Spongebob Squarepants and his assorted undersea friends, neon green Crocs on her feet. "Where's Rachel? My mom called and said one of the neighbors told her she saw the coroner's van pull up…" Her voice got louder with every word, as if she was building toward hysterics.

Oh hell, Erica thought, spotting the resemblance to Rachel in the shape of the woman's face and the line of her nose. Her aura was barely visible even to Erica's gaze in the bright afternoon sunlight, but red and yellow churned through it. *At least she had nothing to do with the murder. She's hurting way too much to have been involved.*

Jake stepped forward, intercepting the woman, and held out a hand. "Deputy Jake Nolan."

She took it and gave it a single squeeze. "Elaine Royce. Rachel's my sister. Is she all right?"

"Let me get some information and someone will be

out to talk to you…"

Elaine's eyes narrowed. "You sound like me trying to avoid telling a patient bad news. Is she dead? Did the son of a bitch kill her?"

"What son of a bitch?"

But Erica barely heard Jake's suddenly intent question. Her attention had fallen on the small group of neighbors clustered behind the woman. Their collective aura -- hard to separate with everyone standing so close together -- shone dimly in the shades of green that usually meant curiosity or excitement, swirled with red and yellow from those who knew Rachel and worried about her.

Except for one swirl of pale ice blue tinged with pink surrounding someone in the back of the crowd. Colors that denoted satisfaction and pleasure. She'd once seen a similar aura around a terrorist bomber watching a girl's school burn.

Unfortunately, Erica couldn't quite see whoever owned this particular betraying aura. Intent on getting a closer look, she started toward the aura's owner. The crowd shifted uneasily as she approached. A tall, older man in the back of the crowd moved aside, revealing someone standing behind him. Erica broke step.

Thinning hair swept back from a long, bony face with a crooked nose and a weak, scarred chin. *And there you are, you son of a bitch.* Pasting a carefully neutral expression on her face despite the anger blasting through her, Erica made a beeline for the suspect.

His eyes widened, and his aura yellowed with alarm. Dropping his gaze, he turned and strode in the opposite direction, both hands thrust in his jacket pockets. *I don't think so, jackass.* Erica lengthened her stride, barely noticing as the crowd ducked out of her path, radiating curiosity and alarm. "Sir!"

He lengthened his stride, his shoulders tensing

under his jean jacket. *He's getting ready to run.* She broke into a jog. "Sir, I'd like a word." *And if you don't give me one, I'm going to kick your ass.*

He threw a glance over his shoulder. As if realizing how guilty he looked, the suspect stopped, turning toward her with a patently fake expression of surprise on his face. "Is there a problem, officer?"

"I'd say so. What your name? Can I see some ID?"

The yellow in his aura intensified, suggesting building panic. "My name's Keith Ormond." He started to reach into his pocket.

Erica tensed, but there was no silhouette of a gun against his aura. He pulled out his wallet and thumbed through it, visibly stalling for time as he tried to think.

"How do you know Rachel Bryer?" Erica demanded, her tone as icily suspicious as she could make it. Sometimes it paid to scare the hell out of a suspect just to see what shook loose.

He glanced up, hesitating just a heartbeat too long. "We used to date. Broke up a couple weeks ago. She okay?" The tone was concerned, but the flare of satisfied ice blue rolling through his aura suggested he knew damned well she wasn't.

"Keith? What the fuck are you doing here?" Elaine hurried toward them, her eyes narrow and suspicious. "Did you have something to do with this?"

Jake followed a pace behind her, close enough to grab the woman if she lost it. Erica was glad to see him. She had the feeling she was going to need his considerable muscle.

"I don't know what you're talking about," Ormond snapped. He turned back to Erica. "This bitch is crazy."

His defensive tone sounded suspicious as hell, even to someone who didn't know him. It must have sounded even worse to Elaine, whose eyes flew wide as the furious red of her aura flared until it was almost blinding white.

"You did it, didn't you, you bastard? You killed my sister!" She leaped at him, her hands curled into claws.

Keith lunged to meet her, one fist drawn back. "You watch your fucking mouth!"

Erica plunged between them, throwing up an arm to block his punch. Before it could land, Jake locked a big fist in the collar of Keith's jacket and jerked him backward. "I don't think so."

Grabbing the suspect's wrist with the other hand, he twisted it behind the man and jacked it up hard between his shoulder blades, forcing him onto his toes.

"Let me go! That bitch ain't talking to me like that!"

"Murderer!" Elaine screamed, fighting to get at him as Erica struggled to control her without doing damage. "You beat her and now you fucking *killed* her! I told her you were a no-good son of a bitch, and I was right! *Murderer!*"

Keith threw a wild look around at the neighbors who stared at them, many with hard-eyed expressions of belief.

"She told me she was afraid of him," a pregnant redhead called. "Christopher plays with my Jimmy all the time, and I've seen Rachel wearing bruises from Keith's fists more than once."

Ormond's aura went egg-yolk yellow with panic, laced with orange swirls of deception. "That's bullshit! I didn't do nothing. A witch killed her! There was a pentagram..." He broke off, his eyes widening with sick realization.

"Who said anything about a pentagram?" Jake asked in a silken voice.

He was searching Keith, Erica comforting the sobbing Elaine, when Johnson walked up. "What's going on?"

"I didn't do nothing! They're lying!" Keith bellowed.

Erica saw Johnson's eyes widen, and she knew the

sergeant had just recognized the man from her sketch. She frowned. *Now why did* your *aura just go yellow?*

* * *

"I'll take care of it." Virginia Laurel's voice sounded cold and flat as a serial killer's.

Roger's hand tightened convulsively on his cell as he paced the length of his garage. "What are you going to do?"

"Nothing you need to worry about."

He didn't believe her. But what the hell was he supposed to do about it?

"You've been quiet a little too long," she told him. "You're starting to make me uncomfortable."

"I've never given you any reason to doubt my commitment."

"Not so far."

"What are you going to do?"

"I don't think you need to know the details. If it makes you feel any better, you can take care of the guilty party afterward." The line went dead.

Johnson sagged back against his car. A thought flashed through his head, making his stomach clench even tighter. If Erica Harris survived whatever Virginia had planned, would the next drawing show his face?

Maybe he'd better have a word with Scott Clary. It might be useful if the deputy and his three Humanist thugs went after Harris. Might not help, but if they could bully her into snapping, maybe she'd get herself fired.

Which would be better than getting killed.

* * *

"I thought you said that little bitch didn't have any power!" Virginia Laurel's voice sounded a bit high through Adrian's Bluetooth earpiece, as if she was edging toward panic. "What if she draws something that identifies me?"

Rocking back in his seat, he contemplated the sketchpad and the tattoo design he was working on: The

Angel of Death, complete with flaming sword. "Calm down. You'd have to actually shed blood at a crime scene for her to sketch you." *And you never handle your own dirty work.* He leaned in to add a swirl of detail to the flames. "Anyway, it won't be a problem because I'm going to take care of her. I have a couple of --"

"I don't want to know."

He rolled his eyes. *You lost plausible deniability a long time ago, lady.* Not least because of the Pearl Harbor File he'd been keeping for the past year. He had no intention of using it, but it paid to be prepared.

When push came to shove, people like Virginia tended to throw the hired help under the bus. He had no intention of listening to the crunch of wheels. "You have nothing to worry about," Adrian lied. "Discretion is part of the service."

"It had better be."

He hung up, beating her to the punch again.

Frowning, Adrian beat his pencil on the sketchpad. He had underestimated Harris, much as it pained him to admit it. She had more juice than he'd thought if she could draw an accurate forensic sketch at a murder scene. Why in the hell was she working for some podunk police department when she could be making a lot more money in the private sector?

Must be another idealistic idiot. There were entirely too many of them in this town. They were becoming a pain in his ass. Frowning, Adrian doodled a sigil in one corner of the sketch -- the swirling sigil for death.

The question was, how was he going to take care of the cop? Normally, the simplest ways were best. Find a good spot near her house, set up with the sniper rifle, and pop her when she headed out to her car in the morning. Since he'd brought his Spook Suit in case he needed to be invisible, she'd never see him coming. And neither would any inconvenient witnesses.

Unfortunately, anyone with that much magical sensitivity might very well sense she was being targeted. That wouldn't do at all. If she ducked at the right time and he simply wounded her, she might be able to sketch him.

Cops being cops, her department would promptly release the sketch to the public. There were people who knew him in this town who might drop a dime on him. He wasn't worried about the HHers, who were firmly under his control. But one of his neighbors was a different story. Or, hell, the guy who worked in the convenience store where he bought his coffee. Anybody.

No, Adrian couldn't afford to pull the trigger himself.

Luckily, that's why he'd cultivated the HHers -- the possibility he might need disposable accomplices. The trouble was, none of them were professionals, which made it entirely too likely they'd fuck it up.

Adrian needed to come up with a plan that was both simple enough for them to pull off, with multiple built-in opportunities to kill her if they screwed one up. Which was going to require some thought.

It took him an hour to figure out a plan with a decent chance for success. Then he started making preparations.

First he phoned Virginia and asked her to nail down Harris's patrol zone with her sheriff's department contact. She called back half an hour later with the information he needed.

Too bad he couldn't simply call the contact directly and find out where she'd be at a given time. Unfortunately, that would be the equivalent of setting up a flashing neon sign over his own head if the cops ever started putting the pieces together.

Next, he headed for Garrison's restaurant. Located in a long brick building with a sign out front that read *VITTLES*, it was an old-fashioned Southern meat-and-three. Ten bucks got you an entrée, usually fried, with three vegetables, at least one of them covered with gravy or cheese. Still, Garrison's wife was sent such a good cook Adrian had fallen into the habit of eating there a couple times a week.

With closing time in fifteen minutes, the dining room was empty except for a lone husband and wife dawdling over a meal. One of Garrison's daughters ran a carpet sweeper over the floor, while a son-in-law bussed booths covered with red vinyl tablecloths.

Adrian gave both a friendly wave and headed for the swinging door into the kitchen. Garrison's wife, in the middle of mopping, gave Adrian a cool nod. He nodded back.

Cindy didn't like him much. He suspected she considered him a bad influence on her husband. She was, of course, right.

Garrison looked up from the prep counter he was wiping down. "Hey, Andy." The HHers knew Adrian as Andy Jones.

"Bill. Need to have a word."

The Norm tilted his head at back door. "Let's step outside. Need to smoke anyway. Cindy hates it when I do it in here."

It always amused Adrian that restaurant Bill was so different from HHer Bill. Made him wonder which Bill was the mask, and which the real man.

Maybe they were both were, and Garrison just kept them ruthlessly compartmentalized.

They stepped outside Vittles into the cold night air. Bill sighed in relief as he reached into a pocket of his stained white apron for his cigarettes and lighter. "Jesus, it gets hot in there."

"Busy night?" Adrian watched him pull a cig out of the pack and light it, then tuck pack and lighter away again.

"Pretty good. I think our message is finally getting out. Traffic's gone up here, and it's down some at the Cauldron." The Cauldron, owned and operated by a Talent who used magic in her cooking, had been his biggest competition for years. Good as his wife was, Cindy wasn't a witch. Adrian suspected that forcing the Cauldron out of business was Garrison's main motivation for his Humanist activism.

"What's wrong?" Garrison asked, exhaling smoke off to the side. "Because I can tell there's something."

"Tattooed a cop today," Adrian lied. "You know the bitch that arrested Carson?"

Garrison's lip curled. "The one the news is calling a hero?"

"This cop says she's a witch."

The glowing tip bobbed as he stared, then jerked the cigarette from his mouth in outrage. "You're shitting me. Gable hired a witch?"

"Yeah. Cop said she made Carson confess." He shrugged. "Witches, they can do all kinds of shit."

Garrison put the cig back in his mouth and puffed. "You think she had something to do with his heart attack?"

Adrian shrugged. "Maybe. Maybe she figured she needed to get rid of him before he got out and tried again."

"That fucking bitch."

"I'm thinking she's a problem, especially with the march coming up. You've gotta figure some of us are going to get arrested. If that witch started questioning people, casting spells…"

"That is a problem." He exhaled twin plumes of smoke from his nose.

Adrian brushed a tendril of aura over the sigil tattooed on Bill's head. As the spell activated, he said, "I think maybe we better do something about her."

Garrison's pupils expanded under the dragon's tattooed glare, signaling his receptiveness. "What do you want me to do?"

Chapter Ten

It was past one in the morning when Erica walked out of the sheriff's department feeling fried. Twelve-hour shifts were a bitch, though there was something to be said for the longer weekends. Given that she'd caught a killer -- and spent most of the day ass-deep in paperwork -- today had been particularly exhausting.

So she was less than thrilled to see the four deputies gathered around her patrol car where it was parked in solitary splendor at the other end of the lot. She was even less pleased when she recognized them: Tom Green, Scott Clary, Mary Hampton, and Bob Martin.

The four Talent-hating cops Jake had warned her about.

The hair rose on the back of her neck. For a moment she was ten years old again, back home in Screamer Mountain, North Carolina.

The gang of kids surrounded her on the playground. "Witch! Witch!" They knocked her down, kicked her, punched her, despite her desperate fists and feet. The sharp, bright pain in her broken nose, the taste of blood from her cut lip, pain jolting her dislocated jaw every time she screamed defiance...

It hadn't been the first time. It wouldn't be the last.

The muscles of her shoulders tightened, but she forced herself to walk toward the four cops as if she felt no fear at all. *I'm not that kid anymore. I'm an Arcane Corps veteran. If they fuck with me, I can fuck back.*

Besides, if her childhood had taught her anything, it was that you didn't back down from a bully. They loved a sense of power like Clarence loved catnip, and they'd go after her even harder if she showed weakness. She didn't let her steps falter, drawing on her Talent to study them as she approached.

The blend of colors floating around them suggested Clary felt cruelly amused, Hampton resentful, and Green nervous. But the one who worried her was Martin, a big man with so much crimson in his aura, he obviously balanced on the blade-edge of violence.

Despite the cold evening air, sweat rolled down her back. The deputies of Charlie shift were already on the road, while their lieutenant was at his desk in the depths of the building. If the situation went sideways, she wouldn't have backup.

Don't be ridiculous. They won't do a damn thing. There are cameras mounted all around the parking lot.

Assuming I didn't park in an area the cameras don't pick up… She kept the thought off her face and gave them her best good ol' girl drawl. "You folks need something?"

Clary's easy smile might have seemed comforting, if not for the vicious amusement in his aura. He was a tall, lean man with the build of a marathon runner, thick, dark hair, and a mustache that reminded her of a 1970s porn star. "We just wanted to congratulate you on catching that killer."

"Bet you think you're some kind of hot shit hero like your freak boyfriend." The red roiling Martin's aura made it difficult to see his features clearly. He was a head taller than she was, with a broad, square face that looked even broader and squarer thanks to his auburn brush cut. He carried enough muscle for an NFL lineman; rumor said he liked to use it.

Erica looked at him and slowly lifted a brow. "Jealous?" If he took a swing at her and the cameras caught it, he'd hand the sheriff that firing offense Gable wanted.

"I wouldn't touch you with a ten-foot pole."

"I'm crushed."

"If you think they'll make you a detective 'cause of those busts, think again." Mary Hampton was a beefy blonde woman an inch or so taller than Erica. She had the kind of snub features and round face often described as cute in children and pleasant in adults, but the look in her narrow eyes was neither. "There's no way the sheriff is going to promote a freak."

She didn't look away from Martin and his psycho's aura. "I'm just happy the killer's in jail."

Resentment tightened Clary's mouth. "That case could've been solved just as well with normal police work. Ormond had multiple domestic violence charges. We'd have caught him regardless."

Erica lifted a brow. "We? Don't you mean Sawyer? Because you were running your usual speed trap over by the women's college. I understand you get a lot of dates that way."

Clary stiffened, sullen red anger sparking in his aura.

"I'll bet the witch just saw a picture of this boyfriend at the vic's house," Hampton announced. "That's how she drew that sketch. Then she pretends to be a 'psychic.'" Her fingers sketched air quotes.

"Either I'm a witch or I'm a fake. Make up your mind, Deputy."

Hampton jolted forward until they were almost nose-to-nose. "You'd better watch your mouth."

"And what if I don't?" Erica smiled slowly, seriously tempted to give her an aural zap to teach her to keep her distance.

Maybe something of what she was thinking showed in her face, because Hampton's eyes flickered. "We'll shut it for you."

"You sure you want to try that? Because it looks to me like you're scared. There's fear in your aura. Lots of pretty yellow." As all four of them stared at her, Erica bared her teeth. "I'm an Arc, remember? I see auras. I see what you're feeling."

"Auras?" Martin rumbled, and the red blazed brighter in his. Shouldering Hampton aside, he lifted one bunched fist. "I'll make you see stars."

The nice thing about people who hated witches was that they were easy to bluff. "You'd better worry about what I can make you see."

"What do you mean by that?" Clary demanded, looking uneasy.

"Why, nothing, Deputy. Nothing whatsoever."

Now yellow forked like lightning across all their auras.

"What the fuck is going on?"

All five of them jerked around, even Erica.

Jake stood glaring at them. They'd been so focused on each other, they hadn't even noticed him walk up.

"Just congratulating Harris on her excellent police work," Clary said with a completely unconvincing smile.

"Yeah?" Jake's nostrils flared. "So why do I smell bullying asshole?"

Hampton looked considerably less intimidated than her male coworkers. She probably figured -- correctly -- that Jake's sense of chivalry would protect her. "Why do we have K-9s when we could put a leash on Nolan?" She turned her sneer on Erica. "Some cop you are. Always hiding behind your fuzzy boyfriend. How many times has he saved your ass in the past week? You must give really good head."

Jake's eyes narrowed and took on a menacing glow. "I seem to remember an asshole with a tire iron swinging at *your* head last week. He'd have knocked a homer if I hadn't stopped him." They all shifted under his stare. "Yeah, think about it. Next time you need backup, maybe I'll just let you tough guys handle it."

"I think this has gotten a little out of hand." Clary gave Erica an apologetic smile belied by the swirl of enraged crimson orbiting his head. "Sorry about that, Harris. Tensions are high, what with all the Talent violence. You know how it is." He gave his gang a significant glance, and they all turned away.

Hampton gave Erica another dose of sneer. "See you later, Harris. We'll have to have a little girl talk sometime."

"Looking forward to it, cupcake."

"Come on, Hampton," Clary snapped.

Erica stood there, the March chill biting her cheeks as she and Jake watched the four get into their patrol cars and drive away. Clenching her fists, she breathed in, working to control the tremor she could feel building in her muscles. "What the *hell*, Nolan?"

Jake rocked back on his heels in surprise. "What are you mad at me for?"

"I had it handled until you undercut me. Now they think I'm a pussy."

"What do you care what they think? They're bullying assholes."

"Exactly. And next time they'll escalate, because that's what bullying assholes do."

He hooked his thumbs in his duty belt and glowered. "You were outnumbered, Erica."

"They weren't going to touch me. It's the damn parking lot. There are cameras. They'd be fired. They were just mouthing off."

"Yeah, that's why Martin smelled like bloodlust."

"Maybe, but he wasn't *doing* anything. And he wasn't going to do anything. Now I'm going to have to teach the bastards a lesson all over again, and the next time it may be somewhere there aren't any cameras."

As they glared at each other, the softly glowing figure of Clarence wandered out of Jake like a cat door. The lion began to circle, scrubbing his jaw against her hip as he rumbled a low, soothing croon.

Despite her temper, the contact with the Familiar's magic was as comforting as the sensation of fur rubbing over her skin. Knowing she was being played, Erica eyed him. "Quit that."

Clarence chuffed and gave her a head butt that would probably have knocked her on her ass had he been physical. With a disgusted huff of her own, she surrendered, reaching down to dig her fingers in the thick mane behind his ears.

Jake watched her, tapping his fingers on the plastic buckle of his duty belt. "Why *did* they take that risk? Why start something in front of the cameras to begin with?"

Erica looked up from Clarence's insubstantial ears. "It's a power play. Nothing gives assholes at the bottom of the pecking order a buzz like bullying somebody." Her jaw tightened as her temper heated again. "Which is why you should have let me handle it."

* * *

Jake stared at her in frustration. She was wearing that stubborn expression he'd come to know so well when they'd served together. "If you think I'm going to stand back and watch four assholes jump you when I could stop it, you're out of your mind."

"Then they'll never learn to respect me. And that's not doing me any favors." Her gaze met his, eyes big and dark as a moonlit lake as a fine muscle flexed in her jaw.

Deciding to take a chance on getting his head bitten off, Jake reached out and cupped her cheek. Her skin felt like silk under his fingertips, tempting, soft, warm. "This isn't Screamer Mountain, Erica. You're not alone this time." He brushed a thumb over her cheek. "You've got me now. And I'm not going to fail you."

He thought he saw longing flash in the depth of her big dark eyes. Then her gaze cooled. "Not willingly, but things happen."

He shook his head in frustration. "You could at least try trusting me."

"That hasn't really worked out in the past."

Damn it, Bobby. "You haven't tried it with me." He stroked her lower lip. It felt soft against the pad of his thumb, warm and tempting. He wanted to kiss her so badly he could taste it. "I don't play by anybody else's rules."

"I have noticed." Her voice sounded dry.

"So notice this." He lowered his head...

For a moment Jake thought she was going to let him kiss her, but at the last moment, she swallowed and stepped back. "Don't you think we've caused enough gossip for one day?"

He paused, reluctantly realizing she had a point. "Then let's go to my place and talk about it." He wanted to touch her so badly his back teeth ached. But then, he'd been battling various impulses since the moment he'd walked up to see those four dickheads surrounding her, violence reeking in the air. It had been all he could do not to manifest Clarence and roar.

Erica's chin took on that jut, and for a moment he thought she was going to refuse. *Damn it, Erica, I need you...*

As if she read his mind, something in her eyes softened into yearning. "All right. I'll see you at your house."

"Do you know where it is?"

Her smile was a little dry. "Yeah, I know. See you in twenty." Turning away, she unlocked her patrol car, got in, and drove away.

Some of the tension drained out of his muscles, replaced by anticipation as Jake headed for his own vehicle. He was a bit surprised she'd agreed, considering how pissed she'd been. But maybe she felt the same need to burn off a little steam that he did. The memory of those bastards standing around her...

Clarence growled, a low rumble in the depths of his brain accompanied by a complex wave of emotion: anger that anyone had dared to threaten her, pure leonine territoriality, the need to make sure none of those bastards dared touch her. Ever. Again.

And the cat had some definite ideas on how to ensure that last one. "Sorry, Clar, the brass frowns on that kind of thing." His voice dropped to a mutter. "Though God knows I'm tempted."

The idea of Erica in danger made him want to hurt somebody. Badly.

* * *

Twenty minutes later, Jake pulled into the carport with his heart pounding.

Erica had parked under the oak out front. As he got out, she did the same, looking tall and slim and a bit tense with anticipation.

And she wasn't the only one.

The need he felt was ferocious, a hot craving to taste her again, feel her silken body under his hands. He felt acutely conscious of Clarence's low rumble in the back of his mind. Reacting to his emotion, his need.

Jake remembered the way it felt making love to her, the stroke of her power along his own, so delicious and so alien. Maddening, beautiful, proud Erica, too courageous for her own good.

He tried to remember if he'd made the bed.

She moved toward him, tension in the line of her body, a certain heat lingering in her eyes. He thought it was anger, but there was need too. The same craving he felt.

He met her halfway with no memory of closing the distance. It was one of those clear, brilliant March nights, and moonlight silvered the soft curves of her features and glittered in her eyes.

For a moment she just stood there looking up at him, hands down by her sides. Something in her stance suggested she felt conflicted, as if she was second-guessing her decision to come back here with him. "I…" she began.

In the depths of his mind, Clarence growled. Jake agreed. Before she could get the rest of her objection out of her mouth, he covered her lips in a kiss infused with all the seduction he could pump into it. The taste of her made him want to moan, though his conscience muttered. *I'll let her go in a minute,* he told it. *Now I need this.*

If that made him a selfish son of a bitch, so be it. He had to taste her.

To his relief, Erica moaned softly and leaned into him, slimly muscled arms wrapping around his waist just over his duty belt. Equipment rattled and plastic clicked, their gear a frustrating barrier.

Erica opened to him, and Jake angled his head to suckle her tongue with teasing sips. As they kissed, his hands slid up to cradle her face. She made a soft, needy sound against his mouth, and he drank in the sound.

At last she pulled away to slant him a wicked little smile. "I think we'd both enjoy this a lot more without two layers of Kevlar and twenty pounds of gear." Reaching out, she flicked his ASP baton, making it swing beside the thicker bulk of his erection. "Notice I'm resisting the obvious nightstick joke."

He chuckled and brushed his knuckles across her jawline. "I appreciate your self-control." Wrapping his hand around hers, he turned her toward the house.

Anticipation rolling hot through his blood, Jake felt his erection pressing against his fly. It made the task of getting his key in the lock a little more demanding than usual. Finally he wrestled the door open, flipped on the hall light, and led the way into the kitchen.

"Nice house," she commented, though she barely glanced at the room's stainless steel appliances and granite countertops.

"Managed to get a VA loan," Jake said, gaze hot on her mouth. Wanting only to taste it again. "Nickel tour now, or later?"

"Later. I'm a little… distracted."

"Glad I'm not the only one." Resting a hand on the

small of her back, he guided Erica into the hall and up the stairs to the master bedroom. And was more than a little relieved to find the California King neatly made under its pewter spread.

"Damn, Nolan, you could land jets on that bed."

"Hey, I'm a big guy."

"You're five feet ten inches."

He smiled so slowly and suggestively, she snorted. "I see -- you need the extra room for your ego." Her gaze swung and caught below his duty belt. A dark brow rose. "Among other things."

"I find you very inspiring."

"I'm flattered." Erica rose on her toes as he leaned down for another taste of mint and magic. But as their bodies brushed, her ASP baton tapped his thigh again. Erica chuckled against his lips. "Gotta get rid of the armory."

"Sounds good to me" He reached for the wide plastic buckle of her duty belt, clicked it open, then went to work unfastening each of the straps that attached the belt to the leather one beneath it.

While he worked on the belts, she started unfastening the buttons of his uniform shirt, revealing the black bulk of his Kevlar vest. A deep breath reminded him he'd just spent the past twelve hours encased in the thing. It might be April -- he got really ripe in August -- but still. "Want to share a shower?"

"God, yes. I probably smell like a goat."

Jake gave her a slow grin. "Nope. Nowhere near that baaaad." He gave the last word a realistic magical bleat.

Erica wrinkled her nose at him. "What, Dave's writing your material now?"

But when she shed her shirt and pulled open the Velcro tabs of her bulletproof vest, there was nothing even remotely goat-like about her scent, just heated, healthy woman. His erection bucked in hot interest.

They undressed each other slowly, tossing clothing and equipment on the armchair by the bed. He enjoyed the sight of her clothes lying tangled with his. Every inch of skin they revealed was an invitation to touch and kiss, and he lost himself in the taste of her, in the silken textures of her body, the intoxicating scent of sex, Erica and magic.

At last he had her naked, her body slim and strong, with just enough curve to soften the lean athlete's muscle she'd built as cop and soldier. Her breasts tempted his hands with their small berry nipples. So did those long, lean legs and the soft triangle of chocolate hair between them.

He drew her into the master bathroom. It was a thoroughly utilitarian space, with a narrow sink, commode, and glassed-in tub. When he bent to turn on the water, her hands promptly sought out the width of his back to begin tracing intricate patterns over his skin.

Jake grinned over his shoulder at her as the water came on with a hiss. "Working a spell back there?"

Her smile was slow and mysterious, and her fingers moved, gliding over his aura as much as his flesh. The sensation that rolled through him was indescribable, as if she had plucked his soul like a guitar string. His cock hardened even more in response to the surge of stark lust. Jake stepped back with a sweeping gesture for her to precede him into the tub.

She lifted a brow. "Ladies first? Really?"

He flashed her a grin. "Hell, no. I'm just ogling your ass."

Laughing softly, Erica got in, the shift and sway of that beautiful backside every bit as delicious as he'd anticipated. Jake stepped in after her as she turned to face him, backing beneath the spray. Her eyes slipped closed, head tilting back as the water cascaded over her head and shoulders. Rivulets traced shining patterns over her delicate collarbones and down the slopes of her breasts to stream off her nipples.

Unable to resist, he leaned down and took one of those raspberry points into his mouth. The water streamed along his jaw as he rolled his tongue over it. Sweet. She tasted so incredibly sweet.

And I want more.

* * *

Erica stared down at him, entranced by the look on his face. There was such fierce need in those golden eyes. His teeth rasped gently over her captured nipple, and he suckled hard, each pull sending another bolt of pleasure shafting through her body.

Her gaze skated along the width of his broad, wet shoulders, admiring the ridges of tendon, the thick pads of muscle lying over the broad bone.

Jake straightened, kissing and licking his way up her torso as he went, following the line of her throat up to her chin and from there to her mouth. His big hands closed around her waist and pulled her closer as he took her lips, his tongue thrusting deep.

Erica caught his lower lip between her teeth and bit down gently. His mouth seemed the only soft part of his entire body as he pulled her flush against him. All that slick, hard muscle was intoxicating, intriguing. Delicious.

Unable to resist the need to touch him, Erica stroked her hands up his ribs up to the tight beads of his small male nipples. She flicked her thumbs over them, and Jake rumbled against her mouth, sounding like Clarence. And returned the favor, his hands cupping her breasts, his touch exquisitely gentle.

As they kissed and teased each other, the warm spray cascaded down their bodies, pooling here in the bend of an arm, streaming along the curve of her breasts, beading like gemstones in his chest hair and along the length of his proud cock. Each touch branded itself on her consciousness.

Making love to Bobby had never felt like this. Making love to *anybody* had never felt like this.

Erica thrust the thought quickly away, knowing it would lead her places she had no desire to go. Not with Jake standing so deliciously naked and male against her.

She needed this too much to be distracted by dark memories. Needed Jake's heat, his male carnality, his humor and his intelligence. She'd been alone too fucking long...

Jake dropped to his knees in front of her. Erica blinked down at him as he flashed her that dimpled grin and wrapped one big hand around her knee. She braced her hands against the wall of the shower as he lifted her leg and hooked her thigh over his shoulder, then leaned in and covered her pussy with his mouth. With one of those deep rumbles that always drove her crazy, he stroked his tongue the length of her folds and parted her labia. The incredible flashing pleasure of each hot lick made her eyes roll back, a shudder running the length of her body.

Leaning a shoulder against the wall of the shower, Erica watched in dazed delight as he ate her, his eyes closed, his expression intent. Completely focused on the taste of her. His tongue swirled over and around her clit, each little flick shooting another hot burst of pleasure jolting up her spine. The sensation was so intense it made her knees go weak.

Jake's probing fingers found the opening of her pussy and thrust deep, forcing her to grab his head with her free hand. His hair felt like wet silk under her palm. "Jake!" she gasped, tightening the grip of her lifted leg across his back as she fought to keep her balance.

God, it felt so good...

He ate until the knee of her supporting leg quivered in helpless reaction. His free hand reached up to cup her breast, his thumb flicking her nipple, the pleasure echoing the intense swirls of his tongue over her clit.

Her climax began with inner muscles clenching deep, every pulse making her entire nervous system ring like a bell. Until she had to grab for the showerhead or fall flat on her ass.

She wrapped one hand around the faucet and held on for dear life as his ruthlessly skillful mouth suckled and bit and tasted. Squeezing her eyes shut, Erica chanted through clenched teeth, "Oh God, oh God, oh God…"

She wanted to touch him, had to touch him, but she knew that if she let go she'd fall. So instead she reached out with her aura, let it play over the whirling rose and violet of his.

Jake growled softly against her pussy, the sound a dark male rumble. Staring down at him, she glimpsed the head of his cock, pressed hard against his belly. A wicked thought occurred to her, and she sent her aura questing out to wrap around the thick, flushed shaft.

Jake jerked in reaction, muscle rolling all along his broad shoulders, fingers tightening on her breast and convulsing in the depths of her pussy. Closing his lips around her clit, he sucked hard.

"Jake!" she groaned, almost tumbling into orgasm before she caught herself and retaliated with the gliding stroke of her aura along his balls.

His head jerked back, and his eyes blazed up the length of her body, brilliant gold. His mouth looked wet from her juices as he rasped, "You do like to live dangerously."

Scooping her leg off his shoulder, he steadied her with a grip on her hip. Erica, staring down at him, thought she saw the glowing swirls of a lion's mane curling around his shoulders as he gripped her hips and turned her back to him, then pulled her down.

"What are you…" she began, just before she splashed to all fours in the bottom of the tub.

With a leonine growl, he caught the back of her head and pushed it down. Shocked and aroused, Erica braced herself on her forearms.

A heartbeat later, Jake drove the entire rock-hard length of his cock into her wet pussy, stuffing her full in one ruthless plunge.

"Jake!" The sound was raw with shock and hunger.

His only response was a fierce growl as he drew back, dragging his thick length out of her. Only to drive in again and again, plunging, digging deep. A low rumble filled the air as he grabbed a fistful of her wet hair with one hand.

Erica should have been pissed off. Should have been offended by the raw masculine dominance in the gesture. And if it had been any other man, she would have been. But it was Jake, and she was more turned on than she'd ever been in her life.

Braced on her elbows, feeling the water slosh around her as the spray beat her flesh, hearing the hiss of the shower and his low growls -- it all felt incredibly primal. Each digging stroke of his cock spread her slick tissues, speared her with delicious friction. Her eyes felt so wide they burned, watching each furious thrust send water splashing up the tub walls.

God, she was sooooo close… So frustratingly close…

"Jake, Jake, Jake…" She heard her own voice moaning, sounding raw and desperate.

And as he fucked her, the currents of his magic flowed through and around hers until it seemed to reach parts of her far beneath the skin.

Erica wanted more. Wanted it all. Craved the savage, burning orgasm that trembled just out of reach. She threw herself open, releasing the mental shields that usually protected her. And closed her eyes.

Their joined magic spun around them like a whirlwind, a dozen shades of violet, rose, and blue, his denser, brighter than hers, surging and tumbling together.

With each pumping swirl of magic and cock, she felt the orgasm coil tighter in the base of her belly, so frustratingly close she started throwing herself backward to meet his thrusts, making her breasts dance. She felt the prick of something sharp on the skin of her hip.

He swore, and the pain faded. He must've manifested claws, then retracted them. "Are you all..."

"Don't stop!" She screamed it, so close to the edge she could feel inner muscles clamping, pulsing...

He didn't question her, just pounded, deep and grinding. The lingering sting inflicted by his claws combined with the fierce stroke of his cock and the blaze of their magic, shooting her higher, higher until...

Erica screamed, coming, as her magic exploded behind her eyelids, a boiling light show that flared out of her body -- and engulfed him.

Chapter Eleven

Magic tore through Jake like a firestorm, feeling as if every cell of his body was involved -- flesh, bone, muscle and soul.

He cried out in a human yell that grew louder, deepening into a roar. He roared until his chest and throat ached with the force of it as the magic blasted him and his balls emptied in her slick, hot depths. Pumping and pumping until nothing was left.

When it was over at last, he sagged against her, folding over her bent body, catching himself on the bottom of the tub with a splash.

For a long moment neither of them moved, too busy fighting to breathe.

Jake wrapped one arm around her and laid his cheek against her back, listening to the furious pound of her heartbeat as it slowed. The warm water of the shower pounded against his back.

He felt at peace, and was struck suddenly by how rare a feeling that was. This time they'd avoided the pitfalls of guilt and grief that had sabotaged the moment the last time -- the ghost of Bobby's sins...

The thought brought an ice-cold burst of realization. *Oh, fuck, I manifested claws! Just like Bobby...* Jerking upright, Jake twisted to look down at her hip, at the spot he remembered gripping when he'd felt the magic dig deep. To his relief, the five marks looked no worse than pinpricks. *Thank God.*

It still bugged the hell out of him that he'd lost control. *Again.* "Are you okay?"

Erica turned her head to look at him, a sated smile on her face. "Oh, yeah."

The purr in her voice made Jake grin. "You look downright smug."

The smile broadened and tilted into a wicked grin. "I

am."

He sat back on his heels, wincing a little as his knees protested grinding against the tub floor. "As much as I hate to break this up, if we don't get out of here, we're going to turn into giant prunes."

"I'll risk it if you will."

"You'll change your mind when the hot water runs out." Rising to his feet, he bent to catch her around the waist, meaning to help her up.

"I've got it." Erica pulled free and sat up.

Not about to start an argument on that score, Jake stepped out of the shower and walked, naked and dripping, to the vanity. He pulled out a couple of clean towels and tossed her one as she emerged from the shower. She made a hell of a view, lean and naked, water beading her full, perfect breasts, dripping from her pert nipples.

"Hello, gorgeous." Unable to resist his need to touch her again, he walked over, flipped the towel over her head, and began drying her off.

By the time he was done, her short, damp locks stood up in tufts, and her eyes gleamed lazily at him. She treated him to the same stare he'd just given her, gaze lingering here and there -- mostly *there* -- as she looked him up and down. "*Mmmm.*"

Lifting the towel, she started running it over his chest and shoulders, drying him in turn. The rasp of the thick, soft fabric sent a delicious little swirl of heat down to his balls. "If you keep that up, we're never going to get any sleep."

"I thought you like it when I keep you up."

Chuckling, he started drying her long, lean torso, enjoying the way her soft breasts bounced as he blotted away the water. He ran the towel over her slowly as she worked on him, enjoying her purr of contented approval.

"My mom has a cat that sounds just like that."

She gave him a mock glower. "You did not just mention your mother after we finished making love. That's a major violation of sexual etiquette."

"Etiquette?" He grinned. "I don't know this word, 'etiquette.'"

"Barbarian."

"Didn't seem to bother you much a minute ago." His smile faded at a new thought. *Fuck it, might as well just ask.* "Are you staying the night?"

The silence stretched on so long, he was beginning to think she'd refuse. "I'd like that."

Tight muscles loosened across his shoulders, and he smiled.

* * *

Erica made use of his hairdryer and one of the spare toothbrushes left over from his last trip to the dentist, then joined him on the California King. She curled against him, her head on his shoulder, her long fingers playing sleepily with a strand of chest hair.

He'd spent the time she'd been drying her hair thinking about what he wanted to say. What he needed to say. What he'd *better* say if he wanted them to have any kind of chance.

If they didn't clear the air, he wasn't sure their fragile relationship would survive.

"I remember the first time I watched you disarm a MEED," Jake said softly. "We'd all watched Sergeant Castillo die that way just a couple months before, and we were all scared shitless we were about to watch you do the same. But you handled it, just like you handled all the others I've seen you disarm since."

"I notice you didn't try to protect me from it." Her voice sounded a little dry.

"Of course not. I knew I couldn't without getting you *and* me blown to hell. And you demonstrated you were up to the job. You had the guts and the skill and the sheer power."

"I'm sure it came as a shock." That observation sounded even drier than the first one had. Then she snorted softly. "But I'm not that damned powerful. Genevieve…"

"… Wouldn't have the faintest idea how to disarm a MEED. Besides, for certain kinds of jobs, that much power gets in the way, which is why she has a hard time detecting more delicate magical structures. You don't."

She lifted her head from his chest and eyed him dubiously. "Nolan, are you trying to flatter me?"

"My point is I do respect your abilities." He gave her a long, steady look. "On the other hand, if somebody manifested, say, a fucking polar bear, I trust you'd stand back and let me handle it."

"I'm not an idiot." After a pause, she added, "Though I'd also be furiously trying to work a spell to trap the son of a bitch."

"Exactly my point. You'd build a trap, so I could run him into it and finish him off at my leisure. That's why we make a good team." Jake sighed. "I didn't mean to undercut you with those assholes tonight. If I'd had any sense, I would've hung back and watched -- only stepped in it looked like things were going to get messy. The thing is, it *was* about to get messy. That asshole Martin…"

"Yeah, I was worried about him too. And I do appreciate the backup. Knowing you were there made me feel a hell of a lot safer." She gave him a long look. "But that doesn't change the fact that your stepping in made me look as if I couldn't defend myself. And that is not a message you want to send bullies."

"The next time it happens…" Jake's first impulse was to give her an easy assurance that he'd stay out of it, but he realized he'd be lying. And she'd know. He broke off and started over. "You know, I'd have done the same thing if they'd been giving Dave a hard time…"

"None of those little fucks would've had the gall to

say one word to Dave Frost."

He laughed. "Oh, not *now* they wouldn't. But back in the day…"

"… When he'd still been human."

"He *is* still human."

She had the grace to look embarrassed. "Of course, he is. I meant when he'd still been a biped."

A memory surfaced, and Jake grinned. "Remember the time he got in that bar fight with those Navy SEALs? Dave was in his civvies, so they didn't realize he was a Feral, and the bar was dark enough they didn't notice his eye color…"

"As I recall, everybody waded in on that one, including me."

But since it was fellow serviceman they were fighting, none of them had used magic; that would have been cheating. "It wasn't until it was over that Dave manifested his cat. Then he said…"

Erica finished the quote, grinning. "'You boys need to remember you're not the Frogs of the Jungle.' I laughed until I cried."

"Point is, none of us stood back, including you."

"That was different. Those boys needed a lesson in manners."

"Pretty much what I was thinking tonight."

She sighed, her breath blowing warm across his nipple. "Will you at least wait until I ask for help?"

"That depends. Will you get around to asking for it?"

Now she looked annoyed. "I call for backup plenty."

"On the street. I'm talking about when it comes to the asshole brigade. I'm afraid you'd be so intent on proving the size of your brass balls, you'll be lip deep in shit before your ego lets you call me."

Anger flashed in her gaze, only to fade into a sigh. "Just promise me you'll try to let me handle it."

"I'll try."

They fell silent, and he stroked one hand up and down the length of her bare back until her breathing deepened into the rhythm of sleep.

Just how much danger *had* she been in from Martin, Green, Clary, and Hampton? Jake knew the scent of the various flavors of aggression, from bullying all the way to murder. He had the ugly impression that confrontation had been about more than some stupid dominance play designed to put her in her place.

Yeah, maybe Green and Clary were just giving her shit, and Mary Hampton hated her guts. But Martin... Martin had scared the fuck out of him.

And it hadn't been the first time. On several occasions, Jake had been forced to report the bastard to Johnson for losing his shit with somebody. You didn't hit a handcuffed suspect, period, no matter what said suspect might have done. Not only was it against regulations, it was just fucking wrong.

Most cops were decent people. Many were idealists who actively wanted to make the world a better place. But there was also a certain segment of the asshole population who had no business with a badge. Martin was one of those.

Which was why Jake really hadn't liked the way Martin had smelled during the confrontation with Erica. At all. It had been the sheer vicious anticipation in the bastard's scent that had driven him to interfere. He didn't think Erica realized how close the situation had come to spiraling completely out of control.

If it came right down to it and Erica really was in danger, Jake would do the same thing again, no matter how much it pissed her off.

He'd lost Bobby. He was damned if he was going to lose Erica. One midnight regret over a lethal mistake was enough. So in the final analysis, he'd do what he had to do. And hope she could forgive him for it.

* * *

It was just before noon when Erica answered a call at a strip mall on the outskirts of Laurelton. It wasn't that big, as Laurelton strip malls went, consisting of a consignment shop -- New 2U Treasures -- a used bookstore, and something called Killer Ink.

A gray haired woman who looked like someone's grandmother stood on the sidewalk, arms folded in a pink pea coat worn over yellow polyester pants. A couple of plastic shopping bags hung from one elbow, and a white leather purse bumped her hip. She was a head shorter than Erica, with a soft, rounded figure that suggested she probably gave excellent hugs.

Just now she wasn't in the mood.

When Erica parked her patrol car and got out, she found the old lady's hazel eyes snapping with anger. Her mouth was drawn in a tight line that pleated her face in deep wrinkles.

After Erica identified herself, she snapped, "I want to report a witch."

Oh, brother, here we go. Erica wished she could hide that damned pentagram pin. *The job's to serve and protect, Humanists included.* "Yes, ma'am." She pulled out her notebook and a pen. "But I'm going to need to look to get a little information first. Do you have any ID?"

Some folks would have immediately started ranting something like, "I'm not the one who committed the crime," but the woman just reached into her purse and excavated her billfold. "Of course."

Ten minutes later, Erica had Wanda Jeffries' name, address and phone number, and was ready to get down to business. "Were you the victim of a crime, Mrs. Jeffries?" *Because being a witch isn't illegal.*

"Yes, I was." Opening one of her shopping bags, she pulled out something small and handed it over.

Erica examined the object, eyebrows climbing. It was a cocktail ring, with a green-tinted chunk of faceted glass the size of her thumbnail mounted on an imitation gold band.

"Meghan O'Reilly, the owner of that shop there --" Mrs. Jeffries jerked her head toward New 2U Treasures -- "told me this was a real emerald. And I believed her." She grated the last words with such outrage, it was obvious that was what she found most offensive about the whole situation. Pointing a gnarled forefinger at the ring, she demanded, "Now, does that look like an emerald to you?"

"No, it's obviously glass." Frowning, Erica looked up, studying the angry swirl of the woman's aura. Mrs. Jeffries believed what she was saying: there was no trace of orange.

"Exactly. But that woman charged me four hundred dollars cash for it."

Erica raised her brows and eyed it again. "I'd be surprised if it's worth twenty bucks." And nobody but a five-year-old would think otherwise. Wanda Jeffries didn't strike her as that gullible. "And a real emerald that size would be worth thousands. How did she know you had that kind of money?"

"I'd just cashed my Social Security check, and she saw the money in my wallet when I bought a scarf for my daughter-in-law. So then she says, 'I've got something really special you might be interested in,' and brings out the ring. Now, I may be old, but I'm not senile. It's obvious that's not an emerald, but I didn't even question it."

Yeah, sounded like Mrs. Jeffries had been scammed. This kind of bullshit was the reason Norms thought all Talents were con artists and thieves. "Do you have the receipt?"

"Yes." Mrs. Jeffries reached into her shopping bag and pulled out a cash register slip. "The dollar amount says forty. Which is definitely not what I paid."

"What happened then?"

"I left the shop and got in my car. I was so excited, I wanted to look at my ring. And then I saw... *that*." She gestured contemptuously at the trinket. "I about had a heart attack. That's when I realized she must've put me under a spell, because there is no way I would've fallen for such an obvious lie otherwise."

"What did you do?"

"I went back in the store and demanded my money back. She said I was crazy, that I hadn't given her any four hundred dollars. Well, if she thinks I'm going to let her get away with this..." Now a swirl of yellow rolled through the red in her aura, so intense with worry Erica felt a stab of pity. "Look, I *need* that money. How am I supposed to buy groceries or my medications or..."

And what kind of asshole preyed on an old lady? "Let's go have a word with her." All but growling, Erica headed for the shop and pushed open the door, Mrs. Jeffries at her heels. Bells jingled merrily, announcing their entry.

New 2U Treasures looked like the set for an episode of *Hoarders*. Scanning the place, Erica noticed items ranging from dented metal Coca-Cola signs, to delicate ceramic figurines, to antique furniture -- even a yellowing wedding dress in a transparent plastic garment bag.

At the heart of it all, a long glass counter supported an ancient cash register. There was no sign of the proprietor.

Erica's instincts twanged. There was barely enough room to swing a cat anywhere else in the shop, yet the floor around the counter was completely bare. When she reached for her Talent, she wasn't surprised to see dim glyphs orbiting it.

Mrs. Jeffries had been right.

Examining the symbols, she realized the spell was designed to make anyone standing inside it trust the person on the other side of the counter.

Erica lifted her voice and let it ring over the shop. "Meghan O'Reilly? I'm Deputy Erica Harris, and that's an illegal spell. I suggest you get out here and talk to me, because otherwise I'm arresting you."

As she'd expected, rapid footsteps sounded as the shopkeeper emerged from behind a hulking armoire. Dressed in a cheerful red sweater over neat black slacks and rubber-heeled black shoes, the woman was about forty, a couple inches shorter than Erica, with a long face carefully made up under artistically cropped brunette hair. "That's ridiculous," she snapped indignantly, though she looked a little pale. "I'm not a witch."

"I am," Erica said flatly. "And judging by your aura, so are you."

O'Reilly tilted her chin up and lied, even as vivid orange pulsed through her aura. "I have no idea what you're talking about. There's no spell here."

"Don't insult my intelligence." Erica gestured at the rotating glyphs. "That's an active spell."

Mrs. Jeffries frowned down at the floor. "I don't see anything."

"That's because there isn't anything to see," the witch lied, trying to sound outraged. She wasn't a particularly good actress even without the telltale orange in her aura.

"No, it's because you painted the spell circle on the floor in ultraviolet paint that's invisible in normal light. But to activate the spell, you had to infuse the paint with your own dried blood. Which will show up when the crime scene investigator sprays it with Luminol. A DNA swab will prove you're the one who cast the spell." She took a step closer, deliberately looming over the shopkeeper. "This ends one of two ways. I can charge you with breach of trust by magical means, a felony carrying a minimum of five years..." The witch blanched. "Or you can give Mrs. Jeffries back her four hundred dollars and scrub that spell off the floor." Erica gave the woman her best icy cop glare, letting the rage she felt show. "I'd better not find you've repainted it when I come back. And I promise you, I will be coming back a *lot*."

"This is…" The shopkeeper paused to swallow. "This is all a misunderstanding. I… I didn't take anything, but I'll be happy to refund the money to clear this up."

Erica turned to Mrs. Jeffries. "Is that acceptable to you?"

The old woman blew out a breath in relief. "Yes." A smile dawned across her face. "Yes, I'd be fine with that."

The shopkeeper pulled a bank bag out from under the counter and counted out four crisp hundreds, then handed them to Mrs. Jeffries. The old woman thanked her with automatic courtesy, said goodbye to Erica, and started toward the door.

"I'll walk you out," Erica told her, then added coldly to O'Reilly, "I suggest you start mopping."

Once they were out on the sidewalk, Erica said, "Most of us aren't like that."

Mrs. Jeffries waved a wrinkled hand. "Of course not. My daughter-in-law's an Arcanist, and she'd never use her Talent that way." She sighed. "Unfortunately, there are a lot of crooks in the world. And they keep giving the bigots ammunition." When Erica blinked at that, Mrs. Jeffries gave her a smile as she started toward a twenty-year-old Mercury Sable. Over her shoulder, she added, "Thank you, dear. I had no idea what I was going to do without that money."

"Glad I was able to help." Erica watched her drive away, then turned on her heel to stalk back in the shop.

O'Reilly looked up from her mop bucket and glared, muttering something under her breath.

Erica folded her arms. "What was that?"

"Do you enjoy selling your own people out to the Nazis?"

"You are *not* 'my people.' And you just tried to rip off a little old lady on Social Security."

"Norms steal from Norms all the time!"

"And it's illegal when they do it too." She curled her upper lip. "I'm not bluffing. If I *ever* walk in here and find another spell circle on the floor, your ass is going to jail. Because we both know this isn't the first time you've defrauded one of your customers."

"Not for anything big!" Meghan threw her a flaming look over one shoulder. "So maybe they pay a few dollars more…"

"Four hundred isn't a few. And it's a hell of a lot to an old woman on Social Security."

The Arcanist's cheeks flushed. "I wouldn't have done it, but my boyfriend's a real prick, and he told me if I didn't bring in at least --"

"Shut. Up. The only reason you're not going to jail right now is if I charged you, Mrs. Jeffries' money would have to go into evidence until the trial. She can't afford that. But this is the one and only break you're going to get."

The woman subsided, growling. Erica growled back, putting plenty of Clarence into the sound.

* * *

With O'Reilly squared away, Erica continued on her patrol of the businesses, neighborhoods, and schools that made up 22 Zone.

At two o'clock, she started toward Wooten Elementary School, where she usually parked somewhere obvious on the side of the road. Nothing like the sight of a black-and-white to deter those who might otherwise blast through a school zone.

As she drove, her mind drifted to X-rated memories of her night with Jake. The shower had been only a warm up, followed by another session in the *USS Jake's Bed.*

After a surprisingly sound night's sleep in his arms, she'd awoken to the rough wet velvet of his tongue swirling over her nipple.

Beats the hell out of an alarm clock.

Erica smiled, but before she could drift into another delicious memory, a red Camaro shot past on the two-lane road. She stared after him a moment, her jaw dropping. He had to be doing at least ninety. "What the fuck?"

She hit her lights and sirens with one hand and scooped up her radio mic in the same motion. Stomping the gas, she sent her black-and-white roaring after the speeder. "Dispatch, Laurel Alpha 22 in pursuit of a red Camaro going approximately..." She paused to do an estimate. "... Ninety-five in a forty-five zone."

Her heartbeat thundered as adrenaline flooded her body. *What the hell is he doing? What kind of idiot passes a marked car at that speed on a double yellow line? He's just begging me to chase him. I do not like this at all.*

Her instincts had good reason to howl. High-speed chases were extremely dangerous -- and even more so when pursuing someone who seemed nuts to begin with. Even aside from trying to catch the subject, adrenaline had the physiological effect of causing tunnel vision, until you saw only whatever was directly ahead. It became physically impossible to see something approaching from a cross street -- with potentially fatal results.

To make matters worse, it was two o'clock on a school day. *Should I break this off before this asshole slams into a school bus?*

Even as that thought flashed through her mind, Erica realized the Camaro was slowing down. She blew out a breath in relief as the car pulled onto the shoulder and stopped. Her heartbeat began to slow as she parked behind it.

Sitting back in her seat, Erica paused to do a minute of tactical breathing, bringing her heart and respiration back under control with a series of deep, slow breaths. Once her voice was steady, Erica picked up her mic and told dispatch she'd successfully pulled the car over, then rattled off the tag number.

That done, she reached for the laptop mounted on the passenger side of the dash and swiveled it closer. Logging into the state's Department of Motor Vehicles system, she typed the Camaro's license plate number into the search field.

Frowning, Erica studied the results. The car hadn't been reported as stolen, but that not might not mean anything. Could be the owner just didn't know it was missing yet.

A quick check of the National Crime Information Center revealed no outstanding warrants connected with the car's owner, but she wouldn't know for sure until she ran the driver's license information from whoever was driving the car.

Her heart began to pound again as she got out of the car, activating the body cam clipped to the front of her shirt.

Now for the tricky bit: finding out why this fucker *wanted* to get pulled over.

Chapter Twelve

Car stops were arguably the most dangerous part of the job, because they were also a boring routine -- right up until an officer inadvertently pulled over a killer with a body in the trunk. The cop might not see the danger until the killer opened fire. And that was aside from officers who got struck and killed by cars driven by some texting asshole.

As Erica started toward the car, she realized the Camaro's driver hadn't pulled far enough over, which meant she'd have to step further out into the road than she'd like. Fortunately, there was very little traffic. Hearing the sound of an approaching vehicle, she looked back to see a blue pickup. The driver was already slowing down, probably worried about hitting her.

Returning her attention to the Camaro, she stared warily through its rear window. The driver appeared to be alone, though it was possible someone else sat hunkered down in the passenger seat.

Damn, she wished she could make out the driver's aura, but the glare of sunlight on the glass made that impossible. Reaching the vehicle's rear, Erica started to circle out around it -- just as the hair on the back of her neck rose. Three overseas tours had taught her to listen to her instincts. Her hand dropped to her weapon, thumb flicking open the snap on the retention holster. The suspect had both hands firmly on the wheel, but...

Behind her, the rumble of the approaching pickup became a howl.

She didn't even glance around, just threw herself at the Camaro, one hand bracing on its trunk as she vaulted for the shoulder of the road. Something brushed the sole of one shoe, followed by a crunch as the car rocked. The Camaro's driver's side mirror tumbled by as the dark blue Dodge Ram pickup barreled past.

Cursing, Erica jerked her Glock out of its holster as she hit the ground beside the car and spun. Before she could fire, her instincts shrieked again. She ducked.

BOOM! Fragments of safety glass pelted her face and uniform as the Camaro's rear window exploded. She dove into the ditch just as the shotgun thundered again. An engine roared, tires squealing in shrill protest.

Erica came up firing, but the Camaro was already accelerating in the same direction as the pickup. She grabbed her shoulder mic and ran for her car. "Laurel, Alpha 22. Code 1. Dark blue Dodge Ram pickup truck attempted to hit me as I approached the Camaro. Camaro driver fired at me, blew out his rear window. Sounded like a sawed-off shotgun. Returned fire. Don't know if I hit anyone."

"Alpha 22, are you injured?" The dispatcher's voice sounded tight with suppressed alarm.

"Negative." She jerked the car door open and slid into the front seat. Slamming the door, she threw the car into gear and hit the gas as she activated lights and sirens with her free hand. "In pursuit." The howl of the cruiser's engine was barely audible over the siren's banshee shriek as she shot after the Camaro. *Question is, what the hell am I going to do when I pull it over? Because those fuckers just tried to kill me. Twice.*

The siren's shrill wail jerked her nerves tighter and tighter as she blasted down the road. Trees blurred past on either side as her heart kept time in frantic, pounding beats.

Two o'clock on a school day was a lousy time to have a car chase, but Erica didn't have a hell of a lot of choice. She remembered a phrase from her academy training: "Shoot at a cop, and we'll chase you until the wheels fall off."

Wooten Elementary was two miles away. On another street, true, but that was still too damned close for comfort, given these assholes had already proved they were willing to kill a cop.

The road curved, and she slowed fractionally, knowing there was a four-way stop ahead. She rounded the bend just as a school bus pulled into the intersection.

Right into her path.

Her heart barreled into her throat. Cursing, Erica braked, shuffle steering the wheel in a desperate attempt to miss the bus. The shriek of tires competed with the siren's howl and her own cursing. A wall of pines loomed in front of the car's hood, and she sucked back a scream, stomping the brake to the floor...

The car jolted to a stop, its front bumper overhanging the ditch that would have launched her into the trees like a ski ramp.

A metallic taste filling her mouth, Erica jerked her head around. The bus had stopped squarely in the middle of the intersection. The driver stared at her through his side window, his jaw gaping, eyes wide. A dozen terrified young faces peered at her. If she hadn't veered, she'd have T-boned the bus.

Flinging the door open, Erica ran toward it, knowing the violent stop might have injured one of the kids. The door creaked wide and she leaped the steps in a bound. "Anybody hurt?"

The driver glanced back over his shoulder at his charges. "Anybody?"

"No, ma'am!" a ragged chorus answered.

"Did you see a red Camaro or a blue pickup truck?"

"Yeah, going like a bat out of hell." The driver pointed right. "That way."

"Okay, you can go. Thanks." She leaped back down the steps and raced back to her car, mentally noting the bus's number. Gears ground as it lurched off on its way.

Erica slid behind the wheel and backed up, then straightened the car out again. "Fuck. Fuck fuck fuck." She turned left on Pineheart Avenue, grabbing the mic to update the dispatcher.

And promptly ran into a stream of traffic heading to and from the school. Lips lifting off her teeth, she squealed to a stop at the nearest intersection, scanning for her suspects. She spotted neither.

Goddamnit, they could have gone anywhere. *Calm down, Harris. There's still a chance. It's a long shot but...* Drawing in a deep breath, Erica closed her eyes and reached for her magic. Got the faintest impulse to turn left. Could be just some random neurons firing, but at this point she had nothing to lose. She turned left and wove around the stream of cars to the accompaniment of her siren.

Five minutes later Erica left the worst traffic behind. As she accelerated, her gaze swept the road ahead, alert for another potentially lethal brush with another vehicle. As the last of the traffic thinned, she hit the gas. Judging by the radio traffic, other units were searching for her two attackers, but nobody else seemed to be having any luck either. Frustrated, she growled aloud, "Where did the sons of bitches go?"

Obeying another niggle of instinct, Erica turned right onto yet another two-lane road, rounded a corner...

And spotted the Camaro sitting on the side of the road, parked behind the pickup truck. Both had their drivers' doors open. The bastards had obviously bolted, but they might have left useful evidence behind.

Erica picked up her mic. "Laurel County, Alpha 22. I've spotted the Camaro and the blue pickup at..." She looked up at the GPS unit attached to the windshield to get the street name and nearest intersection. She rattled them off and pulled over, well back from both vehicles. "Requesting backup."

A deep, familiar voice drawled, "Laurel County, Alpha 23 en route. ETA five minutes."

Jake was coming.

Tension released its stranglehold on the back of her neck. Judging by the view through the busted rear windshield, there didn't appear to be anyone in the car. That said, she had no desire to step into another ambush.

This time, she was waiting for Jake.

* * *

"I had her!" John Reese pounded his big fists on the dash of the minivan, his face dark with rage. Adrian ignored the ex-Marine's temper tantrum as he drove sedately along. No sooner had Reese and Garrison pulled over at the agreed-upon location than he'd swung by to pick them up. They'd abandoned the two vehicles without a backward glance.

The three had spent the morning stealing the Camaro, the Dodge, and this minivan. Adrian always kept an eye out for any employees of local businesses who were in the habit of working through lunch. You never knew when you might need to appropriate a car.

The muscles of Reese's jaw worked in frustration. "I was aiming right at her. That blast should have taken her head off, but she ducked like she knew it was coming."

"She's a witch, boy," Garrison growled from the backseat, sounding just as frustrated and worried. "I thought I had her too. It's like she's got eyes in the back of her head."

Adrian mentally blessed his own paranoia. Once again, it had saved his ass. *Harris really is sensitive. If I'd tried to take her out myself, she might have realized another Talent's involved.*

"You think she's gonna be able to find us?" Reese threw him a worried look. "During the war, I heard witches could draw people who did bombings."

Adrian hesitated a moment, trying to decide what an HHer tattoo artist would reasonably know about magic. "Dunno. Lying low might be a good idea. We'll get another chance sooner or later. At least you didn't get caught, and nobody saw you."

Which meant the two were still usable. They weren't bad tools, all in all. They'd followed directions, avoided getting caught, and hadn't choked when they'd pulled the trigger or hit the gas. Sometimes amateurs lost their nerve at the last moment, which could really fuck up a good plan.

In the meantime, Adrian had gained information he hadn't had before. Now he just had to come up with Plan B. A professional didn't let that kind of shit get to him.

He dropped the pair off one by one where they'd parked their cars, abandoned the minivan, and walked to where he'd left his own beater. On the way home, he considered his options.

Better not try again, at least not immediately. She'd be looking for it now.

The Human Heritage protest coming up next weekend had possibilities, though. A few thousand pissed-off people, half of whom hated the other half, all chanting and working each other up. It would be a perfect opportunity to cause some casualties.

Of course, the situation was also as potentially unstable as a truck bomb, and just as likely to blow up in his face as to succeed.

And that, perversely, only added to the appeal of the idea. Nothing like the challenge of trying to engineer the results he wanted from chaotic circumstances. It took split second timing, intense planning, and plenty of pure luck.

What he needed was to calm down, read the currents of the magic, and wait for the outlines of the plan to come to him. A call to the Alchemist might be in order.

He pulled over and got out his cell, then opened the messenger app and began to type. *"I need to take a walk."*

The Alchemist messaged back within minutes. Like any good businessman, he was never far from his phone. *"How long a walk do u want?"*

He considered the question. *"Around an hour."*

"Come @ 10. I'll take u."

"*OK.*" Adrian nodded in satisfaction, dropped his cell in the cup holder, and turned toward his shop. He needed to do some brainstorming.

* * *

Jake and Erica moved cautiously toward the abandoned Camaro, their weapons drawn. He gave her a familiar sweeping gesture, one of the hand signals they'd used in the Arcane Corps. Nodding, she stepped around to approach the car from the left.

Magic flared, golden and bright, as Clarence's full manifestation appeared. The lion seemed to balance on his hind legs, encasing Jake like glowing armor. The cat's magical shell could withstand a sustained burst from an AR-15 before their melded magic finally collapsed. Or until Clarence ate the gunman, whichever came first. Either way, Erica's money was on Clar.

"Police!" Jake barked as they reached the vehicle. But a check of the front and back seats confirmed it was empty. Exchanging a look, they headed for the Dodge, only to confirm it, too, had been abandoned.

Erica holstered her weapon. "You think you can catch a scent?"

"I've got one now. Just not sure it leads anywhere." He went to one knee beside the open truck door and leaned in, careful not to touch anything. As she watched, he drew in a deep breath, then duck-walked away from the truck a few feet. Frowning, he got to his feet and returned to the Camaro, where he repeated the procedure.

When he finished, Jake shook his head. "I got a pretty good scent on them, but the trail ends a couple yards away. Probably got in another car and left."

"Which suggests either they had a car waiting for them, or somebody picked them up."

"My money's on somebody picking them up. Otherwise they would've had to know where to leave the third vehicle."

"You didn't by any chance pick up a blood scent? I fired at the dickhead in the Camaro a couple of times."

"Sorry, no."

"Figures." She turned back toward her patrol car. "I'm gonna try a sketch."

"You think you can get anything, given the lack of blood?"

"Worth a try." Erica opened the front passenger door of the car, where she kept a bag of ticket books, incident reports, and her sketchpad. She pulled out the pad and a pencil, then started back toward the Camaro. "Wish I'd managed to wing the son of a bitch." If he'd bled, her magic would have something to get a fix on. As it was… But maybe she'd get lucky. "Why don't you call for the crime scene van?"

Jake nodded and keyed his mic as Erica made for the Camaro. She would've preferred to sit in the driver's seat, but she didn't want to risk contaminating any evidence that might remain. With any luck, the bastard had left behind fingerprints, hair, or fibers they might be able to collect.

Sinking to one knee beside the open door, Erica started to reach for her magic when Jake called, "Wait a minute. I want to keep an eye out while you do that."

Yeah, she should've thought of that. Sitting back on her heels, she waited.

"Ready?" he asked, moving to stand behind her. Just the sound of his deep voice made her feel less vulnerable.

Blowing out a breath, she closed her eyes and concentrated on opening herself to the magic.

Which turned out to be a lot harder to do immediately following a massive adrenaline dump. That was no surprise. The Caliphate War had taught her it was hard to achieve a mystical calm after the shit hit the fan.

Still, she hadn't forgotten the tactical breathing techniques she'd learned in the Corps. Drawing in air through her nose, she held for a four count, then blew out again. Repeating the process until her mind stilled its frantic circling, she managed to silence the little voice screaming *I almost died*. Finally she let her consciousness reach for the swirling patterns of magic that made up the world around her.

There was Jake, blazing like a psychic torch just behind her. Filtering him out, she focused on the car -- on its empty front seat, on the pungent smell of nitrocellulose from the fired shotgun. An oily chemical scent of antifreeze drifted in the air, suggesting her bullet had hit the radiator.

At last, eyes closed, she put her pencil to the paper and began to draw. But instead of the bold sweeps she'd managed at the scene of the yesterday's murder, the movements of her hand today were slow, tentative.

Worse, the image she saw was vague. By the time Erica gave up and opened her eyes, the sketch was little more than a few broad suggestions of the shape of eyes, the line of the nose, a thin mouth. None of which was strong enough to support an accusation like attempted murder. "Fuck."

"Nothing?" Jake asked as she rose to her feet.

Disgusted, she handed over the sketchpad. "Next best thing to nothing, anyway."

He studied the pad, then shook his head. "Well, we knew it was a long shot."

"I was hoping it wasn't quite that long."

Approaching sirens drew their attention. They watched as a patrol car and the crime scene van parked behind Jake's car. A familiar tall, graying man got out of the unit and headed toward them.

"Oh great," Erica muttered. "It's the sarge."

Johnson's lips were tight, an air of barely suppressed agitation swirling around him. His attention fell on the sketchpad in her hands, and he broke step.

Erica instinctively checked his aura. Streams of yellow streamed across it, swirling like storm clouds. *What* is *it with him?*

He gave her a tight nod, then gestured at the sketchpad. "You got a drawing of the gunman?"

"Not really." She handed over the pad, watching the yellow cool into green, then calm blue as he studied it. "The shooter didn't leave me enough to lock onto." *And why are you relieved? What the fuck do you know about this?* But it wasn't a question she could ask.

Her gaze slid past him to collide with Jake's. The line of her lover's jaw was tight, a muscle rolling as if he ground his teeth. His nostrils flared as he locked his gold eyes on the sergeant's face, and she knew he was drawing in Johnson's scent.

The crime scene investigator walked up. Deborah Owens was a tall, slender African-American woman with steady dark eyes. Dressed in a green utility uniform, boots, and Nitrile gloves, she carried a large tackle box full of gear.

"Did y'all touch anything in the car?" the CSI asked.

"No," Erica assured her. "We just looked inside."

Owens grunted, moved over and started dusting the car door for prints.

Johnson handed the sketchpad back to Erica and straightened his shoulders, every inch the supervisor. Instead of, say, a man who might know more than he should about her attempted murder. "All right, exactly what happened?"

You don't know? She bit back the question and briefed him, each sentence as clipped and professional as any report she'd ever given in the Corps. But as she spoke, Erica watched yellow swirl in his aura, accompanied by the searing reds she associated with anger. *Are you angry they tried to kill me, or angry they didn't succeed?*

Johnson asked her a couple of questions she suspected were more for form's sake than anything else, then told her to head back to the Sheriff's Office. "Sheriff Gable and Lieutenant Williams want to talk to you about this. You'll need to go in."

He turned to Jake. "You'll have to work both zones, but be aware Gable intends to call a full meeting of all available sworn officers tonight. He wants you two attending. I'll send somebody out to cover both your areas."

"Yes sir." Jake's tone sounded frigid enough to give the sergeant freezer burn.

"Get going." Johnson headed back toward his car.

Jake started to open his mouth, then hesitated, caught Erica's eyes, and jerked his head in a signal to follow. They moved out of Owens's hearing.

"He smelled guilty as fuck." There was a distinct rumbling undertone to his voice that suggested Clarence was very close to the surface.

"Maybe. There was a lot of yellow in his aura that calmed down when he realized the sketch wasn't worth a damn. Later when I was describing what happened, his reactions were a little harder to track. He was definitely pissed and worried, but it's possible he reacted that way because I came so close to getting killed."

Jake snorted. "Yeah, I could tell he was terrified for you."

Erica shrugged. "When it comes to interpreting aural patterns, it's easy to misread. I thought he had some guilty knowledge too at first, but I'm not sure it's that cut and dried."

"Maybe not, but something's sure as fuck not right. Watch your step."

She forced a grin, despite her own tension. "Always."

"Sell that to somebody who doesn't know you."

Erica laughed and watched him walk off, his broad shoulders rolling with that easy male stride of his. But as she turned and headed for her own car, the smile drained from her face.

What the hell was going on with the sergeant? *And if he's dirty, what are we supposed to do about it?*

* * *

As Roger turned his car around and headed back to the department, he started to reach for the personal cell phone on his duty belt.

Then he let his hand fall away. He really didn't want to know. The little witch sensed emotions, and Nolan could smell them. Suspecting Virginia had tried to have Erica Harris killed was bad enough. If he *knew* she had, Harris might spot that knowledge in his aura and go straight to Gable. He'd be under investigation so fast, he'd get whiplash.

God damn Virginia anyway. It was one thing to rough up Talents, try to create such a hostile environment they'd leave town. But murdering a cop, even a witch cop... *This isn't what I signed up for.*

Unfortunately, it no longer mattered that he'd had good intentions when he'd let the politician talk him into this. He'd come painfully close to becoming an accessory to Harris's murder. As it was, he was hip-deep in a conspiracy that could send him to prison for a very long time.

What would happen to Doris if he was arrested? And it would kill his eighty- year-old father. Dad had always been so proud of "my son, the cop." He'd be a lot less proud of "my son, the murderer."

So you'd better make Goddamn sure you don't get caught, because the innocence ship has sailed. You ain't on it anymore.

Something had to be done about the Talents, even if it was something he'd rather not do.

* * *

Scott Clary listened over his private cell as Sergeant Johnson explained the situation. "We can't afford to keep playing softball with those two," Johnson said. "This is getting serious. Our mutual friend wants them gone."

Meaning Virginia Laurel. Doing favors for the next Governor of South Carolina wouldn't hurt Clary's career at all. Assuming she managed to get herself elected, anyway. And if he did something to help her get elected, that would be even better.

"What do you have in mind?" Scott asked. "We've been working on Nolan for a while now, but we don't have much to show for it. He's harder to play than you'd think."

"You haven't had the right lever," Johnson said. "Harris is the key. He's got a thing for her. Work that angle right, and he'll do something stupid. Be even better if you could get him to lose it in front of witnesses."

Scott curled his lip. Only an idiot would let a woman get so far under his skin that she made a useful handle. "I'll sic Hampton on it. She hates the fuck out of Harris, and it's mutual. If anybody can light Nolan's fuse when it comes to his girlfriend, it's her."

Better Mary than him. If Scott himself pushed the cat too far, he could end up dead. Nolan had enough delusions of chivalry not to seriously hurt Hampton, but the Feral might lose it just enough to get himself fired. Not that Scott really gave a shit. Mary could be useful, but she was also a flaming bitch.

And not even that good in bed.

"He's got really sensitive hearing," Johnson said thoughtfully. "If Hampton says something inflammatory in a low enough voice -- maybe at the meeting the sheriff's called this afternoon -- that might do the trick. But she'll have to be careful nobody else hears her, or it'll backfire. We do not want to attract suspicion, especially given the fuckers who just tried to kill her. Besides, since Faraday Square, a lot of people in the department admire that big bastard."

Scott smirked. "Don't worry, we know exactly how

far to push. And how not to get caught pushing further."

"Good. Give the witch a good shove." Johnson hung up.

Thoughtful, Scott watched the traffic stream out of the women's college. Power was all about relationships. You built relationships with the powerless to build a power base, and you built relationships with the powerful to hitch a ride on their coattails. Between Laurel, his brother-in-law, Johnson, and his three fellow deputies, Scott had the beginnings of a very useful network. Who knew how far it would get him? Sheriff was a distinct possibility. Maybe even governor, in a decade or so. And after that... Well, he was only thirty. He had plenty of time.

The trick was knowing how to tie all those relationships together. Friendship wasn't good enough -- people betrayed friends all the time. Fear, though... Fear was good. Make people afraid of something, and they instinctively wanted to find allies against it.

A whole lot of people were afraid of Talents. He wasn't. Cautious, maybe, but not fearful. But he was more than happy to use other people's fear.

A red convertible BMW peeled out through the college's iron gates. Its young driver's blonde hair whipped behind her like a flag.

Clary grinned wolfishly, hit his lights and sirens, and accelerated after her.

* * *

Two hours later, Jake sat in the sheriff's office briefing room by Erica's side, watching the video of her fighting for her life.

He kept having to remind Clarence she'd survived. *She's sitting right next to me. She's fine.* Judging by the low moaning sound the lion kept making in their bond, Clarence wasn't convinced.

Then again, Jake wasn't all that comforted either. His hands coiled into fists as they rested on his thighs, and the muscles of his shoulders knotted. From the corner of one eye, he saw Erica glance at him, frowning. She'd probably heard Clarence moan.

On the flat screen television hanging on the wall, the dash cam showed Erica approaching the Camaro, one hand on her weapon. *Why in the fuck didn't she call me for backup? She must have known there was something off about this stop.*

On second thought, he knew exactly why she hadn't called him. She was still trying to prove herself to Johnson's bully squad -- and that machismo had almost gotten her killed.

On the recording, Erica approached the car on the driver's side. An engine roared. Without looking around, she threw herself at the Camaro, braced a hand on the trunk and vaulted over it. A Dodge Ram pickup blasted through the space where she'd been.

She landed, drew her weapon, and threw herself to one side again as shotgun pellets blew out the Camaro's back window. A blast from the shotgun's other barrel missed as Erica darted aside, returning fire. The Camaro accelerated away. Whirling, she raced back to her patrol car, lips peeled off her teeth, eyes narrow in rage.

And I was miles away. I should have been with her. Protecting her. Clarence growled, echoing the thought.

Jake watched the chase unwind, teeth grinding, his hands gripping his thighs as she pursued her attempted killers.

When she swerved the patrol car toward the trees to avoid the bus, he had to work not to manifest claws, knowing he'd puncture his own skin.

Suddenly a soft hand landed on his where it gripped his leg under the table. Erica's fingers felt long and cool and soothing -- and reminded him that she had, after all survived. He turned his hand over so he could grip hers. The muscles in his aching shoulders relaxed.

The room was dead silent, none of the other deputies

making a sound as they watched Erica's efforts to catch the shooter.

Next came her body cam's version of events. It looked even more chaotic and terrifying than the dash cam had. Clarence's psychic growl grew louder until it was all he could do to keep it from vibrating the air around him.

Then, as the shotgun blasted out the Camaro's rear window, a female voice whispered in a breath of sound so soft he doubted the Norms in the room heard it at all. "Too bad the asshole wasn't a better shot."

Jake's head whipped around to stare at Mary Hampton, who sat with the rest of her gang directly behind him and Erica. Hampton, Tom Green, Scott Clary, and Bob Martin must have slipped in after the two of them. Meeting his outraged glare, Hampton smirked. And blew him a kiss.

Rage, hot and overwhelming, ripped away his control as Clarence flooded his mind. Blazing into full manifestation in a shower of sparks, the lion roared at the four deputies, his voice so thunderous, every cop in the room jumped.

Oh shit!

"Jake!" Erica hissed.

Jake didn't answer as he clawed for control of his Familiar before Clarence could go over the conference table at Hampton. *Stop it!* Clamping down on his Talent, he fought to make the manifestation vanish despite Clarence's raging determination to teach Hampton that Erica was off limits.

As Jake struggled to force his Familiar out of his head and back to BFS, he was vaguely aware that half the cops in the room were on their feet, hands on weapons, tense and cursing. He gripped Erica's hand hard as he fought to control the enraged lion.

Her free hand found his forearm, nails digging in so

deep, he wondered if she was drawing blood. "Damn it, Jake!" she hissed through her teeth, "Get rid of that cat!"

At the anger in her voice, Clarence vanished like a popped soap bubble.

"Sit. Down!" Sheriff Harry Gable's roar did not permit any argument whatsoever. "Nolan, have you lost your damned mind? What the hell was that?"

Oh shit, I've really fucked up this time. "Sorry, sir." His voice sounded hoarse, growling. "It won't happen again."

"It had damned well better not. See me after the meeting." Judging by Gable's icy tone, this would not be a conversation Jake would enjoy. The sheriff's rage was no surprise. Jake might as well have drawn on a fellow officer.

Great. Just fucking great. Did I just get myself fired?

Chapter Thirteen

As Jake silently cursed himself, Gable moved to the podium at the front of the room. He was a big man with the build of a defensive lineman and a broad, beefy face under thick red hair. As he scanned the room, leaning against the podium with its Laurel County Sheriff's star, his cool blue eyes measured his deputies. He let a long pause develop, forcing them to focus on him. "I don't need to tell you what happened to Harris is a serious situation. This isn't just a car stop gone bad. It was a coordinated murder attempt with at least two perpetrators. That much is obvious from the fact the truck deliberately tried to hit her, and when that failed, the Camaro driver opened fire. Both vehicles were stolen somewhere around a half-hour to an hour earlier, apparently so their owners wouldn't have time to report the thefts before the attack. A third vehicle, a 2013 Honda Odyssey minivan, was stolen earlier, though we can't be sure it was connected to the others. I do not like the way that smells."

The cops muttered among themselves, obviously not liking it either.

"Then there's the fact that the location is so close to Suellen Wooten Elementary, suggesting they intended to use school traffic to frustrate pursuit. According to outraged calls from parents, a Dodge pickup and a Camaro drove through the school zone at a high rate of speed, even veering into oncoming traffic to get around stopped cars."

A muscle rolled in Gable's jaw as he visibly ground his teeth. "The fact that the Camaro and the Dodge were found abandoned together, while the minivan was found ten miles away half an hour later, suggests that the perpetrators used the minivan as a getaway vehicle before abandoning it, as well. That suggests there are at least three individuals involved with this: the drivers of the two stolen vehicles, and whoever picked them up."

Gable scanned the room, letting the implications sink in before he continued. "There can be no doubt they intended to kill a cop. It's not immediately clear they intended to kill Harris in particular, but we can't disregard that possibility either. We also can't ignore the possibility that each and every one of us is a potential target."

But even if we're not, Erica definitely is. Jake turned to study her, but her face was expressionless, coolly controlled.

She'd released his hand after he'd calmed down. Now it was his turn to reach for hers beneath the table. As he encircled her fingers with his, she looked at him, startled, and gave him a smile. It looked a little tight, but it was something. He returned it, hoping she could see his determination to protect her.

"Given that, you *must* maintain situational awareness at all times," Gable continued, his tone dead serious. "And when you're conducting a car stop, do not approach from the driver's side. Walk along the shoulder of the road. Stepping into the roadway puts you in danger of being hit even by people who don't intend to hit you. Something about blue lights hypnotizes some people. That's aside from murderous shits like these three."

He leaned forward, curling one huge hand around the edge of his podium. "Also, I want to stress that whenever you do a high risk stop, you've got to call for backup. When the little voice in the back of your mind starts screaming, *listen to it*. If Harris hadn't had excellent instincts, we'd be putting black ribbon on our badges right now."

The reminder made Jake feel sick. He wasn't surprised to see Erica's expression had gone stony. She probably didn't appreciate having her mistakes during the car stop pointed out.

"Needless to say, I want those bastards found. Yesterday." Gable straightened away from the podium, which creaked as his weight lifted. "Unfortunately, that's not the only thing we've got to worry about. There's that Human Heritage march coming up next weekend. That's an all hands on deck situation, so don't even think about requesting Saturday off. Fortunately, we have ten departments from surrounding jurisdictions sending manpower to help. And we're going to need every bit of it, because not only do we have HH to worry about, the local Talent community has sought a permit to counterprotest. Adding those two groups together is going to make for some nasty math."

He tapped the top of his podium with a stiff forefinger. "Or rather, it will if we drop the ball. I have no intention of being the lead story on CNN because somebody got killed. We're going to keep those Humanist jokers and the Talents well apart. If they want to scream at each other, they can do it across us.

"Speaking of HH…" He looked down at the sheet of paper in front of him. "There have also been reports of anti-Talent graffiti and harassment in the county."

"Damn Talents probably trying to get their fifteen minutes of fame," Martin muttered.

Before Jake could turn to glower at him, Erica's long fingers closed around his forearm. He subsided, knowing she had a point. The last thing he needed to do was get Clarence stirred up again.

But Gable, it turned out, had heard the remark. The sheriff leaned an elbow against the podium and glared. "*Any* reports of Talent harassment are to be taken seriously. Talents pay taxes just like Norms. They're entitled to our protection when they're threatened. And if some idiot tries to take advantage of the situation, we *are* going to investigate. What we don't do is assume there isn't a genuine threat." He straightened his big body as if coming to attention. "I will not put up with bigotry in my department."

He scanned the room, his gaze stern. "You would be well advised not to push me on this, ladies and gentlemen. Now, get back to work." Gable's lips twitched slightly. "And as they used to say on *Hill Street Blues* before most of you were born: 'let's be careful out there.'"

A babble of voices rose as cops stood and started filtering out. As Jake and Erica stood, Gable's gaze met his. The sheriff jerked his head in a come-with-me gesture, and he stepped out from behind the podium.

Oh hell, here it comes. Keeping his face expressionless, Jake followed Gable from the room.

As he left, he was conscious of Erica's worried gaze.

* * *

Damn it, Jake. Don't get fired. Biting her lip, Erica watched him go.

"Hey." A hand touched her shoulder, and she turned, automatically bracing herself for another confrontation. But it was Katilia Sharp, dark eyes concerned. "Are you okay? That video… Oh, damn, that was close."

"She's not kidding." Jason Ferris paused on his way out, his long, homely face just as appalled. "How the hell did you know what was coming? I'd have a face full of buckshot if it'd been me."

"Damnedest thing I ever saw," another cop agreed.

With that, she was surrounded by deputies, slapping her back and expressing their sympathy and support. Despite her worry for Jake, her heart warmed. *Damn, they actually care.*

When the small crowd finally melted away, only Katilia remained, looking troubled. "Hey, what set Jake off? That's not like him. I went to school with that guy, and he doesn't lose his shit like that. And he certainly doesn't whip out the fur without a damned good reason."

"Yeah, I know. They train Ferals to keep a tight grip on their Familiars for that very reason. I have no idea why he'd manifest."

On her way out, Mary Hampton paused to give Erica a nasty smirk. "Maybe you need to look in the mirror."

Realization struck. "What did you do?"

Hampton just laughed and walked away. Erica stared after her, temper flooding her in a burning wave.

"Two thoughts," Sharp said. "First, what a bitch. Second…" She flashed very white teeth in a very wicked grin. "Jake's got it bad if he lost it just because that bimbo bad-mouthed you."

Erica rolled her eyes. "Terrific."

* * *

Jake stepped into Gable's office and closed the door behind him at a gesture from his boss. The big man settled down at his massive oak desk, leaning back in the executive chair with a grunt.

The room was decorated with framed newspaper clippings, photos of Gable's wife and kids, and his diploma from the University of South Carolina. There were also the usual plaques and certificates from the South Carolina Criminal Justice Academy and assorted law enforcement training courses the sheriff had taken.

Jake fell into parade rest in front of the big mahogany desk, fastening his eyes on a framed photo of Gable in a football uniform back when he'd played for the USC Gamecocks.

"Sit your butt down, Nolan." As he obeyed, the sheriff growled, "You want to explain to me why you lost your shit?"

He hesitated for a split second.

"Nolan."

Recognizing the warning tone in the sheriff's voice, Jake surrendered. "Hampton whispered it was too bad the subject was a lousy shot, sir."

Gable closed his eyes and rubbed a thumb between his brows as if his head hurt. "Yeah, I had a feeling it was something like that." He braced his muscled forearms on his desk blotter. "Look, I put you on that shift because I thought you were levelheaded enough to keep an eye on those idiots without letting them get to you. Was I wrong?"

"Harris almost got killed, sir." Jake clamped his mouth shut. He hadn't intended to say the words, and he certainly hadn't intended to say them in that tone.

"Yeah, she did. I'm not even sure how she managed to stay alive. Three different attempts to kill her in the space of five seconds." The sheriff shook his head, then lifted a thick red brow at Jake. "That some kind of magic thing, or just combat experience?"

Jake relaxed fractionally. It didn't sound as if Gable was about to fire him despite Clarence temporarily losing his fuzzy mind. "She's always been like that. Her instincts saved our asses more than once during the war. I don't know whether it's magic or what, but we learned to listen to her."

The sheriff eyed him so long he started to get uncomfortable. "I know you two served together. Is that all this is?"

Jake stiffened.

This time there was a distinct snap in Gable's voice. "If you're thinking that's none of my business, it damn well is if it makes you pop claws like Wolverine and go after a fellow deputy. Do *not* do that shit again, Nolan. I'd suspend you, but I don't want to leave Harris hanging in case somebody *is* trying to kill her specifically instead of just cops in general. Are we clear?"

Jake straightened. "Yessir."

"Don't let your dick get you fired. Now get your ass out of my office and get back to work."

"Yes, sir. Thank you, sir." He pivoted, eager to

escape before the sheriff changed his mind.

"Yeah. Don't make me regret it."

* * *

Out in the hallway, Jake closed the door behind him with a suppressed sigh of relief. God, he needed caffeine. He started down the hall toward the break room.

"Jake!"

He looked around as Erica hurried up, her anxious gaze searching his. "Is everything okay?"

"If you mean did he fire me, no. He didn't even suspend me."

She blew out a relieved breath. "Thank God. When Clarence manifested, I was afraid you were screwed. What the hell did Hampton say? I know it was something -- she all but bragged about it."

He repeated the comment, and she glowered. "Why did you let that idiot get to you?"

Jake ground his teeth. The fact that she had a point did nothing to soothe his temper. "Maybe it had something to do with you almost getting yourself killed trying to prove the length of your dick."

Her jaw dropped. "I beg your pardon?"

"Why the fuck didn't you call for backup?"

She made a chopping gesture. "Keep your voice down!"

Jake stepped closer, dropping his volume to a hiss. "You knew that was a high risk stop. For Christ sake, the Camaro passed a cop going ninety in a forty-five on a double yellow line! But instead of requesting backup, you pranced out there…"

"Pranced?"

"You know what I mean! You almost got killed three times! What the fuck would I have done, huh?" They stared at each other in frozen silence. He was breathing hard. Somewhere in the depths of his mind, Clarence moaned in distress.

Erica straightened. "This is a bad idea."

"What do you mean by that?"

She looked up at him, her face so expressionless he knew she was hiding something that hurt. "Cats are territorial as hell of anything they view as theirs. If you can't keep Clarence under control, we need to break it off before he gets you fired."

He stared. "You want to end it because I lost my temper?"

"It wasn't your temper you lost control of. It was Clarence, and that's a hell of a lot more dangerous. Jake, you *manifested* in a roomful of armed cops!" She raked both hands through her short hair. "You want to talk about *me* almost getting killed? If Clarence got away from you…"

"But he didn't. I reestablished control and I sent him back to BFS. Yes, maybe I lost it for a minute or two, but I didn't let him tear into that little bitch no matter how much she deserved it."

Erica whirled, throwing up her hands in frustration. "Christ, you'd think after Bobby I'd have more sense."

Jake clenched his fists. Feeling the prick of claws digging into his palms, he loosened his grip. "*I am not Bobby.* Anyway, this isn't about Bobby, this is about your ego."

She turned very slowly. Stared. "What?"

"You're so intent on proving to those assholes that you're as good a cop as they are, you put yourself in a potentially lethal situation. You've got to quit fucking around, Erica. You *know* better than this. When you need me, I expect you to *call me.*"

"You don't give me orders," she growled, her voice low and seething. "You're not in my chain of command. The fact that we slept together does not give you any right to tell me what to do."

"Oh, that's good. Tell the whole fucking department we're involved."

"Not anymore. This is it. This was a bad idea from the start."

It felt as if Clarence had sunk his claws into Jake's heart and jerked. Pain exploded in his chest, cold and shocking. A full minute went by before he could even speak without screaming at her like a lovesick crazy man. "Fine. It's your call. But the next time you need backup, you had better goddamn call me. Or I will be all over you every time you answer a fucking call."

"Don't you threaten me!"

"I'm not threatening you." His lips felt oddly numb. "I'm trying to keep your ass alive, and you are not cooperating. We're zone partners. Backing each other up is part of the job. So is knowing when to ask for backup when the situation is spinning out of control."

"Fuck. You," she snarled, her dark eyes blazing. "I do my job. I do my job *well*."

"Yes, you do. But that's not the issue. You want to talk about keeping something under control? You need to control your ego more than I need to control my cat. Because if you don't, it's going to get you killed."

"Go to hell." She whirled and stalked from the room.

Jake stood frozen, staring after her, wondering distantly how many people had overheard that argument. His hands burned like a son of a bitch.

He looked down and opened his clenched fists. Blood filled his palms from four sets of puncture wounds. *Great. Popped my fucking claws again.*

Jake headed for the sink to wash his hands and look for the first aid kit.

* * *

The Alchemist lived in a brick split-level in a thoroughly middle-class development. His neighbors would have been shocked if they'd known he brewed illegal potions in the basement.

Adrian pulled into the paved driveway, got out, and headed into the garage, but before he could open the kitchen door, Ray Carlisle jerked the door open, stepped outside, and slammed it behind him with a thunderous bang.

"Ray, damn it…" A female voice yelled from somewhere inside, sounding a little panicky.

"Shut up, Meghan!" Ray bellowed back. "I don't want to hear your bullshit excuses." Stalking past, he told Adrian, "Come on out back. I've got your Stroll."

Brows climbing, Adrian followed the other Talent out of the garage and behind the house.

A massive play set built of cedar loomed in the center of the back yard -- a mash-up of a tree house, a slide, monkey bars, and swings, all jutting off the central structure at various angles.

"This is new." Adrian settled into the wooden seat of one of the swings, which was more than sturdy enough for his weight.

Ray plopped down the next swing over. "Meghan bought it for the brat." The Alchemist was a pudgy man nearing forty, with a round face, thinning red hair, and bitter blue eyes. He wore jeans and a T-shirt that said, *Want to see my magic wand?* The lettering glowed faintly phosphorescent.

One of the most talented Alchemists Adrian had ever known, Ray could have been making good money in pharmaceuticals. Unfortunately, he'd gotten himself fired from his last such job for punching a supervisor and threatening coworkers. Self-control wasn't Ray's best thing. "Here's your nice long walk." He handed over a plastic bag full of a familiar selection of exotic plant life, including a variety of magical marijuana he grew in his combo grow room and alchemist lab.

Closing his eyes, Adrian studied the bag's magical contents. The leaves emitted shades of green that ranged from emerald to peridot. Reaching into his wallet, he extracted a few hundred. The drug was well worth the money if it helped him brainstorm a solution to the Harris problem. Nothing encouraged his creativity like smoking a bag of Stroll. It also brought him down enough to sleep, which had become something of a problem on this job. "Looks like a good batch."

"Have I ever sold you one what wasn't?" Ray demanded, his tone biting.

"What did you say?" Adrian stared at him, letting enough of his true personality show that the Alchemist looked unnerved.

"Sorry. Sorry, man. I didn't mean anything by it. It's that bitch, Meghan. She smoked a whole fucking cookie of Tink Wednesday. By herself."

Adrian blinked, startled out of his irritation. "It's a miracle she's still alive. That much Fairy Dust…"

"Four hundred dollars worth of Dust, man. I spent two days brewing that shit. I told her she'd better fucking well pay for it. So what'd she do? The dumb bitch tried to rip off an old lady at her store and got caught. She's lucky she wasn't charged. Christ, she's stupid. I've had about enough of her." He held up a plump hand, thumb and forefinger a fraction apart. "I'm this far from using her precious brat in my next spell." Judging by his tone, it wasn't an idle threat.

Adrian blinked, intrigued. The boy was seven. "What the hell spell would you work? Be a shame to waste that kind of power on a potion. Like using a brick of C4 to kill a wasp's nest." And considering human sacrifice was a capital crime, it wasn't the sort of thing you did for shits and giggles.

"Spell's not the point. Teaching that bitch a lesson about stealing from me is the point." His eyes narrowed. "Hell, I could use the blood connection to take out Meghan too." A slow, nasty smile spread over his face. "Do it in a spell circle and make her watch. Bleed the kid. Do it slow."

Adrian's eyes widened as inspiration struck -- and he hadn't even had to smoke the Stroll. "How'd you like to make a shitload of money, Ray?"

* * *

Erica spent the rest of the shift mentally reliving her assorted close calls like a rat on an exercise wheel.

Diving across the trunk of the Camaro... The howling instinct that drove her to duck the instant before the shotgun thundered... The terrified faces of those kids when she'd almost hit the school bus... The cluster of trees looming in front of the hood of her car as she fought to stop in time.

Yet even after all that, what really made her want to scream was the fight with Jake. Damn it, she'd thought they had something. Thought that after all the years of loneliness, she'd found what she was looking for -- a man who understood where she was coming from because he'd *been* there.

The times they'd made love... God, it'd never been better with anybody, not even Bobby. Not just because of Jake's incredibly sexy body, face, and skill in the sack. She'd felt a *connection* with him. They fit together like puzzle pieces. When they made love, he'd seemed to touch parts of her she hadn't even known were there.

The problem was Clarence.

When she'd gotten involved with Jake, Clarence had started seeing her as a member of his pride, just like the two lionesses. And a male lion would not put up with anybody encroaching on his females.

That possessiveness, added to the tremendous power of a Feral, created a package roughly as explosive as fuel oil and fertilizer. Add the fuse of Jake's emotional reaction to her close calls, and it was no surprise he'd lost his shit.

He could have gotten away with a certain amount of that crap in the Arcane Corps. Ferals were expected to maintain discipline when it came to their Familiars, but senior officers were also inclined to cut them a little slack.

Plus, unlike Hampton, people in the Corps knew better than to poke a fucking lion with a sharp stick.

But she and Jake weren't in the Corps anymore. He was lucky he hadn't been suspended for roaring at Hampton. What was worse, that possessiveness would only get more extreme as they got more involved.

Like it or not, Erica couldn't afford to let either of them destroy their careers for the sake of sex. No matter how good that sex might be.

And yet the thought of walking away hurt. Hurt so damn bad.

By the time she got off shift, she was almost vibrating with the need to hit something -- anything.

She considered heading home to the bottle of white zinfandel she had in the fridge, despite the hangover she'd probably suffer in the morning. Unfortunately, drinking really wouldn't do a damn thing for the stew of frustration and anger she was barely keeping contained.

But she knew what would.

* * *

Erica walked into the sheriff's office carrying the bag of workout gear she kept in the trunk, ignoring the metal detector that beeped as she strode through the double doors. The desk sergeant buzzed her in.

The narrow hallway's beige corridor walls were lined with framed photos of past sheriffs and recipients of department service awards, interspaced with corkboards covered with everything from bake sale flyers to wanted posters. She headed past the offices of various divisions and admin offices, rounding one corner after another in the warren of hallways.

When she passed Mary Hampton on the way to the stairs, she seriously considered stopping to feed the bitch her fist. *Better not. Don't want to end up suspended.* Erica pulled the metal door open and clattered down the steps instead.

The Laurel County Sheriff's Office had once been the

corporate headquarters of a manufacturing firm that had moved to better digs. In exchange for a sizable tax break, the company had sold the sprawling building to the county for use as a law enforcement center. The LCSO and its three hundred sworn officers had long since outgrown the basement of the county administration building that had been its previous headquarters.

All that extra room had allowed the sheriff to indulge in some luxuries. The LCSO gym occupied what had once been the building's cafeteria, while the kitchen had been converted into a pair of locker rooms.

Erica shouldered through a swinging door marked "Women." Long and narrow, painted in shades of slate blue and oyster white, it was barely big enough for a single wall of lockers, a couple of showers, and a toilet. The men's version was decidedly larger, since there were far more male deputies.

She dropped the bag on the bench, stripped, and changed into black shorts, cross trainers, and a LCSO T-shirt. Taking a seat by the bag, Erica spent the next ten minutes encasing her hands with layer after layer of fabric hand wrap. The wraps were designed to reinforce and immobilize the small, relatively fragile bones of the hand so they wouldn't shatter when they slammed into the thicker bones of someone's skull. Since she fully intended to beat the shit out of something, she needed that protection.

Hands thoroughly encased, she banged out the door and into the gym, with its assortment of equipment donated by various Laurel County businesses. Mirrors covered three of the walls, showing multiple reflections of Erica when she flipped on the lights. At one end of the room stood a couple of racks of free weights, four weight benches, two treadmills, and three exercise bikes. Erica headed for other end, where the department conducted hand-to-hand training. It was mostly empty, except for several exercise mats rolled up and stashed along the wall. An eighty-pound Everlast heavy bag dangled from a thick chain, beside a speed bag attached to a metal platform bolted to the ceiling.

Just what the doctor ordered.

Erica started slow, tapping the speed bag with the side of her fist, letting it rebound on the board three times between strikes. Working the little bag was an exercise in eye-hand coordination more than power, a good warm-up for the heavy bag that was next on the menu.

She settled into a comfortable rhythm, speeding up gradually, the bag rebounding faster and faster with rhythmic *thump-thump-thumps*. There was something almost soothing about it, like a Zen meditation for the fists.

Erica's muscles warmed as her blood flowed faster, wrapped hands stinging from multiple impacts. She began punching faster and faster until the bag blurred, each blow a matter of rhythm and instinct as the stress of the day bled away.

Maybe after an hour of this, she'd be exhausted enough to sleep without hearing that damn shotgun go off in her ear all night...

"Well," an unpleasantly familiar female voice sneered. "Look, y'all, Witchybitch thinks she's Rocky."

Jolting, Erica lost her rhythm and missed her next swing. She turned, silently cursing herself. She'd been concentrating so hard on the bag she'd lost situational awareness. Not a smart thing to do with Assholes R Us in the building.

Hampton, Clary, Green, and Martin stood smirking at her, all four dressed in some combination of athletic wear -- LCSO sweats, shorts, and tees.

Erica silently cursed herself, remembering that she'd passed Hampton on her way downstairs. The bitch must have realized where she was going. Evidently they'd decided this was a perfect opportunity for an ambush.

And they might be right. Shift change was over, and the cops of the second shift were already out on the road by now. True, the desk sergeant and Charlie Shift's lieutenant were still in the building, but both were upstairs. They'd be unlikely to hear if things got out of hand.

And Johnson's pet thugs looked as if "out of hand" was exactly what they had in mind. Hampton smirked like a possum perched on top of a full trashcan. Scott Clary looked smug, Tom Green uneasy... and Bob Martin's eyes gleamed with ugly anticipation. His aura burned psycho red.

Oh, fuck.

Chapter Fourteen

"Heard you and furboy had a lover's spat," Hampton drawled "And here you are, nursing your broken heart."

Goddamnit, I should've kept my voice down. "What in the hell are you talking about? I'm here to work the heavy bag." Flexing her fists, she stalked to the weight bench where she'd dropped her athletic bag. She knew better than to attempt the speed bag with those four in the room. Not that she was in real danger. They wouldn't try anything in the sheriff's department; senior officers were too likely to intervene. No, they'd jump her on the street like the bullies they were.

Erica's eyes narrowed in sudden calculation. If she could make the bastards think twice now, they might hesitate to try anything later. *Certainly worth a try. Besides, I owe Hampton a mouthful of fist for trying to get Jake fired.* Unzipping the bag, she pulled out a pair of boxing gloves Bobby had bought her for Christmas one year. The question was, what would be the best way to maneuver one of them into a fight? "Unless you'd like a little boxing practice?"

"Why not?" When she looked up, Hampton flexed her fists. "I promise not to hurt you. Much."

That bitch caused this. If she'd kept out of it, I'd be in bed with Jake right now. She gave Hampton her best psycho stare, the one she'd perfected at age ten for the mini-maggots who'd tormented her. Hampton, after all, was only a taller version of those childhood bullies. "You won't get the chance."

The deputy's smile wilted at the edges before she hid her unease and widened her ugly grin. Yellow flickered in her aura. *Seems I haven't lost my touch.*

Clary gave her a nasty grin. "Guess I'll referee."

"Guess you won't," Erica retorted. "Whoever hits the

ground first loses. No kicks, no hitting below the belt."

Hampton smirked. "Then this won't take long."

"We'll see."

Clary eyed her. "You are an arrogant little Witchybitch, aren't you?"

"I have a lot to be arrogant about." Erica reached into her bag and pulled out the padded head guard. She pulled it on and tightened the chinstrap so it cupped the sides of her face protectively. Amping up the psycho, she met Clary's gaze. "And if you call me Witchybitch one more time, I'll demonstrate just how much of both I really am."

"I'm shaking." Despite the sneer in his voice, uneasy yellow swirled in his aura.

"You're smarter than I thought," Erica said silkily.

Martin glared, flexing huge hands. "Well, I ain't afraid of you."

She lifted a brow. "You, on the other hand, are not."

Martin stared at her, his cheekbones going red, his nostrils flaring as his eyes narrowed dangerously. He jolted toward her, his aura paling toward white.

Oh, fuck, I may have miscalculated. She might be able to handle Hampton, but Martin would be a real problem. He was several inches taller than she was, and most of his considerable weight advantage was muscle.

On the other hand, bullies had a cowardly streak, and the best way to make them think twice was to act as if you had no fear at all.

Erica held her ground and kept her face expressionless.

Looking alarmed, Clary stepped into the big man's path and braced a hand against his chest, leaning close to whisper something urgent. Martin glowered at her, seething. To her relief, his aura darkened, though red still burned in it.

Hampton smirked and blew her a kiss.

Erica turned her back on them all and bent to dig in her bag for the plastic case that held her rubber mouth guard. As she slipped it between her teeth, anger began to heat her blood again, replacing the unease.

I've fucking had enough. I don't care if these assholes do kick my ass later, I'm taking Hampton apart. She picked up her boxing gloves and slid her hands into their thickly padded confines, then tightened their Velcro straps. *She's going to pay for what she tried to do to Jake.*

Pounding her gloves together, Erica walked over to the bare open area reserved for hand-to-hand training. When she glanced back, she saw Green helping Hampton wrap her hands.

Erica drew in a deep breath for a count of four, then blew it out slowly, centering herself. She did it again, ignoring the taste of rubber in her mouth from the guard. Rolling her head on her neck to loosen her muscles, she repeated the breathing exercise.

This was a fight she had no intention of losing.

Erica reached for her Talent, letting her awareness of the magical patterns around her increase. The workout room was so brightly lit, it was difficult to see the auras, but she could still make out the swirls of color around the four.

They were all feeling confident. The last traces of yellow had drained away, replaced by the burning blue and greens of pleasure. In Martin's case, there was also the dark rose of sexual excitement. *Man, he's really looking forward to watching Hampton kick my ass.* Erica slapped her gloves together. *Sorry, buddy, you're not going to keep that boner long.*

Green finally fastened the Velcro on the last hand wrap. Hampton put on her gloves and head guard, then slid in her mouth guard. It seemed she, too, habitually carried her boxing gear in her workout bag. That, or they'd intended to pull something like this all along. Given the way Hampton had deliberately goaded Jake, it was possible.

Still, even with the protective gear, Erica knew she couldn't afford to hit the other woman full force. Whether or not Hampton deserved it, the sheriff wouldn't be happy if they put each other in the ER.

Clary clapped his hands, grinning like a used car salesman. "Let's get this show on the road, shall we, ladies?"

Hampton swaggered toward her, aggression and excitement swirling through her aura. There was very little yellow.

Overconfident. Let's see what I can do with that. She started toward her opponent, which was when white light flared on the right side of Hampton's aura, right over her fist.

The woman charged, swinging her right fist out and around in a haymaker obviously intended to lay Erica out before the fight even started.

Pivoting left, Erica ducked under the taller woman's punch. As she came up, she whipped her left fist over Hampton's extended arm to nail the blonde in the side of the head. The impact jarred the length of Erica's arm even though she'd pulled the punch.

Hampton staggered, knocked off balance in the middle of her charge.

For a moment Erica thought the fight would end then and then there, but the woman caught herself. Face contorted in a snarl, she went after Erica in a flurry of punches: a right, a left, another right. Erica tightened her guard, letting Hampton's fists slam into her lifted forearms twice before she bobbed clear of the assault.

The woman wasn't fucking around. Every one of those blows had struck at what had to be full force. This wasn't just sparring. *Hampton means to send me to the ER, then claim it was an accident. "Sorry, Sheriff, guess I don't know my own strength."*

Yeah, no. Sidestepping another haymaker, Erica powered her left fist into Hampton's ribs so hard, she had the satisfaction of hearing her gasp.

Cursing, the blonde swung out a wild backhand that caught Erica across the side of the face. Despite the padding, the blow staggered her. If it hadn't been for the head guard, Hampton would have blacked her eye. *Damn, the bitch can hit.*

The blonde charged in again, aura swirling chaotically as she threw punch after punch. Erica backed up, avoiding some of the blows by pivoting to one side or the other, deflecting others with her arms. Making Hampton chase her -- and tire herself out.

A punch slammed into Erica's shoulder with numbing force, but she ignored the pain and kept moving, backpedaling, weaving, so the bigger, slower woman barely managed to touch her at all. Waiting for the opening she needed.

"Look at her run like a pussy," Martin sneered. "Coward."

No, strategy. Hampton was taller than she was, not to mention more powerfully muscled, but she was also breathing harder, her face going red. *Too much time in a patrol car, too little time in cardio. And I'm going to demonstrate why that's a bad policy.*

Though to be fair, Erica was breathing hard now too, sweat beginning to slick her heaving ribs. No exercise was quite as exhausting as close quarters combat.

A fist streaked toward her ribs. Erica dipped to one side to take the punch on her left arm, then powered in a right, driving up through her thighs and into her hip, slamming her body's momentum into a vicious uppercut that snapped Hampton's head back.

The blonde staggered, but didn't quite go down.

Had to pull it just a little too much, Erica thought in disgust. Hampton might not care if she gave Erica a concussion, but Erica wasn't willing to risk doing the same. *Which probably makes me a dumbass.*

With a screech muffled by her mouth guard, Hampton swung a vicious right at her face. Erica danced back a step...

Her shoulders smacked up against the wall behind her. *Fuck.*

Hampton's mouth pulled wide in a grin that showed black mouth guard, as she rammed a punch into Erica's jaw. Rolling with the blow, Erica slid sideways. Tasting victory, Hampton stepped in, drawing a fist back...

The instant her guard dropped, Erica threw herself off the wall, driving a right at her opponent's jaw with the full weight of her body behind it. The blonde walked right into it. The jolt of the landing punch jarred bone all up and down Erica's arm.

Hampton fell flat on her ass and toppled onto her back.

Erica stared down her a moment, watching her blink up at the ceiling, fighting to breathe. She looked dazed. Which was no surprise. Erica hadn't pulled that last punch at all.

Spitting her guard out into a gloved hand, Erica told Hampton, "You might want to get that looked at."

"Shit!" Alarmed, Green hurried over and dropped to one knee to help the blonde.

Erica pivoted on her heel and started toward her athletic bag. Her ribs ached, and she suspected a bruise was coming up on her jaw. It was all she could do to draw a breath.

Damn, she'd forgotten how much boxing hurt. She'd had more bruising at combat practice -- one or two memorable lessons from Bobby sprang to mind -- but this one hadn't been a party.

She almost walked directly into Martin's broad, beefy chest as he stepped into her path. Erica looked up to see his aura burning dangerously pale with rage. *Fuck.*

Her first instinct was to back the hell up, but that would lose whatever ground she'd just gained. Glaring up at Martin, Erica wondered if she had enough juice left to give him a magical jolt in the aura. She doubted it. The fight had taken too much out of her, and he was fresh. Not to mention fucking *huge.*

"I served two tours killing sorcerers, asshole," Erica growled. "Think about it."

As the words left her mouth, she realized she wasn't bluffing. Exhausted or not, she'd give the son of a bitch enough of a jolt to make him think he'd been Tased. She started drawing magic...

Martin blinked, and she saw the faintest swirl of yellow in his aura. "I ain't scared of you."

"You should be." Giving him a snarl that would've done Clarence proud, she stepped around him, grabbed her bag in one gloved hand, and headed for the women's locker room.

* * *

Dizzy, humiliated, Mary Hampton listened to the door thump closed behind Harris.

"Damn," Green said, shaking his head. "Who knew the bitch could fight like that?"

"You getting your ass kicked was not the plan." Clary pursed his lips, a note of cool disapproval in his voice. "You were supposed to put a hurting on Harris so bad, Nolan would do more than roar. We need something Gable can't blow off."

"I know what the plan was," Mary snapped. "Harris must've put a spell on me or something."

Clary snorted. "She didn't have time." Despite everything, there was a smug note in his voice. He didn't think women had any business being cops. He just fucking loved it when Mary failed, on his side or not. *Prick.*

"You should've let me do it," Martin growled. "She

wouldn't have beat me."

"The idea was to get *Nolan* fired, not you," Clary told him. "You're on thin ice is it is."

That was a legitimate point. If Martin had put Harris down, he wouldn't have stopped until she went to the ER -- or the morgue. His control issues had almost gotten them all suspended more than once. Luckily the other times had been with suspects, and the brass had given him the benefit of the doubt.

Mary dreaded the day someone live-streamed one of Martin's temper tantrums. They'd all be cooked.

Green examined her with concern. "You want to go to the ER?"

She glared at him through the eye that hadn't swollen shut. "Fuck, no. Harris barely hit me." She hobbled over to weight bench and sank down, trying not to wince from the pain in her battered ribs. She'd be black and blue tomorrow.

She fumbled with the boxing gloves until Green sat down next to her and helped her pull them off. She thanked him automatically, then started unwrapping her hands. Despite the wraps, her knuckles throbbed almost as much as her face. God, she hoped that little bitch hurt as bad as she did.

Harris could probably wave her magic wand and make all the bruises disappear.

Fucking Talents. Even when Mary was a kid, her bitch sister always got away with murder thanks to her magic. Janice was the golden child, the Talent who sailed through school, went to college and got a fancy corporate job.

Mary had been the powerless one, the one the magic skipped. The whole reason she'd become a cop to begin with was that she figured she wouldn't have to worry about Talents on the force. Witches wanted nothing to do with cops.

But no sooner had she started making a place for herself than Harris flounced onto the scene with her magic and her pretty face. She'd probably be a detective inside a year, thanks to that fucking Talent of hers.

Mary had been positive she'd be able to kick the little bitch's ass. She'd thought it would prove to that smug fucker Clary that she could pull her own weight, female or not.

Instead, the whole thing had blown up in her face.

Fucking witch. Somehow, someway, Mary was going to turn the tables on her. And next time, she'd make damn sure she didn't lose.

Next time Harris would be the one who bled.

* * *

It was well past midnight when Jake drove through the gates of BFS. Kurt had given him permission to come by whenever he needed to see Clarence. The lion needed him tonight. And to be honest, he needed the comfort too.

He parked his truck in the empty lot and got out, heading for the winding paths that led between the enclosures to the one Clarence shared with his two lionesses.

It had been a long and depressing day. After Erica had broken up with him, Jake had spent the rest of the shift driving around and brooding.

To make matters worse, it had been one of those utterly boring nights when absolutely nothing happened, despite his fierce need for distraction. He'd spent the last couple of hours doing nothing but checking doors on closed stores and businesses to make sure they hadn't been broken into.

As he walked along, Jake considered dropping in to see Kurt and Genevieve. He could use his friend's advice right about now. Unfortunately, it was so late the newlyweds were probably asleep.

Or not in the mood to be interrupted.

Reaching Clarence's enclosure, he opened the

padlocked door into the unoccupied section. Each cage was divided in two sections, so the animals could be kept in one half while the other was cleaned. Jake strode to the door of the second section, drawing on Clarence's night vision to avoid trees and brush in the darkness.

He found his Familiar and the two lionesses waiting patiently for him by the gate.

Unlocking it and stepping inside was the kind of thing that could get an ordinary human killed. Fortunately, Jake was a Feral. As far as all three cats were concerned, he was basically an extension of Clarence.

When he stepped inside the guillotine door, the lion gave one of those miserable moans Jake had been listening to all night. It was considerably louder in person.

"I know." Jake sank to one knee to stroke his Familiar's thick mane. "I'm not happy about it either."

Clarence chuffed, puffing warm breath pungent from the raw turkey he'd had for breakfast. Jake didn't even blink, not after twelve years being bonded to the cat.

"Look, you just can't go roaring at the police. It gets me in a fuck of a lot of trouble."

Clarence rumbled back at him, a borderline growl. Jake had no trouble understanding the subtext, given the images rolling through the cat's mind. "Yeah, I know, Hampton is a huge bitch, not to mention a lousy cop. We still can't threaten to eat her."

"What the fuck did you do that lion?" Dave called. "He's been moaning for hours. There's nothing sadder than six hundred pounds of depressed pussy."

Jake glanced over his shoulder. The tiger stood on the path outside the enclosure, staring at him through the fencing, eyes reflecting gold in the dark. "Long story. We managed to get ourselves in some trouble."

"Yeah, I kind of figured that out when the moaning started." Dave's ears rotated forward in question. "You want to come by the tree house? I just got in a whole crate of those microbrews you like. You can tell me what's going on."

Jake hesitated, absently scratching Clarence behind one fuzzy ear, digging for the itch he could feel through their bond.

Talking to Dave wasn't a bad idea. He could use a dose of his friend's snark and common sense, though he had no intention of admitting as much. Dave would gloat. "Yeah, sure. Give me half an hour with the pride and I'll come by."

"Great. It's unlocked." Dave sauntered off to his own enclosure.

Jake watched him go. He never quite understood why living in a cage didn't seem to bother Dave. His friend always swore the fencing was more for his protection than the public's. *"Otherwise I'd have to sign all those autographs."*

The reality was that people tended to freak if they saw a tiger wandering around loose.

Jake shook his head, thinking of everything Dave had lost when Bobby killed him. "Damn, I wish I hadn't frozen when Bobby triggered that fuckin' spell."

Unfortunately, just like his fight with Erica, it was too late now.

* * *

Half an hour later, Jake climbed the stairs to the enormous tree house that dominated Dave's enclosure, not far from the lake his friend treated as his own private tub. Tigers loved water, unlike other big cats, and Dave spent a lot of time swimming.

The house was built of thick, heavy wooden beams, the better to support two tiger occupants. Since Kurt's Familiar, Stoli, had been killed during one of the terrorist attacks the year before, Dave had it to himself now.

Kurt and his father had spared no expense making the tree house as comfortable as possible for Dave. It had heating, air, electricity -- even Wi-Fi. The furniture consisted of a couch for human visitors and an enormous round tiger bed Kurt had built for the cat on a raised wooden platform. The mattress itself was made of thick rubber to withstand Dave's claws, well-stuffed for comfort.

There was also a fifty-inch flat screen television with a satellite connection, two gaming systems with controllers, and a refrigerator and microwave. There was even a small bathroom for human visitors. Dave made use of the bushes outside, since no toilet ever built could accommodate a six-hundred-pound tiger.

Lounging on his giant cat bed, he looked around as Jake entered. "You get Clarence and the girls settled?" Manifesting a glowing arm, he picked up the remote and cut off the Hulk in mid-roar. "Get us some beers and tell me what the hell is going on."

Wordlessly, Jake pulled the refrigerator door open to discover it was filled with magical microbrews from Potions, along with several containers of Chinese take-out. Kurt must've picked it up for him. It was for damned sure China Garden didn't deliver to the tree house.

Snagging three longnecks, Jake poured two of them into one of the bowls Dave kept on a wooden cart beside the fridge, then carried the bowl and his own bottle over to his friend. He put the bowl down by the bed, then headed for the couch and fell onto it with a tired grunt.

Dave lowered his head to lap thirstily. Though he could pick the bowl up with his manifestation's hands, his mouth wasn't designed to drink from it as a human would.

Jake twisted off the cap on his own and took a long swig, then held it in his mouth to savor the taste of yeast, hops, and magic. His shoulders relaxed for the first time since he'd heard Erica's radio call that she was in hot pursuit. He swallowed another mouthful as the buzz of magic made his situation seem less grim. *Potion's microbrews are worth every dime.*

Between sips, Jake told Dave what had happened. For once, his friend kept his mouth shut and let him tell the whole story without the usual jokes and sound effects.

Finally Dave sat up from his empty bowl, his tail flipping in irritation. "Let me get this straight. You've been together one whole week and you've already broken up?" The tiger shook his great head. "God, what a pair of dumbasses."

Even through the beer's spell, Jake felt a niggle of irritation. Under the circumstances, that probably illustrated just how potent the beer was. "Hey, it wasn't my idea."

"Maybe not, but you didn't exactly help." Dave sighed. "Look, get your head out of your ass and think about it from Erica's point of view for a couple of minutes. She came damn close to getting killed at least five times this afternoon." Holding up a manifested fist, he raised fingers one by one. "Almost got hit by that truck; asshole shot at her *twice;* nearly T-boned a bus; almost ran head-on into a tree. As if that wasn't enough, she wasn't able to catch the people who tried to kill her before they got away, *and* she couldn't sketch the killers."

"That wasn't her fault. There wasn't enough blood on the scene for her to work with." The words rumbled.

"Don't growl at me, Jake," Dave snapped back. "I'm not one of those Goddamn humans you terrorize."

Now his irritation was becoming a serious case of pissed off. "You…"

"Shut. Up. My point is that she'd had a really fucking bad day, *and* she had to watch you almost get yourself shot because you can't keep a leash on Clarence."

Jake's face grew hot. "It wasn't exactly a party for me either."

"Yeah, well, she'd just had two solid hours of

adrenaline overdose. It's not surprising she said shit she probably already regrets. You need to give her time to calm the fuck down."

A little spurt of hope zinged through Jake, but he forced himself to be realistic. "She sounded pretty damn definitive that we're over."

"Let me ask you a question. Do you have four legs and a tail?"

"Occasionally."

Dave lifted an enormous paw and flexed. Three-inch razor claws slid out. "I mean all the fucking time."

Jake sat back and eyed him. "No."

"Do people regularly tell you that you have too many legs for a sexual relationship?"

Wincing, he realized that particular joke must have worn thinner than they'd realized. "No."

"Then it's not too late. You can still get her back -- as long as you don't give up."

"I think they call that stalking."

"Your other car is a lion. You're good at that."

"That's not fucking funny."

"Neither is..." Dave broke into a perfect imitation of Genevieve's voice. "'Ewwww! Too many legs.'"

Yeah, definitely time to tell Gen and the volunteers to drop *that* joke.

"I've seen you two together," his friend continued. "There's so much sexual tension between you, you make my fangs ache."

"There's more to a relationship than sex."

"Yeah, but sex is the reward for getting through the other stuff. And right now, the other stuff includes demonstrating you can control Clarence. After that, you need to show her you know she's capable of defending herself. Do you ever call her for backup?"

Jake stared at him. "The last time I needed backup was a fight with a magic polar bear. Besides, I used her for backup all the time overseas. Erica knows I respect her Talent."

"Yeah, against Caliphuckers. The issue is *now*. You keep acting like she can't handle herself. No wonder she's pissed. You've got to prove you respect her. Lecturing her about not calling for backup was stupid, Jake. She already knew she screwed up -- the sheriff just told her so in front of the whole department. That was one of the reasons she got so mad."

"So I was supposed to let Bob Martin beat her head in to spare her ego?"

"No, you were supposed to treat her the way you would a male cop in the same situation. Would you have said any of that if she'd been a guy?"

"Yeah, because not calling for backup was dumb."

"Really? In the exact same words, in the exact same tone? Because I fucking don't think so."

Jake started to open his mouth, then closed it again.

"And the light dawns." Dave sighed. "You're going to have to repair the damage. Apologize for being an asshole. A little strategic groveling wouldn't hurt. Then let her cool off for couple of days before you try to worm your way back into her good graces. Preferably on your belly."

"I'll give it some thought."

"You'd better. Because I swear to God, if you don't quit throwing away a good thing, I'm going to bite you right in the ass. And I promise you, it'll leave a mark." He shoved his bowl forward with a big paw. "In the meantime, use those opposable thumbs and refill this, would you?"

Jake sighed and did as he was told.

Maybe there was hope for his romance with Erica. Still, he didn't fool himself. She wasn't going to make it easy. "Easy" had never been in the woman's vocabulary.

Chapter Fifteen

Erica woke the next morning with sore muscles and aching ribs from her fight with Hampton the night before. The only bright spot was that the deputy hadn't managed to give her a black eye. She found herself hoping Hampton couldn't say the same.

With a sigh, she rolled out of bed and got ready for work.

The problem with a twelve-hour shift was that sometimes it seemed to go on forever. Yes, the three- and four-day weekends were nice, but you had to get through the weekdays first.

Elsewhere in the county, tensions were running high among both Humanists and Talents, in part thanks to those coming to town for the protests. The result was even more bar brawls, arguments, and general pissiness than usual. Her zone, however, remained stubbornly quiet, leaving Erica entirely too much time to second-guess her decision to break up with Jake.

Her mind kept drifting back to making love to him in the shower. Those big hands caressing her wet skin, cupping her breasts, stroking her nipples. The way he'd loomed over her, his thick shaft pumping deep, their magic interacting in a swirl of energy and heat that made the pleasure that much greater.

The glow of his eyes. The wink of that dimple in his smile. The deep male boom of his laughter. The way he'd stood at her back like a brick wall, hard and steady, a man she could absolutely count on whenever things went to hell.

She had to keep reminding herself of the moment he'd stood there fully manifested, every cop in the room pointing a gun at him. Scaring the fuck out of a bunch of heavily-armed professional paranoids wasn't good for your life expectancy. Which was why a relationship with

Jake just wasn't a good idea for either of them.

And yet her mind kept drifting...

Erica wrapped her legs around his broad back, digging her heels into the thick muscle as she reached for his head with both hands. The short, curling strands of his hair felt like raw silk, cool and tempting...

Dragging her mind out of the delicious memory, she scanned the street ahead of her and listened to the radio, hoping for a call. This would be a terrific time for a good drunk-and-disorderly. Anything to get her mind off her failed love life.

As if on cue, a Toyota ran a stop sign right in front of her. She hit her blue lights and accelerated after him, wondering if she should expect another murder attempt.

The driver promptly pulled over, demure as an old lady headed to church.

Erica got out of the car with her adrenaline pumping, one hand on her holstered weapon as she walked around to the passenger side. With every step, she kept expecting to hear the boom of a shotgun blast.

Instead, the Toyota's windows hummed down to reveal a skinny sixteen-year-old African-American kid, wide eyes fixed on her weapon hand in stark terror. His license and registration shook as he held them out.

Erica let him go with a verbal warning to pay more attention to stop signs. *And yes, I do feel like an asshole*, she thought, watching the Toyota drive slooooowly away.

It was after dark before she finally got the call she was waiting for. "Laurel County, Alpha 25, requesting backup and the assistance of Alpha 22 on a Code 61, possible Code 76. 34 Edgefield Court, Colton."

Erica frowned. From the sound of the call, Katilia Sharp was dealing with a fight. A Code 76 meant a magical crime. She picked up her handset and keyed it. "Laurel County, Alpha 22 en route."

"10-4, Alpha 22."

"Laurel County, Alpha 23, en route," Jake's voice

said crisply.

Great. Just what I need -- another painful conversation. But she lost the snarl as it occurred to her that given the possible magical crime, having Tooth Tank backup could come in handy.

She hit lights and sirens and floored it.

Thirty-Four Edgefield Court was located in a middle-class subdivision in Colton, one of the unincorporated suburbs surrounding Laurelton. The house itself was a Cape Cod, with gray vinyl siding, white trim, and slate blue shutters. Two gabled windows that reminded her of wide eyes stared at the brick split-level across the street.

Sharp's patrol car sat in the driveway, but there was no sign of the deputy or anyone else. Judging by the line of cars parked in front of the split-level, it looked like someone was having a party.

This could get ugly. *Nothing gets a cop's adrenaline pumping like a fight involving a dozen people and alcohol.* That suspicion was reinforced by the sound of angry voices coming from behind the Cape Cod.

Erica got out of her car and keyed her mic just as Jake pulled in behind her. "Alpha 25, what's your 20?"

"We're around back at the gray house," Sharp said, before adding to someone else, "If you don't calm down, sir, you're going to jail." She sounded frustrated, but not as tense as she'd be if she were actively in danger.

"On our way," Erica said, glancing at Jake as he stalked toward her.

He met her eyes, and for a moment his expression lost its stony cop professionalism to pain. Then his face hardened again. "What have we got?"

"No idea. Let's find out." She unsnapped her retention holster as they both headed up the driveway and behind the house.

Once again, they fell into the familiar rhythms established during a hundred patrols. Despite last night's fight, Erica felt something inside her relax at his big, comforting presence.

The house was surrounded by emerald grass and flowerbeds in a wild riot of brilliant blooms, looking like a rainbow brought to earth. Following a hunch, she scanned the yard, detecting a brighter than normal magical glow that suggested an Arcanist had used her Talent to encourage the lush springtime growth.

Glancing back over her shoulder at the split-level next door, Erica saw no sign of magical gardening. There were just the standard daffodils and azaleas, no thicker or more profuse than usual. *Bet it's tough to win Yard of the Month when your neighbor's an Arc.*

"My granddaughter loved that cat," a man's voice snarled. "She cried for days."

"I didn't have a damn thing to do with Tinkerbell dying," the woman snapped back. "I like cats."

"Yeah," sneered another man. "Black ones!"

A chorus of voices started yelling accusations and insults, most of them involving the word "witch."

"Terrific," Jake rumbled.

When they rounded the corner, Katilia stood between two groups of people in a pool of illumination from the floodlights around the house.

On one side stood a ragged half circle of nine or ten people, all of them tense and smelling of beer and grilled meat. Seemed somebody had been having a cookout. Checking auras, Erica saw red swirls of aggression seemed with pockets of yellow fear. If any of the crowd had a magical Talent, it wasn't much of one.

Opposite them stood a harried blonde woman in a T-shirt and jeans, flanked by a pair of teenagers, one a girl in a peach tunic, green leggings and boots, her face pale with anxiety under a fall of long red hair, her hands in fists. She looked maybe thirteen. The other was a lanky young man in a green polo shirt and chinos who seemed vaguely familiar.

All three had power. Based on the pattern of the auras, Erica suspected the two kids were Bards, while the mother was probably an Arcanist.

A handsome, graying man in a polo shirt and black slacks took a menacing step closer to the Arcanist. "Admit it -- you sacrificed Tinkerbell to fuel whatever spell that thing is." He pointed at something in the grass a few feet away.

It was a ring of flat, dark gray paving stones, the kind of semi-permanent arrangement some Arcs used for spell work. Sigils were drawn on the stones in chalk, then erased once the spell was done. Eying the circle, Erica saw the magic wasn't active.

"Terrific," Jake said in a low voice. "Humanists living next to a witch. Because that always works out." He gestured at the young male Bard. "Hey, isn't that Shannon? The server from The Cauldron?"

Erica shot a look at the boy and realized he was right. "Yeah, I think so."

"Oh, great. Well, might as well get this shut down." With that, he stepped into the light of the floods, big and dark in his uniform. "What's going on?" His sudden alpha male bark shut everyone else up.

Katilia turned toward them, her dark face lighting in relief before she hid her reaction behind a professional mask. "Good timing." She turned back to the group and gestured at Erica. "This is deputy Erica Harris, the department's Arcanist."

"Just what we need," the graying man grumbled. "Another witch."

Katilia eyed him icily before indicating Jake. "And that is deputy Jake Nolan. You might remember him from the Faraday Square massacre, where he saved a *lot* of lives."

The whole crowd went dead still, staring at Jake's

gold eyes and Feral patch. To Erica's satisfaction, the anger and aggression quickly bled away from their auras, replaced by the yellows of unease and alarm.

The three Talents, on the other hand, looked relieved.

The gray haired man squared his shoulders and lifted his chin. "I'm Dr. Henry Robertson, and I'm a dentist." He indicated the slim, pretty woman at his side, who wore a long sleeveless maxi dress covered with sunflowers. "This is my wife, Barbara." He rattled off the string of names belonging to his backup. Most of them seem to be brothers or sons of his, along with their wives.

Still with that self-important air he pointed at the Arcanist. "Kim Biggerstaff sacrificed my granddaughter's cat to power a spell she used to call down a lightning strike on my house. It blew out my television. I want her charged with animal cruelty and vandalism."

Erica stared at him in disbelief. "Say what?"

"That spell." He jabbed a finger at the circle. "I told Ms. Biggerstaff I don't like her practicing magic in our neighborhood. The next thing I know, I find my granddaughter's cat with her belly ripped open. When I said something to Kim about it, lightning struck my house that night. It fried my seventy-inch 3D television. That was a three thousand dollar set! I'm suing and I want her charged with animal cruelty and destroying my property."

Erica drew in a deep breath and counted to ten. "First off, that's not possible."

"The tree in front of my house has a lightning scar all the way down where the bolt hit. Take a look at it and you'll see. It's probably dead!" He gave the Arcanist a glower. "She killed it."

Idiots. I hate idiots. "Then you need to have a word with God about that, because I can assure you no human is responsible."

"This is why witches shouldn't be cops," someone

growled. "They cover for each other."

Erica's ribs ached, and she was standing far too close to the man she could never have. She'd had had just about enough bullshit. "When was the last time you heard of a Caliphate sorcerer throwing lightning bolts around?"

The whole bunch stopped muttering, looking startled.

"Yeah, right: never. You know why? Because *nobody* can do that kind of magic. It's impossible."

Robertson thrust a finger in Jake's direction. "*He* turns into a giant glowing lion."

"Which is completely different than tossing *lightning bolts*. Why do you think the Caliphate used magically-amplified chemical explosives? If lightning bolts were possible, I assure you they would have hurled them."

"They brought down the World Trade Center!" Robertson snapped.

"With MEEDs in backpacks planted all over the building."

"The cat is dead!"

"Because, *as I keep telling you*," Kim told him icily, "the neighbor's dog got her. For God sake, you're a dentist! Don't you know bite marks when you see them?"

"Then what does that spell do?" Robertson shot back, pointing at the circle of stones, his face reddening. "I know it's something. This neighborhood has gone to hell since you and those witch kids moved in…"

"You leave my kids out of this!" Her eyes flashing, Biggerstaff jolted past Katilia, fists clenched.

Robertson and his friends surged forward, eager anger burning in their auras as Erica and Jake exchanged an *oh, fuck* look. But before anyone could land a punch, a high, ethereal voice rang out in crystalline purity.

Amazing grace, how sweet the sound…

They all froze. Kim's daughter was singing, her eyes

closed as she belted out the old hymn. Her brother joined in, his surprisingly deep voice winding around hers, adding strength and power to her angelic sweetness.

> *'Twas grace that taught my heart to fear,*
> *And grace my fears relieved,*
> *How precious did that grace appear,*
> *The hour I first believed…*

A wave of goosebumps rolled across Erica's skin. During her childhood, her mother had dragged her to church every time the doors opened, yet she had never heard the old hymn sung with such conviction and beauty. Awe filled her, just as it shone so plainly on the faces of everyone around her.

It was a spell. She could see the magic pouring from the teens to engulf their listeners in a wave of tranquil turquoise blue. In that exquisite peace, it was suddenly possible to sense a vast presence surrounding them. It was not simply good, it was distilled love. Concentrated justice.

It felt like God.

> *When we've been there,*
> *Ten thousand years,*
> *Bright shining as the sun,*
> *We've no less days*
> *To sing God's praise,*
> *Than when we'd first begun.*

> *Amazing Grace…*

Not even Erica was immune. As she listened to the Bards' song, the anger and anxiety she'd carried since yesterday's brush with death drained away, leaving a perfect, floating serenity.

When the last words of the chorus faded away, silence didn't so much fall as ring like a bell.

People stirred and wiped their eyes. "My mother loved that song," Robertson's wife said in a ragged voice. "Maybe you can sing for my church sometime." To Kim, she said, "I'm sorry about all this. It won't happen again." Wiping her eyes with the tips of her fingers, she added to her husband, "I'm done with this Humanist crap. You need to stay off WitchHunter.com. Nobody evil could sing a hymn like that." She stalked past him, evidently headed for home.

"Barbara…" He turned and hurried after her. Looking shamefaced, his family members followed.

"Wow," Katilia said to the two kids, who unsurprisingly looked exhausted. "Want a job? Also, you two seriously need a recording contract."

Shannon gave her a shy smile. "Thanks."

"She's right. That was…" Erica had to stop the clear her throat. "… really impressive." Which was something of an understatement. Her brain was still vibrating like a tuning fork.

"I've never heard anything like that," Jake told the teens. "You've got real talent -- in both senses of the word."

Shannon shrugged, looking uncomfortable. "We got lucky."

"Yeah," the girl agreed. "I tried that with the wrong song once and made the situation worse." She frowned a little. "I just hope Mr. Robertson doesn't come back tomorrow, mad because I used magic to calm them down."

"He won't." Jake's eyes glittered in a way that didn't bode well for Robertson. "I'll head over there and inform him that you saved him from going to jail for disorderly conduct and trespassing. Which was exactly where he was headed before you started to sing."

"Thanks." Kim said, before laying a hand on her daughter's shoulder. "I'm proud of you, Sarah. But you have school in the morning. Better go study."

Sarah rolled her eyes. "Trig. Ugh." She gave the deputies a wave and headed up the steps into the house.

"'Night, everybody. It was nice meeting you."

Shannon smiled at them as he followed. "Thanks, y'all. I was afraid we were toast."

Kim watched her children vanish into the house before turning her attention to the three deputies. "My son's right. If you hadn't stepped in and made them back off long enough to give the kids a chance to sing, it would have turned out a lot worse."

"Glad we could help." Jake flashed both dimples full blast.

"But from now on, it's probably best if you do any spell work inside the house," Erica added.

Kim blew out a sigh of frustration. "It's harder for me to draw on the earth's magic through the floor. But I guess you're right. Using any kind of magic these days is like waving a red flag in front of a bull." She frowned. "And somehow I don't think one song is really going to change Henry Robertson's attitude."

"We'll talk to him," Jake told her.

* * *

All three cops headed over to Robertson's house to reinforce the point, where they found the party was already breaking up. Henry stopped trying to make up with his wife long enough to assure them he'd leave the neighbors alone.

Erica wasn't sure she believed him, though his aura looked as if he meant it. Still, the kids had given him something to think about.

"That was entirely too close," Katilia commented as they headed back to the cars. "There are way too many people in this town spraying gasoline everywhere and lighting matches. I am not looking forward to that protest."

Jake grunted. "Neither is anyone else with any sense."

"Thanks for the help. And watch your backs." Sharp drove off, leaving the two of them alone.

Erica slanted a look at Jake they walked toward their cars. The light of the full moon outlined his profile in silver. Longing stabbed her. *Don't start*. She groped for something to say. "That was one hell of a spell. Must be handy to be able to combine magic like that."

"Yeah. Genevieve's done it a couple times. Kurt even manifested his tiger around her during that last fight with the terrorists."

Erica stared at him. "That sounds about as safe as sticking a fork in a wall socket."

"Yep. But she managed to hold it long enough for him to take Indigo out." Jake glanced at her, and his gold eyes flared, reflecting the moonlight. "It might be worth it to see if she can teach you the technique. I can think of all kinds of situations where it'd be handy if you could draw on my magic."

Their joined magic spun around them like a whirlwind, a dozen shades of violet, rose and blue, his denser, brighter than hers, surging and tumbling together...

Erica swallowed. "I'll give it some thought." They'd reached her car, and she pulled out her key fob to unlock it. "Well, I'd better get back to my zone. Good night."

"Erica." The rough note in his voice made her look back at him. "I want to apologize for the way I acted. I shouldn't have raked you over the coals."

Eying his aura, she decided he meant it. She sighed and admitted, "Yeah, but you had a point."

A flash of hope darted through his aura in shades of electric blue.

Erica winced. *Better to be honest.* "Unfortunately, I'm not sure it changes anything. Neither one of us can afford to get so emotionally involved that we get ourselves fired." She made herself meet his gaze. "You're a good cop, Jake. The department needs good cops."

"We're both good cops. And we're even better together."

Staring up into his glowing Feral eyes, she

remembered the feel of his big hands riding her body. *Maybe we could make it work...*

But she knew better. She was too vulnerable to him. And Bobby had taught her just how high the cost of that vulnerability could be. "No. I can't." Before he could say anything more, she slid into the driver's seat and started the car. As she drove away, she glanced into the rearview mirror to see his eyes glowing in the dark as he watched her go. Pain stabbed her.

Cut it out, she told herself brutally. *It's over. Get used to it.*

To divert her mind from her bitter longing, she thought about Jake's suggestion that she learn how to draw on his magic. Ferals did have a ridiculous amount of power, but they couldn't direct it the way an Arcanist could.

Could I have saved Bobby if I'd known that trick? If she could've kept him from bleeding to death just a little longer, maybe he would've survived...

As a cop, Erica was first responder to all kinds of potentially lethal scenes, ranging from car accidents to attempted murder. If there was any way to keep someone alive long enough for EMS to arrive, that was an ability she desperately needed.

Erica pulled into the parking lot of a church -- closed at this hour -- and started searching her contacts for Genevieve's number. As the phone dialed, she realized it might be too late to call.

Genevieve answered before she could hang up. "Erica! Is everything all right?"

"I hope I haven't called a bad time."

"Nope, your timing's terrific. Kurt's out of town picking up a new cat, and Dave and I are watching Netflix. What can I do you for?"

Erica related her conversation with Jake. "You think you could teach me that technique?"

"I don't see why not. Would you like to come by after your shift?"

Go home to toss and turn all night thinking of Jake, or distract herself with magic lessons until she was tired enough to sleep? "I don't get off until midnight. Is that too late?"

"Nope. Working a little magic is the only thing that wears me out enough to sleep when Kurt's out of town." Gen sounded as if she meant it. She probably did, considering Erica had just been thinking the same thing.

"Great! I'll see you then." She hung up.

The rest of her shift was so quiet it was all she could do to get through get through it without her mind drifting to memories of making love to Jake. The last thing she needed was another crying jag.

* * *

It wasn't quite 1 a.m. when Erica found herself in the center of Gen's backyard magic circle. The two women sat facing each other on a BFS blanket spread over the frosted grass, knee to knee.

Dave sprawled a few feet away, wearing a toothy tiger grin. "Oh, come on," he coaxed. "You know it's a witchy tradition."

Genevieve gave him the side eye. "For the last time, we're not going skyclad."

"A guy can dream, can't he?"

"Furvert," Erica accused, smirking.

"Hey, I'm only human -- more or less." He grinned back, thumping his tail on the grass.

"Ignore him," Gen told her. "Concentrate on the magic." She took Erica's hands in hers and closed her eyes. Her aura suddenly blazed up like a campfire sprayed with gasoline.

Every hair on Erica's body rose as the spell circle activated, the sigils rising from the earth in three concentric rings of color. Slowly, they began to orbit around the two women, casting a soft glow over the spring grass.

She glanced over at Dave -- and was startled to see a man standing half submerged in his body like a ghost. It was Dave's human manifestation, the equivalent of the Clarence version Jake often summoned. The figure glowed so brightly it almost appeared solid. The magic circle must be boosting Dave's power too.

"Reach for the magic," Genevieve said softly. "Open yourself to it. Draw it in."

Obediently, Erica concentrated, sending a curl of her aura toward the slowly rotating sigils. As she neared the closest glyph, it radiated warmth like a campfire. The instant she touched it, the heat blazed up, almost searing her fingers. She recoiled, jerking back her aural probe like someone who'd touched a stove.

"No, not like that," Gen said patiently. "You don't want to drink it directly into your mind. This spell amplifies it too much. You want to use your aura as a conduit -- like this." Genevieve extended a hand, reaching toward the nearest sigil. The magic flowed through her aura and began to burn brighter. "You have to shield yourself with the innermost layer and use the outer to manipulate it."

Examining her, Erica realized it was the outer shell of the Arcanist's aura that shone the brightest, churning with furious color. The layer beneath it glowed more dimly and didn't swirl as fast. "Like a magical oven mitt."

Genevieve laughed. "Exactly."

Nibbling her lower lip, Erica worked to separate her aura into two layers, one directly over her skin, the other an inch or so further out. It was similar to the glowing shell Ferals created when they generated a manifestation. The trouble was, the outer layer was so weak she wasn't convinced she could do anything with it.

Still, it was with a try. She stretched out another tendril and touched it to the surrounding spell's innermost ring. Heat flashed through her, and sweat broke out over her skin. For a moment Erica thought she was going to lose control, but she gritted her teeth and resisted the impulse to drop the probe.

It didn't seem to help. The heat intensified.

"Use it," Genevieve told her. "Burn some of it off and it won't bleed through."

Erica swirled a hand through the air, leaving a glowing trail of sparks behind. The burn backed off. Encouraged, she pulled in more magic and began to draw a serpentine shape in the air. Working fast, she started adding detail -- scales, wings --turning the snake into a dragon and sending it winging around them. Its long tail whipped as it flew, wings flapping, shedding a rain of sparks.

"Oh," Genevieve breathed, "That's nice."

"Too bad I can't do a damn thing with it. It's just a light show." Frowning, she added, "And I won't have access to your spell circle in the field."

"I can teach you how to draw the spell. Besides, the real idea is to be able to pull on a magical power source in an emergency. Like Jake."

Erica snorted. "Jake would fry me like a mosquito in a bug zapper if I tried to manifest his power. You may have the juice to do that, but I don't."

"I don't mean you should try to create a Feral manifestation. You're right -- I damn near roasted my brain trying that trick. I wouldn't even have tried it if Indigo Ford hadn't been holding a blade to my throat. What I'm talking about is establishing a link with Jake, a conduit for his power. You could use it to reinforce a ward or…"

"Or heal?" Erica remembered Bobby's eyes staring up into hers, wild and desperate as he died.

Genevieve hesitated a long moment before she shook her head. "Maybe. I don't really know. God knows you have the control, but I'm not sure you'd have time in an emergency."

"I'm not talking about working a healing spell. I just want to be able to keep somebody from bleeding to death long enough to get to the ER."

Genevieve considered the idea a moment before nodding slowly. "Yeah, that's possible. Let's give it a shot." She gestured Dave closer. "That's your cue, fuzzy."

"One striped Energizer Bunny coming up." The tiger padded over to them, accompanied by a bass drum thump. His human manifestation knelt so that he and Erica were eye to eye. His long, angular face glowed so brightly it almost looked solid.

"You look like a bug zapper waiting for a mosquito," Erica joked, to cover her unease.

Dave's manifestation gave her a reassuring smile. "If I start smelling bacon, I'll let go."

Erica took a deep breath and reached out a hand. He wrapped glowing fingers around hers, and she inhaled sharply, smelling ozone. A psychic buzz vibrated through her, the same feeling she got whenever she touched Jake's manifestation.

Concentrating, Erica worked to split her aura into two layers again before sending a tendril of energy to brush his mystical form. Even shielded, the burn was fierce and immediate. Though the circle's magic was far greater -- drawing as it did on the power of the earth -- Dave's was so much more concentrated.

Erica gestured, drawing another dragon, this one even bigger and brighter than the last, then sent it soaring around them. Drawing on Dave's power as cold sweat rolled down her spine, she fed it more and more magic.

"Take more," he murmured. "Don't be afraid of it. I won't let it hurt you." He grinned. "Jake would never forgive me."

Setting her jaw, ignoring the acid burn beginning to

spread over her skin, she drew in more and more Feral magic, feeding it to her dragon. The magical construct began to radiate a rainbow of colors, growing as it flew, its wings beating faster as it circled them.

An image flashed through her mind -- Bobby staring up into her face, his eyes impossibly wide. His face shifted, taking on the sharper angles of his brother's, until it was Jake staring up at her, begging her to save him. Pleading for forgiveness.

The magic shifted in her grip, escaping her control to plunge into Dave's. Distantly she heard his startled gasp as pain screamed through her, searing the base of her brain in an explosion of light.

She screamed. Everything went black.

Chapter Sixteen

Erica opened her eyes to see a tiger's massive head blocking out the sky. She jerked with a yelp of alarm.

"Hey!" Dave said, as the tiger quickly retreated from her wild stare. "Hey, it's me. You're okay. I think you're okay." He looked around. "*Is* she okay?"

Genevieve bent over her, replacing the cat. Her aura blazed, and Erica felt the feathery brush of her friend's magic. "Looks that way. Are you all right, Erica? Anything hurting?"

Her skull was throbbing in time to her pulse, and she groaned, dropping back down to cover her eyes with both hands. "God, my head is killing me."

"I'm not surprised, considering how fast you were pulling power at the end. You've got to be more careful when you do that trick. Can you sit up?"

Erica lowered her hands and considered the question cautiously. "I think so."

"Let's give it a try." Genevieve took one of her hands and slid an arm around her waist, helping her into a sitting position.

Erica groaned as her head thumped like a bass drum. "That wasn't the smartest thing I've ever done. Got any Excedrin?"

* * *

Fifteen minutes later, she was sitting in Gen's kitchen, polishing off a glass of water to wash down the aspirin.

"You never did have a well-developed sense of self-preservation," Dave told her.

"Look who's talking."

He flicked his tail and shook his huge head. "You and Jake really are made for each other. Both of you are stubborn as hell."

Erica stiffened.

Genevieve's red eyebrows climbed. "Well, that's not a happy expression. What's the King of the Jungle done now?"

"Jumped her because she almost got herself killed." Dave rolled over on his back so that all four feet were in the air. He covered his eyes with one big forepaw. "I swear, that boy could fuck up a wet dream."

"He also can't keep his mouth shut," Erica growled.

The tiger lowered a paw to glare. "You're no better. We've talked about this."

"He roared at another cop!" She held up two fingers pinched together. "He came about this far from getting fired. Cops must keep their heads or people get killed. And Jake and I are really lousy for each other's self-control."

Dave flipped over onto his stomach and stared up at her, ears rotated forward. "So what you're saying is it's not just him who's got a problem."

Erica ground her teeth. "No, it's not just him."

Genevieve headed to the refrigerator and pulled out a bottle of wine and a Mellow Microbrew, then reached into the cupboard for a pair of wineglasses and a bowl. Digging a corkscrew out of a drawer, she asked, "So what are you going to do about it?"

Erica opened her mouth to tell the Arcanist she didn't want to talk about it -- only to realize she did. Maybe talking it out would help. "Only thing I can do. I broke it off."

Genevieve filled Dave's bowl with beer and put it down in front of him, then poured wine in their glasses and strolled over to hand one to Erica. "And that's going to make you happy?"

Erica sipped the wine -- a chilled, fruity Riesling -- before she answered. "Sometimes it's not what makes you happy. It's what makes you less miserable."

Genevieve sat down and sipped her wine, her eyes

very green and direct. "I'll admit a romance with a Feral can be pretty damned complicated. Sometimes it's downright dangerous. But it's got its rewards too." One corner of her mouth quirked up. "And not just *that*."

"But if you want to talk about *that*," Dave said brightly, looking up from his beer, "I'm here for you."

Genevieve reached down, grabbed his twitching tail tip and gave it a tug. "Shush."

"You have no shame," Erica told him with a reluctant grin.

He widened his big gold eyes in an attempt at innocence that failed completely. "Shame? I'm not familiar with this concept."

"Yeah, we noticed."

Gen toyed with her wine glass a moment. "Are you really so sure giving him up will make you less miserable?"

Erica opened her mouth to answer... and hesitated.

"I didn't think so. Maybe you need to give that one a little more thought."

* * *

The next morning, Jake was trying to keep his mind off Erica when the call came in. "Alpha 23, Laurel County dispatch. I have a 911 hang up at 320 Blackstone Court. The female caller was screaming at someone when the call cut out. Sounded like a man."

"Laurel County, Alpha 23 en route." He put the address in his GPS, activated lights and sirens, and hit the gas.

Nine times out of ten, a 911 hang up turned out to be someone's four-year-old playing on the phone. But the raised voices suggested this was a domestic, and domestics could get seriously ugly.

As he accelerated, Erica's voice spoke. "Laurel County, Alpha 22. Backing up Alpha 23. ETA ten minutes." Which put her at roughly the same distance from the address as he was, since it was on the outskirts of his patrol zone.

Evidently, Erica hadn't liked the description of that call any more than he had. Despite the situation, his heart lifted. He knew he was being ridiculous. Any zone partner would do the same. But the more often he and Erica worked together, the more chances he got to prove they *could* work together without him fucking it up...

Damn it, Nolan, keep your mind on the job and off your dick.

Some instinct made him kill his siren as he drove into the development. It was a thoroughly middle-class neighborhood, a blend of new construction and older homes. Which meant absolutely nothing when it came to domestic violence. The middle-class and the rich were just as likely to beat their wives as anyone living in a trailer park.

Jake slowed the cruiser as he approached the house, killing his blue lights. He'd rather not find the homeowner waiting at the door with a gun.

He had the feeling this was that kind of call.

A cranberry-red Honda Accord was parked halfway on the grass, half on the driveway that sloped upward to the house. Black skid marks striped the concrete leading from the garage, as if the driver had peeled rubber pulling out, only to lose control of the car.

"I do not like the looks of that," Jake muttered. He parked the car diagonally in the drive, passenger side toward the house, in case he needed to use the unit as cover from gunfire. "Laurel County, Alpha 23 on scene."

"10-4, Alpha 23."

Clarence? he thought, reaching for their link as he got out of the car. With a soft chuff of greeting, the lion filled his consciousness and burst into full manifestation around him.

Better than a bulletproof vest.

Jake straightened, magically drawing on the cat's acute leonine hearing, and scented the air. He didn't hear anything but Clarence's psychic growl of warning, but there was a faint hint of something magical and rank on the air. He drew his Glock.

A car engine rumbled as Erica's cruiser rounded the corner and pulled into the drive. She parked diagonally next to his car and got out, staring at the house, eyes grim. He gave her a hand signal to follow and moved toward the car.

Erica drew her gun, aiming it at the ground in a two-handed grip as she followed. "Somebody's working some really dark magic in that house." She nodded at the Accord. "And it's affecting whoever's in that car."

Jake stopped, tensing. "Is there a MEED?" The last thing he wanted to do was trigger a magical bomb. *Or, God forbid, a spell trap that drives me crazy as Bobby.*

She hesitated, frowning. "I don't think so. It looks like a feedback loop, as if magic is flowing from the house into the driver and back again."

Closing his eyes, he looked toward the car. A sullen red magical nimbus surrounded the vehicle, but he couldn't tell what it did. Which was no surprise. If Erica couldn't identify it, he certainly wouldn't be able to.

"Shit." Her voice took on an urgent, alarmed note as she switched on her body cam, holstered her weapon, and moved fast toward the car. "Whoever that is, I think they're dying."

"Oh, hell." Transferring his Glock to his right hand, he activated his own body cam, then grabbed his mic to radio Dispatch. "Laurel County, Alpha 23. I need an ambulance at 320 Blackstone Court, and we need backup. It looks like a Code 76 with unknown injuries. I'll give you the details as we get them." As he spoke, he shadowed Erica, ready to step in and surround her with his manifestation if things went sideways.

There was a tense pause as the dispatcher digested the fact that the department's magical heavy hitters were calling for backup on a magical crime. "10-4, Alpha 23." There was a definite *oh shit* note in her voice. "Be advised multiple units are tied up with a search for a subject who fired on a deputy in Daniels."

Fuck. The town of Daniels was on the opposite end of the county. God only knew how long it would take backup to arrive from there. Jake bit back a curse. "10-4, dispatch."

As Laurel County dispatch went into a flurry of radio traffic, Erica jerked the Accord's door open. A woman sat slumped in the driver's seat, her head lolling, her face slack.

"Ma'am?" Leaning in, Erica laid two fingers on the woman's throat, searching for a pulse. "Meghan. Meghan O'Reilly?" So she must know the woman from somewhere. "Can you tell me what happened? Who's doing this to you?"

"Wha..." O'Reilly stirred, then jerked as if coming awake, a note of panic entering her voice. She lifted her hands as if to ward off a blow. "Ray... no, Ray, no... Not Noah..."

"Meghan, who's Ray?" Erica's voice sharpened into a demand. "Who's Noah?"

"My son," the woman moaned. "Bastard's sacrificing... my son... in a spell..."

Oh, holy fuck.

* * *

Muscles clenching, Erica stared into Meghan O'Reilly's bruised face. Somebody had hit her in the jaw at least once. Her skin was pale, clammy with shock to the touch, her green eyes vague over bloodless lips. She didn't look like the same defiant shop owner who'd tried to rip off Wanda Jefferies over a cocktail ring last week. *Did you try to scam the wrong guy this time?*

Because someone was using magic to kill Meghan as well as her son.

"Who's sacrificing Noah?" Erica demanded. She and

Jake needed more information if they wanted to save the boy. If they charged in blind, the Arcanist might murder the kid on the spot, or trigger a booby trap that could kill them all. "What's the spell do?"

"Ray... my boyfriend... He cut Noah. Bleeding him for the spell... Ray's a drug dealer. Al... chemist..." Her eyes narrowed, and dull recognition flickered in her eyes. "Wait... I know you. You're that... cop. Told you I needed the money. Your fault. He's doing this because a' you..."

No, he's doing this because you moved in with a drug dealer with a taste for human sacrifice. Erica drew a look over her shoulder at Jake, still surrounded by the blaze of his manifestation. "Spell must be targeting her through her blood link to her son."

"We've got to get in that house now," Jake growled, his deep voice reverberating with Clarence's magic. "We can't afford to wait for backup. I'm not even sure any's on the way. You call Lieutenant Williams while I put her in the back of my car. She needs to be prone with her legs raised or she's going to code."

Erica stepped back and plucked her department cell off her belt. The Alpha shift supervisor picked up on the first ring. "Harris? What have we got?" Lt. Williams' voice was crisp with tension. He must have been listening to the radio traffic.

She briefed him quickly. "Nolan and I are going in. Judging by O'Reilly's condition, the boy must be in pretty bad shape."

"You think he's still alive?"

"Yes, or his mother would already be dead." She looked toward the house, eyeing the stream of burning red energy now swirling around Jake's patrol car since he'd put the woman in the back seat. It had gotten brighter in the few moments they'd been here, probably building strength as this Ray bled the boy. "I'm afraid if we don't get in there in the next five minutes, we'll be too late. If I can break the spell fast enough, we may be able to save him."

"Do it. I'm mobilizing SWAT and sending all the manpower we can spare from that search. Be careful. And good luck."

They were going to need it.

* * *

The front door was locked. Jake slammed a booted foot into the thick door beside the knob, and the deadbolt shrieked as it ripped through the wood frame. The door flew open to bounce against the inner wall.

Fully manifested, he stalked inside, Erica at his heels. Weapons drawn, they scanned for attackers. "Laurel County Sheriff's Office!"

A short foyer lay before them, an arched doorway on the right. Erica let Jake lead the way. His manifestation would deflect any gunfire short of a sustained burst with an AR-15.

"Keep your fucking distance!" a male voice shouted, pitched a little high with a kind of manic hysteria.

"I don't think so." Jake prowled into the room, the shell of his lion glowing around him.

A pudgy redheaded man knelt in the center of a triple ring of revolving sigils, the sprawled form of a child lying in front of him. The boy looked perhaps nine years old, a sturdy-looking kid in a sweatshirt and jeans. He stared at them, his green eyes dazed in a face smeared with tears, snot and blood. Erica saw a resemblance to his mother in the eyes, the shape of his mouth, and the curve of his jaw.

The two were surrounded by a pool of bright red on the gleaming blond hardwood floor. The blood welled from slashing cuts in Noah's left forearm.

Ahead of her, Erica saw Jake's big shoulders tense inside the glow of his manifestation. "If you don't let that child go, I'm going to fucking *kill you!*" The last two words emerged as a shattering leonine roar that made the killer jump.

Noah cried out, his weak voice inaudible as the house vibrated with the echoes of Jake's rage. Instinctively, Erica reached out with her aura, trying to touch the boy's, soothe his terror. But when her power hit the outer ring of sigils, light exploded in her head as if she'd run headlong into a brick wall.

Yeah, not good. Erica stepped to one side, trying to get clear of the blinding nimbus of Jake's magic. She needed to see the spell Ray had cast.

Erica frowned, eyeing the blazing sigils rotating in the air. The working was far brighter than it should've been, given the power of Ray's aura. Had Meghan helped him cast it?

No, the witch didn't have that much power, either.

Great, a third Talent is involved in this shit storm. But when she reached out with her senses, she didn't detect anyone else in the house either. *Thank God for that. We're going to have our hands full as it is.*

Ray stared at Jake, one hand holding a knife with a wavy blade and a black handle -- an athame, or ritual knife. His blue eyes were too wide in his round face, which was stubbled as if he hadn't shaved in a couple of days. Sweat slicked his skin, and smears of blood marked his forehead and cheeks as if he'd tried to wipe it away with bloody hands.

Judging by the bloodshot eyes in the blown pupils, he was flying very high on something. Probably Tink, the illegal stimulant some Arcs used to enhance their magical abilities. Fairy Dust was addictive as hell, with long term use triggering paranoia, psychosis, and, eventually, heart attacks.

"Keep your distance, Simba, or I'll cut the kid." Ray pressed the tip of the knife against the child's chest. Noah stared up at the bloody blade, his eyes huge and hopeless.

"You don't have a prayer of getting through my wards."

Erica ground her teeth. *We'll see about that, motherfucker.*

Whoever had created that spell circle had known what they were doing. As Jake and Ray exchanged insults and threats, Erica studied its outer ring, looking for any sigil that was dim or misshapen. If she could find a weakness, she could use it to disrupt the spell and crack the ward like an egg.

Damned if she saw one. Each one of the sigils was as sharp and bright as though someone had formed them with laser beams. She didn't...

Wait. *There.* There was a gap between two of the sigils that was a fraction greater than the space between the others. Extruding a tendril of her aura, Erica shaped it into a long, thin spear, drawing on her magic to feed more and more power to the probe. *Good thing Ray's high on Tink and thoroughly focused on Jake, or I'd never get away with this.*

Sweat trickled down her spine, cold against her heated skin. *If it doesn't work...*

She sucked in a breath, gaze fastened on the weakness orbiting toward her. As it started to revolve past, she flung the spear of power into the gap with all her strength.

The probe bounced off the spell like a raindrop against a car windshield. Pain exploded behind her eyes and she staggered, barely catching herself in time to keep from hitting the floor on her ass. *Shit piss fuck!*

She'd never hit a ward with that much juice. *I don't have the power to break it.* Genevieve might, but BFS was on the other end of the county and it would take her half an hour to get here. Judging by the crazed glitter in Ray's eyes and Noah's weakening aura, they didn't have that much time.

The amplification spell!

She sidestepped over behind Jake, who was glowing in full manifestation like something out of a Spielberg movie. He made a damn good distraction.

"Let me in," Erica murmured, knowing his Clarence-enhanced senses would make out what she was saying. Ray didn't hear her. He was too busy ranting about Meghan smoking a cookie of Tink worth four hundred dollars… Suddenly she remembered Meghan's excuse for ripping off Wanda Jeffries, something about owing money to her boyfriend. *Meghan, you have lousy taste in men.*

The back of Jake's manifestation thinned, and Erica stepped into it, knowing Ray wouldn't be able to see her from his spell circle. Leaning in, she murmured, "That's one of the strongest wards I've ever seen. No way can I break it by myself, but Genevieve showed me how to draw on someone else's magic. If I can use yours, I think I can do it."

"Then do it," Jake told her, without taking his eyes off Ray.

"You'll have to drop your manifestation to feed the magic to me. I'll be drawing a lot of juice, and it may knock me on my butt, but it won't hurt me. If I go down, you stay focused on the asshole. Take him down and grab Noah."

It occurred to her that she was giving him orders -- normally the kind of thing that could set a cat off -- but Jake only nodded, his Glock steady in one big hand. "I'll take care of it."

And he would, too. She laid a hand against his broad back, wishing she could feel his body through his winter jacket and bulletproof vest. Pushing the thought away, she reached into his aura as he opened his consciousness to her.

The ability to touch another's thoughts was the core of Feral magic -- the Talent for twining your soul with another's. She felt the soundless mental click of connection, felt for a moment the dark male swirl that was Jake and his cat -- the strength, the stubborn nobility. And under it all, his hunger for her.

The last time we did this, we were making love.

But she didn't have time to explore those seductive feelings, so she stepped back. He thinned the manifestation to allow her to leave, but even as she moved away, a thin shining cord of aural energy stretched between them. The weapon in his hand was unwavering, though Ray's spell could probably bounce a bullet, just like Jake's manifestation.

"I told the little bitch what I'd do if she didn't get my money, but she didn't listen," the Alchemist snarled. "Now she's going to learn her lesson. And so are all of you…"

He broke off as they stepped closer to the rotating sigils of the ward. "What the fuck are you doing?" Ray lifted the athame, his face contorting in a snarl. "Do you want me to kill the brat?"

Peering through the spell's glow, Erica saw Noah's eyes were closed, and he lay too still. At least his chest still rose and fell. *This had better fucking work.*

The gap in the spell drew level with them. Erica sank a hand into Jake's manifestation, which vanished as he blasted his magic into her.

The power slammed into her in a white-hot explosion of pain that seemed to sink fanged jaws into her brain. Teeth clenched, Erica snatched the power into a spear and drove it into the gap between the sigils. As she blasted their joined magic into the spell, the pain increased, burning, blinding until she could have sworn she smelled smoke. Gasping, she jerked away from Jake, trying to break the link between them.

Ray's spell popped like a soap bubble. She tripped as her knees went weak, and she went down hard. Crushing pain tore a scream from her throat -- feedback from breaking the spell.

* * *

From the corner of one eye, Jake saw Erica hit the ground with a cry of pain, but he didn't dare look away from Ray as the Alchemist rose with a screech of outrage. "My spell! What the fuck did you do my spell?"

In the depths of his mind, Clarence roared his need to make the bastard pay for torturing the child. Jake's lips peeled off his teeth as he shared the cat's craving to manifest and rip the bastard apart. He clamped down hard on their shared rage. *We'd never be able to clear the distance in time!*

"I warned you!" Ray's wild eyes narrowed as he raised the knife over Noah's chest. "The kid's dead, fucker! And it's all on --"

Jake shot him. Twice.

The double blast thundered in the enclosed space, hitting his Clarence-amplified ears like a fist.

The Alchemist looked down in shock, then collapsed with a crimson splash. Jake leapt into the circle, boots slapping down in the red puddle of Noah's blood. Kneeling, he unbuckled the Alchemist's belt, dragged it off, and whipped the leather strap around the boy's forearm below the elbow. Pulling his ASP baton, he slid it beneath the strap and began to twist the makeshift tourniquet. The child didn't stir.

Jake laid his fingers on Noah's throat, and was relieved to feel his pulse still throbbing, if dangerously weak. In the distance, he could hear the distinctive wail of an approaching ambulance.

"Fuck, that hurts." Erica sat up, bracing her head with both hands as if it might fall off.

"You all right?"

"Fine. Is Noah okay?"

"No, but I hear an ambulance pulling into the development. I hope they have enough blood on board, or he's not going to make it." Glancing at the sprawled corpse of the Alchemist, Jake wished he could kill him all over again. With a sigh, he rose and started to collect cushions from the couch pushed haphazardly against one wall, evidently to clear a space for the circle. They needed to elevate Noah's legs to keep his blood pressure from sinking any further.

Erica began to swear in a string of profanity so inventive, his Arcane Corps DI would have been impressed. Alarmed, he stared at her as she reeled to her feet. "What?"

"The inner ring of that spell is still active. And it's pumping a hell of a lot of magic somewhere."

"Oh, crap." Jake closed his eyes and looked with his magical senses. Sure enough, sigils still revolved slowly through the air. "I thought you broke it!"

"I broke the ward, but I wasn't able to touch the inner sigil rings." She paced around the spell, studying the sigils in frowning worry.

Jake bent to tuck the cushions under Noah's legs. "What does the spell do?"

"What does any human sacrifice spell do? Collects the life force released when someone's killed."

Jake stared at her, feeling sick. "You mean I just fed it by shooting the son of a bitch?" He frowned. "Wait a minute, that makes no sense. If the Alchemist is dead, who's it feeding power *to*?"

"I have no idea, but I'm going to have to try to break it as soon as I get my magical wind back." Erica stepped into the circle and stalked over to the Alchemist's body, staring down at it. Her eyes widened, and she bent to jerk up the man's T-shirt, baring a hairy potbelly and a pair of man boobs. "Oh, fuck me!"

He rose to look over her shoulder. An upside-down pentagram was tattooed in the middle of Ray's flabby chest. Judging by the raised red flesh around it, the tatt was no more than a couple of days old. "He's a Satanist?"

"No, the pentagram's camouflage for a sigil tattooed underneath. And it's active." She looked up at him, her expression grim. "This bastard was working with somebody."

Chapter Seventeen

It was like taking a hammer to the face. White exploded in his skull, and Adrian Fleming hit the cement floor on his back with a high, wheezing scream of pain.

Backlash. Somebody broke my fucking spell!

Magic poured into him, a searing wave of psychic energy that bowed his spine. He dimly realized it was somebody's life force, being funneled to him through the circle at Ray's house. But instead of triggering the usual intense orgasmic pleasure, the power collided with the backlash, searing his brain.

Adrian convulsed, his body writhing in the center of the magic circle. One kicking foot hit one of the bottles standing around him. It flew out of the circle, hit the wall, and shattered. The air filled with the smell of spilled vodka.

The agony went on and on, feeling as if someone had turned his brain inside out and was dragging it out of his skull through his eye sockets by the optic nerves. Minutes went by before the pain faded enough that he could think again. He lay on his side in a pool of something that stank. Grimacing, Adrian rolled out of the vomit, wiping at his bare skin in disgust. The nauseating reek warred with the potent odor of spilled alcohol.

Panting raggedly, he stared up at the basement's ceiling, trying to figure out what the hell had gone wrong. His head ached as if his skull was the clapper of a huge bell, banging against the bronze walls.

It wasn't the first time he'd suffered backlash, of course. Nobody in his line of work escaped having a spell broken. But it *was* the first time he'd experienced it on top of having someone's life force driven into his brain using the same magical conduit. Turned out that was a really bad idea.

Moving like an arthritic old man, Adrian struggled

to sit up and arrange his legs in the lotus position. Glancing around, he saw only six of bottles of liquor had survived. He'd have to make do.

He badly needed to talk to Ray, but he didn't want to call the Alchemist if the man was surrounded by cops. And he must be, because it certainly wasn't Ray who'd broken that ward.

In the distance, Adrian could sense the two inner rings of the spell circle still operating. That wouldn't last long. Whoever had dropped the wards would take the rest out next.

Gingerly, he reached out along the link to Ray's tattoo. He'd had a hell of a time talking the Alchemist into that tatt. Ray, unlike the Human Heritage suckers, knew exactly what Adrian could do with something like that. He'd agreed only if the sigil was strictly one way. It could send energy *to* Adrian, but Adrian couldn't use it to send *Ray* a magical heart attack. Even so, the Alchemist had charged him $10,000 to piggyback on the sacrifice.

There was no sense of Ray's magic on the other end of the link.

"Well, shit. He's dead," Adrian said aloud.

What the hell had happened? Somehow the cops had gotten wind of the plan to sacrifice the kid. They must have brought Genevieve Briggs on board to break his spell. Harris didn't have the juice.

Damn it. He'd known there was a risk Nolan and Harris would show up, simply because Ray lived in Nolan's patrol zone. That was why he'd sent John Reese and Bill Garrison to the other end of the county to take potshots at cops and bystanders from the thick woods there. The idea wasn't so much to kill anybody as to stir enough shit to keep every cop in Laurel County busy for hours.

It should have worked more than long enough for Ray to take his time with his sacrifices. If things had gone according to plan, no one would have found the bodies until Ray was halfway to Cuba.

Meghan must have managed to get out a 911 call, the bitch. He hoped she'd died hard. That was the whole point of the entire scenario -- not just to kill Noah, but to do it as slowly as possible, inflicting the maximum amount of pain and despair to harvest as much juice as possible from both mother and son.

All of which should add up to a fat magical payoff for Adrian, which he could use for the next step of his plan. It was too bad Ray had died, but in the plus column, he now had even more life force to use. And he was going to need it for the spell he had in mind.

Except… Adrian frowned, considering the psychic sizzle of magic he could feel burning in the background of his consciousness. The life force of three people should have a greater kick than…

"Ray, you fuck up!" he snarled as realization hit. "You didn't manage to complete the sacrifice, did you?" Judging by the amount of power the spell had liberated, it felt as if Ray was the only one who died. Still, if the kid ended up dying of his injuries before Genevieve Briggs broke the rest of Adrian's spell, he'd…

The hammer came out of nowhere and hit him in the face again. It was even worse than the first time.

* * *

Erica sat on the living room floor, ignoring the cops bustling around the crime scene collecting evidence as she struggled to draw whoever had cast the lethal spell. She was willing to swear it wasn't Ray. She doubted the Alchemist had had that kind of power, judging by the strength of his aura.

Unfortunately, the sketchpad, like her mind's eye, remained stubbornly blank. She was having a hell of a time drawing on her magic through the waves of pain throbbing in her temples.

At least she'd finally managed to break the two

remaining layers of the spell circle, the one to gather the life force of Ray's victims, and the second designed to transmit it to the sigil, which would have then sent it to whoever engineered the whole revolting plot. Unfortunately, the second session drawing on Jake's magic had kicked her ass even harder than the first. Her Talent seemed to be out to lunch, which meant no sketch of Boss Asshole.

Though Ray had been the one to spill the child's blood, any third party would have had to use his own blood in the spell itself. But she couldn't pick up shit right now. By the time her magic recovered, the remaining magical energy would be too degraded to use.

Maybe she should have tried the drawing first, but she'd been afraid if she left the spell running, Boss Asshole might use it to kill Noah. She didn't regret the decision, but it meant no sketch.

It didn't exactly help her concentration that her uniform pants were sticky with drying blood, making her stomach roll at the meaty smell of it. She'd never craved a shower more desperately in her life.

At least Noah and his mother were on their way to the hospital, and both were still alive. So far anyway.

"Oh, fuck this," Erica groaned and threw the pad aside. Letting her elbows rest on her knees, she massaged her throbbing temples.

"Anything?"

She looked up to see Grant Sawyer watching her. The detective had a notebook in his hand and a sympathetic expression on his face. "I can tell you one thing. Somewhere in this town is someone who uses magical tattoos to work death magic." Wearily, she got to her feet. "Have the pathologist sample that ink for DNA that doesn't belong to Ray. For the spell to work, the tattooist must have used his own blood to create magical ink. We also need DNA swabs of the spell circle itself. All of which means when we catch him, his defense attorney is going to have a hell of a time arguing his innocence."

Sawyer's brows rose. "Wait, this guy tattoos people with his own blood? Isn't that a good way to spread HIV?"

She shook her head. "Not with the spells on the ink. Arcs have been doing magical tats for hundreds of years. The Corps uses them to amplify the Talents of some of our special ops guys."

Sawyer perked up. "So all I have to do is find out who in this town does magical tattoos, compare the DNA and…"

"Maybe." Erica considered the idea, then shook her head. "But I doubt it." She gestured at the floor, where the crime scene investigator had sprayed Luminol to reveal the remnants of the spell's blood-infused paint. Each of the sigils was intricate and crisply drawn. "Honestly, I don't think any of the local guys would have the juice to do something like this. Laurelton's got some good Arc tattooists, but this working is on a completely different level. It's a dense, professional spell backed by a hell of a lot of power."

He looked disappointed. "So looking for local artists is a waste of time?"

"I wouldn't say that, but don't get your hopes up. This spell looks too much like stuff I saw in the war -- the kind done by serious sorcerers. I wouldn't have been able to break it if I hadn't drawn on Jake's magic."

Sawyer stared at her, his eyes widening. "Are you saying we're dealing with another terrorist?"

Erica winced. If there was one thing guaranteed to spray gasoline on an already explosive situation, it was the prospect of terrorist involvement in Laurel County. The whole county had PTSD from the last time. "I don't know, Sawyer. I hope not."

He scrubbed a hand over his face. "And we've got

that Humanist march next weekend. This town is going to go up in a fireball."

They contemplated that for a moment in glum silence. At last, Sawyer sighed. "You really need a shower before someone shoots cell phone video of you looking like the last reel of the *Texas Chainsaw Massacre*."

Erica glanced down at the stiff, sticky fabric of her uniform. "Well, at least the black fabric doesn't show the blood -- much."

"That's probably the idea."

"Probably. Have you seen the sarge? I need to ask him if I can swing by the house to change."

He smiled crookedly, as if knowing exactly how little she was looking forward to any conversation with Roger Johnson. "I think he's outside talking to Nolan."

Erica winced, wondering how much shit the sergeant was giving Jake. "Thanks. Give me a call if you need anything."

But he caught her elbow as she started past. "You did a good job today. Keep that in mind if Johnson starts giving you a hard time."

She smiled at him, pleased with the compliment. "That means a lot."

As usual at any major crime scene, the front yard and the street beyond looked like a cop convention. Police units lined the road, and crime scene tape encircled the house. At least this time she hadn't had to string it.

Jake and Johnson stood with their backs to her. Based on their stiff posture, whatever conversation they were having wasn't pleasant. Checking their auras, she saw a storm cloud swirl of red in various shades, ranging from irritated to seriously pissed off. Jake was the pissed one.

Yeah, the sarge was being charming.

Which meant an interruption was in order. Erica headed toward them, her own anger working its way through the waves of her headache. "Hey, Sergeant?"

He turned and looked at her, his expression icy. *What, no attaboy for saving the civilians? I'm shocked.*

"You able to sketch whoever cast that spell?"

Erica shook her head. "I wasn't able to pick up anything."

The blue swirling in his aura looked a lot like relief. "That's twice you came up empty."

Jake turned, eyes narrowing, and Erica caught a flash of Clarence's mane around his shoulders. "Considering she just saved a nine-year old and his mother from becoming human sacrifices, I think she came up aces."

Johnson's head whipped toward him, and the two men locked gazes.

Erica's muscles tensed as anger boiled through Jake's aura, brightening visibly with Clarence's contribution. *Oh God, don't manifest!*

"That goes without saying," Johnson said at last, his tone clipped.

Jake's aura dimmed, and his expression flattened with concentration. *He's making Clarence retreat.* Even as her shoulders relaxed, she frowned at herself. Well, of course. She'd seen Jake retain control under a lot worse circumstances than this -- like when he didn't eat Ray.

He's not Bobby, damn it. Maybe I need to quit acting as if he is. Anyway, even Bobby didn't start losing it until he melded with Selena. Cut the man a break.

The sergeant turned to her. "You look like you rolled in blood. Go home and take a shower, then head back to the department. You've got a lot of paperwork to do, and I'm sure the sheriff is going to have questions." He flicked Jake a look. "You too, Nolan. We can't have the civilians think you've been eating people." He walked away.

Erica and Jake exchanged the same what-an-asshole look they'd employed about certain Arcane Corps superiors. Then his brows lowered in concern. "You've got a migraine, don't you?"

"Yep." She sighed. "I couldn't get a damn thing on

that Arc. I didn't have anything left."

"It was worth a try. You do realize they're going to put both of us on administrative leave for at least a couple of days?"

Erica straightened in alarm. "They don't think the shooting was justified?"

He waved that concern away. "No, no, leave's just standard procedure in any officer-involved shooting. For one thing, they figure you need a couple of mental health days after something like this." He grimaced. "And they're right."

"You're not feeling guilty about killing that asshole?"

"God, no. I'd rather have arrested him, but he didn't give me that option." Jake frowned, troubled. "I just keep thinking about what Noah went through, how terrified that child must've been. Judging by all those shallow cuts and the amount of blood, Ray spent at least half an hour torturing him. Makes me want to kill the bastard all over again."

"Can't say as I blame you."

He sighed. "I keep second-guessing every additional minute we took. Even putting Noah's mother in the car left him at the creep's mercy a few minutes longer."

"I know, but breaking a ward like that is like defusing a bomb. It could've been designed to kill Noah the minute we tried to take it down. I had to know what it did before I could touch it." She raked both hands through her hair. "Do I wish Genevieve had been there? Oh hell, yes. She probably could have broken it the minute she walked in the door."

Jake met her gaze with such intensity he seemed to stare at her soul. "Erica, I would not have wanted anyone else at my back today. And that includes Genevieve. She's come through in some nasty situations, and God knows she's got power, but you've got the training. And you're tough."

Even with her temples banging like a kettledrum, the compliment made her smile. "Thanks." She hesitated. "You kept a handle on Clarence just now, didn't you?"

"Yeah. Yeah, I did. I'll admit he wanted to take a bite out of Johnson, but we're not stupid. Both of us learned our lesson the last time."

"And that wasn't the first time today you controlled Clarence either. After I dropped the ward, I could see him trying to manifest, even as strung out as I was. I could feel how much he wanted to rip Ray's throat out."

"He wasn't the only one," Jake admitted.

"But if you'd manifested, Ray would've stabbed Noah before you managed to clear the distance."

"Yeah, I had to haul pretty hard on both our leashes in order to shoot him instead."

Erica looked him in the eye and told him the truth she'd realized when she watched him take Ray down. "I was wrong when I said we couldn't afford a relationship. I think… I think part of it was because I'm afraid." She looked away. "Losing Bobby…"

"Yeah?"

"I think Dave's right. I think it's time I grow a pair."

He pretended to recoil in horror. "Oh, God, don't do that!"

She gave him the side eye. "Do you and Dave have the same gag writer? Jake, I'm saying I want to try again."

"Yeah?" Jake's aura lit up like the Fourth of July in shades of electric blue delight.

"On one condition…"

"What?"

She smirked. "You promise not to eat anybody."

Dimples flashed. "With one exception, I hope."

"Just one."

* * *

The rest of the day was as exhausting and frustrating as she expected. First came the paperwork -- and there were reams of it for an officer-involved shooting -- then the interrogation. To avoid a possible conflict of interest, Sheriff Gable had asked the South Carolina Law Enforcement Division, AKA SLED, to handle the investigation. SLED was basically South Carolina's answer to the FBI.

Agents Thomas Romero and Sabrina McPherson were both scrupulously polite and painstaking in their questioning, which meant Erica spent an hour narrating the body cam footage to explain what she'd done. Fortunately, Romero was a Talent, and both were specialists in investigating magical crimes.

"So far it all looks pretty cut and dried," Romero told her. A distinguished older man, he was a veteran Arcanist who'd retired from the Corps to pursue a second career in law enforcement. "There are a few more things we need to check, but it seems to me you're in the clear." He smiled at her, dark eyes crinkling at the corners. "Good job breaking that ward, by the way. I saw the crime scene photos of that thing. It must've been a bitch to take down."

She grimaced. "Pretty much."

Romero's partner, a plump African-American woman with shrewd, cool eyes, gave her an approving nod. "That boy and his mother owe you their lives."

Erica's grimace morphed into a smile. Noah was out of critical condition, and his mother had been released from the hospital. "Thanks."

When the agents finally declared themselves satisfied, Erica found Jake waiting in the Alpha bullpen finishing up his report on the shooting. She gave him a searching glance. "How are you doing?"

He straightened and rolled his shoulders as if his back hurt. "Could've been worse. Those SLED agents could have been Humanists, which was what I was afraid of." With a sigh, he shut down the laptop. "Let's get out of here before somebody remembers another form I have to fill out."

Outside, the moon hung cold and bright in the cool April darkness. Erica paused, drawing a deep breath of the fragrant air.

Jake slanted her a look. "Would you like to come over?"

Her head was pounding, and she felt battered, wrung out. And yet she longed desperately to feel those strong, warm arms around her. Wanted it so badly she was tempted to kiss him right now, parking lot cameras be damned.

As if mistaking her longing for hesitation, he took a step closer. "I'm not asking you to make love tonight -- I know you're not up to it. To be honest, I'm not either. I'm fried." He met her gaze, his eyes reflecting the glow from the nearby streetlamp. "I just need to hold you." The words came out so low and rough, they almost thrummed. "I need to sleep with you in my arms -- or I'm not going to be able to sleep at all."

"God, so do I. And I really want to get the fuck away from the security cameras, so I can kiss you. Let me swing by the house to shower and pack an overnight bag. Give me about forty-five minutes."

His face lit despite his obvious weariness. "I'll have a couple of Mellow Microbrews waiting."

"Bless you."

* * *

Jake met her at the door wearing only a pair of faded jeans, his blond hair damp and dark from his own shower. She paused on the doorstep, just drinking in the sight of the muscled Vee of his chest, broad and dusted with golden hair.

"Hi. Didn't you say something about a kiss?" he asked, dimples flashing.

With a growl of strangled need and desperation, she went into his arms. Jake tasted of toothpaste, as the scent of shampoo, magic and masculinity flooded her head.

Her magical senses detected Clarence's chuffing somewhere in the distance.

Jake drew her backwards, freeing one hand just long enough to swing the front door closed. She barely heard the bang, too intent on the taste of his mouth, the press of his erection. He felt so damned good. Why in the hell had she stayed away?

When he turned her toward the living room, she wrapped her arm around his lean waist with a sigh. "You know it's been a bad day when you need three showers."

"At least there was less blood the third time." He grimaced. "Though I still reeked. Nothing like an interrogation in a Kevlar vest to give your deodorant a workout."

She frowned. "They told me it was cut and dried."

Jake took her hand and pulled her after him into the living room, where two cans of beer sat on the coffee table. Handing her one, he said, "Yeah, but I still shot a man. They couldn't go easy on me."

Erica settled down on the couch next to him, admiring the broad, muscled contours of his bare chest. Her gaze slid downward, and her eyes widened in anticipation at his impressive erection. "Why, hellloooo there." With a mischievous smile, she reached to trace her forefinger along the length of his bulging zipper.

Jake caught her wrist and gave her a crooked smile. "I don't think that's a good idea."

"My headache's really not that bad."

"Yeah, no. Last thing I want you to feel making love to me is pain. I'm not into that."

"That's not what I heard. Wasn't there that nurse…"

To her delight, his cheeks reddened. "Bobby told you about that? Anyway, she asked *me* for that spanking."

"The way I heard it, you were more than happy to give it to her."

"That was then. Now I'm into whatever you're into."

"Maybe I'm up for a little adventure too." She gave him a seductive smile, ignoring a warning pulse from her temples.

"Ask me sometime when you don't have that headache line between your eyebrows, and I'll be happy to play whatever games you want." His smile turned dark and wicked. "In fact, there's nothing I'd like more. But not tonight."

"So what do you want to do tonight?"

"We could try something really radical. Talk. Drink a beer or two. Unwind." He lowered his head, a smile curving his lips. "Kiss."

Erica smiled back. "Sounds good."

* * *

An hour later, pleasantly relaxed from a couple of Mello Micros, they stripped and settled down in Jake's big bed. Erica half expected the moment to segue into delicious sex, and headache or not, wasn't averse to the idea.

He arrested her roaming hands with his larger ones. "Sleep. I promise to make it up to you in the morning." His voice dropped into that wonderful low register he used. "I want your undivided attention when we make love."

"Hmmmm. Well, okay, if you insist." With a sigh, Erica wrapped her arms around him, nestled against his hard warmth, and closed her eyes, listening to the comforting thump of his heart.

A soft psychic rumble sounded in the darkness, and she glimpsed Clarence's maned head above them in a swirl of golden light. He chuffed at her and vanished.

As Jake's breathing deepened and slowed, it occurred to her Bobby would never have turned down sex if she'd offered it, headache or not.

Three days. They had three days of administrative leave. Then after that they'd need to work the Humanist protest -- it was going to be all hands on deck for that little party. But in the meantime they'd have three glorious days together. Nobody shooting at them, no Humanist assholes giving them a hard time.

Whatever will we do with ourselves? Erica grinned into the dark.

Chapter Eighteen

Erica woke lying on her side with the feel of Jake's big body warm and strong along her back. His erection pressed against her ass, solid and tempting. "Good morning." His voice rumbled in her ear, low and rough with sleep.

Her breath caught. "Good morning." She tried to turn in his arms, but his grip tightened, holding her in place. When she rested one hand on his biceps, his upper arm was broader than the length of her entire hand. He nuzzled her hair, his breath rolling over her skin in warm gusts.

"Have I mentioned how much I love the way you wear your hair?" He bit gently at the curve where neck met shoulder, then began to press a string of tiny bites along her nape. "It leaves so much sensitive skin so delightfully bare." His teeth closed on the lobe of her ear. "It's really hot."

"You find everything hot."

Jake chuckled, the sound so dark and suggestive she felt her heart begin to hammer. "Only where you're concerned." He propped himself on one elbow, but when she again attempted to turn to face him, he held her still. "You're not going anywhere. I've finally got you where I want you."

She grinned over her shoulder at him. "Yeah? What exactly do you have in mind?"

"Oh, this and that." One big hand swept the length of her body, long fingers dancing over her ribs with the perfect pressure to make her squirm. Jake hummed in approval. "Sensitive. This has possibilities."

She licked dry lips, watching the rose and violet of his aura swirl around her. "For what?"

"This and that." He found the jut of her hipbone and swirled a circle around it, tickling. She laughed and squirmed, fighting his hold, but he held her still with no effort at all. Erica wasn't exactly weak, but she was nowhere near a match for Jake Nolan. Somehow the reminder of how much stronger he was made her breathless. She felt hot, restless, and wet.

Jake rolled his hips, and she felt his erection grind against her ass. She gasped as her excitement spiked.

He leaned down and sampled the curve of her ear again, his breath gusting hot against her skin. His teeth closed over her lobe. Tugged, just short of stinging. One hand reached up and curled around her throat. Not tight. Just hard enough for her to feel the calluses on his palm, on those long fingers.

His free hand found her nipple, fingers trapping it, tugging with the perfect pressure to send sweet little darts of delight up her spine. He cupped her in his palm as he milked the eager tip, first gentle, then hard, until her eyes slid shut. The rose of her own arousal wheeled before her eyes. "I've always loved your breasts." His voice sounded even deeper than usual. She could feel the reverberation of it in his chest, against her back. "Your skin's like silk. And these little nipples drive me crazy."

"Your body's not bad either." The teasing tone she'd intended was ruined by the strangled note in her voice.

"Why, thank you." Jake found a cord in her neck, nibbled, breathed. She shivered. "I was wondering," he asked, his breath gusting warm on her throat, "Did you mean it when you said you were interested in a little adventure?"

"Depends on what kind of adventure you've got in mind."

"Well," he drawled, "I couldn't help but notice you seemed to like it when I pinned you down in the tub and took you from behind."

She swallowed. "It had its moments."

He inhaled as if drawing in her scent like a cat.

"Apparently. You seem to be getting wetter."

Oh boy. "Maybe."

"How'd you like to try little bondage?"

Her heart was pounding so hard, she was pretty sure he could feel it. "Oh, God, tell me you don't have a red room…"

He chuckled, warm against her ear. "You don't need a dungeon when you're sufficiently creative."

"Yeah, you've never suffered from a lack of imagination."

He released her to roll out of bed. As she twisted around, he snagged the belt from the pants he'd left on the bureau the night before. When she gave it an uneasy blink, he rolled his eyes. "Please. I said bondage, not discipline."

"Do I need to give you a safe word?"

He grinned back. "Actually, that's not a bad idea."

Erica dropped her gaze to the jut of his erection. "Kielbasa."

He laughed and pounced, but she flipped clear and scrambled off the bed to dart for the door. "Sorry, not that easy!"

With a growl, he leaped after her. "We'll see about that."

Laughing like a loon, Erica raced down the hallway toward the stairs, Jake in hot pursuit. The wall ended in a balustrade on one side, and she vaulted over it, hitting the floor five feet below. She took off like a rabbit an instant before the considerably louder thump as Jake hit the ground and pounded after her. The buckle of the belt jangled merrily as he roared, "Don't make me chase you!"

She laughed and spun aside, narrowly avoiding his hand as he snatched for her. "Who are you kidding, lion boy? You love a good chase!"

"I must -- I've been chasing you long enough." He pounded after her as she veered into the great room. She darted around the sectional couch, but he vaulted over the back of it to land squarely in her path. Yelping, Erica threw herself aside, but he tackled her, taking her down right on top of the huge beanbag chair that sprawled in front of the TV.

Erica tried to throw him off, but the enormous bag was full of memory foam beads, and she couldn't get any leverage. Between its enveloping softness and Jake's massive everything, she found herself pinned facedown, giggling helplessly as he wrapped the belt around her wrists and buckled it.

Then he jerked upright to throw both arms in the air in triumph. "And *that's* how I won the calf roping contest."

"Calf roping?" Lifting her head off the bag, Erica aimed a mock glare at him over one shoulder. "Really?"

"Wanna see my buckle?"

"I'll buckle you." She got a foot free and kicked at him. Laughing, Jake jumped back off the bag, his cock bobbing. It might have looked a bit silly -- if the veined shaft hadn't been even thicker than the flushed, bullet-shaped head. And if she hadn't remembered how it felt, grinding hard into her...

He grabbed her hips, hoisted her butt in the air, and nipped her on the ass.

"Jerk!" she squawked in outrage.

But the squawk became a gasp as he repositioned her ass up across the bag and spread her thighs. "What are you doing?" she demanded, her voice a little muffled by the fabric.

He stopped and craned his neck to look down at her. "Can you breathe?"

"Um, yeah."

Jake rolled her forward her over the bag until her face was free of the fabric and her butt was in the air. Spreading her thighs wide, he nuzzled between them, his hair tickling her thighs.

Erica's eyes widened as he went exploring, breath gusting over delicate folds. His mouth covered her pussy, hot and wet, making her sigh in delight. His tongue tip circled her clit, then flicked back and forth. Each tiny flutter sent a pulse of pleasure surging up her spine.

"Jake!" She moaned and squirmed, but he planted a big hand on either butt cheek and held her still like Clarence pinning a rabbit.

Engulfing her clit, he began to suck in strong, hard pulls as he tongued the exquisitely sensitive nub. Erica jerked, longing to clutch a fistful of the bag and anchor herself against the storm of delight, but she couldn't escape the belt. She could only gasp as he painted fire over and around her clit, each stroke increasing the pleasure and building her maddening arousal.

Writhing in the soft grip of the enveloping bag, Erica bucked, hungry for the orgasm blazing just out of reach. She didn't think she'd ever gone from 0 to 60 so fast in her life…

He released her clit to sweetly ask, "Having a good time?"

The orgasm receded. "Don't stop!"

"Yeah, I've got other plans." Jake flipped her over. She lifted her head to glare at him incredulously as he gave her a smug and wicked grin. "And since you're the one tied up and I'm not, I'm in charge."

"You…" But before she could finish the sentence, he landed on top of her like Clarence on that hapless bunny, hands braced on either side of her head, knees astride her thighs. He loomed over her with a devil's grin and dipped his head toward her mouth…

Frustrated, she snapped at his lower lip. Cat-quick, he jerked out of range. "Uh-uh. Bad witch." Dropping onto his elbows, Jake grabbed her head between his big palms, immobilizing her.

Breathing hard, ferociously turned on, she tried to glare up at him. But as the gold glow of his eyes burned into hers, fierce and hypnotic, she swallowed, hunger drowning irritation. "Jake. God, you're driving me crazy!"

"Good." He kissed her slowly, and she tasted herself, salty and little astringent. His lips felt velvet-soft, seductively warm and wet, coaxing hers open for the stroke of his tongue. Erica moaned, kissing him back, her tongue swirling around his. The yielding cup of the chair pillowed her body, keeping their combined weight from crushing her arms.

His free hand slid down the length of her body, found the point of her nipple. As he toyed with the sensitive flesh, their tongues danced, lips pressing and stroking. She could feel the solid weight of his cock against her belly, and her cunt clenched in frustrated need. Helplessly, she began to roll her hips against him, craving the rough stroke of his shaft, the delicious grind and dig.

When he broke the kiss at last, she groaned, "Fuck me. For God sake, Jake…"

"Not yet," he murmured and began to kiss his way along the line of her jaw, down the curve of her throat. "I want to make you as wet as you've made me hard."

"Jaaaake!"

Gold eyes flashed up at her. "Don't expect sympathy from me after all the years you've made me wait." His mouth found her nipple, teeth closing just short of pain, lips tightening to suckle hard.

Erica's eyes rolled. "God, I've been a moron."

He laughed, an intimate puff of warm breath on her breast. His tongue tip drew a swirling pattern over the areole, then flicked back-and-forth over the tip, each sweep sending another arousing jolt through her body.

She threw her head back, grinding it into the bag,

hissing through clenched teeth. "Jake. God, please…"

"I'll never get tired of listening to you beg."

Her hands curled into fists, gripping the fabric of the bag so tightly her knuckles ached. Her hips rolled as she writhed, maddened, hunching furiously against his belly and the head of his shaft so maddeningly out of reach. "Jaaaaaake!"

"You talked me into it." He thrust himself up on his palms and moved into position between her thighs. Reaching down with one hand, he positioned his cock at the opening of her pussy and entered her slooooowly, his jaw tight as if he fought not to drive in up to the balls in one lunge.

Erica sucked in a breath at the feeling of being filled an inch at a time, slick walls yielding to his powerful thrust. Lifting her legs, she wrapped them around his hips to dig her heels into the hard muscle of his ass. Urging him on.

Clarence rumbled, a psychic vibration against her aura. Jake's pupils dilated until only a thin ring of gold surrounded them. Not quite human.

Finally, he was seated as deeply as he could get, and she was deliciously full of him. He seemed to cover every inch of her with hard, sculpted muscle and warm satin skin. She felt surrounded by him.

And God, it was sweet.

Jake stopped and bent to kiss her. With a moan, she opened her mouth as she'd opened her body. Still kissing her, he drew out, his shaft feeling endless as it retreated from the tight clasp of her pussy. Erica stared up into his face, the tight line of his jaw, his burning gold eyes.

In again, hot and sweet and slick, filling her so full, the sensation hovered suspended between pleasure and pain. Licking her lips, she unwound her legs from around her hips, the better to brace her feet on the bag and grind upward, meeting his thrusts. Something about the position of her body and his caught her clit with the perfect pressure, the perfect friction. He picked up the pace, muscle rolling and working in his broad shoulders and strong arms.

Inner muscles begin to pulse and clamp, her skin tingling with the electric build of the orgasm.

"God, Erica," he rasped, his voice sounding ragged. "You drive me crazy."

"Yeah, yeah, you…" But she couldn't manage anything more coherent than that with the orgasm building momentum, every hair on her body rising, her heartbeat pounding like a kettledrum, her breath rasping.

Erica's eyes slipped closed to savor the feel and the smell and the taste of him. She heard a distant leonine rumble, and magic flared in a sudden psychic explosion, her aura reacting to his, a crackling discharge leaping between them. Shades of violet and rose exploded behind her closed eyelids as leaping magic showered sparks through her consciousness.

She convulsed, the breath tearing out of her in a muffled shriek as Jake bellowed, shoving to the balls. Coming, pouring himself into her, the magic bursting around them like tsunami waves throwing great fountains of light.

Clarence roared in her ear, the sound deafening as it triggered a deeper magical detonation that wrung more pleasure from Erica's straining body. She arched upward into the heat and hardness of Jake's cock shoving deep.

As their bodies heaved and writhed, their magic twined together, until it seemed their very souls flowed together, melded as Ferals meld, magic blending cat and man and woman.

In that shining moment, Erica *felt* Jake. Felt all that he was -- the courage and the intelligence and the aching loneliness. Felt his need for her. A need that reflected hers. She'd been alone since she'd been a bullied child seeking the love and approval of a mother who'd had little time for her.

He'd longed just as desperately to be more than the responsible big brother riding herd on reckless Bobby. Longed for someone to love him for *him*. To love him and his cat, accepting them both as the package deal they were. Someone with the intelligence and the courage to fight beside them.

Jake had recognized Erica as that woman from the first. It had frustrated him unbearably that she had seen him only as a reflection of Bobby for entirely too long.

Now at last she saw *him*.

Panting, her heart thundering, Erica stared up into Jake's strong, handsome face as he stared down into hers. Feeling his heart hammer through the muscled wall of his chest where it rested on hers, as a drop of his sweat landed between her breasts. But it was his eyes that riveted her, the radiating rays of gold and honey and amber as their gazes locked.

"I love you." She said it even as he did, the words a ragged, unplanned chorus.

Erica's jaw dropped, and she stared up at Jake, who stared down at her, looking just as stunned. "You do?" she asked.

"Yeah." Jake reared off her, out of her, and flipped her over on her belly. As she gasped into the bag, feeling stunned as the world seemed to swoop and whirl around her, he whipped the belt off from around her wrists. Then she was on her back again with no memory of turning over, and Jake's mouth covered hers in a kiss that blazed violet and rose. Moaning, she wrapped her arms around his neck and kissed him back, watching sparks dance behind her lids as she wound her legs around his waist. Holding him hard in the cradle of her body, feeling his muscled arms secure around her, feeling as if he never intended to let her go.

When he drew back at last, he rested his forehead against hers. For a long moment, neither of them made a sound.

Until Erica licked her dry lips "What do we do now?"

"Fuck if I know." His mouth curved in a brilliant smile. "But I'm looking forward to figuring it out."

She found herself grinning back. "Me too."

* * *

They were cleaning up the breakfast dishes when the doorbell rang. A dog barked, and Jake groaned in frustration. "Damn it, Ma. Couldn't you call first?" He dropped the washrag in the sink and headed toward the front door to a chorus of frenzied barking. The dogs sounded less warning than ecstatic. Erica followed, curious to see the source of the canine racket.

Jake opened the front door to reveal a blonde woman with Feral gold eyes flanked by a pair of German shepherds the size of Shetland ponies. Judging by the eye color, both animals were Familiars, one with standard shepherd markings, the other a deep, gleaming black.

"So you *are* alive." The middle-aged woman lifted a blonde brow at him and stepped inside, accompanied by a good three hundred pounds of enthusiastic Feral canine. She was comfortably plump, dressed in jeans and a blue sweatshirt printed with the white silhouette of a German shepherd and the words *Nolan K-9 Training*.

Erica had seen photographs of Jake's mother often enough to recognize Diane on sight. Though her face was round where Jake's was angular, her mouth and the stubborn angle of her jaw looked very much the same. So was the intelligence in those gold eyes. She wore her streaked blonde mane tied back in a ponytail that bounced jauntily as she rose on her toes to kiss her son on the cheek. "Considering that god-awful story on the news last night, I was afraid you'd been sacrificed to Satan."

"I told you I was fine." Jake knelt to pet each of the

dogs and get his face thoroughly licked.

"That was a text," his mother retorted, studying Erica with interest. "That doesn't count." She thrust out a hand. "Since it seems I failed to instill any manners whatsoever into my son, I'll just introduce myself. Diane Nolan. And you must be Erica. I've heard so much about you."

Her grip felt strong, steady, and warm around Erica's. "I can definitely say the same. I wish I could've come to Bobby's funeral."

"It was the middle of a tour. I understood." Grief shadowed the older woman's eyes before she made an obvious effort to banish it.

The two dogs looked up at Erica, their ears pricked with interest, though they were too well trained to jump up or jostle closer. No stranger to dealing with Familiars, she presented her hands for a good sniff. They obliged her thoroughly with obvious interest.

"Want breakfast?" Jake asked his mother, as he turned to lead the way back into the kitchen. The dogs followed at their heels, claws clicking on the wooden floor. "There's bacon. And I'd be happy to scramble up some more eggs."

"Nah, I had a sausage biscuit. Anyway, I can't stay long. I'm on my way to a planning session for my Talents' Rights group." She threw Erica a considering look. "But a cup of coffee would be welcome."

"Sure." He headed for the coffee pot, which still held a few cups.

Diane studied him a shade anxiously as he reached into a cabinet for a mug. "The reporter last night said you were on administrative leave. You're not in any trouble, are you?"

"No, it's just standard procedure at the department when there's an officer-involved shooting."

She blew out a breath in relief. "That's good.

Everybody's gone so nuts with anti-Talent hysteria, I was worried they'd be gunning for you."

Dimples flashed. "I'm the hero of Faraday Square, remember?"

"That's not as comforting as it used to be, what with all the nasty crap VirginiaLaurel is saying. That old bat is determined to stir up as much anti-Talent resentment as possible, so she can ride it into the governor's mansion." Diane dropped into a kitchen chair, the dogs flopping at her sneakered feet. "Which is why we're trying to mobilize as many counterprotesters as we can."

Jake hesitated as he handed her the filled mug, then pushed the cream and sugar closer. "Mom, I hate to ask this, but would you consider staying home? It'd be one thing if the protestors were garden variety Humanists, but we're expecting a contingent of Human Heritage, and those guys are violent. The sheriff is afraid it's going to get ugly. We're not going to allow anyone to bring guns or weaponry, but things could still get out of hand."

Diane's blonde brows lowered, and her chin took on a familiar jut Erica recognized from Jake's in a similar stubborn mood. "I have no intention of letting those jerks scare me off. The First Amendment still applies to Talents -- at least for the moment. But if we keep rolling over for these assholes, we're all going to wind up in camps."

"Nobody's going to put us in camps, Mom."

"Did you listen to the news last night? That's exactly what some HHers are saying -- that we all sacrifice children like that fruit loop you shot. And since the Humanists got that damned Talent Registration Act passed, they know who we are and where to find us. It would take no effort at all to round us up and stick us on cattle cars."

"There are five million Talents in this country, and millions more who carry the gene for one ability or the other," Jake reminded her, his tone patient. "Logistically speaking, there's no practical way they could pull something like that off."

"I don't care!" At Diane's feet, the dogs growled softly, reacting to her anger. "I'm tired of people suggesting I've made a pact with the devil. And I swear to God, I'm gonna slap the crap out of the next person who asks me if I'm a terrorist."

"Please don't. I'd hate to have to bail you out of jail on assault charges."

Diane opened her mouth for an indignant reply, then caught Erica's gaze and closed it again, a blush spreading over her face. "You probably think Jake's mom is a crazy person." Sighing, she sipped her coffee as if making a conscious attempt to calm down. "I'm sorry, dear. It's just... you wouldn't believe what people have been saying on my Facebook page. And don't even get me started on Twitter. I'm fifty-seven years old, and I've never felt this way. Like there's a target on my back." She forced a smile. "Though I realize I have no business complaining to someone who was shot at a couple of days ago."

Erica gave her an understanding smile. "Believe me, I get it. A lot of people are saying really irresponsible crap."

"And the results aren't good." Diane frowned down at her coffee as she stirred it, the spoon clinking against the mug. "Used to be, law enforcement wanted K-9s with Feral ancestry. They're bred to be so much more intelligent and empathetic than ordinary dogs, even without a Feral handler. But I had a police chief tell me today he didn't want a dog with gold eyes because some people would think it was possessed." She sighed. "If this keeps up, I'm not sure I'll be able to sell my animals. How can I feed them without that income?"

Jake nodded grimly. "Yeah, Kurt's in the same boat with BFS."

"At least my dogs don't go through fifteen pounds of meat a day each. I have no idea how the man does it."

He leaned toward his mother and met her gaze, the dark yellow of worry threading through his aura. "Mom, seriously… I'm working that march. How am I supposed to keep my mind on the job if I'm worried about you getting in a fistfight with some HHer?" A low growl rumbled in the air, distinctly leonine. "Clarence doesn't like the idea much either."

His mother sighed. "I'll think about it, dear. But I can't just back down from these assholes. I'm every bit is entitled to my opinion as they are." A cell phone chimed a ringtone, and she started. "Speaking of which, that's my alarm. I've got to get going if I don't want to be late for my meeting. See y'all later. Stay safe." She hopped up from her chair, then bent to press a kiss on her son's cheek and gave Erica a wave before heading for the front door. The dogs trotted behind her, claws clicking.

Jake followed. "Look, at least caution your buddies not to get carried away -- because they will go to jail. Or worse, end up badly hurt, which isn't going to help anybody."

Diane paused on her way out the door to give him a smile. "I'll pass it along."

As the door closed behind her, he sighed. "Sure you will."

Erica gave him a sympathetic smile. "I see where you get it."

* * *

Friday night's party at Killer Ink was in full swing. Adrian circulated through the crowd, watching and listening is the HHers whipped each other into a frenzy, growing drunker as they did so.

"Fucking Talents," one huge bearded man growled. "What sick bastard sacrifices a kid, for fuck's sake?"

"We need to round up every last one of the freaks and put them somewhere where they can't hurt anybody," John Reese agreed, a definite slur in his voice.

"Fuck that. Shoot the whole goddamn lot of them."

"We got to run them the hell out of town." Bill Garrison's face was ruddy from the whiskey he was drinking, and his eyes glittered under the tattooed gaze of his dragon. "Thing is, Satanists look like everybody else. We need to tattoo them or something, so you know who the hell they are."

Adrian gave him a sunny smile. "Absofuckinglutely."

Chapter Nineteen

There's nothing like being in the middle of six thousand pissed-off people to make you paranoid, Erica thought grimly. The Humanists and Talents filled the green bowl of Laurel Park in two restless, hostile packs separated by a thin barrier of twitchy, grim-faced cops. On the outskirts of both groups, teams of news camera crews waited for something to blow up.

She hoped her feeling of dread was a product of everybody else's mood. Instead of, say, a witchy precognitive warning that something ugly was about to happen.

At least Kurt and Genevieve were here. She'd spotted the two talking to Diane among the Talent counterprotesters, looking as pissed and worried as Erica felt. Though she wished Jake's mother had stayed home, the couple would make good backup if things went to hell.

She and Gen had spent the previous day practicing drawing power from the Ferals. The guys had even discovered a technique to feed the magic slowly enough that it didn't knock the two women on their asses. That trick might save their collective skins today.

The four of them, plus Dave, had celebrated that accomplishment with an impromptu cookout. Then Erica and Jake had returned to his place, where they'd spent another glorious night the way they had the previous two: making love.

There was something to be said for administrative leave.

Too bad it was over. Today was going to suck, though the cops had done everything possible to make sure the protest wouldn't get out of hand.

Gable had pulled Jake and Erica aside during a planning session early that morning. "You're my secret weapon," he told Jake. "If things start getting out of hand, I want you to go full-out King of the Jungle on these idiots. I'm not saying eat anyone -- just roar like hell. They'll be so busy pissing themselves, it should calm them right the hell down."

Turning to Erica, he'd added, "Keep an eye out. If anybody starts using any magic, I want you to put a stop to it."

"I'll check the park grounds beforehand, make sure nobody's set any traps." She wished she could tell him the counterprotesters wouldn't stoop to violence, but any population had its criminals and psychotics. The Fords had proven that when Talents went bad, they could do a hell of a lot more damage than your average asshole.

That was part of what made the Humanists so infuriating. Amid all the lunatic conspiracy theories was just enough truth to make their paranoia sound almost justified. So, while teams of cops with metal detector wands searched the protesters and counterprotesters, Erica had worked her way over the Laurel Park grounds, searching for spell circles or MEEDs.

Nothing, thank God. They probably had more to worry about from the HHers.

"Why the hell did it have to be a beautiful day?" she grumbled to Jake. "A good thunderstorm would've kept some of these idiots at home."

"Maybe you should have tried a rain spell."

"Too bad it wouldn't have worked." Morosely, she looked around. Spring had officially sprung, and the day was just cool enough to be comfortable. The dogwood, crabapple, and magnolia trees of Laurel Park were in full bloom, surrounded by azaleas and daffodils that filled the air with a rich floral perfume.

This part of the park was a natural amphitheater, with a grassy hillside sloping down to form a bowl. Here and there, granite outcroppings protruded from the hill, offering places to sit or picnic.

In the center of the grassy hollow stood a wooden gazebo where musicians performed during the summer. Just now, though, Virginia Laurel was doing her damnedest to whip up the mass of Humanists, while chanting Talent counterprotesters tried to drown her out. Meanwhile, camera crews from a dozen news organizations circulated through the crowd, transmitted her message to live trucks idling in the nearby parking lot.

Erica had to admire the old bitch's sense of theater. She'd created a hell of a backdrop to announce her gubernatorial campaign.

Laurel was dressed like someone's favorite aunt, in red slacks and a blue-and-white silk tunic, her blonde hair styled in a deceptively simple bob. Though she was in her sixties, she looked much younger. Either she had an excellent surgeon or an Arcanist painter on the payroll, despite her anti-Talent rhetoric.

As she spoke, her voice rang from the amplifier, resonant and rich. "For too long, these so-called Talents have used their magical abilities to unfair advantage. How can even the most skilled *cordon bleu* chef compete with a cook whose every dish is infused with magic? All our education, hard work, and ability means nothing when the playing field can never be level."

A woman's voice rose from the crowd of counterprotesters. "Oh, bullshit, Virginia!" Glancing around, Erica was amused to see Diane bellowing between cupped hands. "Y'all run the damn government! How are we supposed to compete with *you*?"

Next to her, Shannon Biggerstaff and his mother, Kim, booed lustily along with the rest of the Talents. Erica made a mental note of the Bard's location. He might come in handy, given the way he and his sister had calmed down their irate neighbors.

Virginia ignored the hecklers. "Just last year, terrorists killed seven people and sacrificed them in a spell designed to assassinate President Roth and every member of Congress. Virgil Ford has admitted their objective was to terrorize Norms, to make us fear Talents and prevent us from protecting ourselves against them. Well, they failed."

Yeah, thanks to Jake, Genevieve, Dave, and Kurt, Erica thought.

"Now we learn that a drug-dealing Alchemist has attempted to sacrifice a nine-year-old child and his mother in an act of Satanic magic. How long are we going to permit the Talents among us to commit these crimes? We need more stringent laws to prevent them from using their magic on normal Americans. We need to quit turning a blind eye to their crimes, and we must stop polluting our bodies with their magic -- with their microbrews, their food, and especially their drugs. We need to crack down and make it clear to them that they cannot continue to take advantage of normal Americans. We must make it a felony for them to use *any* magic at all on us."

She paused to let the Humanist crowd shout approval.

The Talents booed. "We are what democracy looks like!"

"Norms are becoming second-class citizens in our own country, and we can't allow it to go on. If you elect me governor, rest assured I will do everything in my power to level the playing field for God-fearing South Carolinians! I…"

A few feet away, one of the Humanists bent over and vomited onto the grass.

I'm right there with you, Erica thought dryly. *She makes me sick too.*

A ripple flowed over the crowd, accompanied by the

sound of someone else being noisily sick. When he straightened, he stared at the ground in horror. "Fuck, I'm bleeding!"

A videographer pivoted in his direction, focusing a camera with a CNN logo on his shocked face.

More sounds of vomiting. At the edge of the Humanist crowd, a man turned toward Erica, his eyes wide as he swiped a hand across his nose and looked down at the blood on his fingers. "What the fuck?" Taking a staggering step to the side, he toppled to the ground. A stir rolled over the crowd, as more cameras planned over protestors collapsing with blood smearing their faces.

Crap. Erica's training took over, and she hurried toward the nearest victim. Kneeling beside him, she saw his eyes had rolled back. The pulse at his throat thumped too fast against her fingers. *What the fuck is this, some kind of drug? Poison?*

Good thing there were EMS units standing by. She reached for the radio mic clipped to her uniform shoulder and triggered it. "I need a paramedic for an unconscious white male, bleeding from the nose. Not sure of the cause." Frowning, she looked around, aware of the sound of people retching and calling out. "A lot of these people seem to be experiencing some sort of gastrointestinal…"

"You did this!" a man's voice snarled in rage. "You fucking *witch!*"

Erica jerked her head up. A middle-aged man loomed over her and the unconscious Humanist. His face contorted in an expression of insane fury beneath the blue dragon tattoo that wrapped its wings around his bald head. "You did this!" He drove his fist at her face.

Erica swung up an arm, knocking the punch aside. "Are you out of your…"

"I should've killed you when I had the chance!" He leaped on her as she started to rise, knocking her flat with his greater weight. His next punch connected in an explosion of white stars and stunning pain. "Missed with the truck, but this time you're dead!"

Wait, what? Erica blocked another wild blow and hit him in the jaw, knuckles splitting as they ground against teeth. He didn't even seem to feel it. When she checked his aura, it was batshit-crazy white. *Oh fuck.*

She threw up both arms to protect her head and started to hook both legs around his hips, intending to wrench him off her. But before her thighs could get a grip, she heard a rippling, leonine snarl.

The man vanished, jerked into the air like a rag doll. He hit the ground facedown, Jake astride him and seriously pissed off. "I don't think so, asshole!"

"I'm gonna kill you, you fuckin' freaks!" the Humanist screeched, writhing. "You ain't getting away this time!"

"You're under arrest." Jake ground his knee into the small of Dragon Head's back as he jerked a pair of zip ties off his duty belt with one hand, the protester's wrist clamped in the other.

"I'll do it. You hold him." Erica took the plastic strips so Jake could use both hands to immobilize the man. Even so, the Humanist fought like a rabid dog as she bound his wrists and ankles. If it hadn't been for Jake's Clarence-enhanced strength, she doubted they could have controlled him.

"You're dead, witch!" Dragon Head bellowed, spittle flying. "Next time I'm not going to fuck around running you over, I'm gonna blow your brains out! You're gonna die!"

Jake stiffened, staring down at the man, eyes narrowing. *"What did you say?"* His voice rumbled with that deep, leonine undertone.

"Fuck you, freak!" DH snarled. "And you too, witch!"

"*So* not my type." Blowing out a breath, ears still ringing from the punches she'd taken, Erica sat back on her heels. And froze, her breath catching as she stared around in growing horror.

In the few minutes she and Jake had been busy with Dragon Head, the park had become a battlefield. Knots of cops fought with Humanists who punched, kicked, clawed, and bit in an insane frenzy.

Nor was it only cops versus protesters. Many of the Humanists seemed to be fighting each other just as viciously. One coldcocked a cameraman, who went down like a felled ox, his camera crashing to the ground beside him.

Every protester's aura glowed a blinding white. Erica had never seen so many raging psychotics, not even during firefights with Caliphate sorcerers.

A single person in a psychotic frenzy was one thing, but it looked as if hundreds of these people had lost their damn minds. *No way is this natural,* Erica thought, appalled. *It's got to be magic. But I checked the park, and there was no sign of booby traps.*

But something unnatural had sure as hell happened, and it didn't bode well for the cops.

Off to her right, Katilia Sharp gave a man in a Human Heritage T-shirt a faceful of CAP-STUN pepper spray. The stinging, choking oleoresin capsicum should have stopped him in his tracks as his eyes swelled and teared, but the HHer didn't even appear to notice as he charged her, fists swinging.

Erica leaped forward to grab the Humanist's arm before he could land a punch. Jerking him in a circle, she cranked his arm behind his back and up between his shoulder blades, then crashed into him, forcing him to his knees. She and Katilia forced him face down on the ground, ignoring his howling rage. Jake planted a knee on his ass and put him in an arm bar, immobilizing him long enough for the women to get him zip tied.

Panting, one thigh aching from a vicious kick, Erica studied his aura. Like far too many of those around them, it burned white. But against that background, she spotted an unnatural magical current zipping through his field. It wasn't his magic -- the man had no Talent at all. "Yeah, he's definitely under a spell."

"What?" Katilia shouted, evidently unable to hear her over the angry howls and curses of battling cops and protesters.

"What kind of spell?" demanded Jake, who must have been drawing on Clarence's hearing.

"Not sure." Frowning, she sank her hand into the protester's churning aura, extending a magical probe to explore.

ZAP! The tingling burn felt like an electrical shock. Hissing a curse, Erica resisted the instinct to jerk back. "I don't think this is an Arcanist working. It feels more like... Alchemy maybe. Like something he drank or smoked. Some magical drug."

Katilia stared at her. "You mean all these assholes are under the influence of something?"

"Yeah, and it's nasty, whatever it is." A few feet away a South Carolina highway patrol trooper went down, felled by a punch from an HHer the approximate size of a grizzly bear. "Damn it."

They ran to help the cop. By the time they got the attacking HHer down and zipped, Erica had added yet another bruise to her collection. But she'd also confirmed her suspicions, because the HHer had the same magical patterns as the previous jerk. "Yeah, that's a spell," she told Jake. "If we can't snap them out of it, somebody's going to get hurt."

"Sounds like my cue to roar." Gold sparks exploded around him as Clarence flashed into view. This wasn't a dim partial manifestation Erica alone could see, either. He blazed like a spotlight even in full sunlight, ten feet long plus three feet of tail, his head waist high on Jake. He reared, covering her lover in a bulletproof shell of blazing magic.

And roared.

The raw power of the sound could have been heard five miles away. Erica was no stranger to pissed big cats, yet it made even her inner cavewoman gibber in terror. She wasn't surprised to hear screams from Talents and cops alike.

But the Humanists didn't stop. They kept right on attacking cops, Talents, camera crews and each other, frenzied by whatever potion they'd been given.

Jake roared again, and this time Kurt answered him from among the crowd of Talents. Turning, Erica saw his tiger manifestation looming over the crowd, bright as an acetylene torch. The cats' bloodcurdling chorus should have sent anyone with a lizard hindbrain diving for cover.

The Humanists kept right on attacking anything that moved.

Erica's heart sank. *We're so fucked.*

* * *

The roaring chorus of two big cats was so loud it was all Adrian could do to control his reflexive jerk. Fortunately, he was no stranger to painting sigils when all hell was breaking loose. That was why he used stencils in such situations; otherwise it would be far too easy to ruin a spell.

And he sure as hell didn't want to ruin this one. If it worked, it would be perfect. Not only because of the effect it would have, but because it was so fucking ironic.

He glanced over the edge of the stone outcropping and smiled in satisfaction behind the full-face mask of his Spook Suit. Judging by the chaos of battling bodies that filled the park, the Demon in all those spelled bottles of liquor had worked just as Ray had promised. Demon not only caused psychosis, it gave its users inhuman strength and no awareness of pain whatsoever. This batch had been the Alchemist's last creation, brewed while Adrian had painted the spell on the floor of Meghan's house.

Then, of course, there were the bottles laced with Bleeder, which had made the other members of the crowd so violently ill. Ray really had been a hell of an Alchemist.

Adrian had served both potions during the HHer party last night, accompanied by a spell to delay the activation until noon.

Now all those news cameras were getting lots of great video of poor Humanists being poisoned and driven crazy by some evil Talent spell. Virginia Laurel would ride that footage all the way to the South Carolina governor's mansion. Roth and his Humanist allies might even be able to use it in the next legislative session.

Which was pretty much the whole point of this little exercise.

Forcing himself to take his time, Adrian chose the next stencil, then dipped the wide brush in the jar of ultraviolet paint. Breathing deeply in and out to keep his hands steady, he stroked the paint over the plastic cutout he'd laid on the stone. His blood seemed to fizz with a delicious combination of fear and exhilaration. If even one of those Talents in the crowd glanced up at the outcropping with their eyes closed, they'd see the magical glow of the Spook Suit that rendered Adrian invisible in normal light.

The suit had cost him all the profits from the assassination of a South American warlord, but it'd been worth every dime. No one had any idea he was up here, and they weren't likely to. Only the most sensitive Arcanists could see the suit's magic without closing their eyes against the glare of daylight.

Not until it was too late.

* * *

As Jake rescued another cop from yet another

Humanist, Erica scanned the crowd of Talent counterprotesters beating a wise retreat from the riot...

There.

She broke into a run until she caught up to her quarry on the edge of the crowd. Grabbing the young Bard by the shoulder, Erica pulled him to a stop. "Shannon, I need your help!" It was a damn good thing she'd caught him and his mother before they escaped the park with the others. "You've got to help me stop this."

Shannon Biggerstaff's dark eyes widened. "Me? What can I do?"

"Sing." She started towing him toward the chaos.

"Are you nuts?" His mother stepped into her path, frowning ferociously. "Nobody'll be able to hear him in all this!"

The woman had a point. Erica could barely hear herself over the howling Humanists, roaring cats, and bellowing cops. Her gaze fell on the gazebo, where Virginia Laurel had been speaking to the crowd over the PA system. The politician had disappeared -- no surprise -- leaving the amplifiers and mic unattended.

Unfortunately, several hundred crazy Humanists separated them from the sound system.

Following her gaze, Kim scowled. "If you think you're taking my kid into that," she jerked her chin toward the melee, "You're out of your mind!"

She was right again. But they had to do something, damn it, or people were going to die.

Erica's attention fell on Jake, who stood back to back with Kurt, both fully manifested. They were fighting at the head of a flying wedge of cops trying to push their way through the crowd, swinging batons and fighting hand-to-hand with protestors.

"Disperse! Disperse or go to jail!" The two men's voices rang over the howls of the crowd, reverberating, inhumanly deep, amplified by their magic.

Jake snatched up a Humanist as if he were a toddler, jerked his wrists behind his back, and held them there as another cop zip tied them. "If you don't disperse, you're going to get hurt!" Every word he spoke blasted over the screams and curses of the battling Norms.

Inspiration hit. "Shannon, wait here. We can get Jake to amplify your magic."

The Bard's eyes widened. "Jake?" She'd never been so glad to see hero worship on a kid's face.

"Oh, hell no!" Kim told her son. "Don't even think about it."

"Mom!"

Erica didn't stay to listen to the argument. She just plunged into the crowd, screaming Jake's name.

She passed a white-faced cop, blood pouring from a cut on his forehead, as he swung his baton at one of the protesters. This time she didn't stop to help. Every moment this continued, somebody could -- and probably would -- get hurt much worse. "Jake! Jake, I need you!"

The lion's huge glowing head turned toward her. "Erica?"

He said something to Kurt, then pushed his way toward her as the cops separated to let him through. "What?"

"I need you to play amplifier for Shannon!"

His eyes widened. "That could work!" Then his brows snapped down, and he whipped out a huge glowing paw that missed her by inches.

Startled, Erica turned to see a protester behind her face-plant on the ground.

"He was about to punch you in the head," Jake told her, as he started clearing a path through the crowd. Erica followed, ducking and blocking attacks as he picked Humanists up and tossed them aside. A woman with a network news camera trailed them through the scrum, her lens pointed in their direction.

To Erica's relief, they found Shannon and his mother waiting for them at the battlefield's edge. She'd been afraid Kim would drag the boy off -- and she'd probably have been justified.

Even Shannon seemed to be having second thoughts, his eyes wide, his face white with anxiety. "I'm not sure I can do this," he yelled.

"He can't -- these idiots are crazy," his mother shouted. "If he had the kind of power he'd need to influence them, he'd already have a recording contract."

"He won't be doing it alone. Jake and I will help. Or do you want to just stand there and watch cops get killed?" Erica shot a finger at the riot. Blood flew as cops and Humanists fought with berserk desperation. *"A Talent did this.* And Talents are going to have to stop it -- or we *are* going to end up in those fucking camps!"

Kim stared at her, then at the brawl. Muttering something that was probably a curse, she gave her son a tight nod. "Do your best."

"Thank you!" Erica planted one hand on the teen's shoulder, then reached for Jake's manifestation and started forming the conduit they'd practiced last night. Unfortunately, she'd never done anything involving a Bard. She was just going to have to make it work anyway. "Now sing!"

Shannon threw his head back and obeyed.

Erica had never experienced how a Bard's magic actually worked. Now, as deep magical vibrations rolled through his aura, she realized how similar it was to the way Dave, Kurt and Jake manipulated sound.

She let her own aura resonate with Shannon's, adding her power to his and passing it on to Jake. There was a nerve-racking pause, as if Jake was trying to figure out what to do with that thrumming energy. Just as she was starting to worry, his manifestation began to vibrate. Shannon's voice blasted out of him to roll across the park with the same thundering power as one of Jake's roars.

As the words of "The Old Rugged Cross" rang over the chaos, the tight, frightened faces of the surrounding Talents began to smooth, fear draining away. Even the woman videographer stared at Shannon in awe.

Turning toward the battle, Erica spotted an entranced deputy gazing at the Bard as if hypnotized. He didn't see the fist-sized rock that flew out of the crowd to slam into his head, dropping him like a hammer to the head.

Oh shit. Erica concentrated harder, trying to amplify the Bard's magic with more of her own. *Damn it, the drug's too strong. He's not going to be able to overcome it.*

"We can help!" Genevieve and Kurt emerged from the crowd, already linked; her fingers were sunk into her husband's manifestation, and magic leaped between them like tiny forked lightning. Their joined auras made Erica's eyes tear. "We just need a singer…"

"I can do it." A woman Erica didn't recognize hurried up. Genevieve took her hand as the Bard began singing in a pure, ringing soprano, joining Shannon's in an exquisite duet.

More Bards streamed out of the woods, singing as they came, gathering around the Ferals, Erica, and Gen. And Christ, it hurt. Each additional singer increased the throbbing burn growing behind Erica's eyebrows. Without the layering trick Genevieve had taught her, she suspected her brain would explode like an aerosol can in a microwave.

She ignored the pain as she drew in the Bards' magic and fed it to Jake, who sent it thundering over the riot.

The videographer who'd been shooting the group stepped back, her expression dazed. Then she lifted her camera and started filming them again, the look on her face a tortured blend of exultation and determination.

The fighting began to slow.

First one Humanist and then another turned in their direction, eyes startled as the magic finally overwhelmed the potion's effects. More and more of them stopped fighting to listen entranced as the Bards sang, until they all stood frozen, silent tears rolling down their cheeks. Drunk on magic.

* * *

Adrian ground his teeth in rage. Goddamnit, he'd been afraid some fucking Talent would pull something out of a hat, but he hadn't dreamed they'd figure out a way to stop the fighting completely.

Good thing this is only the first act.

For the hundredth time in his long, black career, he found himself blessing the tattoos that made him resistant to other Arcs' mental magic. He was lucky his mother had been so fucking good with a spell.

Which reminded him -- it was time for the next phase. Adrian started down the hillside into the trees where the Talents had retreated from the riot. The Spook Suit ensured nobody saw him, even when he knocked more than one idiot out of his way.

And there she was. Slipping up behind his victim, he reached into his belt pouch and pulled out a small metal tube. Adrian popped the cap off, removed the plastic needle cover from the syringe, then jabbed it into the thin skin of her neck.

"Oww!" She slapped at her nape as if trying to kill a mosquito. Adrian dropped the syringe on the ground and flipped the spelled blanket he carried over the woman's head. The Talents, thoroughly enthralled by the Bards' song, didn't even notice her vanish behind the blanket's magical camouflage. Clamping one hand over her blanket-covered face, Adrian muffled her outraged yell as he wrapped the other arm around her to contain her struggles.

Barely a minute passed before the drug took effect and she went limp in his arms. Adrian bent and swung her over his shoulder in a fireman's carry, grunting a little from her weight. "Damn, woman, you could stand to lose a few pounds."

As he turned and started back toward the outcropping where he'd made his preparations, his gaze fell on Jake Nolan.

Who had no idea his mother had just been kidnapped.

Chapter Twenty

As the last notes of the song faded away, Jake sagged in relief. His head throbbed, and he felt drained. Amplifying the chorus's magic had been the most complex thing he'd ever done. As a Feral, manifesting Clarence was effortless; all he did was release their combined magic.

But this had been something altogether different.

At first, as Erica had sent the exotic, alien power rolling through his aura, he'd been afraid he wouldn't be able to do the job at all. In desperation, he'd finally treated it the same way he treated Clarence: he got the fuck out the way and let it pour through him, reshaping his magic as it would.

He wrapped one arm around Erica for a fierce, relieved hug. "I can't believe that worked!"

"It wouldn't have if it hadn't been for Shannon." She turned a dazzling smile on the young Bard, who was practically glowing. "Thank you so much." Looking around at the exhausted, exhilarated Bards, she called, "Y'all saved a lot of lives today. I'm sure I can speak for Sheriff Gable when I say thank you all!"

As the Talents shared hugs and grins, Jake scanned the battlefield. The Norms blinked and looked around -- cops, Humanists, reporters and videographers alike, all a bit dazed and confused from the various spells they'd been subjected to. Some clutched injuries while others collapsed to the ground in pain and exhaustion. He heard one HHer ask, "What the fuck just happened?"

"Yeah," Jake muttered, "Just what I was thinking."

"All right," the sheriff's amplified voice crackled through a bullhorn. "Everybody who hit a cop is under arrest until we get this thing sorted out. Officers, take your zip ties and get to work."

"Wish Shannon could've used that fucking bullhorn

instead of us," Kurt told him, rubbing his forehead as if it hurt. Judging by Jake's headache, it probably did.

Evidently overhearing, Shannon explained, "A bullhorn distorts the sound too much. Anyway, it wouldn't have been loud enough."

Now that it was safe, EMS crews began working their way across the field, triaging the injured and going to work on those hurt the worst. There were a lot more crews than they'd started out with. Evidently dispatch had realized things were going sideways and called in every unit in the county.

Remembering the guy with the dragon on his head, Jake glanced around, narrow-eyed. He'd heard the guy say something about failing to kill Erica the *first* time. Yeah, he wanted a word with that dickhead.

"Jake Nolan!" The amplified voice was badly distorted in a way he recognized as a product of yet another bullhorn. "Hey, Simba! I've got your mommy."

What the fuck? Jake scanned for the source of the sound, seeing nothing but a bunch of injured, exhausted and confused people. There was no sign of his mother at all.

"I'm not joking, kitty. Make some noise, Mom."

"Oww! Damn it, let go, you bastard!"

"Shit!" Jake exchanged a look with Erica as his heart lurched. "That's Mom." In the depths of his mind, Clarence roared as his exhaustion disappeared in an explosion of adrenaline. The manifestation burst from him again, sweeping him up and enclosing him in a glowing four-legged leonine cocoon.

Around him, cops turned, drawing weapons, scanning the area, looking for the source of the voice. Over the radio, Gable growled, "Nolan, what the hell he's talking about?"

Jake grabbed his handset. "He says he snatched my mother."

"Shit."

"I'm not joking, Nolan," the kidnapper called. "You'd better get your magical ass over here, or Mom's gonna have issues."

"I'd bet money that's the Arc asshole who engineered all this," Erica said in a grim, low voice.

"Here, kitty, kitty, kitty!"

"Damn it, stop!" Diane snapped, her Familiars adding a canine snarl to her voice. A chorus of furious barks sounded as if she were trying to manifest. She didn't use her dog form often -- it was nowhere near as strong as his -- but when she did, you knew she was pissed.

"Watch it, bitch, or I'll feed you a bullet!"

Diane made a high, pained sound.

Shit. Canine manifestations were too small to provide bulletproofing; their magic just wasn't strong enough. Mom wouldn't be able to keep the bastard from shooting her.

Ignoring the alarmed exclamations from the crowd, Jake sprang into a trot, headed in the direction of the kidnapper's voice. It seemed to be coming from the hillside that bordered the park in a natural amphitheater. Several granite outcrops protruded from the hill like fingers, providing convenient spots for an audience to perch or picnic. His eyes narrowed, focusing on one rock that had to be twenty feet tall. If he were an assassin, that's where he'd be. Great view from there.

The outcrop appeared empty, but with an Arc, that didn't mean much.

From the corner of one eye, he saw Kurt loping beside him, Erica and Gen on his right, running to keep up. Off to either side, more cops moved cautiously after them.

"Better get a move on, Simba," the kidnapper called. "You don't want me to get bored and put a bullet in

Mommy's head."

"Jake!" Erica stared up at the hillside. "There's a weird magical shape up on that big outcrop. I think it's somebody under a camouflage blanket."

"A what?" Genevieve asked, as Kurt cursed.

"Bends visible light like a Spook Suit. The military used 'em during the war to hide gun emplacements."

Slowing, Jake closed his eyes, staring at the outcropping. An odd, lumpy shape appeared to hover in midair about twenty feet up. It didn't look like a shrouded weapon, and it seemed to be moving, "What the fuck *is* that?"

Erica was right -- it did look like a spelled blanket with someone struggling underneath. The odd shape that protruded from it was probably the head and shoulders of an Arcanist wearing a Spook Suit. Bastard must be standing behind his mother, using her as a shield.

"Nolan, give me a vowel," Gable demanded over the radio.

Erica triggered her handset. "I think that's the Arcanist who's behind all this. He's got a hostage."

"Yeah, I picked up on that part," the sheriff said dryly. "Let's try not to get anybody killed. Back 'em up, officers, but nobody open fire until you can see what the hell you're shooting at."

Kurt veered closer, until the Ferals' manifestations trotted shoulder to magical shoulder. Voice low, he muttered, "You can almost see the giant neon sign hanging over his head: 'this is a trap.'"

"Goddamnit, I know that," Jake snapped. "But he's got my mother."

The sheriff's voice rang out over the bullhorn. "Let the woman go! There's no way you're getting out of this. We will shoot you if you don't turn her loose."

"And sacrifice the hero's mother in front of all these cameras?" He laughed, the sound grating and mechanical. "Besides, you can't even see us."

The four Talents slowed to a walk as they approached the base of the outcropping, all too aware of the danger of running head-on into a MEED. Glancing back, Jake saw some of the cops herding people out of the line of fire, while others melted into the trees, seeking cover they could shoot from.

Meanwhile the four of them stood here like targets. At least he and Kurt were bulletproof.

"Take cover between us," Kurt told Gen and Erica, evidently realizing the problem at the same time he did. "Crouch down."

As the two women obeyed, Jake asked, "So if this is a trap, where is it and what is it?"

"I can't quite tell." Erica sounded pained, uncertain. She probably had a savage headache from the magic she'd already used. Did she even have juice to disable whatever trap this fucker had created?

Kurt murmured, "Should we have the sheriff bring the bomb suit?"

"I don't think it's a bomb. I'm not seeing any sign of wiring or mechanical parts. The only magic I see is the blanket. Trouble is, that thing's so bright I might not be able to make out other nearby spells." She glanced at Genevieve, whose eyes were closed as if she, too, was trying to scan for magic. "You see anything?"

"Nada. That blanket really is bright."

"I'm starting to get bored," the Arc called.

With that, Jake's mother appeared out of thin air, blinking and dazed, as if he'd jerked the blanket off her. "Let me go, you bastard!" She jerked as if fighting an invisible hold.

Closing his eyes, Jake saw the glowing figure of a man standing with one arm wrapped around the smaller glowing figure that was Diane. The Arc's other hand held something pressed against her head. Probably a gun, also hidden by the Spook Suit's camouflage field.

"Let's get interesting." The Arcanist's voice, no longer distorted by the bullhorn -- he must have dropped it -- sounded amused, mocking. Jake didn't recognize it.

"Jake?" His mother sounded dazed, frightened.

"Shut up, bitch!" The kidnapper clubbed her hard with his gun hand. Diane fell with a cry, landing on her side at his feet.

Jake tensed in rage, his own and his cat's. His fury was all the hotter for the terror boiling under it. He ached to leap onto the outcrop and take the bastard out, but kidnapper and victim were twenty feet up and about five feet ahead. An impossible jump even for a flesh and blood lion the size of Clarence. If he missed…

The glowing figure planted a foot on the side of his mother's face, pinning her there as he aimed his invisible weapon down at her. Diane being Diane, she beat at his calf. "Get off… me… you jerk!"

The Arcanist laughed. And drew back a foot to kick her. "That's no way to…"

Oh, fuck this. Jake got a fix on his target's location, opened his eyes, and sprang. His human body could leap a hell of a long way carried by magical leonine muscle, but he'd never tried a jump that far.

Glowing paws hit the lip of the outcrop, scrambled, almost lost their grip -- and caught. Roaring, Jake powered himself onto the stone in a furious surge. Snapping his eyes closed, he saw the Arcanist standing astride Diane.

Cursing, the kidnapper aimed the gun at him and emptied the clip as fast as he could pull the trigger. Bullets ricocheted off Jake's manifestation in an explosion of magical sparks. He lunged at the bastard, striking out with his claws, glowing jaws wide to display his armory of teeth. "You keep your fucking hands off my mother!"

With a defiant howl, the Arc leaped into a

spectacular spinning kick aimed at his muzzle. Jake swung a forepaw, batting the Talent out of the air like a tennis ball. He went flying, hit a pine tree with a melon thump, and fell in a senseless heap.

Jake came down twisting to avoid Diane, who lay coiled in a ball with both arms thrown over her head, and hit the stone with all four legs apart. He had a moment to feel triumphant relief...

Until the magical trap sprang shut around him in an explosion of sparks and rotating sigils. He barely had time to think, *Oh shit!*

His brain seemed to detonate in a white-hot blast. Jake had never felt such blazing, frenzied rage, such a bloody craving to make someone pay. The bastard had dared touch Diane Nolan -- the single mother who'd worried and struggled and fought to give her sons a better life, only to be forced to bury one of them.

The magic-using shit had tried to *kill* Jake's mother.

He deserves to die.

Head low, the air around him vibrating with his snarl, Jake stalked toward the Arcanist, eyes closed to let him focus on his prey. The man stirred feebly, a bare twitch of his chin.

I'm going to bite the little prick's head right off his shoulders...

"Jake?" The voice was a hoarse croak, and he opened his eyes to look around, lips rippling with his snarl.

The middle-aged woman lifted herself on her elbows, her face white everywhere it wasn't bruised and scraped. "Don't, Jake! He's unconscious. It would be murder."

"You can't tell me..." He broke off, and for a moment he recognized her through the bloody haze clouding his vision.

Until another wave of fury tore through him, ripping the moment of sanity away.

He roared.

She jerked her gaze away and huddled submissively, her voice going high with anxiety. "You're under a spell! Like Bobby. Just like Bobby. Please, please, don't. I've lost one of you. I can't lose…"

That's Mom. I can't hurt Mom. He froze, shaking, trying to see her through the red-hot firestorm that hazed his vision with the need to rend and tear and kill. With the craving for blood.

Mom's blood. An icy bolt of horror jolted through his madness. *Get the fuck away before I hurt her. Start killing, won't be able to stop. Like Bobby.*

Somewhere on the ground below, a voice spoke, reverberating with magic. "Jake? What's going on?"

Kurt. Kurt's down there. Kurt can stop me.

Wheeling, he ran toward the end of the outcrop and threw himself over the edge.

* * *

Her head felt as if it was about to topple off her shoulders if she made one wrong move, but Diane Nolan managed to crawl to the edge of the granite outcrop.

Twenty feet below, Jake's manifestation crouched, tail lashing, as he faced off with Erica, Genevieve, and Kurt's tiger.

Her son roared, the sound louder and more inhuman than she'd ever heard it. Whatever spell that bastard Arc had cast on her boy, it was bad. *No, damn it. Not again. I'm not losing you, too.*

Teeth gritted with effort, she reeled to her feet. And damn near blacked out again from the vicious pressure against her eyes. *Suck it up, Diane.*

She needed to get down there, try to talk some sanity into her child. Teeth clenched with effort, she began to hobble down the length of the rock. She was not looking forward to trying to climb down that slope.

Wait, where the hell was the kidnapper? The last thing she needed was for him to come after her. Diane closed her eyes and turned slowly, searching with her aural vision…

There he was, huddled on the ground at the foot of a tree, dead or unconscious. *He's lucky Jake didn't eat him.*

She started to turn away, only to realize he might regain consciousness and escape, especially given the Spook Suit. *Damned if that jerk's getting away after what he did to my son.* Diane hobbled over and bent to wrap her fingers in the fabric of his full-face mask, almost face-planting in the process. Bracing one hand against the tree, she finally dragged it off. It peeled off slowly, revealing a bleeding scalp wound.

As she straightened, his head appeared, looking decapitated. When she stepped away holding the mask, the spell broke and the entire man appeared, looking like an abandoned rag doll in black body armor. He was a big man -- dark haired and bearded, about forty, with the heavy muscularity of a boxer. His chest still rose and fell.

At least Jake didn't kill him. Not that he doesn't have it coming. Still, it would be better if he were alive to be questioned.

Shoving the mask into the back pocket of her jeans, Diane turned to stagger along the line of the hill, searching for a way down.

With the sound of her son's menacing roars echoing in her ears, she knew she'd better hurry.

* * *

Erica latched onto Genevieve's arm and jerked her friend back away as the two glowing Ferals circled each other, muscles tense, heads low. She'd heard Jake roar a lot over the years, but he'd never sounded so thoroughly inhuman. Every time that savage, thundering sound raked her eardrums, it was all she could do not to flinch.

"Jake, you're under a spell," Kurt said, his magic amplifying his voice. "Remember what happened to Bobby? Remember what he did to Dave? I don't want to have to kill you to keep you from killing someone else, and you don't want to end up living in the tree house with Dave for the rest of your life. You finally have Erica. Don't screw that up."

Genevieve leaned in and yelled into Erica's ear, fighting to be heard over the Ferals. "We've got to break that damned spell! We're going to have to get closer."

"You can't do it! It's going to have to be me. He won't kill me."

"Bobby killed Dave!"

"Bobby wasn't in love with Dave." She grabbed her shoulder mic and triggered it. "Sheriff Gable?"

"Any luck getting Nolan back under control?" He sounded as grim and desperate as she felt. "We're still trying to evacuate, but the crowd's on the verge of a wholesale panic."

"Warn them that if they run, they could trigger him to attack. Besides, Hussein Bolt couldn't outrun a manifested Feral. Walk slowly and calmly. If he charges, get down on the ground, cover your head with your arms and roll into a ball. Do not move. Do not make eye contact. Kurt will keep him from hurting you." *As long as Jake doesn't kill him.* "And I'm going to break the spell as soon as I can get close."

"How are you going to do that without getting mauled?"

"Magic."

Jake lunged at Kurt again, and the glowing tiger leaped back, ducking a vicious slice of leonine claws. Roaring in frustration, the lion jolted after him, but the tiger danced away, probably hoping to exhaust Jake with a chase until his manifestation simply collapsed.

It might even work.

Erica licked lips gone dry with terror. She had to figure out how to break that spell, assuming she had the juice left after what she'd done with the Bards. Her head still throbbed like a kettledrum, but at least sheer terror had given her a second wind.

Jake's back was to her now, and she edged closer, reaching for her Talent to examine his aura.

Oh fuck.

White burned so hot in his skull she could see the frenzied heat through the golden blaze of his cat. Crimson sigils orbited him like moons around Jupiter. Deciphering them, she realized the spell was every bit as bad as she feared. It was designed to overwhelm the human half's centers of judgment and self-control while maddening the cat half. Probably the only reason it hadn't affected Diane too was that her Familiars were dogs.

Studying the spell, she took another step closer…

The lion's great head snapped around, glowing eyes narrowing in rage. His muscles tensed. Erica froze.

"Oh, fuck no!" Kurt charged, plowing into his friend. As Erica and Genevieve leapt away, the fight was on in earnest.

* * *

The cats' roars hit his ears in a sonic assault that made Roger Johnson's hands shake with the need to run. Instead, he forced himself to help a reeling Humanist stagger toward the parking lot they were using to evacuate the civilians.

You're a cop, damn it. Do your damn job and get these people out of here.

But an image flashed through his mind for the tenth time in the past few minutes: the bear Feral dragging Steve across Faraday Square as the cop howled in agony and terror.

Roger tightened his grip on the Humanist's arm to keep himself from shaking. He could almost feel fangs sinking into his own flesh.

Today was going to be another nightmare to add to his collection.

All around him, desperately quiet men and women streamed into the woods around the park. A guy in an HH T-shirt stopped to take the elbow of an elderly woman in a polyester pants suit, steadying her when she tripped. If he realized she was a Talent, it didn't seem to matter.

A thin hand clamped down on Roger's forearm, manicured nails digging into the flesh. "Did the cat kill him?"

He jerked around to see Virginia Laurel glaring up into his face, eyes wide with fury and desperation. "Who?"

"Adrian!" she hissed.

"Adrian who? What the hell are you talking about?"

She leaned in and rose on her toes until she could snarl in his ear. "The Arc terrorist. Did Nolan kill him?"

Rogers jaw dropped as he suddenly had a whole new reason to be horrified. "*What?*"

"Shut. Up." Virginia tried to drag him away from the humanist he was guiding. He released the man and followed her until they were clear of the streaming crowd. Finally she turned on him and demanded, "Did the cat kill the terrorist?"

"Who the fuck knows? I couldn't see from where I was."

She wrapped a bony hand in his collar and jerked him down until she could snarl in his ear, "You've got to make sure he's dead. Find him and kill him."

Roger tried to pull away, but she wouldn't let go and he didn't want to attract attention by ripping out of her hold. "You are out of your fucking mind."

"You're involved in this up to your badge! If that little bastard takes me down, you're going with me. Get up there on that hill while everybody's distracted." A deafening roar sounded, and another replied. "With all the noise the cats are making, nobody will hear anything they shouldn't."

She released him and gestured impatiently. Glancing around, he saw Clary, Green, Hampton, and Martin standing, waiting for her orders. A more sinister collection of cops he'd never seen in his life. "Go with him," she told them. "Make sure."

Clary's jaw tightened, but he gave her a jerky nod.

Satisfied, she hurried off to disappear into the trees with the rest of the evacuees.

Fuck. Fuck fuck fuck. He felt sick. It would be a miracle if they weren't caught.

Martin bared his teeth. "You heard the lady. We got a job to do." And judging by the look on his face, if Roger didn't do it, Martin would -- and kill Roger while he was at it. He didn't have a choice. If Laurel said she'd take him down with her, she meant it.

Besides, the psycho she'd evidently hired had it coming for doing all this shit.

* * *

Damn it, the Arcanist bastard had known his business. Erica scanned the spell, but she could see no misshapen or badly spaced sigils.

Jake charged Kurt, who ducked aside, whipping out a paw to rake across his friend's glowing muzzle. Jake reared as Kurt leaped, and the two manifestations slammed together in an explosion of sparks. Wrapping their paws around each other, they ripped, clawing, fighting to puncture one another's magical shell and reach vulnerable flesh.

Jake began to muscle Kurt backwards, and the tiger released him to bound away. Erica's heart sank. Kurt was moving more slowly, his manifestation no longer as bright, while Jake's lion shell burned as hot and moved as fast as ever.

I'm running out of time. If he takes Kurt down, we're all screwed. Erica edged closer to the fighting pair, knowing she risked drawing Jake's lethal attention, yet desperate to see the spell more clearly. Every muscle tensed as she prepared to leap away if he turned toward her.

Then, at last, she saw it. One sigil wasn't quite as

bright as the others. *There you are, you little bastard.* Not much of a weak point, true, but it was going to have to do. She started forward...

Jake's great maned head whipped toward her, gold eyes blazing, lips pulled back from fangs longer than her fingers. Erica froze, remembering the sight of Dave's lifeless body lying on the cave floor.

Leonine muscles tensed...

"Jake..." she whispered. Pleading.

His eyes widened as recognition flashed in their mad depths. His lips relaxed down off his teeth. "Eri..."

"You're not touching her!" Kurt landed on him in an explosion of sparks, all four legs encircling Jake's torso as he dove for a grip on the back of the manifestation's maned neck, jaws wide, fangs glowing.

Roaring, Jake twisted in a move no human could have matched, throwing himself to the ground and rolling. Sparks exploded as the cats twisted together, roaring in a deafening chorus, claws digging for purchase. Jake's rear paws raked the tiger's belly, leaving dim gashes in the manifestation where they penetrated.

Shit. Kurt's manifestation's definitely failing...

Sensing the danger, Kurt released him and leaped away. Jake rolled to all four paws and dove for the tiger's throat. They tumbled as Kurt fought to escape, writhing and biting. But Jake got him pinned on his back, immobilizing him with fangs sinking into his throat. Kurt's shell darkened beneath the pressure of those glowing teeth...

The vulnerable sigil rotated into view. Erica raced toward the battling cats.

Insane, this was insane, but it was the only chance they had...

"Erica!" Genevieve's voice rang with helpless terror for her husband, for Erica, for Jake himself, but Erica knew she couldn't stop. A thought flashed through her head: *If I don't have the juice to pull this off, he's going to kill me.* But she couldn't stop, or Kurt would die -- and Jake would be destroyed as surely as Bobby had been.

Thrusting out a hand, Erica sank her fingers into the dimmer sigil barely a foot from the lion's huge glowing head. And hit it with all her strength.

Nothing happened.

Jake's eyes rolled toward her though he didn't let go of Kurt's throat. One forepaw released its grip on the tiger and lifted. *He's going to rake my legs open.*

Too fucking bad. She'd survive that. She wouldn't survive letting Kurt die. And neither would Jake. She shot her will toward the earth as Genevieve had taught her, fighting to draw power even without a spell circle. *More, I've got to have more...*

A feminine hand landed on her shoulder, nails digging in hard. "Erica!" Gen cried. "Take mine!"

Power blasted into her, a great blazing wave of it, nothing held in reserve, backed by all Genevieve's desperate love for her husband. Pain blazed through her, but Erica ignored the vicious burn as she grabbed her friend's magic like a drowning woman. Drinking it down, feeding her own into it, she blasted it into the sigil, backed by the raw force of her will, her furious determination not to lose either man.

The sigil blasted apart, vanishing in a cascade of sparks. Their joined magic burned right through the kidnapper's spell, splitting it wide, dissolving its sigils into glowing mist.

Jake's eyes widened. He froze, the grip of his jaws going slack. With a convulsive heave, Kurt drove his rear legs hard into the lion's belly, throwing him ten feet through the air. Leaping up, he drove a shoulder against Erica's hip, sending both women stumbling away.

Kurt whirled, planting himself between them and the lion. "Are you insane?" he shouted, without looking around at them. "Get the fuck back!"

Jake snarled, but the white blaze of psychotic rage burning in his head had dimmed.

I've just got to snap him the rest of the way out of it. Ignoring the tiger's warning rumble, Erica headed toward Jake, sidestepping Kurt's lunge for her arm. Her gaze lowered, she sank to her knees until her head was lower than Jake's -- a gesture of submission. Slowly, she extended a shaking hand.

"Are you nuts?" Kurt snapped, starting toward her.

Jake snarled and tensed to spring...

* * *

Rage leaped high in his mind again like another gust of burning hurricane wind. He growled at the glowing tiger, knowing only that it had hurt him, tried to kill him. Was getting too close to *her.*

"Jake!" the woman said, her low voice shaking with desperation. "Jake, please, don't!"

He knew that voice. Knew it mattered. The fury that had ripped through the cat's consciousness faded a little before the knowledge that she needed him. Almost enough to let him remember who she was. Who he was...

He stared at the slim, straight figure kneeling in the grass, her head lowered in submission. Slowly, she lifted one delicate hand, and he tensed, a warning growl vibrating through his manifestation.

She lifted her head. Dark eyes met his, deep and warm. And he knew her. *It's her... It's...* The thought spun away into confusion as he struggled to remember.

A cool breeze blew into his face, carrying her scent -- rich, female. Familiar. He took a step closer, drinking in the taste of her on the wind. The rage that had bathed his consciousness in flame cooled again as he stared into those fathomless eyes. Stepped closer to that delicate, trembling hand. Drew in a deep breath.

Tasted fear. He tensed, his hackles rising.

"You're not going to hurt me." Despite the fear scent,

her voice was steady. "You're not Bobby. Your control is better than that. Stronger than that. You won't hurt the people you love." A current of air teased him with her scent as the fear bled from it.

And he recognized her. Knew her. Almost knew her name...

"Come back to me, Jake. Come back."

He edged closer until his glowing nose touched those long fingers. They no longer shook.

"I love you, Jake." The words were low, clear. "Feel me. Know me. The way I know you."

Magic. Her magic. Rolling across his mind like a cool rain pouring over desert sand. His breathing slowed as her power danced along his. Calling him.

He wanted her. He didn't know why, but he knew that. Knew she was his. Knew he needed her. Had to have her.

"Erica..." The word rumbled, deep, hoarse. *Yes. Erica. It's Erica.* Memory bloomed through him -- the touch of her hand, silken on his skin, the intimate scent that lay behind one lovely ear, the taste of her nipples on his tongue, the salt and sex of her pussy...

"Yes," she breathed, exquisite eyes staring into his. "Jake. Jake, I love you. Come back to me. Please. I can't make it without you." Her voice vibrated with a note of pain that shook him to his core. "You're the best part of me."

Clarence moaned, a deep note of distress. Yes, Jake thought. *She needs us.*

He released his manifestation. The glowing shell vanished, leaving the man kneeling before his kneeling lover.

And Jake had his first sane thought since he'd leaped into the kidnapper's magic circle. *What the fuck had just happened?*

The last thing he remembered was his mother, curled

in a terrified ball at his feet as he fought his horrifying thirst for her blood.

Oh, Jesus, what did I do? He stared at Erica as she knelt before him. Proud, strong Erica, who never submitted to anyone. "What... what happened? Did I hurt you?" Jake rose, caught her by the shoulders and pulled her to her feet. Frantically, he scanned her body, breathed deep of her scent, searching for blood. But all she smelled of was... joy.

And relief, the kind of relief you feel when you almost die -- and don't.

A brilliant smile burst across her face like sunlight escaping storm clouds. "You didn't hurt me." She laid a trembling hand on his cheek. The love in her eyes shook him to his heart. "You'd never hurt me."

"Good. Good. Oh, God, I love you!" Jake threw both arms around her, knowing only that he had to kiss her, had to anchor his consciousness in that hot, soft mouth. His mouth took hers, and to his inexpressible relief, she kissed him back, hot and frantic. As wild relief surged through him, he was distantly aware of the sound of applause and whistles from the watching audience of cops.

"Thank you, Jesus!" From the corner of one eye, he saw Kurt grab Genevieve and kiss her with the same desperate hunger he felt for Erica.

Where the hell had they come from?

Erica pulled back just enough to laugh softly against his mouth. "We're never going to live this down."

"I don't care," he gasped, and kissed her again.

* * *

Sergeant Roger Johnson knelt and put two fingers against the kidnapper's carotid artery. His pulse was a little fast, and his head still bled sluggishly, but he didn't move. Studying the black suit the terrorist wore, Roger realized it was made of Kevlar. *I'll have to shoot him in the head.* He swallowed, feeling sick.

"Fuck," Clary snarled in disgust, lifting his weapon. All of them had their guns drawn. "He's still alive." His lips twitched, and his eyes glittered with a nasty light. "We've got to do something about that."

Roger stood and took a step back. In the distance, he heard the sound of applause. "Sounds like the fight's over. We can't shoot him now. They'll hear the shot."

Hampton toed something in the leaves at her feet. Glancing over, Roger saw a gun. "We can always tell everyone he was going for this."

"It'll raise questions." His mouth was painfully dry, and he licked his lips.

Clary laughed. "Nobody will ask shit. And if they do, Virginia will get the investigation quashed."

He was probably right. Roger looked down at the man's body and his stomach lurched. It would be cold-blooded murder. He'd done a lot of things he shouldn't have over the years, but he'd never killed a man. Especially not a helpless, unconscious man.

I used to be a good cop.

He remembered the day he'd talked a suicidal domestic abuser into releasing the man's wife and children unharmed. Remembered the day he'd graduated from the South Carolina Criminal Justice Academy, and seeing the pride on the faces of his wife and parents. Remembered the people he'd helped over thirty years as a cop -- the men and women and children he'd defended, the lives he'd saved. How had it come to this?

But he knew the answer to that. *I gave up my soul one tiny piece at a time.* For fear and rage and hate.

"No." Roger holstered his weapon.

Clary stared at him, incredulous. "Are you out of your mind? I'm not going to jail. Look, if you don't want to do it..." He pointed his Glock at the man.

Roger reached up and activated his body cam, making sure they saw him do it. "One thing you may not know about body cams. They run all the time, they just don't save. But when you hit the button, it saves *everything*, including from thirty seconds before you activated it."

"Fuck. You. We'll smash it." His face contorting with rage, Martin took a step toward him, aiming his pistol at Roger's head.

"Go ahead. I really don't give a fuck." Roger half-hoped the bastard would do it. It would save him going to jail.

Green stepped up behind Martin and shoved his gun against the back of the psycho's head. "Yeah, no."

Martin froze, his eyes widening in astonishment.

Hampton stared at Green in blank shock. "Tom, what the fuck are you doing?"

"I'll tell you what I'm *not* doing -- I'm not going to be an accessory to another cop's murder. This is fucking bad enough as it is. I should never have listened to you to begin with," he told her bitterly. "You're worse than the fucking Talents."

Well, damn it. Hell of a time for him to grow a spine. Roger's shoulders slumped, and he reached for the handset of his radio. "Sheriff, we've got a problem."

Chapter Twenty-One

Jake stood beside Erica, watching an EMT check his mother's pulse. They'd found Diane sitting on the hillside not far from Johnson and his henchman, still a little dazed from one too many blows to the head and whatever drug the kidnapper had used to carry her off.

He could hear Gable's deep voice reading the sergeant his rights. It was a good thing the five assholes hadn't seen his mother, concealed as she'd been by the huge, flowered mound of an azalea bush. They'd probably have killed her.

"… If you can't afford an attorney, one will be appointed for you. Do you understand these rights?" Gable finished as he handcuffed Johnson, his expression grim.

"Yeah." The man looked haunted, defeated. Hampton, Clary, Green, and Martin were already in cuffs, their expressions variously sullen, dazed, resigned, or enraged.

Jake was a little surprised he wasn't in cuffs himself, but when he'd asked if he was under arrest, Gable snorted. "Don't be an idiot. That damned Arcanist set the whole thing up to sucker you into that trap. The only thing I'm pissed about is you fell for it, but I guess if somebody'd been pistol-whipping my mother, I'd have done the same." He'd shaken his head. "That dickhead's lucky I don't put him *under* the jail."

Another EMT was checking the kidnapper's head wound. The man was conscious and surprisingly alert. Apparently he'd come to just before Johnson and his pals found him but decided to play possum. Smart move.

Nearby, a crime scene tech was busy photographing the spell circle, revealed by the Luminol she'd sprayed on the stone outcrop.

"I underestimated you."

Surprised, Jake looked around, realizing the Arc fucker was talking to him. His immediate impulse was to tell him where to go, but far be it for Jake to dissuade a dickhead from incriminating himself. "How so?"

"Never worked with a Feral big cat, just Virgil Ford. Didn't know you bastards could jump like that. I expected you to run up the hillside and around."

"Bastard," Diane growled, her voice reverberating with a distinctly canine note that came straight from her dogs.

Jake shot a questioning glance at Gable, who gave him a watchful nod. "What exactly were you trying to accomplish?"

"What I was hired to do. Frame the fuck out of you." He snorted, then winced as if his head hurt. Given the head wound, it probably did. "I thought I was so damned smart, hitting you with the same kind of spell the Caliphuckers used on that brother of yours."

"You knew about that?"

The man shot him an offended look. "I do my research. Thought I'd pay you back for the Fords."

Gable spoke up, his gaze cool and suspicious. "You're being awfully damned chatty all the sudden."

"Because my employer double-crossed me." A note of outrage colored his voice as he nodded at the handcuffed cops. "Sent her goon squad there to shut me up. You don't do that to a professional. I wouldn't have talked -- but I damn sure will now." His lips stretched into a smile with something vicious around the edges. "What she didn't know is I keep Pearl Harbor files on all my clients."

"What now?" Diane murmured, confused.

"A file that government workers keep in case they're betrayed by their superiors," Erica explained. "Takes its name from the attack on Pearl Harbor, and the admiral who got the blame."

"Exactly," the Arc said in grim satisfaction. "In my case, betrayal means somebody tries to have me killed. Or thinks they can leave me to face a capital magical murder charge while they skate free. Yeah, not happening." He turned to eye the sheriff, jerking his chin toward the pile of personal effects they'd already put in evidence bags. "If you'll uncuff me and hand me my cell phone…"

Gable studied him coldly. "Why?"

"Because I want to show you a sample of what I've got to trade the prosecution. Or rather, *who* I've got to trade the prosecution." His lips tightened. "And not even the FBI can crack the security on that phone without my help."

Gable turned to Erica. "Is it safe?"

She hesitated, then nodded slowly, her gaze on the phone. "I don't see any spells on it. It's probably okay."

The sheriff nodded. "Uncuff him."

Jake's fists clenched, but he didn't object as she moved behind the Arc, pulled the key from her belt, and unlocked his cuffs, though she left one bracelet attached to a wrist.

At a word from Gable, the crime scene investigator put on a fresh pair of Nitrile gloves, opened the evidence bag, and handed him the phone.

The Arc thumbed the screen until an audio file began to play. "Fleming?" The voice sounded familiar, but Jake couldn't quite place it. "We've got another client for you. Virginia Laurel. She's a member of the South Carolina House. Needs a little help running for governor."

Gable's eyes widened. "Is that…"

The Arcanist smirked. "President Roth's chief of staff."

Holy shit.

* * *

All Jake wanted was to go home, but he and Erica had promised Gen and Kurt they'd drop by to brief them. Dave met them at the front door of Kurt's house. "I told you that you should take me with you."

Erica gave him a look through eyes squeezed to slits of pain. She looked as if she was going to collapse any minute. She'd managed to keep it together through most of the day, but by the end of their shift, only willpower was keeping her on her feet. Jake had no idea how she'd kept going this long. He was running on fumes himself. "Dave, the sheriff didn't let the protesters put sticks on their signs. He sure as hell wouldn't have let the Talents bring six hundred pounds of fangs and claws."

"And how did that work out for him?" A glowing arm emerged from Dave's shoulder and pointed at Jake. "At least I could've helped distract the Lion King. But nonooooo. I was stuck at home watching the whole thing live on CNN." His voice dropped to a pissed-off growl. "And having a heart attack."

Jake winced. He was going catch shit about this for years. Still, given that the alternative was no one being alive to give him shit, he'd catch it with a smile.

Genevieve emerged from the kitchen, followed by her husband. Unlike Jake and Erica, the Briggs had been allowed to go home after their own question and answer session. Hours ago.

Jake and Erica had faced a lot more paperwork, not to mention a couple of Arcanist FBI agents who hadn't been in the least amused by the situation. Waiting for those two to show up had been one of the reasons they'd been so late getting to BFS.

"You look like hell," Gen told Erica. "You desperately need an hour in the circle."

"It could wait until tomorrow," Erica said, sounding exhausted. "It's past midnight and you guys have to feed the cats in the morning."

"We took a nap when we got home." The look she gave her husband made it clear the nap had been about a lot more than sleep -- or even sex. "But if you don't spend some time recharging, you're going to feel like hell for days. Come on." She caught Erica's shoulder, turned her around, and pushed her gently back out the front door.

"I thought the spell circle was in the backyard," Jake said as the door shut behind the two Arcanists.

"No, that's the healing circle," Kurt explained. "Gen created a new one in the memorial garden specifically designed to help her recover from working a lot of magic. She's already used it once tonight."

"Come on," Dave said. "I want a beer."

"Oh, God, so do I," Jake said, meaning every word.

As he led the way into the living room, Dave informed him, "By the way, video of your little catfight has been running on all the cable news stations all damn day."

"Terrific." He could barely remember anything beyond blind, overwhelming fury, a desire to kill reinforced by Adrian Fleming's magic and Clarence's rage. Jake's anger had fed the cat's in turn, creating a kind of murderous emotional feedback. He felt sick just imagining what he could have done. Even his mother had had a close call at his paws.

Luckily, Mom was tough. The EMTs had given her a clean bill of health and let her go. From what he'd heard, she'd spent the hours since giving television interviews on the kidnapping, telling everybody who'd listen that her son had been the victim of a terrorist spell.

Jake realized Dave was studying him, something in the expression of his furry face giving an impression of compassion. "If it makes you feel any better, you and Erica are officially America's sweethearts."

He blinked, thoroughly confused as he sank down on the couch. Kurt handed him a microbrew and he twisted off the cap. "Wait, what now?" He shook his head. "I mean, I get Erica -- she saved everybody's ass." He jerked a thumb at Kurt. "He's definitely the hero of the piece. And neither of them would've been able to do any of it without Genevieve. I was the one who almost ate people."

"You'd think that, except an interesting piece of audio leaked to the media. It's been playing on a loop, alternating with the *Nat Geo* special you and Kurt threw." Dave headed to the coffee table where the remote sat next to an open laptop. He manifested a hand, scooped it up, and pointed it at the TV.

The big wall screen flicked on. On one side of the split screen, a camera showed Virginia Laurel being perp-walked out of her mansion by Detective Grant Sawyer, her hands cuffed in front of her. The old woman's face was so twisted in rage she looked crazed.

The other side showed Humanist protesters, their faces contorted, kicking and swinging wildly at the cops, who fought back with batons, pepper spray and even Tasers. From what they'd told Gable's people, none of the protestors had even felt their injuries until the Bards broke the spell.

"It's amazing we didn't have more fatalities than we did." Two protesters and a cop had died. The officer had been beaten to death, and the two protesters had been shot by deputies trying to get them off him. There had been more than a thousand injuries ranging from minor to critical.

"You want to hear what's really amazing? Listen to this," Dave told him.

Laurel's recorded voice said, "We need to make it look as if the Talents cast the spell to make the protesters go berserk. I want those witches discredited."

"Actually, I've got an idea about that," replied a voice Jake recognized as Adrian Fleming's. "How'd you like the hero of Faraday Square to kill some people?"

There was a long pause. "Could you do that? Never mind, I don't want to know the details. Just do it. I'd love to discredit that bastard."

Jake's jaw dropped as cold anger flashed through him. "Where the fuck did they get that audio? The sheriff's office sure didn't release that."

Dave gave him a very toothy tiger grin. "Funny story about that. Evidently some anonymous party emailed the audio to CNN about the time you were arresting Fleming."

Jake's eyes widened. "He must've done it when they gave him back the phone."

"That, or he had it set to go automatically unless he stopped it. Mr. Fleming is a liiiiittle bit vindictive."

"Bad man to fuck over."

The camera cut back to a trio of talking heads, one of whom looked more than a little sick. "How do we know Fleming didn't cast a spell on Mrs. Laurel to make her say that? We all know what kind of people Talents are."

The camera cut to a shot of Erica reaching out to lay a hand on Jake's lion manifestation as he held Kurt down, fangs in his friend's throat. A huge paw lifted, preparing to strike out at her, and Jake caught his breath in horror.

He was barely aware of the talking heads arguing as the video continued: Kurt tearing free of him, planting himself between Jake and the two women. Erica deliberately walking around Kurt, then sinking to her knees in front of the lion manifestation and extending a shaking hand to him.

That was the moment she'd helped him break the spell's grip.

The glowing leonine shape disappeared, leaving the recorded Jake on his knees. He leaped up, caught her by the shoulders and pulled her into his arms. He remembered his panic and relief as he realized she was unhurt...

And the sheer giddy joy of kissing her, feeling the hot, soft pressure of her mouth...

"Yeah," drawled one of the talking heads dryly. "Those Talents *are* bloodthirsty."

"Jesus." Jake tilted the beer up and slugged the whole thing down in three long swallows. He put the empty down on the coffee table and looked at Kurt. "Got another one of those?"

Kurt handed over his own unopened bottle. "You're entitled."

"Christ, you really did save my ass." He twisted the top off the beer and took a long swallow. "I don't remember much of that at all."

"I'm not surprised," Kurt told him. "Look, none of this is your fault. And the point is, you didn't kill anybody. You didn't even really hurt me. You might have clawed the hell out of my manifestation, but you never got to skin."

"I damn near got to Erica's."

A big forepaw landed on his knee as Dave sat down in front of him. "But you didn't. And she knew you wouldn't. Think about that for minute -- about what that says about your relationship. *She doesn't doubt you anymore.*"

Jake snorted. "We're talking about Erica Harris. She'd have done the exact same thing if she hadn't known me from Adam's house cat. That woman has a streak of insane courage that goes all the way to the bone."

"Yeah, she does," Kurt agreed. "But when I told her to get away, she told me you wouldn't hurt her."

"And the rest of America agrees with her," Dave said, turning to the open laptop and manifesting arms again. "Witness my Twitter feed." He began to read in a high-pitched imitation of a teenage girl. "'OMG! That was the most romantic thing I've ever seen! When he kissed her, my heart just *melted*.'"

Jake fell back against the back of the couch, both hands covering his face. "Kill me now. I'm going to be hearing this shit from other cops for the rest of my natural life."

"Probably," Dave agreed cheerfully. "Oh, here's a good one." He went back into teenage girl mode. "'Would you just look at his shoulders? He is such a SNACK!'"

Kurt roared with laughter as Jake snatched up a pillow and sailed it at Dave's head.

The tiger ducked, thoroughly smug. "You do realize you owe me a woman," he told Kurt. "I told you he'd pull it off, and he did."

"I didn't take that bet," Kurt objected, as Jake wondered what the hell they were talking about. "And like I told you before, where the hell am I supposed to get this tiger woman? There aren't that many women Ferals with female tiger Familiars. And there are even fewer melded women in the tiger's body."

"Not my problem," Dave told him loftily. "A bet's a bet."

"Still didn't take the bet. Anyway, he hasn't proposed yet, and she hasn't accepted."

"Hey," Jake protested. "Sitting right here."

Dave turned to him. "And *why* are you still sitting right there? Go propose, asshole. I need a woman."

Jake snorted. "Yeah, because I'm absolutely proposing to win you a bet."

"No, you should propose because she's a hell of a woman and you're a dumbass if you don't."

Kurt looked at him. "He's got a point."

* * *

Fortunately, Genevieve returned before he was forced to kill his two best friends, and Jake was able to escape.

He headed for the memorial garden that lay not far from the house, intent on finding Erica. It was a lovely spot, azaleas and magnolias in full bloom, filling the air with their heady scents. Stone markers stood here and there among the greenery, each chiseled with the name of one of the cats who had been buried there. Besides the markers for the strictly non-magical cats, there were larger, more elaborate ones for Lahr, Fred Briggs's lion familiar, and Stoli, who had been Kurt's tiger.

Jake found Erica sitting in the center of the garden under a wooden pergola. Roses climbed the wooden supports of the structure, and long swags of wisteria draped from its lattice roof. The grape-like clusters of blooms screened the circle from the view of the park, probably so the tourists wouldn't be able to tell anyone was working magic inside it.

Erica sat on a blanket in the center of a ring of stones, each carved with sigils Jake assumed were designed to feed magic to whoever occupied the circle. It was evidently working. As he dropped to his knees in front of her, he saw her face no longer held the expression of pain she'd worn throughout the day.

She'd taken off her duty belt, socks, and shoes, which now lay in a pile off to the side. She'd also shed her uniform shirt and Kevlar vest, leaving her dressed only in a thin tank top and uniform pants.

Erica sat very straight in the moonlight, eyes closed, her hands palm up on her knees. Something about her short-cropped hair and the elegant bone structure of her face made him think of Joan of Arc, the French teenager who'd led her country's armies into combat when everyone told her it was impossible.

Thank God things had turned out better for Erica than they had for Joan. It had been entirely too damned close as it was.

In the depths of his mind, he heard a low leonine moan, echoing Clarence's actual voice from the depths of the park. The cat had been desperately unhappy to realize how close they'd come to hurting her ever since they'd come back to themselves.

Don't worry, buddy. We'll make it up to her.

* * *

Erica felt Jake's presence the moment he stepped into the circle, felt the brush of fur against her skin as Clarence silently demanded reassurance. While they'd cooled their heels at the sheriff's office, Erica had tried repeatedly to tell the lion she wasn't angry, but he didn't seem to believe her.

Now Jake himself stood there, the glow of his presence lighting up her consciousness. Before she could open her eyes, his Feral magic touched her -- a slow, velvet stroke, ghosting across her aura. Sharing his aching need for her. Not just for her body, but for her intelligence and courage and skill.

Her.

Telling her without words that she was everything he'd ever wanted. The sheer naked intensity of his emotion made her catch her breath.

Me? He feels that way about me? Deep inside her, the desperate, wounded child who'd never been accepted by anyone froze in wonder, scarcely daring to believe.

She opened her eyes and looked up at him, dazzled. She didn't intend to ask the question -- it was incredibly hard to reveal such vulnerability even to him -- yet she heard herself say the words anyway. "Do you mean it?"

Jake stood looking down at her, tall and strong, the moon pouring silver across his impossibly handsome face. "Yes." He reached out, cupped her face in a broad, strong hand. Brushed his thumb over the curve of her cheek. "How can you even doubt it? I'd be dead now if not for you. Dead or destroyed by that bastard's magic. You risked everything to save me. Didn't hesitate, even when you knew I might rip you open."

Erica stared, startled. She could feel it, see the belief glowing in his aura. "I was never in any danger from you, Jake. Even if you hadn't... loved me, you're decent all the way to the bone."

"Bobby was decent." Pain flashed in his glowing eyes.

"Yes, he was." Erica rose, needing to be on her feet. Needing to look in his eyes so he could see the truth in hers. "But not strong enough to beat the booby trap. You are. All I had to do was crack Fleming's spell, and you were able to beat its effects."

"Barely." He closed his eyes, and a spasm of terror crossed his expression as if he remembered how close they'd come to losing everything. "It was too damn close, Erica. Way too close."

"But you beat it." She rose on her toes and leaned in, bracing her hands on his chest as she breathed against his mouth. "I knew you would. I knew you'd never fail me."

She took his lips slowly, brushing her mouth back and forth across his. Tasting Mellow Microbrew and Jake, inhaling the ozone tang of Feral magic and the ghostly smell of fur. He stilled against her, then opened for her with a throaty groan, swirling his tongue into her mouth. Tasting her. Drinking her. "Erica," he whispered, his voice harsh with emotion. "God, Erica, if I'd hurt you…"

"You didn't. Wouldn't."

Both big hands came up to cup her head between them, fingers tunneling into her hair. Caressing the curve of her skull, drawing her close.

With a low growl, she pulled back a fraction and bit gently at the curve of his plush lower lip, then nibbled the aggressive jut of his chin, a little rough with beard shadow after the long day. Her hand curled into the collar of his uniform shirt, pulled. "I want you out of this."

His closed eyes opened, revealing a glowing gold slit. "All right." His lips curled into a smile. "If you insist."

"Oh, I'm insisting." She stepped back, started in on the buttons, her fingers fast and a little clumsy in her need. He reached down and caught the fabric of her

undershirt, and she stopped her attack on his buttons
long enough to let him pull it off over her head.

So they undressed each other, fumbling a little in
their need, dropping pants and shirts and weapons and
gear, piling them up haphazardly. Until Erica and Jake
were naked in the moonlight, breathing hard, shaking
with the intensity of the emotion they felt.

For a moment they just stopped and stared at each
other like a couple of virgins. Though they'd made love
before, it had never felt like this. Never felt so new and
strange, so naked and strong and... somehow terrifying.

Dry-mouthed, weak-kneed, Erica gazed at Jake's
gloriously sculpted body edged in moonlight. At the
broad shoulders and muscled arms, the ridges of
abdominal muscles and powerful corded thighs. At his
cock, that glorious shaft curving and ready, a pearl of pre-
come glinted on the tip.

He stared back at her, his pupils wide in the glowing
ring of his irises, his lips parted, an expression of wonder
on his tough, confident face she'd never expected to see.

Bare, powerful arms closed around her, pulling her
against his brawny body and trapping his thick cock
between them. Then he was kissing her again, his lips as
soft and warm as his body was hard and hot, his tongue
tracing the seam of her lips and thrusting inside as she
opened them to moan. She wrapped her arms around
him, digging the nails of one hand into his shoulder as
she threaded the fingers of the other into the short, silken
strands of his blond hair.

They kissed with ravenous intensity, greedy tongues
swirling and thrusting, their bodies rolling together with
desperate, yearning pressure. His hands roamed over her,
cupping the curve of her waist, the rise of her ass, lifting
her off her feet. In the depths of her mind, she heard an
ecstatic rumble, felt the brush of the mane against her
aura, the crackle of magic across her skin. She tore her

mouth away from Jake's and groaned, "Too many legs!"

Clarence chuffed a lion laugh and vanished.

Jake chuffed an echo and dropped to his knees with Erica in his arms. He laid her on the blanket and sat back on his heels.

God, he was beautiful, every muscle sculpted in moonlight and shadow, rolling under velvet flesh like music as he moved. His cock jutted straight up, angled by his pose, a long, elegant length, veined and thick and ready. Just the sight of it made her mouth go dry even as wet flesh swelled and tightened between her thighs.

He surged forward, coming down on top of her, catching himself on stiff arms, biceps bulging. Erica drew in a breath of delight as he lowered himself, and she arched to meet him, surrendering stiff nipples to his mouth, to his tongue, to his teeth. She moaned in helpless pleasure as his tongue swirled and lashed each nubbin in turn, alternating with nibbles of gently raking teeth. The silken pleasure made her eyes slide shut and her breath catch.

She wrapped both arms around him, cradling his head, relishing the cool, feathery texture of his hair. Bracing on an elbow, Jake caressed the side of one breast as he sent the fingers of his free hand tracing over the line of her ribs, the jut of a hipbone. Stopped to circle her navel as she writhed at the ticklish sensation with a breathless giggle. He chuckled, his breath gusting over the point of her nipple, warm and arousing.

"God, Jake!" She wrapped her arms around the width of his chest, rolling her hips up to grind against the intoxicating male promise of his cock. It felt so damned good. She couldn't wait to feel him spearing into her, grinding erotically over slick and eager flesh. "God, I want you, I need you. So bad…"

"Not as bad as you're going to," He growled against her breast, and she gasped at the sweet threat. Releasing the captured nipple, he licked and kissed his way downward, pausing here to nibble a rib, there to suck the jut of her hipbone. A quick swirl of his tongue over and around her bellybutton made her squirm and gasp.

And every time he moved, the hair of his chest tickled her skin as his body pressed against her pelvis, brushing over hot, aching pussy.

That was where his mouth was headed. The thought of what he'd do there made her grind her head back into the blanket in helpless need.

But she wanted more than that.

Erica locked the fingers of one hand into his short hair and tugged until he lifted his head to look at her. "Sixty-nine! I've got to taste you!"

He grinned at that, a wicked flash of white teeth and gold eyes. "Demanding wench."

"You bet your sweet ass." She planted both palms against his chest, tightened the grip of her thighs as she twisted her hips against him in a wrestling throw.

Jake let himself be flipped onto his back. Sprawled there in the moonlight, he was broad and muscled and beautifully erect.

Lust flashed through Erica like a lightning strike. She flung a leg across his narrow hips and leaned down to kiss him, unable to resist the lure of his mouth. His cock brushed her naked belly, and she sucked in a needy breath, drinking the taste of him, smelling sweat and fur and magic. Tasted Mellow Microbrew and Jake. Jake, more intoxicating than the beer.

He kissed her back, cradling her face in one broad, calloused palm. When she drew back at last, he gave her a lazy smile. "I thought you were going to let me kiss the other lips."

She grinned wickedly at him. "Oh, yeah. I forgot."

"You *forgot*?" Gold brows lowered in mock anger. "I must be doing it wrong if I'm that forgettable."

Erica laughed in a chuff worthy of Clarence. "Believe me, Jake, you don't do anything wrong." She sat up and rearranged herself, turning her back on his laughing mouth to kneel aside his torso and face the broad, eager curve of his shaft. Wrapping her fingers around his impressive width, she savored its warm, velvet texture.

Then, slowly, anticipating, she extended her tongue and licked a pearl of arousal off the tip of his cock. It tasted salty, astringent, eager.

His hips gave a little involuntary jolt at the feel of her tongue, and she smiled in pleasure. God, she loved making Jake hot.

Slowly, spinning out the moment, she opened her mouth and leaned in, letting him feel the heat of her breath. Letting him anticipate. Enjoying the power his lust gave her. *I'm going to drive you right out of your mind.*

Her plan derailed when a wet male tongue stroked the length of her sex, scooping through swollen, juicy lips. Spreading her lips with his fingers, he lifted his head to lap at her clit. *Time to return the favor.*

Angling his cock up with one hand, Erica began to lick all up and down the shaft, playing her tongue along the thick veins, tracing the mushroom tip, swirling over its exquisitely sensitive head.

To her immense satisfaction, Jake groaned, hunching against her grip. "Damn, you're good at that!" His voice sounded ragged, his breath gusting over her wet flesh.

Erica lifted her head and grinned. "Believe me, it's my pleasure."

Opening wide, she sucked him in, tightening her lips for a long, merciless pull. He grunted against her pussy and began to eat her, just as ravenous and eager. One hand slid down to the erect nipple dancing over his torso, captured it. Skilled fingers milked its hard jut, each tiny pinch spilling more burning delight into her body like flaming brandy.

Erica moaned around his width, pulling her lips off him, sucking hard. Her free hand reached up to find his balls drawn tight and close to his body. Cupping them, she rolled their warmth in her fingers, making him squirm.

He plunged his thumb into her wet pussy as he sealed his lips around her clit, suckling with delicious greed, his tongue dancing wet swirls around it. The sensation made her close her eyes, moaning helplessly around the hefty girth of his cock. Magic danced and sparkled behind her eyelids, all violet, blues, and shades of lusty pink. It gave her an idea, and she sent tendrils of magic stroking the length of his aura, building his pleasure and arousal even more.

With a low, throaty rumble, he pressed his face closer and suckled even harder, thumb and forefinger now thrusting in and out of her pussy.

But what she wanted, what she needed, was that delicious cock. She dragged off him and panted, "Jake… fuck!"

She didn't even get the rest of the plea out of her mouth before he tumbled her off him and onto her back. The next moment Jake was on her, big hands catching her knees, bending her legs.

Spreading her wide.

He paused just long enough to take his shaft in hand and position it between her juicy lips, right at her slick opening. Grabbing her ass in both hands, he lifted her and sank back on his heels.

And impaled her, all in one breathtaking plunge.

Erica cried out in shock and blind pleasure as he stuffed her without any mercy at all. Jake wasn't a small man, and it would've hurt if she weren't so wet, so incredibly aroused.

He froze there, holding her still, his shaft filling her to the lungs. Or at least that's how it felt.

Startled by the raw intensity of the sensation, Erica stared into his wild Feral eyes. "Oh, God!"

"Did I hurt you? I didn't plan to… enter that hard…"

"No! More! God, more…"

Jake's grin flashed, white in the moonlight, and he was moving, lifting her off him so he could roll his hips to spear into her again. Surging in and out, relentless as the tides, sending burning pleasure pulses blasting through her with every stroke.

Erica threw back her head and grabbed his shoulders, digging in her nails as he bucked wildly against her. Each long thrust shoved multicolored streamers of magic into the base of her brain. She could see them behind her closed lids.

Breathless, she writhed, vaguely aware she was screaming, lost and maddened.

The orgasm gathered like a huge rose wave towering over her head, glowing against the darkness. Clawing for it, she ground down on him as he plunged up to meet her, a rumbling growl vibrating through his chest and into hers.

She felt how close he was in the straining tendons of his body, and her eyes flew wide, wanting to watch him go over. Gold blazed as his lips drew back off his teeth in a soundless snarl of erotic effort. The cords of his neck went tight.

Jake roared, freezing, his cock plunged deep, jerking as it pulsed.

Magic fountained around them as the rose wave crashed down, and Erica screamed, lost in the blazing glory of the moment and the gold of his eyes.

When it was over, they clung together, chest against chest, sweat damp and muscles twitching, panting as their hearts thundered as one.

"Oh, sweet holy God," Erica managed at last, unable to think of anything more coherent as they struggled to catch their breath.

"Yeah. Yeah, God." Lifting her carefully in his arms, he pulled himself gently free of her wet depths, then let himself fall backward, still cuddling her close against his chest.

For a long, long moment there was no sound except pumping gasps. She listened to his heartbeat slow its desperate thunder. Sweet peace stole over her, and she closed her eyes, letting herself float.

Until she heard him swallow. She opened sleepy eyes, and found a thread of soft butter yellow winding through the violet and electric blue of his aura. Not fear exactly. Not the right color. More nerves.

She ran a hand in a calming stroke down his working chest. "What's wrong?"

"Nothing. It's just..." He paused and took a deep breath. The yellow bled away, and his aura took on a deep, calm blue. When he spoke, there was certainty in his voice. "I want to spend the rest of my life looking at you." His voice sounded velvety and deep, edged with a hint of leonine reverberation. "I want to wake up next to you every morning and go to sleep beside you every night."

She stared at him, feeling her heart begin to hammer. "Jake..."

"Let me finish. I've been thinking about what to say all day." He gathered one of her hands in his and held it, staring into her eyes. "I want to fight alongside you and protect you, knowing you'll protect me whether I think I need it or not. I want, I *need* forever with you, Erica Harris. Will you marry me?" In the distance, Clarence gave another long, low roar. He sounded a bit peeved. Jake's lips twitched. "Correction -- marry *us*?"

She stared up at him, stunned silent.

When she didn't answer, his gaze flickered. "If it's too soon..."

"No!" The word burst out of her with a note of desperation mixed with a kind of crazy joy. "Not 'no' no -- I mean I just wasn't expecting…" She broke off, trying to recover, trying to think. Only she didn't really need to think, because the answer was obvious. "Yes, Jake. Yes, I'll marry you." She felt a crazy smile spread across her face and watched as rose and violet spilled through his aura, as vivid as sunrise. "I love you, Jake Nolan. You and Clarence and his girls and…"

His grin was blinding, framed by both dimples. "And I love you, Erica. I always will."

Almost giddy with pure, distilled joy, she lifted her head, knowing what she'd see. Clarence sat on the edge of the blanket, glowing and ghostly, the most smug-looking lion she'd ever seen.

Then, from the other side of the tumble of wisteria, a falsetto voice began to sing: "In the jungle, the mighty jungle, the lion sleeps tonight…"

Jake lifted his head. "Damn it, Dave!"

Dave cackled.

When Jake scooped up a shoe and hurled it through the wisteria, big paws thudded on the ground, racing away to the sound of chuffing laughter. "Kurt Briggs," the tiger shouted, "You owe me a girlfriend!"

Angela Knight

New York Times best-selling author Angela Knight has written and published more than sixty novels, novellas, and ebooks, including the Mageverse and Merlin's Legacy series. With a career spanning more than two decades, Romantic Times Bookclub Magazine has awarded her their Career Achievement award in Paranormal Romance, as well as two Reviewers' Choice awards for Best Erotic Romance and Best Werewolf Romance.

Angela is currently a writer, editor, and cover artist for Changeling Press LLC. She also teaches online writing courses. Besides her fiction work, Angela's writing career includes a decade as an award-winning South Carolina newspaper reporter. She lives in South Carolina with her husband, Michael, a thirty-year police veteran and detective with a local police department.

Angela at Changeling: changelingpress.com/angela-knight-a-26

Changeling Press E-Books

More Sci-Fi, Fantasy, Paranormal, and BDSM adventures available in e-book format for immediate download at ChangelingPress.com -- Werewolves, Vampires, Dragons, Shapeshifters and more -- Erotic Tales from the edge of your imagination.

What are E-Books?

E-books, or electronic books, are books designed to be read in digital format -- on your desktop or laptop computer, notebook, tablet, Smart Phone, or any electronic e-book reader.

Where can I get Changeling Press E-Books?

Changeling Press e-books are available at ChangelingPress.com, Amazon, Apple Books, Barnes & Noble, and Kobo.

Changeling Press, LLC

ChangelingPress.com